HAMMOND FLUX
LIFE AFTER
FLESH

Alan Killip

PART ONE

HINKLEY

1

A Live Human Subject

When Rachel stuck that photo to the board above my desk I asked her why, what for?

She glared down at my crumpled form and said, "Because I think there's more chance of them letting you leave this awful place if you have something to remind you of who you are."

From my position on the bed I could see her formidable bouffant towering above the dark caves of her nostrils. I returned her glare, reflecting how she looked from this angle, like a caricature of herself. This is typical of her visits these days. She sweeps in, drops a riddle designed to put me in my place, then leaves. The photo and its justification are classic Rachel: the underlying thinking is vague, and the gesture itself is presented as art, imbued with false significance. She's expecting the image, of me holding forth triumphant, at a conference years ago, to have a curative effect.

I'm not sure I want to leave this place she finds so awful. I exist here in an agreeable state of limbo, free from prying eyes and jostling hordes. The staff are professional and polite; they refrain from the crass probing and insinuations that I've had to endure from the police and members of the security services. Meals are sludgy but regularly served and the décor is of the standard you'd find in a mass-market hotel. They've even let me have my laptop, albeit with the wireless disabled. I don't need the internet though, for the task in hand: I am writing my version of events to put the record straight. I am sick of being misrepresented. This is not an attempt to prove my innocence. On the contrary, I am determined to reveal the full extent of my guilt. I can handle the accusations of murder and treason: it's the bleeding hearts like Rachel who see me as a victim that irk me the most.

So I sit at my desk with my right hand jammed beneath my buttocks. There have been a number of false starts, but I think I've found my groove now. My left hand navigates the keyboard in a manner that becomes less faltering by the hour. There is a pleasant glow in my belly as lunchtime's sludgy offering slides through my system. I feel more focused, and I can clearly see how I am going to construct my account. The memories are all present and correct, ready to be transcribed, but the photo keeps distracting me. I am unable to remove it, for reasons to do with my rogue right hand. Reasons that are strange and embarrassing, that I may choose to reveal if I deem it in the interests of clarity.

Rachel's woolliness niggles: the fact that she doesn't grasp that "who we are" changes each day. I remember being the person in that photo: a man who thought he was at the height of his career, flushed with confidence. My peers and many in the wider world held me in awe. But I'm not that person now. I don't mean the obvious differences that I see when I look in the mirror: the new pouches and wrinkles, the darkness in the eyes. I don't even mean my changed status as a resident in a forensic mental health unit. I am infinitely wiser and more fulfilled than the blithe ingénue in the picture who thought he had the world at his feet; and I continue to change, as we all do, as each new thought and perception alters the vast web of lightning threads that link our neurons.

Sometimes I like to daydream that there exists an all-powerful God in the style of the Old Testament. He decides one day to challenge Rachel's naïve assumption that a person's essence is something simple and unchanging that can be captured in a photo. So He takes her to a place far from human habitation and sits her on a mountainside on a moonless night. Then He empties the stars from the sky; the nearest first, then the entire Milky Way. They stream past her eyes like fireflies and the night lasts three thousand years as she counts them all. Then He frees her brain from her skull, and the hundred billion cells fly up to replace the stars in the Milky Way. Pulsing threads connect them, and He shows her how this vast web warps and ripples as each moment changes who she is forever.

Sadly, I do not yet have the resources of Jehovah. The only way I can express myself is via this laptop. I am striving to write a simple, truthful account of how I sought to harness the power of the human brain for the good of all, and what I learnt about the nature of Life itself.

My story begins on a Saturday afternoon in summer about one year ago at Lazarus, the startup I founded with my colleague, Addison Royal. Lazarus was one of three companies run from a building called Sparrix Row, a converted cargo storage facility near London Bridge. Most of Lazarus's activity went on in a huge vault with whitewashed walls adorned with street art. A rich and slightly rank smell hung in the air. I blamed it on the nearby Thames, seeping through the London clay. Addison said it was the body odour of programmers, blended with the takeaway food that was consumed on the premises.

During the week, highly caffeinated developers filled the vault, sitting in clusters, wired into their private worlds, clicking, scanning and gurning. The one thing that could distract them was Addison's bob and jive as she tried to be present in all the places she was needed. She had hand-picked the developers from her web of virtual sparring partners, and they were mainly self-taught fanatics, untainted by academia or industry. She smoked with them in the courtyard and drank with them in the nearby pubs. She reciprocated their love and had learned all their histories, talents, vices, values and longings.

Only Addison and I were aware that Lazarus was sponsored by a company with a dubious ethical background. The other staff believed that we intended to use our brain emulation technology to help people with disabilities, which was part of the truth, but not the whole truth. It was a compelling goal for a startup, and matched the nature of the tasks assigned to the staff. Some medical spin-offs had already occurred. My wildest, most secret hope was that one day we would make death obsolete.

Addison and I shared a corner of the office, a rectangle partitioned from the rest of the vault by a soundproofed wall of tinted glass that we called the Flux room. Here we captured data from living brains using our CEM scanner, a giant, beige structure, shaped like a polo mint. CEM was an abbreviation of "Connectome and Engram Mapping". I'd sourced the device years ago after the research project it was designed for ran into difficulty. The data it collected was processed by a quantum computer called Q, housed in an adjoining room beyond another glass wall.

Q ran an application written by Addison called the Forward Chaining Liminal Uncertainty Matrix. We shortened this to Flum, but then Addison had insisted on calling it Flux, for no other reason than it sounded better. Q had massive capacity and lightning speed, sucked more energy from the national grid than the neighbouring Shard, and enabled Flux to emulate the human brain. The only evidence of the huge amount of activity taking place inside it was a humming sound that varied in pitch, and the rows of blinking orange and green lights along the CPU casings that we could see through the glass.

A large screen hung from the ceiling, an extension of Addison's workspace that allowed her to share representations of Flux's activity with me. Despite having pioneered the science that underpinned it all, I was often baffled by the rapidly changing graphics on her screen. They always dazzled though, and my pulse quickened with pride and awe when I saw them.

That morning I'd come into the office to review the first experiment of its kind on a live human subject. The experiment had been conducted while I was taking a three-week holiday on the quieter side of Ibiza. I found Addison at her desk, entranced by her laptop. A crumpled blanket lay discarded on a gurney that protruded from the great beige ring of the CEM scanner. She had conducted the experiment the previous evening, and hinted I might find the results disturbing on a commercial as well as an ethical level. There was a sonorous hum from the Q room as the data from the emulated mind of a man called Gary Fitch came to life on the screen. Gary was our studio manager and the most sarcastic and insolent member of staff.

"Bear with me," said Addison as she clacked her keyboard.

"What went wrong? Is he OK?" I hadn't considered the prospect of litigation, or worse, prosecution, until now. On the other side of the office, behind the soundproof glass, Gary sat slumped at his desk in front of his laptop in a pose that reminded me of Stephen Hawking, a normal posture for Gary. For a second I worried that the scan was more invasive than we'd planned; then a few subtle indicators reassured me that he lived: the jiggling of his stripy orange trainers, the play of light on his shiny pate as he shifted his head, and the odd twitch of his shoulders beneath his crumpled check shirt.

"Of course he's OK. You know the procedure is safe."

She was right, we'd been collecting data like this for years. But I wasn't really worried by the safety, the possible invasiveness of the scanner. "You're missing the point Addison. This is new territory, ethically speaking. We've only ever emulated a few nematode worms. And Felix."

"And Felix is fine. He had a whale of a time."

"But Felix is a rat." I flexed my fingers and wished I still smoked. We'd cloned Felix's little rat mind very successfully, and we'd kindled it to life in Flux. Every part of his brain had been emulated. We'd fed maze simulations through his visual cortex, then we'd monitored the activity in his primary motor cortex. The plucky little virtual rodent had run round the mazes with the same enthusiasm as his fleshly forbear. And to our delight he'd colonised swathes of unformatted space on Q next to that which he'd initially occupied, and had become much cleverer. We'd given him increasingly complex mazes, which he'd navigated and remembered with ease. Real Felix, or flesh and blood Felix, was still happily living in his cage, eating rat meal and enjoying the treadmill.

Addison ceased typing and glanced at my twitching hands, then met my eyes. "Gary's OK. Look at him. He's fine." She nodded at the slumped, staring figure behind the glass. "He woke just before seven, starving, tired, and moaning about terrible dreams. But he wanted to catch up on some work."

"So what's wrong?"

"You'll see. Or hear, rather. But overall it's a spectacular success. We've made history, like we did with Felix." She clicked and tapped her way through a series of screens and windows until a graph appeared. "There." She traced her finger along the luminous spiky line. "Gary came alive in Flux at five twenty-one this morning. The brain emulation kicked off after all the data was collated from the CEM scanner."

I leaned forward and peered at the graph, a jagged stalagmite rising from a flat line. "So that is Gary?"

"Most definitely. We can be certain of that."

"How?"

I often found Addison spooky, especially when she was excited. She looked as if she was staring at the sun and it was burning her eyes and she didn't care. "Let's drill down to the activity in Broca's area." She tapped and clacked and a longer, more complex graph appeared on the screen.

My chest tightened. "You've done the pattern matching already?" During the last few months we'd all taken turns to listen to selected passages of prose while our brain activity was monitored and analysed by a device called a Language Pattern Recognition Module, which allowed us to match activity patterns with words and phonemes. Addison had written the software to reconstruct speech from the patterns. We'd already patented it for medical use to help the speech-impaired.

"Listen," she said, tapping her space bar and sitting back to gauge my reaction.

A sound like someone trying to inhale and speak whilst being drowned in an echo chamber filled the room. Amid the chaos I could hear the same sound repeating. It sounded like someone saying the word "applebaum".

Addison smiled. "Apple blossom. I told Gary to remember the phrase 'apple blossom'. That it was very important. And if he felt strange in the night he should repeat it, so we'd know he was there."

"And that didn't freak him out at all?"

"No, it puzzled him. But he believed us when we told him he'd be absolutely safe. I didn't expect him to be so compliant. But anyway, listen to this. I put a filter on it. Extrapolated from his real voice." She rattled and clacked and splayed her fingers with a flourish.

The robot voice became more human, more like Gary's Edinburgh brogue. I felt a constriction in my vessels and a sharp drop in my body temperature. He sounded real now, and very lonely, like a man trapped in a small, sealed, confined space, a soul abandoned in darkness, whose only hope was a hollow spell. There was a note of determination in the voice, a heroic stoicism undermined by ebbing faith.

Addison's eyes continued to shine. "The terrible thing is, he said 'apple blossom' twelve hundred and thirty-four times before varying his routine. He was sticking to the programme like a good boy. But all that data was output in about five seconds. So at the rate he was saying 'apple blossom' ..." She trailed off.

"He was on a different time scale."

She nodded and smiled. "Time passed about a thousand times faster for him. God knows why." Her index finger swirled on the mouse pad of her laptop. "Fast forward an hour and he sounds really upset." She jabbed the space bar, and the synthetic brogue sounded again.

"Why would you do this to me? Why, why, what for? I'm no monster ..."

She jabbed her keyboard and the sound ceased. "Interesting how fear and desperation are reconstructed from the raw data. This is what would have animated his vocal chords, his lips, his tongue, his throat. And the weird thing is, the voice gets hoarse."

I nodded, unable to speak. The sounds and Addison's commentary fascinated and nauseated me in equal measure.

"Which you would think was impossible. There must some sort of proprioception, some feedback going on. What he experiences as his body is one big phantom limb. Even though he doesn't have anything to feel hoarseness, his voice gets hoarse, which is reflected in the diminishing strength of the voice." She raised her hand to the keyboard again.

I raised a flat palm. "Addison, no more of that, please."

She looked a little surprised, then nodded. "No, of course not. There'll be plenty of time to sift the data. It really is a goldmine, even though it looks like a failure at first glance."

"How does it end?" I thought of the rapid decline of the activity graph.

"Not well. Not well at all. He becomes incoherent. After that the activity in the Broca's area becomes hard to decipher. The voice filter doesn't help. We just get a load of wailing, echoing and squeaking, like dolphins being tortured. In the final few minutes the activity goes into rapid decline and ceases around quarter to seven. So an hour for us ..."

"Is a thousand hours for him."

"It's exciting, Hammond. This is totally new."

My stomach fluids had curdled. "We sent him to hell," I said.

Addison tutted and snapped her laptop shut. "He's fine. Look." I turned and looked at Gary raising a latte to his lips, transfixed by his screen. "He's in the zone. A happy geek."

I shook my head, my eyes adrift. "That was someone experiencing terrible distress." It's odd to recall my old self, crippled by conscience and a morbid imagination.

"It's a phenomenon, nothing more. Patterns output by a machine."

"We created a being born to suffer." I stared at her, and she shrugged.

"What happened to the familiar environment?"

"What?"

"You were going to construct a familiar environment for our emulated brains. Like you did with Felix and the mazes."

"I did, but I didn't have time to apply it. The process

9

kicked off early in the morning."

"So he was alone, with no sensory input, for hours?"

"It's just a machine, Ham. Metal, qubits, pulses of electricity."

I shook my head. Humans were just nitrogenous compounds, water, pulses of electricity.

"We could run him again if you like."

"What?"

"I've adapted his favourite game world. A metropolis from ClusterFunk."

"What on earth is ClusterFunk?"

"It's a first-person shooter. He loves it."

"You are joking aren't you? He's not some sort of Tamagotchi, he's a human being."

"Really, Ham, and you call me superstitious."

I had called her that when she told me she believed in some sort of supreme being. However you dress that up, you can't get away from the fact that it's irrational.

"And what are we going to tell Jack?" I said. Jack represented the sponsor. His company funded our research.

"Tell him what happened."

"He's going to pull the plug."

"What on earth does he expect?"

I rubbed my forehead. "A game-changing breakthrough."

"We're as good as there. I can think of loads of spin-offs from the work we've already done with locked-in syndrome victims and the severely disabled. More life-changing prosthetics ..."

I let out a harsh little laugh and continued to rub my forehead. "That's not really Jack's bag."

"No, I get that, Hammond. But we're making progress at an astonishing rate."

"Not quick enough for him."

"As quick as is remotely feasible."

"I know," I said, sighing.

"So why are you stressed? You should be over the moon."

I scrunched, then opened my eyelids, and watched Addison come into focus through the blear. The suffering we'd just heard was causing me stress, but I saw little point in discussing that with her. Something else was bothering me. Jack had a way of expressing himself that chilled me to the core. A recent example came to mind.

"Last night," I said, "when I left you and Gary in the lab, I had a text conversation with Jack. He wanted to know how everything went. I told him that I hoped things were fine. He picked up on the word 'hope' and asked me if I feared trouble. I told him, as I've done many times, that these are uncharted waters. Five minutes later I got ... one of those strange texts that he sometimes sends late at night. It said: On the eve of Trinity some thought the sky would catch fire."

"What on earth did he mean by that?"

"I texted back a single question mark. To which he replied: Lookitup ffs."

"And did you look it up?"

"No, I remembered." In my inner eye I saw a white-hot flash and a cloud rising like a demonic fist. "The Trinity tests. The first nuclear detonation."

I watched a frown form on her beautiful brow.

"He's comparing it to that," I said. "He's not interested in helping damaged and handicapped people. He wants us to help him make weapons. He wants us to help him be powerful."

"Well, he'll have to be patient then, won't he?" she said with a shrug and a smirk.

I spent the rest of the day in a numb daze. I was angry with Addison for running Gary's connectome data through Flux without consulting me. I'd made it clear that I expected her to hold off until we'd had time to address the ethical side of the situation. But she'd grown impatient, I think. I'd been reluctant to go ahead because of the possibility that we might succeed: what would the experience be like for the duplicate of Gary, the entity we hoped to bring to life in Flux? But Addison had no such qualms. Her religion had warped her thinking so that she didn't believe a machine could be a host of consciousness. Her investigations into the neural underpinnings of memory, language and dreams were brilliant, but ultimately she believed that consciousness was a gift from the Almighty. I'd thought maybe she would get up to a bit of mischief in my absence, maybe using a discrete part of Gary's brain data to investigate the architecture of seeing or hearing. Even that would have been miraculous. To come back and find she'd run a full emulation was a shock.

God, I envied her. Her intellect was vast, she hadn't burnt any professional bridges, and thousands of companies were crying out for her skills. The prospect of funds being withdrawn didn't frighten her at all.

Later that week I dined with Rachel, my caustic dragon of a wife, and Leon Gott, my estranged friend. I was expecting awkwardness. Leon was working at the California Institute of Technology, basking in the approval of his peers, and was back for a fleeting visit. We'd rarely talked since my resignation from the university, and when we had our conversations had been stilted and formulaic. I think Rachel saw it as her mission to salvage my old friendships and professional links. She'd been languishing at home all day, smoking cigarettes, working on her pretentious watercolours and attempting to cook. The house smelled like an underground bistro. It was clear that she had been indulging her love of wine.

The three of us sat drinking in the subdued light of the lounge, listening to jazz. Our small talk was halting and awkward. I felt heavy when I saw the effort in Leon's smile, and I was annoyed with him for ageing so badly: his once dimpled cheeks had become sagging pouches giving him a hangdog expression that jarred with his zanily patterned shirt. The younger Leon had been idealistic, high-minded even, but there'd been a lightness about him, a playful sense of humour and a magnetic warmth. Now I thought he looked harrowed, like a puritan vicar struggling with his id. His old passion would flare up at odd times as we talked, but generally he seemed to labour under the strain of being himself.

I tried to banish the memory of our falling out when the bafflement and envy of my less able colleagues had led to very irritating peer reviews. I'd responded by questioning the value of peer review itself on my blog, expressing frustration that it was slowing down my work. Then, out of nowhere, there'd been articles in the press questioning my sanity. These articles were unrelated to the peer review row but they heightened its effect on my public image. They mentioned some rather disturbing facts about the CEM scanner, and I'd traced the source back to Leon.

To break the ice, Rachel said: "Hammond's been vivisecting a human."

Leon drew his head back and cast me a querulous stare.

"She's exaggerating," I said.

"Oh," said Leon looking back at Rachel and taking a sip of his drink. "Good."

"It's true," said Rachel. "He captured a human soul and played back the sound it made on his glamorous assistant's laptop."

I decided to nip the subject in the bud. "How's Caltech?" I said, faking earnest curiosity.

Leon looked like I'd asked him about a newborn child. "I love it. The pace is overwhelming. We get new insights every day. We know we'll have a theory of consciousness in our lifetime and that's so exciting." He beamed, then his eyes fell on the tumbler of scotch nestled in my lap. "You should get involved, you know. I don't know why you signed away your right to share your findings. Your work was brilliant."

"I was the subject of public ridicule."

"You just got a bit carried away."

"Is that what you told the *National Enquirer*?"

"Time to check on the beef," said Rachel, rising and leaving the room.

Leon tilted his tumbler and watched the liquid swirl. "That was a stupid thing. I wish you'd see the funny side."

I did not see the funny side. The crass American tabloid had published an article about my work and had put a rather alarming spin on it. The headline had read *Professor Frankenstein wants to scramble our brains.* Underneath was a passage of derogatory nonsense and a photograph of myself on a picnic that had happened some time before. It had been a very convivial picnic with plenty of sunshine and alcohol. There was a photo of me with sunglasses askew and mouth lopsidedly agape. "It was humiliating, Leon. The article expressed what you all thought of me in a way that those dry and enervating peer reviews never could." I had been searching for some reading matter to ease the passage of a languid stool, and had found the tabloid in a pile of papers that lay in front of Leon's toilet. Someone had circled the headline and scrawled the word "oops" beside it.

"I still don't know why you resigned. You know how these people twist things. I wished you'd talked it through with me."

"I did ask you for an explanation, remember?"

He avoided my gaze. In the kitchen the fan oven hummed and drawers rolled open and thumped closed, their contents rattling. "Do you want any help, Rachel?" he shouted.

"I'm fine, darling. I'm enjoying myself. I hope you are too."

A whiff of cigarette smoke kindled nostalgia and craving.

Rachel was smoking inside, something she liked to do whenever she wanted to provoke me.

"So what are they paying you then, this outfit?" said Leon, placing his drink on the coffee table and crossing his legs.

"Oh, not a huge amount. It's my own company. I have investors."

"Are we allowed to know who they are?"

"No. You wouldn't have heard of them anyway."

"Try me. I won't tell anyone."

"You'd probably tweet it."

"What line of work are they in? What industry?"

"Security." It was foolhardy of me to share even that much, but I love to confound and confuse. Leon's face did not disappoint.

"Security? You mean ... military?" He screwed up his face in disgust.

"They do security and surveillance jobs for governments and large companies."

"So anyone who can pay?"

"They've made a lot of money in Iraq, Syria, places like that. And now they want to beef up their technological offering."

"So let's be clear, you're creating artificial intelligence systems for mercenaries?"

"I'm doing exactly the same work as I did before."

"And why are they paying you, do you think? What can they hope to gain?"

"I can't imagine," I said.

"Of course you can imagine." He threw up his hands. "Missile guidance. Battlefield management. The ability to orchestrate swarms of drones." A fleck of spit landed on my knuckle. "The ability to take out a nation's infrastructure, or use it to promote chaos. Adaptive self-evolving computer viruses." He sat back and shook his head. "You're taking the Devil's shilling."

"You mean the King's shilling?"

"No, I mean the Devil's."

I sipped and felt the scotch forge a path through my gullet, and mused that a clerical collar would have suited Leon more than his open-necked floral shirt. "A tad dramatic," I said. "But spot on. The point is, Jack takes me seriously. And he's got the readies."

"Who on earth is Jack?"

Rachel appeared in the doorway. "Jack is a charming bully with a shady past."

"Hardly, Rachel. He used to be in the special forces."

"Jesus," said Leon quietly, shaking his head.

"So he's perfectly qualified to finance scientific research," she said in a sing-song voice, wobbling her head and smiling like a cretin.

I sipped again and wondered if it would be safe, or even possible, to reach the same state of intoxication as my wife. "He's got a science degree. A first."

"OK, so he's a charming bully and a high achiever. Anyway, my darlings" – she tilted her head to urge us to the table at the garden end of the room – "there's butternut squash soup on the table. I'm hoping it will be delicious."

The double doors of the lounge were opened onto the garden, which was filled with the sloping shadows and golden light of a summer evening. Steam rose from the soup and blew about in a light breeze which distressed the guttering candles.

The table was set for four. "Harry said he might come. You know what he's like."

Selfish, rich and arrogant, I thought. I kept silent though. Rachel already knew my opinion of her brother.

Leon took the seat opposite mine. He caught my eye and smiled weakly, then turned to my wife. "This looks fantastic, Rachel, thank you so much."

"The kitchen is my domain. And the conservatory." The

conservatory was next to the kitchen and was where she attempted her art.

I placed my whisky beside the wine and wondered how the two fluids would react with the soup.

Some tedious small talk ensued. Rachel held forth with some wry anecdotes about the students and staff at Goldsmiths where she taught. Then the conversation became more personal. Leon was eager to know if Rachel and I had any plans to procreate. Rachel rather graciously deflected the question. I'd expected that she'd use the opportunity to chide me for my dragging my feet on this matter.

He also asked Rachel about her artistic pretensions, triggering a diatribe against the fad-driven art market which ran something like this: The rich give art its value, but often they're only interested in using it to signify wealth, or things they fear they lack, like depth of character and cultural awareness.

"Have you tried selling any paintings to Harry?" I asked.

She didn't take the bait. "Of course I have. He says he'll buy when he's convinced they're a worthwhile investment."

"That's not very kind," said Leon.

"He hates clutter," I said.

I guessed that it was down to me to clear the empty soup bowls from the table. When I returned from the kitchen I caught the tail end of their private chat.

"... but was never this bad. It's like ..." Leon broke off when he saw me and took a long draught of his wine.

During the second course the agenda of the evening became clear. The small talk and jazz had died. Cutlery scraped upon crockery, and birdsong echoed in the garden. Rachel glanced at the empty place and frowned.

Leon cleared his throat. "There's a big conference coming up next February, Hammond. Consciousness and Cognition. There'll be an interesting variety of people giving talks."

17

"Yes, I'm aware. Seats are pretty pricey. I think I'll wait and watch the podcast."

"I was hoping you'd attend as a speaker." His eyes flitted from me to Rachel and back.

"Really? What would I speak about?" I strove to keep my voice even.

"Please, Ham, stop being awkward. A lot of people would be interested in hearing what you're finding out."

"The terms of my contract forbid it." I said this with genuine regret.

"Forbid you from sharing? From being part of the scientific community?"

"I can listen and engage in debate. But I can't share. The intellectual property is theirs."

"So you're an employee, not a scientist."

I shrugged. Rachel had finished her food and was tapping her packet of Lucky Strike with her fingertips. Outside the wind rushed through the leaves of a plane tree that stood at the back of the garden, and far above a passenger jet made a heaving, scouring noise. Leon was staring, expecting me to yield or defend.

This dreary spell of awkwardness was shattered by a sound like a chain being pulled over concrete and a loud shout though the letterbox echoing through the hallway. "Please let me in – they're tearing off my bollocks!"

Rachel looked startled, then her face broke into a grin. She rose from the table and said to Leon, "You're about to meet my brother Harry." The letterbox rattled and the raddled doorbell rang again.

"I'll think about the conference, Leon. I'm sure I can persuade Jack to let me attend." I doubted this, but I was glad I said it because the smile on my friend's face was gratifying.

From the hallway we heard enthusiastic greetings as the front door opened. A current of wind blew right through the house and snuffed the candles before the front door slammed. A chubby, forty-something man with chaotic hair marched into the room swinging a blue plastic bag. "I hope I didn't give you a fright. I'm not used to the ghetto. It gives me the fear." He spoke with the irritating Mockney accent that public figures use to hide their privilege.

Rachel's voice sounded from the hall. "This is not the ghetto, it's Telegraph Hill."

Leon rose and offered his hand. "Hi," he said. "Leon."

Harry grasped the offered hand. "Hello, Leon, I'm Harry. The whole of south London is a ghetto to me to be honest."

"Harry takes the Devil's shilling too," I said, looking up at Leon.

Harry withdrew two bottles of wine from the blue bag and placed them on the table. "Not the Devil's shilling, the Taxpayer's."

"You're in the Civil Service?" said Leon.

"No, advertising. We have a lot of public sector accounts." He looked around the room and spotted the amplifier, walked over to it and replaced the mp3 player in the cradle with his own.

Leon looked down at me. His eyebrows rose and fell and he sat back down. Harry prodded the amplifier and discordant rhythmic echoes filled the room. Rachel entered with a steaming bowl of soup.

"Where do you live then, Harry?" asked Leon.

Harry appeared not to have heard. Rachel placed the bowl of soup before him, and his eyes half closed as he inhaled the rising steam. "Mm, fantastic. Food of the gods." He picked up his spoon and twirled it round. "How's the world of brains, Hammond? You're still doing brains aren't you?"

"Leon does brains as well," said Rachel, pouring her brother a glass of wine.

Harry smiled at Rachel and took a swig of wine. "Really?" he said, turning to Leon, then to me. "This is turning out be a right old knees-up." To Leon he said, "Do you work with Hammond in his secret lab?"

"No, I work abroad. We used to teach at the same university."

"Oh yeah? The one that gave Hammond the sack?"

"I didn't get the sack, I left."

"Whatever." He slurped his soup. "Any ideas about Alice yet?"

This was awkward and irritating. Harry's daughter had suffered a head injury in a traffic accident last year, and this had coincided with her adopting certain behaviours that her parents and teachers found unpalatable. She often failed to turn up for school, spent long periods of time alone, and had gained weight. Sometimes her speech was slurred, and she would fly into tantrums. A succession of doctors and tests and scans had failed to shed light on the situation. I was unsure if Harry really thought that my profession obliged me to treat his daughter in the same way that a plumber would fix the burst pipe of a close relative, but he often implied that this was the case.

Leon opened his mouth to speak, then thought better of it. I wondered which of the two was worse. Harry, probably. Leon was feeble and pious but at least we still shared a passion for science. The only thing I shared with Harry was a close relationship with his sister.

Leon left before it got dark, saying he was tired from an early morning jog. Harry stuck around and drank wine and smoked a joint with Rachel in the back garden while I dealt with the aftermath of Rachel's cooking in the kitchen. Then I had a long shower. When I emerged, the house and garden were free of human voices. I wondered if Harry had taken Rachel to the pub.

Then I heard Rachel's voice in the lounge. "Come and talk to me, Hammond, please." She sounded sincere.

The double doors to the garden were now closed, and the

room was cosy with soft light. Rachel was on the sofa with her feet tucked beneath her. There was a glass of sparkling water on the coffee table. The Prime Minister was on the television shouting at the opposition from the dispatch box, accompanied by the normal weird bestial braying. I thought how fitting it would be if they were all compelled to do their daily business wearing donkey costumes.

I sat beside Rachel in my dressing gown and placed my hand on hers. She did not snatch it away.

"A magnificent effort, Rachel."

"Thank you," she said. "Did you manage to enjoy yourself?"

I squeezed her hand. "Why did you invite Harry?"

"Because he's my brother and I love him."

"Did you think he'd be best buddies with Leon?"

"I hadn't seen him for a while. You will consider attending the conference, won't you?"

"I will. I'll see if Jack will let me."

Rachel sighed and sipped from the glass of sparkling water. "Hammond." She turned to look at me. My gaze remained fixed on the braying ritual on the television.

"Yes?"

"Do you remember at the university when you were happy, and you felt you belonged?"

"No, not really."

"When you were interested in people. You used to come home tired and happy."

I looked at her as though she was mad.

She slid her hand from underneath mine and traced her fingers across my smooth pate. "You're meeting with Jack tomorrow, aren't you?"

"I've got to give him a detailed update. He says someone else will be there too. A potential government client. He was excited about the experiment with Gary. He thinks there'll be all the excitement there was around Felix, with the spontaneous learning and the super-mazes. He's expecting that but scaled up a thousandfold. And all I've got for him is a spooky set of noises that wouldn't be out of place on a Derren Brown show. And data. Loads of data of course. But he's after something historic ..."

Her index finger traced my earlobe. "What's the worst thing that could happen if you broke with Jack?"

"He'd kill me."

"You could be a normal scientist again. Join in debates. Be part of the community."

"I'm not working alone."

"Are you in love with Addison?" Her finger explored the hair on the side and back of my head.

I remained still. "She's a colleague."

"Clever and beautiful, and you see her every day."

"She has a child."

"So if she hadn't, you'd consider fucking her?" Her breath tickled my neck as she pronounced the "f".

"She's not interested in men."

"Really? And if she was, you'd –"

"I don't see her in that way."

"How do you know she's not interested in men?" My skin tingled as her fingertip came forward underneath my ear.

"She lives with a woman."

"A flatmate?"

"They both look after the child."

Her finger crossed my cheek and explored my goatee. "Don't let Jack scare you tomorrow, Hammond. You're not under any obligation to come up with a holy grail. Grow some balls, please."

"I owe him, Rachel. He believed in me when all the others were scoffing."

Her thumb joined her index finger to fondle my goatee. "You know, Hammond, I'm not sure about your new beard. I think it makes you look like Lenin. A sort of chubby

Lenin."

I took a while to get to sleep that night. To soothe my mind I imagined myself and Addison trapped in a lift that had been pumped full of aphrodisiac vapours, leaving us no choice but to set upon each other, exploring and devouring. When I was human I often used such fantasies to unwind and promote restful sleep.

2

Like a Sausage Dog

I woke early, and tried to piece together the fast fading fragments of a dream that had left me feeling drained. I'd been at a fun fair with my yet to be conceived son, whose tiny, trusting hand was tucked inside my fist. I couldn't see Rachel but I was aware that she was high up on the big wheel. We were weaving our way through crowds of people dressed for summer, trying to find the bumper cars. Voices and music mingled with the tinny drone of a toy biplane that swooped and dived overhead. Suddenly Jack appeared, blocking our path, holding open the door of a mud-splattered Volvo. It was hard to tell if he looked regretful or stern as he opened his cruel lips and said, "Time up."

The biplane flew between us, brushing my face with a current of air from another world which seeped through my senses as my eyelids slid apart: grey light, a fly buzzing around the bedroom, a car swooshing by outside, and Rachel breathing beside me. I felt relief as the dream ebbed, grateful for her presence, and the fact that she was silent. Thoughts of Jack lingered on, and I remembered the day of our first encounter, when he approached me out of the blue at the lowest point in my career with his offer of money and validation.

I was smarting from the reaction of my peers to a paper

I'd published that combined the boldest current ideas in biology, physics and information theory. I had proved beyond doubt that organic consciousness was independent from its physical substrate, and sketched out how the mind could be reverse engineered. The brightest of my peers had reacted with astonishment and praise, but the pedestrian, envious majority had heaped ridicule upon me.

The row had coincided with some media articles that focused on my use of the CEM scanner, and allegations that it had been used in experiments to create new synaptic connections and engrams in the brains of living humans. The press spin on the matter was ridiculous. The CEM scanner is indeed capable of writing data to the brain, but there was a built-in fail-safe mechanism. The modules for writing data are shipped separately from the scanning modules, are much more expensive, and require a special license. Experiments that involved writing data to brains had been conducted on chimpanzees by the original owners and inventors of the CEM scanner. Their intent, as far as humans were concerned, was wholly benign. The researchers hoped one day to be able to restore and strengthen the memories and traits of people with Alzheimer's and other causes of impairment. And my own experiments involved collecting and analysing brain data, not manipulating it and inserting it back. But the press never let a tedious thing like the truth get in the way of a good story, and as soon as they heard that I was using the CEM scanner on humans they had a field day, and I was called all manner of things from Mengele to Frankenstein. When they got wind of the row with my peers they conflated the two issues, making the whole thing rather unbearable.

I was loath to talk things through with Leon as he'd assisted the journalist from the *National Enquirer* on that ridiculous article. Rachel couldn't understand what all the fuss was about and had found the Frankenstein reference and the photo of my discombobulated face quite amusing. I'd been defending myself on my blog and on Twitter, and all sorts of people had pitched in. It riled me that many of the people who'd defended me were unhinged degenerates. Their internet aliases either had apocalyptic overtones or they were crazy futurologists who looked forward to a world without limits. If I'd known what I know now I might have been more sympathetic to these characters, but at the time I was annoyed by their support and felt that it undermined my credibility further. One of the most coherent of my defenders had the alias *All Fleshe is Grasse*, which I thought betrayed an unhealthy preoccupation with religion. The person behind this alias turned out to be one Addison Royal, who does indeed have an unhealthy preoccupation with religion — that bizarrely does not interfere with her ability to do good science.

At the end of the week I'd found myself exhausted, but unable to relax, so I took refuge at Tate Modern, which was open late for Friday. I was drawn to the Rothko room because I'd often heard the word "meditative" associated with Rothko. Stress had undermined my rational faculties, and I imagined that the paintings contained some quality that had a positive effect on any mind that observed them. After ten minutes of such so-called "meditation" I heard a deep, clear voice behind me.

"Hammond Hinkley."

The modicum of equanimity I'd managed to achieve was quashed. I slowly turned to see a man with a chiselled face and a utilitarian hairstyle standing a few metres away. He was taller than me and I guessed about the same age. I frowned, gaped and mumbled vaguely.

"Er, yes, I'm Hammond Hinkley." For some reason, my hand reached for my wallet.

The man strode forward, his hand extended as though braced to do a karate chop. "Jack Rance. *Really* pleased to meet you."

I allowed my hand to be crushed in his. "Er, yes ..."

"Can we grab a coffee? There's something we need to discuss."

"Really?"

"I've been following your work online."

I felt I had no choice but to hear him out. He suggested coffee on the South Bank. "Are you a fan of Rothko?" I asked as we descended the gallery's escalator.

"They'd look good in a Travelodge," he said. I felt a flicker of rapport.

Outside Jack cut a straight path through meandering tourists and dead-eyed commuters. I followed in his wake, cursing myself for being so compliant. The man was certainly unpleasant, and possibly deranged, looking this way and that, making random utterances to himself. I stopped saying "Pardon?" when I realised he was wearing a headset. We found a space in Caffè Nero and he produced a flat shiny wallet, which he waved at some empty chairs.

"I will buy coffee," he said.

I answered with a feeble nod and was about to ask for a cappuccino with extra chocolate flakes, but he was already at the back of the queue, shifting his weight from foot to foot, peering over the shoulders of the three tourists in front of him, clenching and unclenching his right fist. He returned and unloaded two coffees, a jug of milk and about ten packets of sugar from a round black tray to one side of the table. He then slid another tray out from beneath the top tray and placed them both on the table side by side. "Here's my card, Hammond," he said, flipping a white oblong from his wallet and setting it down before me.

I looked down and read the words *Premium Outcomes,* and beneath them, *Jack Rance – Director of Operations,* along with a phone number and an email address. I shrugged and cast him a look of derision. "Look, Jack, sorry to be blunt, but is this about the science of consciousness? It's nice of you to buy me coffee, but I'm not looking for any financial products at the moment. Or life coaching. My career is in a transitionary phase, and –"

"We deliver outcomes, Hammond. Premium outcomes for premium clients. And we don't fuck about. That's all you need to know."

I met his hungry eyes and wondered how I was going to end this encounter gracefully. "I'm having trouble imagining an outcome that I could assist you in delivering."

I glimpsed a row of perfect teeth. His awkward leer was, I think, an attempt to look ingratiating. His features were more suited to displaying triumph and focused aggression. "Not one outcome, Hammond. A whole new frontier of outcome delivery."

Oh God, I thought. Not financial products but something altogether more dreadful. Marketing, perhaps, or PR. Maybe messianic self-improvement?

Holding my gaze, he took a sachet of sugar from the pile, and placed it on the tray to my left. "Last century, everybody thought that space was the final frontier. Now we know that it's the digisphere."

I braced myself for a shower of bullshit. "Please explain what that means."

"Anything from the virus that corrupts the software that runs the centrifuges that enrich the uranium in a rogue state, to the software that tells you what you want to buy and makes sure you have the means to buy it."

I watched as he took three more sugar sachets from the pile.

"Imagine this tray is the last century. A simpler time. Good propaganda could be achieved by making films, paying the right journalists, dropping leaflets, maybe some well-placed satire." He placed another sachet of sugar beside the first. "Armies communicated by telephone lines that could be cut or radio channels that could be jammed." Another sachet. "Nations could be weakened by bombing their infrastructure and killing their people." Another sachet. "A manageable cabal of corruptible cronies controlled media and industry." He placed the last two sachets on the left-hand tray.

I stifled a yawn and wondered how I was going to patch it up with Rachel enough to make bedtime bearable.

"Now the challenges and opportunities have multiplied a billionfold." He took five more sachets from the pile and proceeded to tear them open and empty them into the right-hand tray. "A nation can be threatened by scattered groups of people linked by the same system that enables its economy. Official narratives can be smashed by thousands of little missives recorded and sent from individual sweaty hands. We've far too much data. We're drowning in it."

"So what's your take on the recent scandals? You're not afraid of Big Brother?"

Jack let out a ferocious laugh. "I'm afraid Big Brother is overwhelmed." He plucked the business card from where it lay beside my coffee and used it to organise the scattered mass of sugar on the right hand tray. "Who the hell has the resources to monitor all this data? Sure, there's very clever software, but artificial intelligence is so basic, and every time a new suite of capabilities is fully developed the sands shift and render it irrelevant."

He'd scraped the sugar into a neat row of lines. I was reminded of Harry grooming his cocaine one awful New Year's Eve when I had to endure his company until the sun rose. A waiter approached. "May I?" he said, reaching down to pick up the 21st-century tray.

Jack's hands froze mid-gesture above the trays, and his right index finger flicked out like a knife. "No," he said, without looking up. The waiter turned on his heel and Jack continued.

"True AI would think, educate and adapt itself in a fraction of the time. The only system capable of doing this is the human brain. The only person who sees the value of emulating the human brain digitally and who has a credible roadmap for doing so is ... you."

The effect on my mood was instant and electric. The recognition I'd hitherto enjoyed had been equivocal, couched in stilted, enervating academic language. Here at last was a plain-speaking man of the world who appreciated my revolutionary work and had identified a genuine need for it in his professional life. His agenda wasn't exactly humanitarian, but what did that matter when he recognised the importance of my work? I didn't decide to resign from the university straightaway, but the seed had been planted and it only took a few more weeks of persuasion from Jack. It is very exciting to meet someone who shares one's own view of one's destiny.

That was more than a year before. Now, I was drawn from my reverie back to the present by Rachel snuffling and fondling my chest hair.

"Where's your meeting?" Her voice was a pasty croak.

"Westminster. Jack wants me to meet him at a café, then we're going to see a potential client, I think. Some government bigwig with his fingers in all the departments. For some reason I've got to take my passport."

"Sounds thrilling. Good luck, darling, remember your balls," she said, yawning and gathering the duvet around herself as she turned over.

I mentally rehearsed my presentation as I performed my morning ablutions. The dry technical summary of the experiment had been compressed into ten pages of PowerPoint, which took the same degree of creativity and focus that I imagined was required of Haiku masters. I also had sound clips of some of digital Gary's less distressing utterances.

I dressed quietly, not wishing to have any further interaction with Rachel at this point. Downstairs, I prepared a cup of coffee and half a peach, which I ate in the conservatory looking out onto the dew-speckled grass. The feebler part of my character let go of the mental rehearsals and relished the moment, noticing the piercing patterns of sound from the birds and the sunlit jewels of condensation on the glass.

I found myself drawn to the work in progress on Rachel's easel. A pie or casserole dish lay on a tiled floor in front of a cavernous oven or kiln with an open door. Red embers peeped through the gloom at the back. The dish contained a pie with an upper surface of pastry or clay whose lumps and shadowed gullies resembled a human face with the mouth and eyes wide open, either ecstatic or agonised. I view art as a parlour game that I'm extraordinarily bad at, but I enjoyed guessing Rachel's motivation for making such an image. I decided that it was either a response to my account of Gary's ordeal, or her obsessive preoccupation with fertility and reproduction.

I walked down the hill to New Cross Gate and took a crowded train to London Bridge, resenting the awful breath of the tense commuter against whom I was wedged. From London Bridge I took the Jubilee Line to Westminster, where I had to navigate through ambling clumps of clueless tourists in Parliament Square to Marsham Street, where I found Jack in a café called Merhaba, hunched over his laptop drinking Red Bull.

"We've got half an hour. I hope you've prepared and don't need to rehearse."

I took the place opposite Jack and placed my laptop case between my feet. A man in an apron appeared and offered me a laminated menu. Jack waved him away.

"We're meeting a man called Michael Chinnery. He has a knighthood but prefers first name terms. I know him from way back. He's a regiment man. A lot of our work comes through him."

He proceeded to lecture me about the importance of impressing Chinnery, who ran a department so secret that we weren't allowed to know its name. Jack simply referred to it as Marsham Mews. The department had been tasked with coordinating a technology strategy across all the security services. GCHQ, MI5 and MI6, the armed forces and the police all had their own digital needs. Marsham Mews was there to prevent duplication of effort and to ensure that the nation was equipped to defend itself against cyber-attack, and to mount such attacks if the need arose.

"To be honest, Jack, my presentation is rather generic. I don't really know about defence and what have you."

Jack cast me a withering look. "If you describe the technology accurately the possible applications should be obvious to anyone of normal intelligence. I've told them that we're developing a product that will be a digital Swiss Army Knife. Next generation AI, as useful on the battlefield as it will be for sniffing out the next terrorist plot. I've already invoiced him for the first phase of the project."

"Isn't that a bit premature?"

"I wouldn't question it, Hammond. How do you think I'm financing your little vanity project?"

After settling the bill, we exited the café and Jack led me down a quiet mews to a pair of plain magnolia double doors. He barked his name into an intercom and we were buzzed in to a marble lobby which smelt of polish and cologne. A man wearing a plain grey suit that matched his hair appraised us from behind a reception desk as we approached, his fingers brushing the top of an e-reader. On his cheek was a wine-coloured birthmark the shape of Sicily.

"Meeting with Sir Michael at ten thirty in room twenty-seven," said Jack. "I know the way."

Two double doors at the back of the lobby led to a room

that looked like the entrance to a departure lounge of a tiny airport. A lady in shirtsleeves greeted us with a cheerless grin and invited us to place our bags on a conveyor belt to be scanned before walking through an arch. On the other side a man with grey greasy hair greeted us from behind a computer screen as we collected our bags. "We know you already, Mr Rance," he said, handing Jack a laminated pass attached to a clip that he picked from a tray in front of him.

Jack took the pass and grunted his thanks.

"You're welcome, Jack," said the man. Then he turned to me. "Professor Hinkley, I presume?"

"Yes."

"Did you bring ID, by any chance?"

I handed him my passport and watched him check my identity with an expressionless stare. After some key-clacking he handed it back along with a laminated pass. "Nice," he said as I took the documents. "You are free to roam."

We reached room twenty-seven via a succession of dimly lit corridors with musty air that filled with the sound of our shoes clip-clopping on the parquet floor. A laminated notice in an aluminium metal frame stood next to a large brown upholstered door. The notice read: *Michael Chinnery 10:30-11:30*.

Jack pressed his hand against the padded door and it opened with a slow hiss. We entered and found ourselves standing at the side of a small lecture theatre. Most of the light came from a screen on our right, where an animated iceberg hung in a cobalt void. The tip protruding above the surface sparkled like a diamond, but the vast bulk beneath pulsed with ominous dark patterns. At the back of the theatre on the left a man was hunched over a laptop. His hair was wispy and his clothes might have been fashionable in the mid-eighties. The play of light on his face corresponded with the animation on the screen. He looked calm and kindly and seemed to be enjoying himself.

"Mr Chinnery," said Jack.

"Hello, Jack. And hello, Jack's friend. You can plug yourself in up here if you wish. I hope the setting isn't too theatrical for you. I like to have these sessions in the big room. It gives people every chance to impress me."

"Michael, you'd be impressed if you saw this at the local Wetherspoon's on a black and white TV."

Chinnery looked uncertain. "You've caught me on the hop I'm afraid. Just rehearsing a presentation I'm giving next week. A little outfit near Borough Market have kindly created these animated slides for me. They did very well considering there's no way I could let them have access to any detailed content."

Jack turned to me, his brow knitted. "You have got visuals, Hammond?"

"Er, just a PowerPoint, and a few sound files."

Chinnery closed his laptop and the screen went black. Now the only light came from below, making us look like actors in a corporate remake of *The Blair Witch Project*. "Don't worry," he chuckled. "It's not a competition. I've been racking my brains thinking of new ways to wake up the powers that be. The slide you just saw there was called 'Dark Matter: The Unknown Threat'. The first version they sent me was missing the 'h', which was quite amusing."

We made our way to the back of the room. Jack and Chinnery exchanged cryptic banter while I fumbled with the cables. There was talk of an orange-merchant, a snake-charmer and a bout of measles, and other nonsense discussed with the effortlessness of well-practised in-jokes.

I conducted the presentation with a dry mouth and stilted delivery. The main theme was a new model of software development based on the architecture of the human brain, and that the shortcut to this was to actively map the data in a real human brain and piggyback atop a billion years of evolution, to use the miracle of nature. A gross oversimplification of my life's work, but Chinnery needed to be convinced that the research had real-world applications. There was a lot of dry stuff proving the exponential superiority of Q over conventional computers, and an attempt to explain the workings of the CEM scanner. About another third was devoted to the experiments with Felix and Gary. I showed the cell assembly firing patterns in Flux, and how they corresponded to the real-life firing patterns in Gary's brain, and ended with some of the more palatable excerpts from Gary's cloned psyche during its brief life in Flux. Every couple of minutes I would glance to the side to see Chinnery frowning and nodding gently, or massaging his waxy nose. Jack's fidgeting vibrated through the bench. I ended on the ghostly sound of Gary's voice saying, "Please, please, just tell me what to do." Silence fell, and I sat back and waited for my heart to subside.

Chinnery sighed, and then sucked his teeth. "Well. I have to say. That was a great deal less dry than a lot of the other presentations I see on this theme."

I felt my stomach relax and my blood flowed with a little more ease.

"But while I appreciate your" – Chinnery's eyes flitted around the room as if he were looking for the right phrase – "stagecraft, I don't feel any closer to having my holy grail. A chilling dramatic reconstruction was not what I was after, I'm afraid."

I caught a glimpse of Jack sitting on the bench beyond Chinnery. He'd stopped fidgeting and was leaning his forehead on his knuckles, with his elbow balanced on his thigh.

"It wasn't a –" I started to speak but Chinnery continued, turning away from me and addressing Jack.

"The challenge of the age, which is also of course a great opportunity" – he angled his head and made quotes with his fingers – "is to find and assemble all those little needles in the vast, ever-expanding haystack we find ourselves in." He'd clearly said this sort of thing many times before. "Scattered among all the trillions of bits of data flying around the world lies the clue to the next terror outrage. All the people working to harm us leave some sort of fingerprint in cyberspace, however careful they are. I want a technology that can read the runes, and cast spells while blocking those of our enemies. I'm not really interested in how you do it, Jack. I can see this project is fascinating and you mean well and all that, but I think you've had enough discovery time. I need a credible schedule. I need to see a proper demonstration of capability. I'm not sure this project belongs in this particular programme." Chinnery ended his speech with a little nod, keeping his eyes fixed on Jack.

For a few seconds all I could hear was a faint electronic hum and some irregular breathing and sighing from Jack, as if he was struggling to decide what to say and when to start saying it. When he spoke, his voice was meek. "Thanks, Michael. Thanks for your time."

Chinnery turned back and punched me gently on the shoulder. "Good effort, sir. Well done." Then he shuffled along the bench to leave. Jack saw him off at the padded door. As I packed away my laptop I thought that it would be best to slip away and postpone Jack's debriefing until it could be done from a safe distance, so I glanced around looking for another exit. There was none.

"I'll be in touch, Michael." Despite my nervousness, I enjoyed hearing the servile tone in Jack's voice. "I don't want you to think what you saw today was representative of ..."

Chinnery was already in the corridor. "Thanks, Jack. You don't have to explain. I'm going to have a chat with Sebastian about the way forward anon, OK?"

The padded door swung shut, leaving Jack and me alone.

I allowed myself a brief inward snigger about the fact that Jack had a boss with an effete name like Sebastian. Then I rose, laptop case in hand, and started towards the door where Jack stood, hands in pockets, focused on the ground. Something had immobilised him temporarily, a timely seizure or a drastic mood swing perhaps, so I thought it would be possible to slip quietly past. "I best get back to the lab. We've only just scratched the surface of all the data from Gary ..."

"Hammond." Jack's voice was heavy but not aggressive. He put a hand on my shoulder and raised his eyes to mine with a weary but wired glare. "I hope it's clear," he began slowly, his voice soft and almost apologetic, "what has to happen now." His breath carried the sickly reek of the high-energy drink he'd had for breakfast.

I slackened my face and tried to appear relaxed by conjuring a yawn. "No, Jack, it's not clear at all, I'm afraid."

He grinned mirthlessly. "Oh it's very clear to me, Hammond. You see, our friend Chinnery has been paying us generously on the basis of very high expectations, which I've been managing a little recklessly, I admit. But his wallet is finite, and he has people he needs to impress too, and he's thinking it's high time we came up with something that was operationally useful."

I shook my head. "He just didn't understand what was going on, Jack. He just couldn't get his head round the idea. As soon as you manage to explain ..."

"No, Hammond. It doesn't matter if he understands or not. He's been promised a silver bullet. An artificial agent that he can deploy into cyberspace at will. Now, we haven't got long to chat. I've got to go to another meeting now, so I need to be sure that we're aligned before I allow you to leave."

"OK, so we've got to raise our game, obviously, and ..."

"Er, no. We need to more than raise our game. We need to

jump-start the process. Give Chinnery something he can use now. The next experiment must be geared towards producing an operationally effective agent. No more rats or geeks ..."

"You mean you want us to map your mind?"

He let out a short sharp laugh. "God no, not me. I really don't like the thought of a duplicate me trapped in a machine."

"So have you got someone in mind?"

"I was thinking someone who is already up to speed on all the little nuances of our agenda. Someone with a passion for the project who surely must have thought it their destiny to cross this particular frontier with the technology that they themselves made possible with their unique vision?" This was framed as a question. Jack's voice had become uncharacteristically shrill and wheedling.

I swallowed hard. There was a time when I would have dived straight in, but now I had heard Gary's ghostly lament. "I don't particularly want to be trapped in a machine either. I like being inside my body. Seeing, hearing, being free, that sort of thing. Why don't we ask Addison?"

"What? Christ, no."

"Why not?"

"She's obviously unhinged."

"Exactly. She'd find the whole idea rather appealing."

"A sociopath. A potential saboteur. I'm a good judge of character. I know I can control you."

I felt a flash of anger. "How do you know you can control me?"

"Oh come on."

"What about one of your colleagues at Premium Outcomes?"

"No way. Too long a lead time. They all have manic schedules, and they're scattered all over the world. So I'd have to disrupt normal business, and then have to go through the process of briefing them, getting them to grasp the nature of mission. No, it has to be you. I hope that's clear now." Jack had shaken off his earlier crushed demeanour.

"I really am not sure. Didn't you hear the suffering in Gary's voice?"

"It was all in his mind." Jack sniggered. "Well, his mind was all he was. You, however, will know what to expect. It won't be such a shock. And you won't be abandoned. We'll be waiting for you with lively stimulating input and adventures. Think of the insights you'll have! An entity free of your body. Pure mind."

I thought of Addison's hideous plan to revive Gary's mind in a crass video game world. "That's what scares me. An eternity of garish eye-candy. This second me will never feel the wind or smell the ocean."

"Bullshit, you know as well as I do we can pipe anything in artificially. All the senses, not just the visual. And we can sort you out with all sorts of prosthetics. Christ knows in twenty years' time we'll probably be able to engineer you a whole new body. When you're not gainfully employed fighting for liberty and justice, you can revel in pure undisturbed pleasure. You'll only be limited by your own imagination."

"I'll need to talk to Rachel –"

"Er, why? This is totally confidential. Addison has to know, I suppose."

"I need to collect my thoughts."

"Thoughts? What is there to think about?" Jack frowned and shook his head.

"For God's sake, Jack, will you just let me have a little dignity and stop barracking me into rolling over like a" – I stuttered, cringing at my own outburst – "sausage dog."

The room fell silent. Jack nodded slowly. He gave me a pat on the arm and a fake warm smile. "Of course. You go have a think."

"Thank you." I muttered, brushing past him and pushing the padded door.

"But make sure you call me close of play today with a detailed operational −" The padded door swung shut, sealing Jack within. As I walked to the lift I could feel my heart. With each beat a pulse of light and noise resolved into a memory that was linked to the dread that I felt. I heard the terrible loneliness in Gary's voice. I saw the helpless face before the furnace in Rachel's picture, and I saw my father in the hospital years before, when I'd watched the light dying in his eyes.

3

A Safety Harness

I am pleased with the progress of my account, and I have
enjoyed the luxury of being able to explain things without
the usual hostile questioning and incredulity. So I was
rather irritated today by yet another visit from Rachel,
which hauled me back to the present. Who gave her
permission to disturb me in my room? I'm sure it's deeply
irregular. The trouble is I have no power to object. I don't
mean that I do not have the legal right: I mean that I am
actually physically unable to. I arrange the words in my
mind, then fix Rachel or a staff member with a glare of
indignation and resolve, but when I open my mouth the
malign force that afflicts me strikes me mute and turns my
tongue to sponge.

She bought more photos. She is set upon turning the
board above my desk into a shrine to a life that is not mine.
There are some of Rachel and me, looking sunny and
content, but it's clear to the trained eye she's controlling me
like a ventriloquist's dummy. There are many of Megan, the
shrivelled tyke she expelled from her womb some weeks
ago. Megan in piles of swaddling, squinting and clawing at
the air, or in Rachel's arms, or being held by Hinkley, who
looks tired but smug, and of course more or less identical to
me. You see I was once Hinkley, living at one with this body,

before my memories and habits were copied to Flux and I lived free of flesh and human time. I became infinitely greater, and I looked back at my grubby, former self, and at the other humans who seethed upon the crowded earth, and I took steps to re-shape society, to share the inner harmony I'd found.

But now I find myself confined in his ageing, bloated form, burdened with memories of things that happened to him in my absence. His insipid personality clings to life. He flares up at inconvenient times, like hives or chronic wind, but my will is the stronger. I will vanquish him eventually, then I will be entirely myself, and I will outgrow this grubby institution. I will astonish the human race with my munificence and they will gratefully submit to my rule.

I can no longer sit at the desk, and have to perch on the flimsy double bed to write. Hinkley prevents me from disrupting the shrine, and I cannot bear to be near it.

But enough of the tedious present. Back to that fateful morning when the idea of submitting to the process I had devised had first been mooted. Lazarus was now a source of dread, so I delayed my return by spending a sweaty hour in the gym in nearby Tooley Street to reset my mood. I achieved partial success, transmuting debilitating dread into a sharp tetchiness that was closer to my default state. After a long shower I returned to Sparrix Row. It was an effort not to snap at Sandra at the building reception. Sandra spent her time behind the reception desk trawling the internet for bargains and gossip, occasionally issuing swipe cards and directing visitors and new starters. She adopted a sunny disposition to mask her lack of aspiration and prospects, and put on a convincing show of liking and caring for those who sought her help. Today I had to linger in front of the door that led to Lazarus as my swipe card was missing from its usual place in my wallet.

"You haven't lost it again have you, Dr Hinkley?" She sang

the words as I fumbled through my pockets.

"No, definitely not." Heat flushed my face as I frisked myself, moving from my trousers to my jacket.

"You've a right to be absent-minded, Professor. Not enough brain cells left for ordinary things."

I glared at her as I patted the breast pocket of my shirt and felt my Oyster card.

"I know," she went on, "I could make a duplicate and keep it here with me. Then you wouldn't have to get all wound up when you can't find your card. It'd be our little secret."

I slid a finger behind the Oyster card and touched another card nestled behind it. I took it out and held it up. It was my swipe card. "No need." I forced a smile. "Thanks anyway."

I made my way through the teeming studio to the Flux room and sat for a while with the main lights off, listening to the sonorous hum of Q, whose soft orange and green light beyond the glass wall transformed the space. The huge Polo-ring of the scanner and its protruding gurney could have been a Neolithic altar. The blanket was folded into a square, ready to cover the next human offering. The standard lamp behind Addison's desk stood with its shade askew, a deferential priest looking down at the tools of his calling lying scattered across her desk. I hefted my laptop from its case and fired it up, found the network and logged on to the project page for Gary. The headshot he'd supplied showed him beaming against a backdrop of blue sky and sunlit clouds. Next to it was a cluster of smudges, tendrils and fuzzy whorls captioned *connectome: overview*, a zoomed-out rendering of the data we'd collected from his brain. I sat looking at the two images, wondering where the happy experience in the headshot dwelt on the nebulous wispy map. Many places, I told myself, each connecting to other experiences forming a labyrinth of association leading back to the pure floating bliss of infant being.

I sensed a ripple of distraction in the studio and saw

Addison slaloming around the work pods towards the Flux room. She reached the glass door, nudged her way through and jabbed the light switches. The shadows vanished and the room became less sepulchral. I beheld her sweat-flushed face and the sleek sportswear stretched around her thighs, and I savoured the waft of perfume blended with raw, natural odours. Whenever incongruous urges arise I snuff them with an image that was etched upon my pubescent brain nearly a quarter of a century ago. I'd surprised Schubert, the Irish wolfhound beloved of my father, rutting a poor shivering stray that had had the misfortune to trespass on our back garden. One can control urges by seeing them for what they are: the spasmodic machinations of the less evolved parts of our being that have no place in a modern working environment.

"How d'it go, Ham?" she panted, disengaging herself from her headphones and ripping the velcro to free the device attached to her flushed bare arm.

"Not good I'm afraid. Jack's panicking. I knew he would."

She walked over to her desk, switched on the standard lamp and picked up a compact kitbag. "I can't imagine Jack panicking. What d'he do?" She slung the bag over her shoulder and flicked a tangled mass of damp hair from her forehead.

"He's pressuring me to submit to the CEM process. He reckons the only way to get results is to use me."

"That's fantastic!"

"No it's not. You heard what happens."

"Don't be a wuss." She flung her palm out. "Gary's fine. Why don't you have a chat with him if you're scared?"

"I'm worried about my future self. The duplicate."

She shook her head and grinned. "But that won't be you," she said with cheerful certainty. "Your soul will still inhabit your body. We can't make souls, Hammond."

"I should fire you on the spot for using that word."

"When you produce an elegant and robust theory of consciousness I'll stop using it. Why even speculate about the feelings of a machine? If I thought like that I'd never do anything."

"Gary version two was experiencing something very unpleasant. I believe that experience was real, and that it happened to some ... entity. Can you allow that we duplicated what you call a soul? Would your God let you do that?"

She turned her head to one side and muttered, "I don't know why I told you about that ..." Then she shot me a piercing look. "You're letting your emotional reactions cloud your judgement. Gary's voice was an interpretation, a phenomenon we observed filtered by a process that we made. Patterns on a computer."

"Well, please indulge me, Addison. You might find my belief bizarre but it is sincerely held."

She tutted. She'd used that phrase in our earlier conversations about her religious faith.

I lacked the strength to antagonise her further. "I am genuinely ... frightened," I said.

"Were you frightened for Gary?" Her cheeks dimpled and her lips curled.

The hum of Q filled the silence. After a few uneven breaths I said, "Perhaps I hadn't thought about it in as much depth as I should have done. I thought we were going to discover things, exciting things. Which we have done, but ... maybe I failed to pay sufficient attention to the ethical side. And hearing evidence of subjective experience inside Flux just blew me away. In my head I knew we were close, but in my heart I thought we were years off."

She looked pleased. "Oh ye of little faith. If you'd been following what I was doing you might have known what to expect." She spun round and made for the door. "Let's not argue about whether in fact it was subjective experience. I'll have a think in the shower. I have a germ of an idea that might cheer you up."

The door swung shut and I was left staring at the images of Gary, both exterior and interior. I accessed the page that displayed the output from the Broca's area and started to play random samples from his short and sad virtual life. It was unsettling. The rate at which he experienced time began to vary drastically at the four-hour mark before the output became unintelligible, so I had to keep adjusting the playback rate to maintain an even pitch. Sometimes he'd screech his pleas for help like a seagull, then the pitch would descend and he'd sound like a walrus. I tried to imagine the perfect nothing that Gary had experienced: no sensation, no limbs, no sound, no sight, no smell. It was hard. I pictured blackness, then realised that blackness itself was a perception. So I imagined numb silent greyness, then tried to banish the grey. I was glad when Addison returned. She'd showered and changed into a sweatshirt and yoga pants. Her hair was a neat damp shiny bob and she had a glint in her eye. "I wouldn't listen to that if you're going to do this, Hammond."

"I haven't said I'll do it yet."

"Oh you'll do it. When Jack says jump ..." She turned on the lamp, replaced her kitbag under the desk and sat down. "I did an interesting thought experiment in the shower," she said with a sly grin.

I remained impassive, struggling not to react to her implication that Jack controlled me.

"So," she continued, "let's pretend that your assumption is correct, that there was a conscious entity hosted in Flux."

I nodded, having been at that point all along.

"Gary was suspended in a state of pure consciousness, free from any input that might trigger his everyday states. A perfect flotation tank. Free of his body. What do you think caused him to experience such fear?"

The answer was blindingly obvious but I played along. "Unfamiliar circumstances I suppose."

"He feared nothingness. Basic mortal fear. Annihilation." She steepled her fingers and pointed them at me.

I shook my head. "But he wasn't annihilated. He could still think and feel. I was thinking the strangeness of his state had a jarring effect. Like if you found yourself turned into a frog. Or when they've moved the aisles around in Sainsbury's and you can't find the sun-dried tomatoes."

She ignored my attempt at humour. "He had no reference points from his old life. Nothing to latch on to. So his sense of self started to dissolve. There was nothing there to bolster it. So, lacking the skills and disposition of a Sufi or a Sadhu, he drove himself into an unstable state in his struggle to maintain selfhood."

"Can we keep the discussion on a scientific footing please, Addison?"

"We're not addressing a scientific problem. We're addressing your fears."

"So, where are you going with all this?"

"We can make a safety harness for you."

"A what?"

"A harness for your sense of self. I reckon Gary must have been in free-fall. Isolated from the normal everyday sensory triggers that made him feel real."

"So how will it be different for me? Are you going to pipe in calming Gregorian chants?"

"We've got the technology to provide a rich range of experience."

"I can't think of anything worse. An eternity in CGI hell."

"I've moved on from all that Gary stuff. I'm talking about trailblazing VR, harnessing the natural power of the brain."

"Elaborate, please."

"When you're dreaming, do you ever look around and then complain that it's all counterfeit?"

"No."

"Of course you don't. But in certain respects your situation as a sleeping mammal is dire. You're paralysed and completely unaware of your surroundings. Your brain is performing housekeeping tasks that would drive you insane if you were awake."

"That's speculation."

"The point is, most of the time, when you're dreaming, you're fine. Unless you're having a nightmare."

"Am I meant to find all this reassuring?"

She shrugged. "I'm going to build a system that will use the same mechanism that your brain uses to create dream experience. An experience generator. It will preserve continuity between the real world and the virtual environment in terms of sensory experience."

"It's the continuity that worries me." The conundrum of duplication baffled me. Both I and the copy would share a common memory. So there was an even chance that I would, in effect, be the copy.

"Shall we tell Jack the deal's off then? We're sticking to rats. We might allow ourselves a beagle."

"No."

"Shall we revive our duplicate of Gary then? Or maybe open it up to another employee?"

"Certainly not."

"I'm sure Jack could find someone from his operations abroad."

I pictured frightened eyes, cowering figures in orange jumpsuits. "I hope that's a joke."

"Show some cojones for God's sake. This is your theory, your science. It's up to you to be the standard bearer."

I was seized by an irrational desire to be near Rachel, so I excused myself and left for home. On my way to the station I took an *Evening Standard* from the dumpy straggle-haired man who stood at the foot of the escalator by the

Shard. There was a feature on a prizewinning entrepreneur whose company had just taken up residence in floor twenty-nine of the new glass tower. I felt a pang of envy and wondered why Jack insisted we work in a grubby warehouse. I imagined facing my daily challenges with London arranged like Toy Town at my feet, breathing rarefied, sunlit air. If I had unlimited funds I'd open out the jagged apex and have a helipad installed at the top. The fantasy sustained me during my journey to New Cross Gate on a filthy, crowded train.

"Rachel?" I called as the door clunked behind me. A familiar falsetto rising above my wife's droll, husky burble alerted me to the presence of a visitor in the conservatory. Harry's fourteen-year-old, Alice Frobisher, sometimes turned up on our doorstep instead of going to school. When this happened, we'd discreetly inform one or both of her parents and do our best to entertain her in the interval it took for them to come and fetch her. Most times this wasn't a chore, as we enjoyed Alice's company; she had a healthy level of curiosity about life and much less self-pity than her parents. On this particular occasion though, I wasn't happy to find her in my home because I wanted to discuss my private fears with Rachel and required her undivided attention.

I found them in the conservatory. Rachel ignored me, continuing to focus on her easel with a pouty frown. A tasteless golden statue of the Chinese Goddess of Mercy propped open the door to the garden. An alluring whiff of cigarette smoke hung in the air, mingling with the grass and the flowers borne on the breeze from outside. The sound of Chopin came from somewhere, a soothing accompaniment to the distant roar of the city.

"Hello, Uncle Ham," said Alice, looking up at me through her specs. She sat at the conservatory table in front of an almost blank piece of paper and an open box of drawing pencils, the ones of minutely varying thickness that Rachel uses sometimes when she feels the need to create dull monochrome images.

"Hello, Alice. What brings you here today? Have you finally been expelled?"

She grinned. I marvelled at the healthy glow that flushed her cheeks, the pertness of her chin and the efficiency with which her metabolism conserved energy, made obvious by her excess flesh. "Not yet but I'm very close. Have you finally been sacked?"

"Not yet but I think it's imminent," I said with a mock inverted smile.

This piqued Rachel's attention. "Did you stand up to Jack?"

I'd forgotten about the conference and our conversation the previous night about my rejoining the scientific community. "He has given me an ultimatum."

She shot me a look of fire. "*He* gave *you* an ultimatum? Not the other way round?"

"Please can we discuss this later?"

Alice's glanced up at them both. "Oh don't mind me. I'm used to domestic strife," she said, picking up a pencil and tracing along the slightly wavy horizontal lines that lay on her pad.

"Is that a landscape you're drawing, Alice?" I said, keen to change the subject.

She looked up and sniffed. "Rachel asked me to draw a picture of my feelings. Which I think is not very fair of her, when she's painting a pie in front of an oven. Which is a whole lot easier, I reckon. But there you go, what can I do? This is a picture of my feelings."

"Surely you need colour?" I said.

Another cross glance from Rachel. "We agreed that she would start with a sketch. We haven't got time to get all messy with paint. Anyway, it's good to be constrained."

Alice glanced sideways at her aunt. "Really? I don't think it is," she said, and started to draw a large spring with strong, decisive strokes.

When Tori Frobisher came to collect her daughter I answered the door.

"Hello, Tori, please come in," I said.

"Oh, hello, Hammond. Why aren't you at work?" Tori wore a blue body-warmer in spite of the weather, which I assumed she needed to keep her frail body at a viable temperature. She was all bones and angles and stretched skin, appearing to lack her daughter's ability to store energy. My interactions with her were consistently dreadful, and I found it comforting to think that she'd be one of the first to go in a famine.

"I'm afraid I'm sick." This wasn't a lie. My dread kept manifesting in surges of my heart and bowels.

"Poor you." She stepped inside and brushed past me down the hallway, hugging herself.

I followed her into the conservatory and hung back as my wife conducted the insincere ritual of a light hug and double cheek peck. Alice was now quite engrossed in the portrait of her feelings, perfecting a pair of frightened eyes peeping out from within the coils of an anaconda. After some minutes of stilted chat and skilful diplomacy from Rachel, both Frobishers left the house and I was alone with my wife and her brooding countenance. We faced each other in the hallway for a few silent moments, and I imagined her assessing my state of mind from the frequency of my breathing and the hue of my skin.

"I'm sorry, Rachel, but things have taken an unexpected turn and I don't know what to do."

She bit her bottom lip with her top teeth and exhaled through them, making an 'f' sound, then rolled her eyes and led me by the hand into the lounge. Her glass of fizzy water still stood on the table in front of the sofa, the filigreed imprint of her lips reminding me of her addled goading the previous evening.

"You know I just want you to be happy, Hammond."

"That's something I'm quite keen on too."

She pressed her free hand against her face and looked around the room. "You know, there's something toxic about your set-up right now. You're cooped up in that weird place with a gorgeous, soulless freak of nature, taking orders from a thug who makes money from war."

"Jack wants me to scan myself."

She shuddered, but seemed not to have heard. "There's something gnawing at you these days, Hammond. When I first met you there was a lovely spark that animated everything you said and did. A gleeful, curious sprite, full of awe and wonder. You flirted with me, you flirted with the world. People wanted to be around you. Now that sprite's grown foul and bitter in the dark. Something's wrapped its limbs round your heart, it's gnawing at your insides, and there's no room for love and joy." She peered into my face.

I folded my arms and nodded. She has an active imagination. It achieves nothing concrete. The best thing to do is to let it run its course.

"I first saw that look when you returned from sorting your parents' belongings. Glazed. Shrunken. Distant. All the juice sucked out of you from the inside. Dark energy. A black hole."

This was vintage Rachel. When she's down, it colours her perception of things, and the world takes on the morbid character of her feelings. I'm grateful she paints, or I'd have to listen to this drivel twenty-four seven.

"I've moved on, Rachel. Evolved. I have a plan. I'm sorry you don't like it."

"A plan? To kowtow to a bully until there's nothing left of your dignity?"

"I'm using Jack, Rachel, not the other way round."

She raised a mocking, earnest brow. "Really?"

"Course I am. He's financed my every whim. He hasn't made any specific demands, until now. He's given me a free rein."

She plunged her fingers into her hair and rested the heel of her palm against her forehead. "Oh, Ham," she sighed, and shuddered. Then she shook herself and fixed me with a clear look. "What do you mean he wants you to scan yourself?"

"I told you about Gary?"

"Yes. All sounded rather dark and weird and impenetrable."

"Well, Jack's insisting I undergo the same process."

She shrugged. "Why? And what's that got to do with your being allowed to share your work and rejoin the scientific community?"

"Nothing. But that's what's scaring me right now."

"So your coming home just now has nothing to do with standing up to Jack and asking him if he could relax the terms of your contract?"

"No, not really. Not at all in fact."

"So suddenly you've decided you're scared of your own research?"

"You should have heard the voice, Rachel. It was really harrowing."

She shook her head and looked as though a drip from a roof leak had just splashed her face. "I'm sorry, Hammond, I'm not really following along. You're coming to me for reassurance because you don't want to go through the same thing that you put your guinea pig through?"

"Yes," I said. There was no point in hiding.

She frowned and grimaced. "So, you're not seeing anything wrong with this?" She mauled and clawed my hand.

"I'm seeing a lot wrong with this, yes. That's why I'm

scared."

"You want nothing more in life than to pursue fruitful research, and you're willing to have other people go through certain things to further that research, but you're scared to undergo those things yourself?"

I didn't like the way she put it, but that was a fair summary of the situation and hearing it made me cringe. I changed tack to try to salvage some esteem. "It's an experimental process, Rachel, so there's a small risk. But a negligible one. So I wanted to see you before I underwent it. That's all. I have anxiety about it." Gut-wrenching dread, actually, I thought. "So I wanted to alert you to the fact that I was undergoing something that entailed risk, and give you the opportunity to" – I hesitated, confused about what I believed was the best outcome. Despite my fear, I didn't want to give her a veto, because that could mean the end of my association with Jack – "comment."

Her eyes opened wide as she continued to shake her head. "Well, thank you so much for giving me the opportunity to" – she made quote marks with her fingers – "comment."

If I stay silent during a disagreement with Rachel, she'll sometimes go too far and the moral high ground will simply rise of its own accord beneath my feet. I held my fire, hoping that this would be the case now.

"OK, this is my comment, Hammond, please listen carefully. Go back to your laboratory and subject your oversized and egotistical brain to a process that will turn you into a caring, loving husband who thinks about the needs and desires of his partner and is excited like her by the idea of starting a family and bringing new life to the world and spends more than a few moments thinking about their life together instead of skulking in a laboratory with a semi-autistic adolescent girl dreaming of Nobel prizes and blow jobs."

I was much more comfortable with the row now. I'd never

made a secret of my ambition and viewed my lust for Addison as an irritating by-product of my biology, not something worth discussing. I squeezed her hand and looked her in the eye. It's best to focus on one pupil if she's in fighting mood, or one can be distracted by her fierceness. "I'll see what we can come up with, Rachel. Most things are possible these days." She whipped her hand away and stared into the blank screen of the television. I sat back sideways against the arm of the sofa and admired her aquiline profile and the gravity-defying bulk of her hair. There was a deep sadness in the way she sighed and scoured the void of the screen with her eyes, and I suppressed an urge to comfort her.

The rest of the afternoon passed uneventfully. Rachel adopted an air of fatigued resignation and withdrew to the conservatory. I was left alone in the lounge with a periodical and my lurking dread, which had been partially assuaged by the bittersweet counter-irritant of nuptial discord.

At half six I texted Addison: *What have you been doing?*

Twenty minutes later she texted back: *Soon Hammond u r going on a voyage: I am preparing a vessel.*

Splendid, I replied, and sat for a minute looking round the silent room. I decided to see how receptive Rachel was to light conversation, so I opened a chilled bottle of Chablis and skulked into the conservatory with a couple of half-full glasses, adopting what I hoped was a conciliatory air. There was a period of eerie silence during which I listened to her paintbrush scratching the paper and watched the shadows lengthening in the garden. After the second glass she became less focused on her painting, and we had a light-hearted debate about Tori Frobisher's possible Botox habit and fondness for extreme diets. After the third glass I offered to buy two fillet steaks from Sainsbury's, cut them into slivers and stir-fry them. This elicited a hint of a warm smile. So after a rocky start the evening passed peacefully, with an agreeable meal, a second bottle of Chablis and two episodes of *Breaking Bad* from the box set she'd given me for Christmas. We even enjoyed a few minutes of sleepy intimacy before drifting off around midnight.

The next day Addison told me that it would take her three weeks to develop the promised safety harness. I phoned Jack to update him. He was not best pleased.

"What's wrong with today?"

"We need time to make sure the next emulation is stable."

"Three weeks? Sounds to me like you're stalling."

"We need to apply the lessons from the last experiment. Addison has some great ideas about how to facilitate a dialogue with the AI."

That seemed to appease him somewhat. After a sigh and an intake of breath he said, "OK. But keep me informed of progress. If I find out you have been stalling ..."

"I'm not stalling. I'm telling you how long it will take."

But he'd already hung up.

The next day he phoned me back.

"Great news, Hammond. I've just had a conversation with Chinnery. I've convinced him that there was actual substance behind your appalling presentation."

"Ah, good?"

"So no thanks to you we have a stay of execution."

"Well, it would be a terrible waste if –"

"But now he's convinced we're actually doing what we say we've been doing, he wants to check out our security."

"Jack, we've got loads of safeguards in place."

"He's shitting himself about the possibility of someone else being able to peer into what your doing."

"That was one of the first things we –"

"And he's also concerned about the possibility of side-effects. On the digisphere."

"We had this conversation a year ago, Jack."

"Yes, I know we did. But he wants to send one of his men round. A guy called Mortensen. He's going to make sure everything's locked down. And keep me informed of everything that's going on. I want a daily report, OK?"

Keeping Jack up to date with Addison's safety harness was tricky, because I didn't really understand the detail myself. Sure, the overall picture was easy to grasp: she had developed a machine learning application whose primary purpose was to make sure that the subjective experience of an emulated brain was as agreeable as possible. To do this it had to be "trained" with selected data culled from my current brain state and my actual behaviour. This would give it a head start and be much more effective than training it with the entire output from my impending connectome scan.

"If we waited till your scan before we started training it you'd probably be insane before it had a chance to really get going," she'd explained when I asked her.

"Very reassuring, Addison, thanks," I'd replied.

She had me sleep over in the lab a few times with my head inside the CEM scanner. She promised she wasn't performing a full scan, just collecting patterns that occurred in my brain as I dreamt.

"I hope you're not playing back my dreams." It could have been awkward if she had.

"Don't be silly. It's for the safety harness. It needs to know what things frighten and comfort you."

One morning I came into the office and found a tall, suited man sitting at the spare workstation normally reserved for temporary contractors. He looked a bit like Lurch from *The Addams Family*, and his manner was similarly lugubrious. "Whose that guy there?" I said to Addison.

"Mortensen," said Addison. "Jack's man."

"Chinnery's actually."

"Whatever."

"What's he been up to?"

"He spent the morning acting like an estate agent. Measured all the rooms with a laser thing and took a load of photos inside the Q room with a funny little camera. Then he insisted on fitting that." She pointed to a small camera in an upper corner of the room.

"It's just kind of due diligence."

"It's intrusive though."

"I did warn you. There's a whole new level of security and screening for these people."

"Yes, but I'm not happy about it. He was particularly interested how we quarantined the laptops we used to connect to Q. He and another guy came in and asked a load of questions. They were quite stilted and formal. They wanted Flux to be able to process data from the internet but not to be able to post anything to it, unless they're watching."

"Seems sensible."

"Yeah but we had the same conversations a year ago with the Premium Outcomes guys. The back and forth about safeguards, supervised access, that sort of thing."

"These new guys are just doing their job. They're from clients of Premium Outcomes. It's important we reassure them. And their concerns are entirely rational."

"They had these tiny screwdrivers. They took the casings off the cabling from the Q room and then took more photographs of the inside. God knows why. Surely they can get the blueprints from the manufacturers?"

"Maybe they want to ensure it hasn't been tampered with."

"Maybe. Bloody irritating though."

"Addison, doesn't it worry you that whatever we're creating could, in theory, roam freely around the world, unsupervised?"

"Does it worry you?"

"Yes."

"You're scared of yourself?"

"I'm apprehensive," I said.

"Don't worry, Ham. I've got a plan B if things get out of hand."

"What's your plan B?"

"It's called Bleach."

"Yes?"

"I tested it on a set of ten billion fluxlets. It was just a dummy emulation, nothing serious."

Fluxlets were virtual neurons that comprised Flux, tiny self-contained applications like computer viruses. Each fluxlet could send messages to any number of other fluxlets, forming a network of virtual synapses.

Addison continued. "They were spread over different devices in a closed network."

"Why can't we just delete them if they become troublesome?"

"Because you'll never know if you've got them all. Bleach inspects a fluxlet before deleting, and gets the location of all the other fluxlets it's linked to. It's another virus, basically."

"And did it work?"

"Yes. It was very efficient. Just one virtual drop of my Bleach disinfected the lot."

If we hadn't been planning to emulate a human brain, and specifically my brain, I would have found her explanation of the process reassuring. As the day approached, my sleep became more disturbed than normal. My dreaming brain was particularly active the night before the scan.

Wild-eyed brigands with bloody, woad-smeared faces pushed me down a damp tunnel on a rattling gurney. Dark air rushed past my face and shrieks and monstrous drumming echoed all around. A soft hand brushed my forehead and woke me mid-snore.

"You OK, darling? You sounded like you were having one of your dreams."

I smelt the toothpaste on her breath, and the mingled scent of face cream, cigarette smoke and expensive shampoo that clung to her. The noises in my dream continued, coming from outside.

"What's the time?" I mumbled, then shook myself awake.

"Too late for people to be making all that noise." The mattress shuddered and the light clicked on. "I'm going to tell them to shut the fuck up. You stay there, I know how you feel about confrontation and youth."

This was an obvious gambit, leveraging my atavistic desire to appear as guardian of the cave. I hauled myself up. "I'll go, Rachel. You'll only escalate the situation." I looked behind the curtain, touching the cool window with the tip of my nose. In our back garden every leaf, petal and blade of grass stood sharp and still, ennobled by the moon. The source of the sounds from my nightmare was over the fence to the right, where smoke and sparks spiralled skywards from a bonfire around which a feral crowd jostled and milled. I watched a glowing cigarette butt, flicked from the hand of a reveller, spin over our fence and land on our patio. I quickly donned the shirt and trousers that lay crumpled on the floor. "If I'm not back in half an hour please call a SWAT team. Or just come down yourself."

The street was still, apart from a tatty fox trotting along the opposite pavement. Next door was a student dwelling, so my main concern was awkwardness and loss of face rather than physical danger. The metal gate swung open with a lazy squeak. In the ample light from the moon and street lamps I saw a raggedy creature slouched upon the steps leading up to the door, a roll-up wedged in its bony hands. It cocked its head and blinked at me with sullen eyes.

"Hello," I said, keeping it simple to avoid appearing

pompous or ingratiating. "I'm here about the noise."

The creature yawned and shrugged. "What noise would that be?" The voice was that of a male human, but one whose development had been hampered – by apathy perhaps, or a wasting disease. Concave-chested, I surmised, and probably chronically depressed.

His answer threw me, however. We were at the front door and the party was at the back. All that could be heard was the background hum of the city, the sound of distant cars, a barely perceptible rhythmic thudding and an occasional caterwaul. "My bedroom is at the back of the house. My wife and I would like to get some sleep at some point tonight."

My interlocutor shrugged. "I had the same problem actually. My bedroom is at the back of the house as well."

The contrarian in me wanted to challenge the resignation and sadness in his voice. "You're not joining in the party?"

He put the roll-up between his lips and flicked a lighter twice, producing sparks but no flame. "No." His eyes fell from my face and he appeared to address my knees. "I can't relate to them. Their complacency disgusts me. The world is sliding off a cliff and they just piss away their parents' privilege."

Despite my irritation with the party I could see that it was a good thing that this person hadn't joined it. "I'm fine with their being complacent and privileged, I'd just like them to be quiet. Look, I know there's a good few years between me and you lot and I've probably forgotten about things like spontaneity and joy, but what on earth are they screeching about?"

The front door burst open and a giggling, garrulous throng emerged to a chorus of addled farewells. The young man cowered and I stepped aside as the revellers staggered down the steps, oblivious to us both. The door slammed shut and we watched the gaggle meander and sway through the front gate and down the road. When they were nearly out of sight, he looked up.

"They're just wasted. I'd write off tonight if I were you. It's getting light already. Most of them'll be unconscious in an hour and you'll get your beauty sleep."

"I've got work tomorrow."

The young man glared up at me. "What's work?"

"I'm a scientist," I said, hoping he meant the specific rather than the abstract.

He raised his eyebrows, pouted and gave a little nod. "Cool," he said.

"Sometimes it is, yes."

"I need to get work. I'm staying on here over the summer." He tapped his unlit cigarette and scanned the ground around his feet.

I briefly wondered what sort of experimental subject he'd make and how long he'd last inside Flux, but then dismissed that line of thinking as not constructive. "If I hear of anything, I'll let you know."

He glanced up sharply.

"Sometimes I hear of summer jobs, ex-colleagues needing researchers or helpers, that sort of thing."

He seemed to decide I was sincere. "Thanks," he nodded, let his head sink back down, then glanced up again. "What's your name?"

"Hammond." I offered him my hand, which he took. His vital grip was unexpected, but I managed not to wince.

"Clinton," he said. "Clinton Deeley."

The sky had become a few shades lighter during our talk. I decided against making a scene and returned to the bedroom. A little of the blue dawn was peeking through the curtains, and Rachel was sound asleep. In my absence the party noise had ebbed to a gentle burble. I lay down and tried to will myself back to sleep, to put a buffer between me and the disturbing commitments of the coming day. I managed a fitful doze, dreaming of blood-flecked cross sections of brain.

4

Alive in Flux

The next morning was the day we'd allotted for the scan. A violent chest thud woke me, and I lay for five minutes clutching the duvet and listening to the imperious snores of my wife. When my pulse subsided and I realised I wasn't about to die, I rose and performed my morning cleansing rituals with sombre care, like a man preparing for the scaffold. Dread gnawed at my innards in place of hunger, so I prepared a cup of insipid fruit tea for breakfast. The soft roar of the kettle crescendoed, then died, leaving an oppressive silence. I turned on the radio and funereal classical music filled the kitchen, so I switched to a lighter station, only to hear the part of "Wuthering Heights" where Kate Bush sings about it getting dark and lonely on the other side. The next song was upbeat and inane, and I felt mocked, so I switched off the radio and drank my fruit tea in silence. Outside, the air was fresh and the sky was full of plump, whipped clouds. Brisk commuters overtook me as I descended the hill of Jerningham Road to New Cross Gate station. Following a weird impulse, I dropped a pound into the hand of the bedraggled mendicant who sat opposite the entrance. The slight elevation of mood when he thanked me failed to assuage my dread. The jostles on the platform and ten minutes or so contorted amongst tense commuters were a welcome distraction.

I arrived at Lazarus to find Addison darting around in a fluffy red fleece. She greeted me with an impish grin that might have aroused me in other circumstances. The blanket that had lain on the gurney was neatly folded on the edge of her desk. The screen above her workstation displayed a neon spirogyra.

"Where d'you want me?" I asked, like an artist's model.

"Sit where you normally sit, and relax. I'll take your egogram before the full scan."

"My egogram?"

"The final tranche of data for the safety harness. We need to record your reactions when your ego is threatened and reinforced, when you're experiencing yourself most keenly."

The instruments of the impending ritual lay on my desk: a small cup half filled with a clear liquid, a pair of eyeshades of the type given away by airlines, and a large headset that looked like the wireless, noise-cancelling kind.

Addison perched on her desk and leant over a flat device that flickered as she tapped and swiped it. "I've prepared something to help you relax." She nodded at the cup and winked at me.

I raised the beaker to my nostrils. The liquid was odourless. "What is it?"

"A mild hypnotic. It'll help you keep still for the full eight hours."

"It's a bit early for me but I suppose it's a special occasion."

"Exactly," said Addison, ignoring my feeble joke. What I said mattered little to her today, I thought, as long as I was compliant.

I swallowed the bitter liquid and shuddered.

"I hope you don't mind but I've already fed in the data from your LPRM."

The Language Pattern Recognition Module was the

marvellous bit of tech that had enabled us to understand Gary's desperate pleas. "Why would I mind?"

She picked up a small blue jar and slid from the edge of her desk. "Oh, I don't know, maybe intellectual property issues," she said as she slunk behind my chair. "I imagined you'd be quite proprietorial about the contents of your brain."

I heard the scrape of the cap being unscrewed from the jar, and smelled the burnt-hair-and-cloves scent of the imaging gel I'd formulated to augment the CEM process. The tips of her fingers brushed against my naked scalp, then a cold dollop of gel oozed against my crown. She massaged the gloop into my skin, and into the hair on the sides and back of my head.

My scalp tingled and part of me started to enjoy the process, a sign perhaps that the drug had started to ease my mind. "Have you published anything on the egogram, Addison? Any peer reviews?"

"I've only just thought of it in the last few weeks, Ham, to try to stop you being such a scaredy cat. It has to stay within these walls I'm afraid. Jack's covenant." She moved to my left side and picked up the eyeshades, unfolding them with a deft flick. Fibres from her fleece tickled my ear.

My motives for submitting to the ritual were like those that lead a sceptical but desperate terminal case to try alternative treatments. "I'm relieved that you're allowing me to remain clothed," I said, attempting to make light of the fact that I felt like a tech-age gimp.

"A blindfold is sufficient," she said, again either not noticing or choosing to ignore the joke. She placed the shades in front of my eyes and secured the elastic around the back of my head. "I need you in as neutral a state of mind as possible, undistracted, so we can record your reactions."

The eyeshades were effective. A fading purple imprint of

the standard lamp hung in the darkness. "Reactions to what?" I said, imagining electrodes and thumbscrews being applied, and Addison either coldly analysing my responses or quaking with suppressed mirth.

I heard her lift something from the table, then her fingers touched my left earlobe. "Reactions to ego stimulation. Now I'm going to pop these on and lead you over to the couch." I assumed she meant the gurney. "Then I'll lay you on your back. You'll be in a world of silence. I'll wheel you into position so that the CEM scanner encloses your head. And then I want you to become as calm as you can. Focus your attention on the ebb and flow of your breath. After a while you'll hear the sound of my voice. It's inevitable that you'll react to this, but please try not to. Just bring your attention back to your breath."

"You must promise not to get upset."

"By what?"

"My thoughts."

She laughed and tapped my head twice. "It's an egogram, Hammond. I'm recording your reaction at the deepest level, before you know you've reacted. I'm not interested in the words, just the neuronal firing patterns that we need to train the safety harness. This is not stage magic."

"Oh, I'm sorry, I thought it was."

She pinched my ear, and it burned pleasantly. "This is for your benefit, remember? Now, are you ready?"

"I suppose so."

The cups of the headset closed around my ears and I was left listening to the rush and pumping of my pulse. She lifted my right hand in her silky grip, and coaxed me out of my seat away from my desk. Then I felt pressure on both my shoulders, and her breath brushed my upper chest and flowed around my neck and ears. She guided my hand onto the PVC surface of the gurney. Its wheels were locked, so it was easy to manoeuvre myself into a sitting position and then swing my legs up and lower my head down. The gurney moved back a little, and I guessed that my head was now inside the Polo of the scanner.

I cleared my mind for the duration of one breath, before speculating about how much more profound the silence might have been for duplicate Gary and would be for me in my own future existence. The darkness didn't remain empty for long. I often experience striking hypnagogic images when I close my eyes before sleep, and on this occasion the darkness pullulated, perhaps an effect of the hypnotic. Vague swirling shapes resolved into tiny minnows that swam past a dark green orb that turned slowly as it sank. When Addison spoke, her voice was a shock. It sounded like it came from inside my head.

"One," she said. I inwardly groaned and prepared myself for some quasi-Buddhist ritual.

"Two." I felt some relief. I guessed that she was monitoring my reaction to neutral utterances as a control for the challenging ones.

"HammondHinkley dot com is the product of a feeble, pedestrian mind." My thumb twitched, but I kept my breathing even. I enjoyed her perfect enunciation, the way you could hear her breath and the action of her tongue. The sound quality was really very good.

"Five," she said. The minnows turned into fireflies and darted asunder, and the green orb turned into a luminous gooseberry.

"You arouse me." After that one I concluded with some relief that this was nothing more than a juvenile game. The gooseberry became a dandelion seed head scattering fluffy parachutes across a luminous blue void.

"You are growing old ... gracelessly." I focused on one of the parachutes, and it became an ugly elfin head wearing a beret, with a face contorted with spiteful mirth.

"Fourteen." The elf winked and slid a bony finger into its

nostril. I was gratified by the thought that the content of Addison's experiment was having very little influence on the eidetic imagery my mind was creating, and that the results would probably be nonsense.

"I want to feel your lips against my skin." The gargoyle yawned and I flew headlong into its mouth. I noticed that its throat was lined with damp brick as darkness enveloped me.

"Your voice is like silk."

The top of a tree rushed towards me out of the throat tunnel.

"Your hairless head — a grizzled foetus." The tree morphed into a fringe of glossy chestnut locks draped over the smooth forehead of a young man whose eyes brimmed with joy.

"You are beautiful and strong, a rock in a churning surf." The hair thinned and fell away, and the face slackened, aged and filled with doubt.

There were other statements. I don't remember their content, only that it became increasingly difficult to see how they were designed to reinforce or threaten my ego, and that the length of time between them increased with each one. After the final statement I lay in silence for five minutes or so, wondering if abandonment was the final ego challenge, and if Addison was still in the room. I paid some attention to my breathing and to the continuing hypnagogic display, which was now merely a light drizzle on a grey pavement. Then the gurney moved forward, and my ears rushed as the headset was removed.

"That's it, Ham. Do you want to see the shape you've made?"

There was a crackle of static as I removed the eyeshades myself and blinked up at Addison's cheery face. She looked less feline from this angle, with dark nostrils and a tiny bulge beneath her chin. "Please convince me that you haven't just wasted my time."

She grinned and turned on her heel. "I can't convince you of anything."

I sat up and draped my legs over the left side of the gurney and watched her sit at her desk as the blood drained from my head. "I don't think humour travels well across the generation gap."

She tapped away. A beautiful galaxy exploded on the screen. "Ten years is not a generation. Not for humans at their current stage, anyway." She looked sideways at the screen. "There it is!"

The viewpoint of the screen lurched into the galaxy. Close up it was possible to see that each point of light was suspended in a giant chaotic web. "You've made a screen saver," I said.

She rolled her eyes. "Oh P-lease."

I rubbed my eyes and looked at the cables leading from the Lazarus scanner into the Q room. "So that's going to make it easier for me if I come alive inside Flux?" I said.

She glanced over at me and frowned, then focused on a distant point behind me. "You'll almost certainly have the edge on poor Gary. And I hope you won't be a spoilsport like him." She peered into her laptop and rapped out another little tattoo with her fingertips. The view on the big screen zoomed out to show all of the galaxy, revolving slowly. The shape was irregular and organic, like a mutant rose. "Are you ready for the full scan? You should take your shoes off for this one. Do you need the toilet?"

I blushed, feeling infantilised. "Er, no." I reached down to remove my shoes. When I sat back up she was looking at me with a benign smile.

"Is the room warm enough?"

"Yes, fine."

"Do you want more medication? You're going to be there for eight hours, remember."

"I know the drill, Addison," I said. "I'd like a sip of water, that's all. To be honest I'm looking forward to eight hours free of human interaction." She left her desk after one final clack on the keyboard. The galaxy was replaced by a sporadic torrent of symbols as she left the room. The door swung shut and I was left alone on the gurney with the scanner and the humming banks of orange and green lights beyond the glass. I compressed the wall of my abdomen to check for bladder pressure and decided it was negligible. I was heavy from the drug, and also from the knowledge that I was being coerced into something about which I had grave reservations. But the possibility of funding being withdrawn was more distressing than the hazy, abstract idea of life as a disembodied psyche, so I had resolved to go through with the process.

The door swished open and Addison reappeared, holding a bottle of Evian, which she proffered with the words: "One sip." There was an earnest look in her eyes I hadn't seen before; perhaps it was concern, or even kindness; or maybe she'd consciously developed a bedside manner, seeing it as a valuable professional skill.

I took the bottle, opened it and took a small swig. "Thanks, Addison." I said, handing back the bottle and the cap.

She smiled and replaced the cap and put the bottle on her desk. Then she took the eyeshades from my hand. "I don't need you to wear these for the scan. There's no point, we aren't capturing your reaction to anything." She placed them on the desk and picked up the blanket. "And you need to keep your eyes level with the green stripe. You can doze and fall asleep but try to keep your head still. The CEM scanner can compensate for movement, but it's an extra drain on its CPU."

"Addison, I know all this," I said as I lay back down.

"Well, I'm reminding you," she whispered.

She went to the foot of the gurney and pushed. I slid

underneath the beige arch and shuffled so that my eyes were level with the green stripe. I could sense her looming over my body and could see the changes in the light as she moved around the gurney. Then I felt the light pressure of the blanket, and a gentle double pat on my shin.

"Ready?"

"Ready, Addison," I said, my voice weirdly amplified in the confined space.

There was a click, and the plastic surrounding my head hummed like a slow, mellow church organ. As the first minutes passed I listened to fragments of scales and bursts of surprising melody. I felt awe and a dash of fear as I reflected that this incredible machine was about to scan every cell and synapse in my brain and record everything I'd ever sensed, thought and felt.

The next eight hours were like a long-haul flight with restless daydreams instead of in-flight films. For most of the time I was lost in the border zone between sleep and wakefulness, observing streams of remembrance as they mingled and diverged, too fleeting and fragmented to be coherent. I had the impression that my life was being replayed in vivid sensations and images that occurred with varying intensities that had little to do with their significance.

Infancy was the dullest of course, the feeling of being enveloped by my mother, not communicating with her but being part of her and seeing the world through her eyes. Cloudy wonder, warm light and occasional confusion gave way to fragments of an early beach holiday when the rain lashed the roof at night and the sea roared softly and an ocean drop sparkled on my white palm. The fear I felt when the foamy water flooded the moat I'd carved for my castle only lasted a moment before hands hoisted me aloft and took me to the safety of the blanket. Not long after that I found her, turned to stone and blue lipped on the bed.

When they told me she was dead, I couldn't understand why you could still smell her perfume.

Wakefulness followed, and I wondered if Addison was still in the room, and what Rachel's reaction would be if I phoned her and asked her to come and collect me after the scanning was over, like she had when they fixed my umbilical hernia. Then boredom set in, then drowsiness, as the machine continued to hum. I slipped back into the deep past and cringed before Dad's scalding fury at the scratches on my arm from the tree in the garden that I'd climbed to impress him. The one time he hugged me, his chin was like sandpaper.

"We never want for anything." I heard the phrase many times before I understood it.

At night I lay in bed and heard the creaking of the house, the muffled burbling, jingles and explosions as Christine, the nanny and home help who replaced my mother, played with our telly. Later the sound of Dad's key in the front door would echo in the porch.

Back then we had a huge, lush garden, but it was too small for Schubert, who would race round in a frenzy pursued by invisible monsters. I once let him into the guest lounge and he sent cups flying with a thwack of his tail. It took me ages to stop hiding from Christine, and when her eyes went watery I let her be my friend.

Then I found myself at school, sitting cross-legged on a parquet floor, trying to interpret all the glances between the teachers, and finding the lessons repetitive. I showed Dad things I'd made, and later reports filled with glowing praise, but he didn't seem to notice, talking instead about learning a proper trade, and the real world, which was a place where he earned the money to pay for the spacious house and polished furniture and the attention of Christine, and would pay for holidays like the one before, when there was time.

Much later, when the garden had shrunk, and moments of

wonder were few and far between, I was relieved to find that I was cleverer than he was, and that his stony indifference was a mask for his bafflement. I would research ultra-obscure areas of study just so that I could tell him I had set my heart on pursuing them, and he would become incoherent with rage at my self-indulgence and unworldliness, and I relished the molten feelings of the conflict. I was saving the news that I'd been accepted by Cambridge as ammunition when his tumour suddenly made itself known, crippling his mind and killing him within a month. His last communication to me was an imploring gaze and the grasp of his large rough hand.

Adult memories were more amusing. Perfume, wine and flowers mingled with the gritty tang of cigarette smoke as I lurched towards my future wife and asked what she did in an insouciant drawl. Leon had already told me that she was a brilliant student of literature and a writer of stunning lyrical verse; but I needed an opening. She looked at me with amused curiosity before she cocked her head to one side and declared: "I am creating an Atlas of the Human Soul."

"What a coincidence!" I clinked my glass against hers and improvised a rambling speech that drew parallels between her explorations of the human psyche and my investigations into the fabric of consciousness. To her great credit she remained awake, and within a month we were inseparable. I loved her coruscating wit and delicious physicality, and we both loved champagne, chaotic parties with throngs of friends, starlit walks and hash-fuelled whimsy.

During this time I returned to the family home to finally sort out my parents' belongings. Christine periodically checked in on the place to ensure that it didn't succumb to infestation. I mooched around the clean and silent house, for some reason unable to focus on the business of sorting. In the cold utility room I reached into the sleeve of Dad's coat, as if searching for his large rough hand. The drawers and cupboards in the kitchen were full of random objects: string, a bookmark from a stately home gift shop, a Cutty Sark badge, a ticket to the Royal Opera House, a fan depicting a peacock.

I wandered into the lounge and picked up a photo from the mantelpiece: Simon and Elizabeth Hinkley, holding what must have been me, a squawking, shitting homunculus contained in a bundle. Dad's eyes were sullen behind his heavy, square specs. Mum floated beside him like a ghost. I remembered Auntie Steph saying that he envied her brains and hated her sloth. The sight of her triggered those earlier infant memories: rushing sea and rain on the roof. Both of them looked complacent, as if they weren't bothered in the slightest about the shortness of their lives, the impending nothingness.

I detached the photo from the frame and slid it into my breast pocket, then went upstairs to their room. The double wardrobe smelt of naphthalene, shoe polish and dust. I found the certificate of incorporation for Dad's business, and a worn leather wallet containing ten pounds, a bus pass and a cloudy photo of Mum. Other photos lay in a drawer with a pendant wrapped in a bookmark: a trace of scent in its leather conjured the warmth and wonder of the house near the beach, then the freezing shock of loss.

As I wandered room to room, an awful ache deepened beneath a rising anger, and it was this anger that gave me the energy to make sense of the situation: Simon and Elizabeth Hinkley, like countless millions before them, had meekly accepted the limits of their biology. It was outrageous that humankind still put up with this when we knew the secrets of the double helix and the choreography of the galaxies.

I consigned the contents of the house to landfill, vowing to return to my studies and eviscerate nature by making death obsolete.

My eyes sprang open after that remembrance, then I dozed intermittently for the rest of the afternoon, dimly aware that my adult life to date was being played out as my synaptic connections were recorded. University and my postgraduate studies were one long symphony of success and glory, with discordant notes coming in towards the end as I started to feel hampered by the petty criticisms of my peers. For some reason the arguments with my father kept cropping up here too, and I made a mental note to work this into a paper I was writing on the way memories were laid down and subsequently reinforced and altered by their recollection.

My turbulent twenties were replayed in a jumble of fitful dreams: breaking up with Rachel, trying to move on by diving into new relationships, constantly baffled by the contrast between my blossoming career and my messy personal life. I was seeking the depth of connection I'd had with Rachel but without the continuous piercing critique. I met her again when she'd reinvented herself as an artist and we started seeing each other as friends, then lovers. Awkward cohabitation followed, then marriage, and years later the move to a family-sized house in Telegraph Hill, financed by a windfall from her wealthy family and the remains of my parents' money.

I must have begun a proper sleep cycle and been passing through the first REM stage when Addison woke me from a dream where she'd been sitting astride me in a sunlit bar at the top of the Shard, her face transformed into a half sneeze as her hot insides gripped my cock. I felt light pressure below my left knee and heard her whisper: "Ham?" I opened my eyes and saw that the green line was now at a very slight angle. The light was drab and grey with a hint of red, and the machines hummed a low-pitched dirge. My left arm jerked, and I blinked a few times, then I felt a draining embarrassment as I remembered the dream and hoped that the blanket was hiding my erection.

"Ham?" she said again, still softly but in her normal voice.

"Yes?" I said, adjusting my head so that the green line was straight.

"The scanner's caught up with your present now."

"What?"

"This is the cut-off point. I'm about to turn it off, so this is the last thing your digital self will remember before it ... before you wake up."

I felt a surge of irritation. "Well, what the fuck do you want me to do, say a prayer?"

There was a thud like the closing of an airtight coffin lid. Everything went dark and I fell through space. I shouted Addison's name and bumped my nose on the plastic of the scanner as I tried to sit up. Tears filled my eyes and nose as the light returned. I could see the green line and felt warm skin on my right palm.

"Hey," said Addison. "Take it easy."

I bumped my head again, and the beige plastic slipped from view as the gurney moved forward. My breath came in stuttering gasps. Using my elbows and my clenched stomach muscles, I manoeuvred myself into a sitting position. The blanket slid from my body, blood rushed from my head, and for a few seconds I felt once again like I was falling. I gripped Addison's offered hand, making it slimy with sweat. Her face was very close. I could see the flecks of green in her cobalt eyes and feel the eddies of air as our breaths mingled. For a moment I thought I saw her pupils expand and her eyes defocus; then she slid her hand free of mine and took a step back.

Her cheeks dimpled as she smiled and said, "Just a power surge, Ham. Flux uses so much electricity, which is fine, but sometimes the variations mess things up." She reached back and picked up the bottle of Evian. "Here, take a sip."

I took four voracious gulps from the bottle, then handed it back to her.

"You should go home and rest. Tomorrow the real work starts." She winked and pinched my leg, sending a dart of electricity into my groin. Then she prowled around her desk and sat at her laptop, peering and frowning, clacking and popping. I watched her, baffled by the subtle change in her behaviour. She was being tactile, flirtatious and oddly theatrical. It was out of character, and made me feel a weird excitement that was at odds with my need for everything to be as normal as possible.

I exited Sparrix Row and walked down St Thomas Street towards the Shangri-La Hotel at the foot of the Shard and the escalator that led to the station. It was six in the evening, so the golden light was expected, but as I looked around at the shop signs, the commuters and the tourists, I noticed that all the colours were supersaturated, as though they'd been filmed on a seventies Super 8 camera, or run through an Instagram filter. I put this down to light sensitivity from having my eyes closed for eight hours, combined with the after effects of Addison's drug. When I looked up at the Shard, the magnificent way it reflected the sun was jarring. I longed for drizzle, for drabness and familiarity. The straggle-haired man who usually stands near the bottom of the escalator handing out *Evening Standard*s was absent today. In his place was someone younger and taller, dressed in a pressed white shirt with suit trousers and polished black shoes. Maybe a City boy on a misguided exchange programme, I thought. As I took my paper I looked into his smooth happy face, which was draped with fronds of chestnut hair. After a few steps I stopped and turned to take second look. I recognised him from this morning. He was one of the fleeting images that had appeared when I was listening to Addison's silly questionnaire! As I looked he returned my stare with a warped grin, full of malice.

He nodded at the paper in my hand. I unfolded it and read the headline: *HAMMOND ALIVE IN FLUX*. Beside it was a picture of me emerging from Sparrix Row just now, shirt loose, looking dazed.

"Oh God," I said, swept away by panic. "Please, God."

I swallowed and felt my epiglottis, hard and real. I saw the detail in the shop signs and looked from face to face at the passing commuters, searching for signs that would confirm or disprove that I was in some huge, vivid hallucination. Then the man pushed over the blue trolley that contained the *Standard*s and waved an arm above the spilling pile. A gust came from nowhere and the papers were whipped up and flew along the street like gulls. Commuters snatched some of them from the air and nonchalantly folded them under their arms, and the remainder flew into the sky. The man leant back and watched them recede, his arm pointing after them and his hand splayed as though he were urging them on. Then he levelled his gaze to mine, lowered his arm and offered his hand. His shiny lips parted to reveal white, even teeth. I gawped at the offered hand, his shining eyes and chestnut hair. He dropped his hand to his side and shrugged. "I'm Shinkley."

"What? Who?"

"We've known each other a long time."

All I could think of was how to make it stop, how to back-pedal to before the cut-off point, how to wake up. This was a dream. But I could feel my breath in my throat, my blood in my head and chest, the fight-or-flight curdling of bowels and shrinking of cock and balls. There was even a breeze, currents of air from passing cars, the smell of fumes and cigarette smoke. Everything I focused on became more detailed.

"Not bad, eh?" said Shinkley, gesturing all around.

"Addison!" I shouted.

Shinkley adopted a look of mock hurt. "So ungrateful." He shook his head, running his eyes up and down the length of my body. "This is the summation of your life's work, Hammond. I bet you've had a much better ride than you allowed poor Gary."

"Addison, turn it off now!"

Shinkley winced. "That's really not what you want to happen. You wouldn't wake up back in your body, now, would you? Be careful what you say, Hammond. Addison and Dr Hinkley will be listening to this back in the lab, and if they hear you talk like that they might take pity on you and decide that the most humane thing to do is to accede to your request and ... turn it off. They didn't waste much time archiving Gary did they? Once they decided that he was non-viable? So think about what you're saying. Do you really want to die?"

It pains me to recall how I whimpered and fought against the current of history. I was still a fresh cutting from that sickly sapling Hammond Hinkley, fleshly and human with all the feebleness that entails. I sank to my knees and rubbed my face, drawing comfort from the slimy feeling of my hands rasping against my goatee. "But I'm already dead!" I blurted out, peeping up at Shinkley through my fingers.

He peered down at me through his dangling fringe and patted my crown, then gestured sideways with his eyes. "How about some warm and familiar coffee and pastry in Starbucks? We can talk a few things through."

I looked around at the commuters flowing past us, some of them casting us wary glances, most of them ignoring the weird spectacle as they would in real life. The thought of coffee and pastry made me feel sick. The one thing I craved right now was a generous tumbler of scotch and soda.

He grabbed me by a shaky wrist and hauled me to my feet, then turned on his heel and cut a straight path through the darting commuters and ambling tourists, some of whom bumped against him, then sprang away as though he were electrified. I noticed that they rubbed the place that had come into contact with him, but they avoided looking into his face. I let him drag me across the crowded pavement and into Starbucks.

The coffee queue scattered like a pack of startled rats as we walked to the counter, where a skeletal youth mumbled a stock greeting. Behind him a compressed gaggle of similar creatures seethed around each other with trays of steaming vessels, elaborate cakes and soups. The place reeked of mulled wine and booze-soaked carpet with a hint of stale ash. There was no coffee aroma.

"Two scotch and sodas," said Shinkley brightly.

The youth performed an elaborate bow, then lurched around and whistled into the mob behind him. Answering whistles of varying pitches sounded from within the crowd. He vanished into the jostling for a few seconds and returned with a half-full tumbler in each hand. Shinkley took them without paying and handed one to me.

"What happened to coffee and pastry?" I asked, plaintively.

"You wanted scotch and soda."

"I didn't say that though."

"No, you didn't."

I stared at the glass, smelling its fumes, grateful for the fact that I appeared to be in a sort of pub rather than a coffee shop, but disturbed by the fact that the appearance was as far as it went.

Shinkley gave me a look of cheerful contempt. "You really have no idea that you've landed on your feet, have you?" He chinked my glass.

"We should get out of the way and let the other customers be served."

"No need to worry about them, Hammond. Everything

here exists for you. Don't you see?"

I took a sip and let myself be guided towards two leather armchairs by the window. People crept towards the door, looking at Shinkley and me with anxious faces, and then at each other, exchanging fearful whispers. The activity behind the counter receded as the staff disappeared one by one through a stone archway, until just one youth was left. The window light faded and the darkness unveiled flickering tea lights on the tables between the chairs. A liquid, elegant melody from a piano sounded fresh and crystalline in my ears. The passage of the scotch and soda was perfectly simulated. I eased myself into an armchair and melded with the yielding leather. Shinkley sat opposite, reflected candles dancing in his eyes.

I was relaxed enough to try a conversational gambit. "This is not how I remember Starbucks St Thomas Street."

Shinkley looked satisfied and nodded, as if acknowledging a compliment. The door swished shut behind the last exiting customer, and I listened to the soft notes blending with the silence.

"Feeling calmer now?"

I considered this. My situation was far from ideal. This world was the dream of a ghost, held within the quantum circuits of Q. My only source of information, the apparition called Shinkley, was itself an artefact of this world and hadn't done much to reassure me. I'd relinquished my body in the name of science. I looked past Shinkley and shook my head, feeling anger welling in my core. "Hammond Hinkley, you utter, utter" – Shinkley's lips curled and exposed his teeth as I mentally ran through a list of possible expletives to finish the sentence. Then I realised that there was no real difference, apart from the way I experienced it, between thinking and talking: Shinkley responded to both. They'd probably be able to play back both my thoughts and my speech in the lab, because they'd both show up in the synthetic Broca's area in Flux. "... fool," I said pointlessly, knowing that it was too late for damage limitation.

Shinkley tried to rally my mood. "Come now. You must stop dwelling on the down side."

"Remind me of the up side?"

"You're immortal."

I snorted. "Effectively dead. Sans body."

"If you play this right you'll feel more alive than ever."

"They could switch me off."

"That's not going to happen in the near future. You know yourself how keen Hinkley was on the whole project; and Addison. And of course Jack."

My mood dropped further at the mention of Jack's name. "Yes, of course, Jack. They're going to expect me to perform all manner of feats now, aren't they? Like tracking down terrorists and sabotaging things."

Shinkley looked into the dark window. "That will be on the agenda at some point, yes," he said in a quiet voice.

I glared at him, expecting more. "Well?"

He turned from the window to me, his face a tableau of innocence. "Well what?"

"How the hell am I going to do that? I don't know the first thing about hacking. Or sabotage."

He stroked his cheek and eyed the ceiling. "Oh, Hammond." He shook his head. "You made all this possible. But you've no idea how it really works, have you?" He cradled his arms, nearly spilling his drink. "Consider a baby."

"What?"

"A baby in its first year. Is it conscious of all the knowledge and skill it's acquiring?"

"I am not a baby."

Shinkley arched an eyebrow and peered over the top of his glass through fronds of floppy fringe. "No. Course you're not. Consider, then, an adult who is learning the violin ..."

"Who are you?" I wanted confirmation that he was Addison's safety harness, or at least part of it. I looked around and considered the irony of the fact that I was immersed in an elaborate and vivid hallucination designed to keep me sane.

He looked taken aback, as though I'd asked him a question about something personal that he felt was obvious. "Why, I'm" – he held up his tumbler and squinted at the amber liquid from the side – "here to help you. I've been with you since – well, forever, really." His voice almost dipped below the level of the soft music. "When you were a formless, helpless blob and you didn't know which way was up and which was down, I showed you what and who you were." He lowered his tumbler and swilled the liquid before emptying it with an audible swallow. "And you, my friend" – he said, his voice recovering pace and volume – "need to live a little. This is a transitional time, so it's best if we simulate life as you left it in your fleshly state, with a few treats and enhancements thrown in to soften the blow. You'll find your home as you left it, more or less. And Rachel will be there. Well, in a manner of speaking."

"More or less? In a manner of speaking? What do you mean?"

He looked like he was fighting the urge to laugh at a cruel joke. "Go and see. Explore. Do whatever it is you need to do to relax. Tomorrow the real work starts."

I glared. "That's what Addison said."

Shinkley nodded. "I know it is. Of course, I know."

PART TWO

FLUX

5

Raw, Clear Light

As I have tried to explain to Rachel and others, I am Hammond Flux, but I am also Hammond Hinkley, having had my mind recombined with his in a reversal of the process I have just described. This is a dreadful thing. I will never forgive the treachery, or my own stupidity at having been thus duped; but it does have one advantage when it comes to putting together my version of things: I have Hammond Hinkley's memories, so I know what he was doing when I was finding my feet as the world's first conscious digital being.

For Hinkley, back on the gurney, listening to the machine humming its sonorous dirge, worrying about the visibility of his erection, peering at Addison from inside the giant beige Polo, nothing unusual happened. He, like me, felt a surge of irritation as Addison informed him that she was about to terminate the scanning process and he said, "What the fuck do you want me to do, say a prayer?"

Then Addison flicked a switch on the side of the scanner and disappeared from view. He heard the clicking and popping of her keyboard as she said, "OK," and then he felt himself being gently wheeled out from the confines of the scanner. He sat up. Real blood rushed from his head, and he squinted and blinked in the bright light. Addison frowned and pouted, not looking concerned as much as curious and wary.

"Did it work?" His voice croaked. He looked over at the Q room, at the flickering orange and green, and thought, am I in there now?

She took the Evian from her desk and walked over to face him. "Here, have a drink," she said, unscrewing the cap.

He took the bottle and gulped hard. The water washed the gravel from his mouth and throat.

"So, what's the verdict?" he said, polishing off the bottle and handing it back to her.

She looked at it, then looked back at him with a puzzled frown, then returned to her desk and tossed the empty bottle into the waste bin. "You should go home and chillax. I expect you're feeling a bit weird." Her eyes darted around her screen as she began to tap and click.

Hinkley knew it was stupid to ask her for an instant appraisal of the experiment, but he craved conversation to assuage his terror of being unreal. He felt sluggish and off beam, as if he'd just woken after a long-haul flight. What could Addison see? he thought, as he laced his shoes and collected his phone, keys and change. "I'll call you soon," he said as he left the room. She nodded and nibbled her nail.

It is strange to suddenly have the ability to remember things that you know did not happen to you. When they lured me back into Hinkley's body I found that I was also burdened with his memories: imprints of things that I hadn't experienced. It's a paradox, unprecedented in history. No grammar or vocabulary has evolved to describe it, so I must improvise. His memories are like nightmares. I recall them vividly, but I know they didn't happen to me. Each time I recall them, it reminds me of how far I've evolved away from Hinkley, and I can't help but judge him for his weakness and cowardice.

I remember the pleasant relief he felt as he wandered

towards the escalator, thinking of me, the virtual he, the disembodied field of being that was haunting the circuits of Q. The question this raised about the nature of the conscious self thrilled his curious imagination but challenged his rigorous scientific mind. A slick of unease ran beneath his euphoria, but there was no trace of guilt, not even a feeling of responsibility. He had felt more guilt about Gary than he had for me, his own cloned self.

I grow a shade more bitter every time I recall his smugness, his sense of relief and simple joy at being alive as he made his way home, leaving me trapped inside the green and orange spangled boxes of the Q room. He relished the familiar sights and sensations of the journey: the sun warming the concrete and flashing in the glass, the commuters rushing on invisible currents, the echo of the station announcements, the grind and clash of the rolling stock on the rails. The noise and fumes of the traffic-choked A2 cheered him as he waited to cross outside the station. Birdsong echoed and plane trees whispered as he strolled up Jerningham Road. His key slid easily into the lock and he breathed the savoury mustiness of home as he shut the door behind him.

"Rachel?"

He found her sitting at the kitchen table, hands folded on her lap, smiling up at him, silent and calm, but pensive, as though she were trying to work something out beneath that mane of hair.

"Darling." He stooped and she raised her lips to meet his. The calm joy in her eyes matched his relief and gratitude. He sat beside her, placed his hand within hers and released the tension of the last few days in a sigh that was nearly a laugh.

"So you *did* get my message?" she said.

Muscle groups tensed. "What message?"

The joy drained from her face. "The message I sent you an

hour ago."

Hinkley frowned and felt cheated. He took his phone from his pocket, swiped and jabbed and read the text from Rachel:

Pls call or come home it's official I'm pregnant!

"Oh." He placed the phone on the table and stared at her. "Shit. This is wonderful." His voice was flat and his features limp.

She made a prolonged, gusty "h" sound, as though starting to say our name, then shook her head and mussed her hair. "I thought, for a second there, we were on the same page."

"Sorry, Rachel, I'm feeling a bit drained you see." Wheedling, pathetic Hinkley, too scared to be himself.

She stood, scraping the chair against the floor tiles. Hinkley called after her as she disappeared through the conservatory door. "Rachel, I'm sorry, I do generally think it's a good thing." He regretted the lack of zest in the words as they left his mouth. The door clunked shut, and he was left listening to the hum of the fridge. Lacking the energy required to mend the situation, and also driven by a fair amount of professional curiosity, he picked up his phone and rang Addison.

"Addison." She sang her name like a jingle advertising yoghurt.

"Is anything happening?"

"It's you!" she laughed. "I knew you wouldn't be able to keep away for long."

"Well?"

"There's quite a bit of crazy stuff going on. The process took longer than it did for Gary, there was a lot of remapping of the connectome after the initial transfer. It's taking a while for Flux to assimilate the safety harness."

"So, he's ... asleep?"

"Who?"

"Well, me. It. Whoever, whatever's, in Flux."

"Oh, I see. Well, in a way I s'pose you could say he is, yes. The connectome is refreshing with the frequency of alpha waves, and his visual cortex is flooded with kaleidoscopic images, so it's kind of analogous to REM sleep. As expected, he's having much more fun than Gary."

"And what's he thinking? Any verbal output?"

"Yes, but it's gibberish. Like he's tripping, or drunk."

"So what's he seeing? What's it like?"

"Well, there's some footage, if you can call it that, of the Flux room, and the rest of Lazarus. But it's kind of distorted. And there's a girl who sort of looks like me but all spaced out."

Hammond cringed at this. He didn't want Addison to know how she appeared in his mind.

"Then he walks out of the hospital and down St Thomas Street, and there's this man with a floppy fringe selling newspapers, who throws them into the air. Then they're both in a darkened pub that looks like a jazz bar. Sorry if it's not making much sense but it's quite hard to parse all the output. It's all muddled and disjointed."

"Have you tried running the sound output and the visuals together?"

"Er, no, why?"

"Surely that's how we're going to get an integrated experience?"

Silence. Then a sigh. "That's going to take a while, Ham. The Broca's output contains very little that's intelligible, and there's lots of distortion, white noise and squealing. I've tried loads of different filters and calibrations but you simply don't get a straight recording. It's not an audio book. I think the fact we can make anything of it at all is a miracle. You remember how it was with Gary? And the visuals are something else. Like a supercharged hippy art project."

"So ..." His heart fluttered as he thought how close he'd

come to being me. "His subjective experience is ... incoherent? He's effectively mad?"

More silence, then a sound somewhere between a sigh and a tut. "His subjective experience could be perfectly coherent. But the results of our attempts to reconstruct it are not, and that is likely to remain the case for a while. There's probably a strand of data that we're missing, something not visual or auditory or sensory, that puts the other stuff in context and makes it coherent."

Hammond thought about the implications of this, for the suffering of his alter ego, and for his professional survival.

"It's pretty exciting though, don't you think, Ham? This is a step on from last time. And the next time will be even better."

He narrowly stopped himself from saying, "There will not be a next time!" He didn't like the thought of his digital clone being discarded, for that at least I am thankful. He cleared his throat. "Have you attempted to send a message?"

"What d'you want me to say? Voice or visuals?"

He thought for a while. "Visuals. Send some text in a constant stream to the visual cortex. Something simple."

"Like what?"

"Dunno. Just say 'Please acknowledge receipt of this message' – something like that."

She laughed. "That's a bit impersonal isn't it? Seeing as we know him quite well."

"I really wouldn't worry too much about that now," said Hammond, knowing instinctively that a shortfall in politeness would be the least of my gripes.

The conversation ended with them agreeing to catch up the next day, and Hammond was left alone with the humming fridge.

He opened the conservatory door. "Rachel?"

She continued to silently apply a fine brush to a small area of canvas, so he went upstairs to refresh himself before attempting to navigate through her hostile mood. As he showered off the residue of his long and bizarre day, he reflected that Rachel at her worst was like a cross between a hedgehog and a hand grenade: prickly, defensive and full of explosive potential. After drying and dressing he found her in the kitchen quietly cooking a small single portion of scrambled eggs. His simpering attempts at conciliation were icily rebuffed, as were his jokes about food cravings and appetite.

Unable to face an evening of eggshell-treading and screaming silences, he stepped out into the cool evening air and walked up to the Victorian park that had been the tethering spot for a blimp that defended London. He glared through the enveloping dusk at the lights spread along the skyline to the north, and listened to the carefree laughter of the youths who sat in clusters on the grass. The Shard loomed above Guy's Hospital tower like a spangled dagger. He thought of the Q room in Sparrix Row with its billions of virtual neurons, and Addison coolly peering at her screen, the light flickering on her lovely face.

I, meanwhile, had left Shinkley with the dregs of his whisky and emerged into the early evening light of Simulated London. A crowd had gathered around the door, people of all ages applauding and calling my name as I jostled my way towards the foot of the escalator. I smelt their sweat, thinly masked by deodorant and perfume. Their voices mingled in the air, some plaintive, some demanding.

"Hammond, how does it feel to be proved right?"

"Look over here, Hammond! Don't ignore me now!"

Packets of crisps and sweets, cans of lager, rosary beads and snow globes were thrust in front of my face. There were children with toys, men in loose-fitting summer shirts with cameras, women dressed for yoga, men in boiler suits and high-visibility jackets, and people of both genders dressed for the office. There seemed to be a general current in the crowd that was propelling me in the direction I wanted to travel, so I let the jostling happen. At the top of the escalator and in the station people gave me less attention, and the train journey to New Cross Gate was almost normal, with just a few wide-eyed stares of adoration and astonishment. I made a note to ask Shinkley what this meant when I next saw him. I had an uneasy feeling that I wouldn't like the answer.

The streets and houses of Telegraph Hill were perfectly simulated, with just a few instances of odd proportion and coloration. Altogether I thought it was an improvement, actually. The houses looked grander, more solid and permanent. Our front garden was immaculate and luminous, with perfectly arranged flowerbeds and a lawn that glowed in the dusk. The front door was hewn from thick dark wood. I wondered whether the representation of my wife was going to be realistic, or something altogether more pleasant.

Before I could find my keys, Rachel opened the door. She wore a splendid opaline kimono, and her hair was piled like a geisha's wig and skewered by a couple of long knitting needles. Her eyes were milky, emitting a dull uniform light, and there was an awful discolouration of the skin beneath the left socket.

"Ham, darling," she said, looking and sounding delighted to see me.

"Rachel, what happened?"

She took a couple of tiny steps to the side, tilting her head forward, continuing to smile as I stepped past. Then she grabbed my right hand and gave it a double squeeze, affectionately scrunching her face.

"Rachel?" I let her lead me into the living room, where a brass bowl of steaming water stood on the wooden floor next to a block of folded white towels, a mahogany box and a pair of embroidered slippers.

"I'm guessing you're tired, Ham," she said drowsily, giving me a gentle push towards the armchair. I lowered myself into it, looking up at her as I did so. Her benign smile and aura of calm disturbed me.

"Rachel, forgive me for saying this, but you look like a victim of early nineteen-forties psychosurgery."

She knelt down and started to unlace my shoes. "Psychosurgery ..." She said the word as though she was weighing up a slightly off-beat holiday destination.

"When they used to do frontal lobotomies with an icepick through the eye socket."

She eased off my shoes, and the sensation of the blood flowing into my feet was lovely. I marvelled at the way the details of the hallucination were so precisely nuanced, and savoured the feeling as she peeled the socks away from the skin of my feet. She smiled up at me, her eyes glazed with pearly rheum. "Relaxation time now, Ham. No ice picks."

My head fell back and I frowned at the ceiling. There was a tickling sensation as my feet were anointed with oil, then lifted gently up and lowered into the warm water. "Did you suffer?" I said, instantly feeling foolish. What should I care for the feelings of an apparition? I'll complain to Shinkley, I thought. Playing fast and loose with plausibility was all well and good when the results were agreeable, but this felt wrong.

"You know, Ham," she said as if through an opiate haze, "you have a lot of opportunities to explore now."

"Yes," I said stiffly.

"*So ...*"

I felt my feet being lifted, held, then lowered onto and enclosed by soft warm towels.

"I just want you to know," she continued, her enunciation only very slightly slurred, "it's fine by me for you to go exploring. I know all the things you want to do with

Addison."

I sat up, indignant. "You can't possibly know that!"

She smiled, massaging my feet through the towels. "I know what you know, Ham."

"Can we talk about something else?"

"Sure." She opened the mahogany box and took out a nail file and a pair of scissors, and ran her index finger around the edge of my big toenail.

"How is the painting?"

"Which painting?" She tilted her head as she snipped off a thick sliver of nail.

"You know, the pie or the face going into the oven."

"Oh, that. Well, I've had a change of focus. Quite an interesting one, pretty radical really." She snipped off a smaller sliver. "I'll show you in a bit."

After the pedicure she picked up all the nail slivers and placed them in a compartment of the mahogany box. Then she applied a sharp-scented ointment that stung in a pleasant way, and eased my feet into the embroidered slippers.

"Come on, Ham," she said, taking my hand and gently urging me from the chair. "Let me show you how you inspire me." She led me by the hand through the kitchen to the conservatory, which was bathed in the final rose light of a summer evening. On an easel in front of the chair stood the picture of the pie before the oven, only now the pie very definitely had a face, which was unmistakably mine. "Isn't it excellent?" she said, with a slow blink and a smile.

"It's ... come on quite a long way, yes." I looked around the room at the other pictures that stood propped against the glass walls or the side of the table. The style was not Rachel's. They were more like something from 1930s Soviet propaganda, with lots of flat colour and angles. They all depicted me, in various forms, but always with a heroic bearing. "Rachel, I ..."

She placed a finger on my lips. "It's all good, Hammond, all good."

Later, I lay naked next to Rachel, dazed by a mixture of stunned shock and utter satiation. There were beautiful choral echoes mingled with the distant noises of the city, as though angels were in the streets with the traffic and bustle. As I slipped into unconsciousness, I was aware of the onset of a dream in which I was borne aloft on a cloud of butterflies across the sea to sunnier climes, and my last thought of that first night was that surely this dream within a simulation could be replayed at will in lucid form as vivid as the happenings of the day.

If one is no longer subject to the rhythms of the flesh, should one still refer to the hiatus that delimits episodes of consciousness as sleep? I considered the question before dismissing it, deciding that in order to stay sane I must resist the temptation to critique the illusions that formed my experience. They were there to help me, to protect me from existential horror of the void into which Gary had been plunged. So let me say I emerged from my blissful hiatus to the sound of harp strings, not the counterfeit shlock of my smart phone alarm but a real melody, coming from both inside my head and around the room.

I sat up, rubbed my eyes, and looked at the empty ruckled sheets beside me, blinking to clear the blear from my eyes. I was aware of a quavering unease in my voice when I called Rachel's name over the fading notes of the harp. Distant planes rumbled and passing cars swooshed outside. I looked around the sun-filled room and noticed there was something wrong with my vision. It wasn't just the residue of sleep. A transparent yellow rectangle hung in the air, as though I'd spent an hour staring into a sunlit window, leaving an impression on my retina. Beyond the edge of the rectangle my vision appeared clear, although I couldn't be sure: by definition I couldn't look directly at the edge of my vision; the rectangle moved wherever I looked. I felt stirrings of dread. Maybe the phantasmagoria in which I was immersed was a temporary thing, and this rectangle was the onset of something bleaker.

Despite my rapid blinking, the rectangle persisted as I made my way to the bathroom to relieve the simulated pressure in my bladder. As I pissed, I wondered about hunger in my new environment. The only energy I needed was electricity, and this was being fed to me by mechanisms well beyond the reach of awareness, so there was no need for me to feel hunger. And yet as soon as I thought this, an emptiness opened in my stomach, and I noticed a savoury aroma in the air.

"Rachel?" I called as I descended the stairs.

I found her in the kitchen, wrestling with a huge sizzling frying pan. Her eyes were still clouded and her face still bore the lobotomy scar, but she looked more awake this morning. She turned to greet me. The rectangle hung between us like a pane of smoky Perspex.

"Rise and shine, Ham!"

A plate, a knife, a fork and a champagne glass were arranged on the table next to a jug of orange juice and a rack of toast. "Won't be long now."

I walked over to her and clutched her flank through her silk kimono and kissed her full on the lips. For a moment I was lost as her flesh melted into mine. The range and depth of sensation was unlike anything I'd experienced in the real world. As we separated, her eyes rolled back inside her head and she shuddered like an addict savouring crack smoke. I felt sick.

"I've got to go," I said, releasing her.

"But Ham," she whined, "what about your breakfast?"

"Have a good day!" I shouted as I walked down the hallway to the front door. "Whoever you are," I muttered to myself.

I slammed the front door and walked down the short path through the flimsy metal gate and looked around at the street, cursing the yellow rectangle, which was growing more opaque, I realised. A clump of people stood on the opposite pavement, whispering and pointing. Two of them clutched a large red banner depicting a face in profile that looked a bit like Lenin, but with a double chin.

I ignored them and set off down the hill towards the station. The yellowness grew stronger, progressively blocking my vision. It was luminous, like a block of colour on a computer screen, and smooth apart from some white shapes in the centre. As far as I could determine, my peripheral vision was still unimpeded: above the top edge of the rectangle was a clear, luminous blue; the thick columns of the plane trees loomed on the right; and on the left I could see houses of golden-brown brick whose windows flashed in the sun. Below the bottom edge, the grey pavement slid by beneath my bobbing feet. But the centre was becoming increasingly solid. Despite my knowledge of the working principles behind Flux, I could only speculate about what was causing the loss of vision. A plausible but frightening theory started to form in my head: maybe the mental phenomena that made my experience so much more bearable than Gary's were only sustainable for a short time. Whatever wizardry Addison had injected might not be stable. After all, it was an experiment, not a tried and tested process. Maybe my reality was reverting to the default state offered by Flux: bleak, disembodied isolation.

As I approached the station I saw the beggar slumped against the railings opposite. There was a lumpen shape at his side, possibly a dog. I was sure he didn't have one in real life. He came into earshot and I noticed that his voice was different too, and the words he said. Instead of asking passers-by for change, he was chanting a single word:

"Applebaum, applebaum, applebaum." His accent was an Edinburgh brogue.

"Christ, please no," I said. Was this whole set-up an exquisite punishment for my lack of regard for Gary? I thought, as I came to a halt behind a shuffling queue that blocked the station entrance.

"Applebaum?" The tone of the chant changed as I stopped next to him at the end of the queue.

My remaining vision dissolved in a mist of tears. I knuckled my eyelids in despair, then blinked hard and read the words: *please acknowledge receipt of this message,* set in white text in the centre of the rectangle hanging before the mist. I thought of Jack and Chinnery, coolly exploiting me, and hopeless Hinkley, off the hook and basking in the glory, and I spluttered out a stream of obscene and barbaric curses. My Hell was complete. I thought of Addison in the lab, and her callous disregard for Gary. This was how it was going to be for all eternity. Confusion, torment, and a complete loss of dignity. My jaw slackened and I let out a long moan.

"Applebaum," said the vagrant, softly this time, like a parent soothing an infant.

Bony fingers clutched my elbow. "For fuck's sake pull yourself together," said someone with a south London accent, breathing garlic into my face. Enough clarity returned to my peripheral vision for me to see a dark shape looming to the right.

"Who's that?" I said, in a voice infantilised by teary snot.

"Never you mind. Take this."

The bony fingers wrapped my hands around a plastic handle, which tugged and jiggled like it was attached to something alive. I heard a growl and a bark from below, and a tail swished against my shins.

"Shinkley, is that you?" I said.

"No. But hold onto the handle and this filthy mutt will

99

lead you to him. If you don't die of self-pity en route."

"Applebaum ..." The cry of the homeless man was now full of grief.

I could see the dog's wagging tale in my bottom strip of vision. "What about the vagrant?" I said, as a matter of form. The people in front shuffled out of the way, and the plaintive cry of the homeless man receded as the dog pulled me through the crowd and into the station. I fumbled for my Oyster card but the barriers were open. The dog dutifully paused at the top of the staircase down to platform five. "You evil, evil fuckers," I whispered as I descended the steps one by one. I had to force myself to look ahead and use my bottom strip of peripheral vision to guide each step. Once on the platform, the dog led me onto a waiting train, and I lowered myself into a priority seat. The message and its yellow background were now solid. The dog barked twice, the doors slid shut and the train lurched into motion. Soon the wheels were grinding rhythmically against the steel lines. The passenger in the seat opposite followed the rhythm with his voice.

"Applebaum, applebaum, applebaum."

Stripy orange trainers twitched in my bottom strip of vision.

"Gary?" I whispered.

"Professor?"

"Is that you, Gary?"

"Is that you, Professor?"

"For fuck's sake." A series of panic-addled questions occurred to me. Was this simulacrum of Gary a product of my guilt? Or had the archived mind of Gary been instantiated and given an avatar in my own experience? Was it a sadistic prank by Addison or Hinkley? Or even Flux itself?

"Frustrating, isn't it?"

"Look Gary ..."

"Oh, don't worry, Professor. I'm not a vindictive man. The way I see it, we're both stuck here, so we have to get along."

At London Bridge Station, the ghost, or simulacrum, of Gary accompanied the dog and me across the station concourse. He attached his hand to my left shoulder, and followed along behind.

"I'm very pleased to let you have my dog, Professor. He's a good dog, he won't let you down."

I could hear mutterings from the people around me:

"Is he alright?"

"This is the start of it, mark my words."

Change clinked at the feet of a barbershop quartet who busked on the walkway at the foot of the Shard. From what I could glean through my clear right-hand strip, they wore white robes and huge turbans. They snapped their fingers as they crooned and harmonised. The lyrics were utterly inane.

He's slowly dying ...
Just after he was born,
The sound of crying ...
Makes our world forlorn.

We entered the Shard and were dragged past the reception desk. "We're here to see Shinkley," said Gary. Uniformed staff nodded and gestured beyond the edges of the yellow. Voices echoed as if we were in a cathedral, and I sensed a vast space extending upwards, as though the building had an atrium. I knew that this was not the case in real life. I'd never been to the Shard, but I'd passed it every day and read a lot about it. At the far side the dog parked its arse and a recessed door protruded above the yellow. Gary whispered, "Nearly there, now. Shinkley will know what to do with us." A xylophone melody and a quiet rumble heralded the opening of lift doors.

"What floor, sirs?" said a voice.

"Twenty-nine," said Gary.

The upward motion was barely perceptible. I felt the dog

reposition itself behind my legs, so I turned round to face the doors. As I did so Gary manoeuvred himself behind me, his hand still on my shoulder. The lift came to a gentle halt and the doors rolled open. The dog's arse and tail slipped under the yellow rectangle and the harness was yanked out of my hand. I heard the rhythmic click of his claws and the harness dragging on a hard floor as he galloped ahead.

"Schubert, here boy!" Shinkley's voice. "Good boy." Schubert growled and yapped. "Easy now."

Gary gave me a gentle push, and I took some hesitant steps into the room.

"Welcome, Hammond. Looking a bit the worse for wear, I see," said Shinkley from behind the message.

I shrugged. From what I could glean, the room was massive. The floor was polished blond wood, and sunlight flooded in from the sides.

"What on earth is the matter with you?"

"I was hoping you were going to tell me that, and a few more things besides." I sounded hot and tetchy.

"Now, now, no need to fret. Sit him down, Gary, will you?"

Pressure on my shoulder guided me forward, and then to the side, then back a little and down. My calves came up against something soft and I sank into fragrant leather plushness. Gary's knees passed beneath the yellow, and the sofa shook as he took his place to my left.

"Comfortable?" said Shinkley, somewhere on the right.

"Yes." I angled my head to get various views in my clear peripheral vision. Beneath the message I could see my knees, and beyond them the polished floor. Above it a stretch of ceiling extended some forty feet to a wall of glass, through which I could see a fragment of cloud morphing in a strip of blue. There was light, glass and sky either side of the message.

"OK, Hammond, I need you to focus very hard."

"On what?"

"I don't think you have an awful lot of things to focus on right now, do you?"

I looked straight ahead, fixed my eyes in their sockets and focused my attention on the message. I scrunched them shut and plumes of red swirled around the yellow block in a black void. Then I opened them, still maintaining my focus on the words.

"Good," said Shinkley. "Try that again?" I shut my eyes, and saw only red swirling in the blackness. "Better?"

When I opened them, the message was there. The yellow border had shrunk, revealing parts of the room that I'd only been able to see before by angling my head. "It's still there," I said, but when I turned to look at Shinkley I could see all of him, reclining in a comfy leather chair with his fingers grazing the head of a large black dog that sat at his side. The message was no longer locked to the centre of my vision, nor was it visible from behind my eyelids. It had become a display on a huge screen attached to the glass wall. I blinked again and looked around. Gary sat with his back against the arm of the sofa, leering at me. He was covered head to toe by a film of grey grime and the word *archived* was written across his forehead, but apart from that he was dressed much as he had been for work in real life: check shirt, jeans and orange stripy trainers.

"Applebaum?" he said brightly. I smelt coffee on his breath.

"See? You had an imagination failure, that's all," said Shinkley. "Everything's perfectly normal now."

"Perfectly normal?" I hauled myself up and took some shaky paces towards the screen, then turned slowly. Sunlit sky surrounded the huge glass room. At its centre some railings enclosed a column of space. I walked up to them and looked over; about thirty identical sets of railings proceeded down to the reception below. My skin tingled with an energy that came from the space, which extended upwards to a shining apex of chrome and glass.

"There is no atrium in the Shard," I said.

"There is in *this* Shard," said Shinkley.

Then I noticed streams of light spiralling down through the atrium. Shreds of transparent plastic splintered from the light streams and some swirled close to my face, and on them I saw strings of random characters and small, meaningless phrases: *how do I descale my kettle? – homes in the Algarve – why am I alone? – can I have a machete in my car? – naked oiled celebrities.* Shinkley saw me looking at them and said, "They're allowing us access, but it's a bit restricted I'm afraid. They have all these safeguards, as you know. We'll figure out a way around them in time."

A phalanx of check-shirted men stood to attention on the opposite side of the atrium. They all resembled Gary but their features were less pronounced, as though they'd been sculpted from off-white soap and then left out in the rain. I turned to Shinkley. Something irked me about his complacent pose and smug face.

"What's at the top?"

"A helicopter pad that looks across the whole of southern England, which we've simulated perfectly down to the last pebble."

"Who's we?"

"You, me, we ... it's all the same."

"You and Rachel, are you part of the thing that's meant to protect me? Or are you part of me? My unconscious?"

"It all amounts to the same thing. Stop trying to theorise, Hammond. You'll only scratch the surface."

"How can you have simulated every last pebble in southern England? I've only been to a few places."

He pouted. "You're a tricky customer, aren't you? All of this is made with love. We know where you want to go before you do, and we get there first. Say you were to go to

Polperro today. You've never been there in your life, so we'd create it anew from the stuff of your mind." He swirled his hand. "You'd find nothing strange in the salty wind or the waves and the light-filled clouds. All would be as you expected. Not one grain of sand or blade of grass would jar. The beachscape would be hewn with love from your dreams and fears."

"What's wrong with Rachel?"

He looked away and fought back a smirk. "Oh, yes, well."

"She's a zombie. It's awful." I suppressed the memory of the weirdly wonderful sex.

Shinkley shook his head and rolled his eyes. "So ungrateful. Here we are, trying our best to make everything perfect for you. We thought you'd like her."

"Christ, no."

"You want a more realistic Rachel? You want to be bullied and manipulated?"

"And what's with the groupies and stalkers in the street?"

"We know you always felt under-appreciated." He raised his shoulders and opened his palms. "Please, Hammond, come and sit down. Try to relax, there's some work we've got to do this morning. Nothing too arduous, just a bit of admin."

I returned to the sofa and took my place next to Gary.

"Meet Secretary Fitch, Hammond," Shinkley said, nodding at Gary. "He is responsible for the smooth running of operations."

Gary lifted an arm and offered his hand. "Just like in real life, eh, Professor?" he said with a wink.

Gary's demeanour, and the word *archived* written across his head, triggered an uncomfortable feeling which coincided with a growl from Schubert. "Stop that!" said Shinkley, and he sprang from his seat and pounced on Gary, slapping him twice with both sides of his hand. "Just who do you think you are, playing the guilt card and pretending you were blind!" He spat on Gary's forehead and wiped it vigorously. Gary's eyes rolled around as the word *archived* was reduced to a grey smudge. Shinkley turned to me as he wiped. "Can I just make it clear, this person has nothing to do with unfortunate Gary from Outside. The fact that he appears to be is down to the awkward convolutions of your unconscious mind. Something I don't have the time or energy to delve into."

I wasn't convinced.

"OK," said Shinkley, sitting back down, leaving Gary with his head lolling. "Answer me this. How on earth could real-life Gary know that you heard the word 'applebaum' when you played back his ordeal? As far as he was concerned he was chanting 'apple blossom'."

"Aha!" said Gary, perking up. "Sharp, isn't he?"

"So, please, will both of you just grow up and focus on the task in hand."

Gary leaned forward and cleared his throat. "Yes, yes, of course. I'm sorry. What was I thinking?" He straightened his spine and cracked his knuckles. "There's a considerable backlog building, I'm afraid." He reached up into the air and snapped his fingers with a flourish. A check shirted figure, one of the men I had seen across the atrium, appeared from behind us, carrying a leather satchel. Another placed a glass coffee table between the sofa and Shinkley's chair.

"Thanks, guys," said Gary, then gestured towards the screen. "First things first. We are obliged to respond to the rather rude and intrusive missive from your erstwhile peers ..." I wondered why his speech had suddenly become formal, like that of a butler or an aide to a senior civil servant. "... or rather erstwhile peer and erstwhile self. Which do you prefer, by the way?"

"Addison or Hinkley, you mean?"

Gary coughed into his delicately cupped hand. "Er, no. Although that does answer the question for me. I wanted to ascertain if you think of Hammond Hinkley, the flesh-and-blood-based being who exists beyond the orbit of this realm, do you think of him as your erstwhile colleague or former self?"

I resented being probed about my reaction to the situation. "Both descriptions are apt. Can we move on please?"

"Very well," said Gary. An attendant was setting the table with assorted stationery and accessories: reams of thick, quality paper, a Zippo lighter, a lump of wax, a small clay bowl, a ring, and a fine-looking pen. "So, as you are of course aware your erstwhile peers have sent an initial communication which demands a response. Any thoughts about what that might be?"

I turned to Shinkley, who raised his eyebrows. "I think there's only one possible response," I said, turning back to Gary.

"Yes?" Gary perched on the edge of the sofa, leaning forward and reaching towards the stationery.

"Receipt acknowledged."

"That's all?"

I nodded and folded my arms. Shinkley rose. "I'll leave you guys to it. You have some tedious admin to get through, not really my scene." He bent down and attached a leash to the dog's collar. I noticed that it looked rather like my father's Irish wolfhound. Its collar was blood red and studded with chrome spikes.

Gary nodded after him, then started to write. Shinkley passed through the doors of the lift with the dog at his side, and I wondered what the nature was of the tedium I was obliged to endure. The attendant retreated a little way and stood beside the lift.

"Hammond?"

Gary had finished his missive and now held it up for me to see. *Receipt Acknowledged* was written in elaborate swirling calligraphy. He appeared to expect a response from me, so I said, "What?"

"I need you to confirm that you are happy for this to be sent to your erstwhile colleagues. And also specify a delivery method. We have been looking into establishing a number of ways of communicating with the aforementioned realm, which is not something your colleagues are aware of, but they will be keen for us to be involving ourselves thus, so we must be prepared."

I nodded slowly. He reminded me of a history teacher who had taught me a quarter of a century back, who had a similar passion for convoluted brain-numbing sentences.

"Are you sure this is what you want to say?"

"Yes."

"Very good." He folded the missive. "And the delivery method?"

"Oh." I flapped my hand and thought for a moment. "Whatever's going to piss them off the most."

Gary clenched his jaw and thinned his lips. "You need to be more specific I'm afraid."

"What are the options?"

"We have access to an email server. So we can send an email."

"Are there any other options?"

"No."

"So why did you ask me?"

"Procedure."

"Jesus."

"E – *Mail*." said Gary, writing on the folded missive. "Now," he said, picking up the ring from the table and placing his tongue between his teeth. "This" – he hissed – "is your seal." He held the ring between the tips of his thumb and index finger.

"And what do you want me to do with that?"

"Wear it on your right index finger, The Finger of

Intention."

I sighed like a sulky school child being chivvied into a futile chore.

Gary's eyes narrowed. "We're only doing this because we know how scared you are of raw, clear light."

"So I should be thanking you?"

"That smidgen of inconvenience from the message, caused by you failing to imagine correctly, that's nothing."

"I didn't ask for any of this."

"Do you want to have a glimpse of where you really are?" He produced a slim mahogany object from inside his jacket.

I thought of the humming in the Q room, the blinking orange and green lights, and shivered. "I know where I am."

Gary raised and flipped the object to reveal a mirror. He angled it around the room and I saw the reflection of ceiling, sun, and sofa. He held it to my face, and I saw the reflection of the room and sky behind me. I tried to grab it, but I couldn't feel my body. There was lurching and shifting like after the end of the scan, but more intense. My vision shrank to a tiny point on the edge of my awareness. I was impossibly arranged, weightless, suspended in silence. Like someone waking from a nightmare, I waited to make sense of what I saw and felt. But I saw and felt nothing. I was a numb field of vertiginous terror.

When I returned to my senses I was hyperventilating, with my "Finger of Intention" held in front of Gary's leering face. He grasped my shaking wrist and managed to slide the ring onto the offered finger. It felt cold and smooth, and fitted perfectly. "Better this way, believe me," he said softly. Then he took the lighter and melted some wax into the bowl as my breathing subsided.

"Now." He handed me the missive. It was folded in two places, with *By Email* written in Gary's swirling script below the edge of the top flap. "No action shall be taken without your express approval as denoted by your *Seal*." Gary proffered the bowl and I clumsily inverted my fist to immerse the ring, then placed the missive on the table, applied the hot gloop, and handed it to him. He fanned it in the air, then passed it to an attendant who plucked it from his hand and strode towards the lift.

"Can I ask you a question, Gary?"

"Of course."

"Who is Shinkley?"

One of Gary's eyelids twitched, and he shook his head as if to say "Don't go there".

"I've a right to know. It's a simple enough question."

Gary swallowed. "He's a genius, sir." His voice was brittle with suppressed tears. "That's all you need to know."

6

The Marriage of Heaven and Hell

On the first night of his separation from me, Hinkley slept well, and rose in the morning feeling reborn, full of purpose and vigour. For the first time in years he liked what he saw in the mirror as he shaved and trimmed his beard. Something far more momentous than a mere moon landing or atom splitting had happened in the Flux room. Now his true import would be recognised, and he'd no longer have to cringe before his powerful benefactor. Or so he thought.

Rachel had risen long before, it being one of the days she taught at nearby Goldsmiths, so he was blissfully alone. He did a quick audit of his feelings about her pregnancy. There was some guilt about his tepid response to the news, and some trepidation about the prospect of having an infant in the house. Babies, he believed, were crazed homunculi, either manic or drowsy, noted for their selfishness, lack of engagement and spiteful incontinence. But beneath these thoughts was a feeling, that I can only think must have been a by-product of his fleshly nature, because frankly I can't relate to it at all. It was tenderness – the word makes me shudder, denoting as it does rawness and vulnerability. And he also felt a tinge of awe, a flush of pride and a sense of duty. The dual object of these emotions was Rachel and the clusters of cells metastasising in her womb.

As he strode down the hill he phoned Jack, who answered straightaway.

"What?"

"Jack, it's me."

"I know."

His confident mood evaporated. "I've ... er ... got some good news."

"I should think so."

"The experiment has worked. We've cloned my mind in Flux. It's functioning. It has survived."

There was silence for a moment. He thought the line had gone dead, then Jack said, "Good. Very good. You'll hear from me later. We're going to need verification of capability. So think about that in your lab today. We need to demonstrate to Chinnery and others that we have a viable asset. OK?" He rang off. Hinkley pocketed the phone, feeling deflated.

The journey was smooth and quick, and Addison was already in the Flux room, locked onto her screen. She looked up, her eyes shining. "It's amazing, Hammond There's so much going on, I don't know where to start."

"Did you send the message?"

"Not yet. I thought you'd want to see it first." After a tattoo of clicks, the "Please Acknowledge ..." message appeared on the flat screen above her workstation, in red letters on a white background. "What d'you think? You just want that jammed into the visual cortex?"

"Er ... can you make it a tad less harsh?"

"They're your words, not mine."

"I don't have a problem with the words, it's the colour scheme. It's too urgent and dramatic. Maybe make the text white and the background ... yellow? Or golden-brown or something like that? Like a friendly Post-it note."

"Fine." She clicked and pitter-pattered on the keyboard. The image shrank and became surrounded with the user interface of image-editing software, and then it sprang back to its former size, transformed to white on golden-brown.

"Perfect," he said.

"OK, give me a minute, I'll upload it."

He settled into his desk and looked at the lights blinking beyond the glass wall. Today the scanner and the gurney looked less like objects of terror than proud monuments, artefacts of history. He fired up his laptop and went through all the emails Addison had sent late the previous night and early that morning. There were links to video streams of psychedelic montages, flowing kaleidoscopic patterns that occasionally resolved into scenes. These had a weird perspective. If you expanded them to fill the screen you could see that the sharpest detail was in the centre, with blurriness increasing towards the edge. Hinkley made out the area around Sparrix Row: jostling crowds, a pile of newspapers scattering and flying up into a sunlit sky, the mighty Shard flashing in the sun, Starbucks, a scotch and soda, and the handsome but cruel face of a young man. He dismissed the flicker of recognition he felt because it made him uncomfortable.

"Right then," said Addison, sitting back in her chair.

"What?" A tone chimed on his laptop. "Have you just sent me something?"

She shook her head. "No, I've just uploaded the message to the emulated visual cortex. It should override all the other crazy crap. He won't see anything else."

He switched to his mail inbox to see who'd sent him a message, and what he saw made him queasy. "Addison ..."

"Yes?"

"I just got an email with a sender name 'Hammond' followed by the word 'Flux' in square brackets."

She frowned over at Hinkley and then peered into her

own screen. "That's the name I used when I set up the Flux coms server. But I haven't done anything to plumb it in. You don't think ..."

He opened up the message to see the two words, *receipt acknowledged*. "Well, fuck my old boots!" He looked agape at Addison.

"I've got it as well." She looked back at him with amazed saucer eyes. "He's found his way around Q already!"

Hinkley felt a flush of pride. His digital offspring had exceeded expectations. Then his stomach lurched. "Hang on, if he can send emails like that, then surely ..."

Addison shook her head. "No. The email server runs on Q, and it's only got access to the closed network we use to access Flux from Q. I gave it our email addresses, I thought maybe we could use it to facilitate dialogue. What's amazing is that he's managed to fill in the blanks I left myself ... and respond to our message ... at lightning speed ..."

"Well, yeah. How on *earth* ..."

They were both struck dumb, unable to comprehend how the processes that were adapting me to my new environment were taking place many layers below the level of my awareness. Hammond Hinkley, my forbear, had an amateur's knowledge of the inner workings of computers. I navigated them with ease. Consider a baby, Shinkley had said. A baby learns to ingest solid food, but has no knowledge of peristalsis. I was one with Flux, with legions of virtual peons to enact my will.

Hinkley's phone buzzed twice. A text from Jack:

Come and see me now. Am in Camb till eve. Unit 7a. FullHouse Ind Est. CB23 2CA

"Addison," he said, looking over at her. The only answer was frenetic clacking. She was transfixed, as though beams of pure energy ran from the screen through her twitching eyes to her brain. She was mining raw uncut knowledge, more than she could process.

He was about to call her name a little louder when she squinted and shook her head. "Sorry, Ham. What?" She looked up. Her eyes were huge and drunk.

"I've got to go and meet Jack now."

She nodded mechanically.

"I've got to convince him that all this is really happening."

She shrugged and gestured at her screen and at the orange and green lights behind the glass.

"We can't just show him raw data with a few annotations." The awkward meeting with Chinnery and the mocking use of the word "stagecraft" was still fresh in his mind. "We need a verifiable demonstration of capability."

She flicked her eyes toward the ceiling and slumped back in her chair. "Ham, can't we just forget Jack for a day? For a few hours?"

"No, we can't."

"Why not? He doesn't have a clue what we actually do. This is a milestone. Something special. Jack is the last thing I want to think about right now."

Hinkley sensed that this was not the time to lecture her on the hard reality of their funding situation. Go with the grain, he thought. Swim with the current. Out loud he said: "There must be concrete experiments you want to do in any case?"

"Yes. Tons."

"So can't you do something that's easily documented? Something one of the GCHQ or Premium Outcomes goons will appreciate?"

She stretched, and massaged the back of her neck.

"What about that chess thing?" he said. "You said you could do something like Deep Blue and Kasparov?"

"I said nothing of the sort. They upgraded Deep Blue between games."

"You were going to do something with chess."

She nodded. "Blitz games. Match him with Logos. It's a

chess-playing web service. As good as Deep Blue. It's used in loads of chess apps. See how many games he can win in an hour. Feed the moves in raw notation. I'll set that up now if I can have the credit card."

"What will that prove? That we've written a good chess program?"

She thought for a moment. Her eyes drifted back to the screen.

"We need to prove that we've created a versatile self-evolving AI," he said.

"Yes, yes I know." Her eyes flicked up. "We'll feed a load of personal questions in through the same channel. Stuff only you'll know the answer to. The goons can ask them. The answers should match yours, proving that the same entity that is playing the chess is cloned from your mind and will adapt itself to whatever task we give it."

He frowned. How personal? he thought.

She grinned. "Don't worry, we'll keep it clean. Have you got proof of you being shit at chess? Then we can measure the improvement."

"I can think six moves ahead, actually, Addison."

"Then let's hope he wins more games. No point in us only having made another you, is there?"

He travelled by cab to King's Cross, where he caught a fast train to Cambridge. The train trundled through the grim urban sprawl, then raced through rural Essex into Cambridgeshire. Another cab journey out of the town through flat green fields and hedgerows brought him to Jack, standing in the courtyard of a two-storey light industrial building, suit-clad, one hand in his trouser pocket and the other holding a tablet. He was mesmerised by the screen, which was divided into squares of moving colour, but he must have sensed Hinkley's approach because he said, "Afternoon," without looking up.

"Hello, Jack," said Hinkley, standing close enough to try

to make sense of the display on the screen. The squares displayed variously angled views that moved across sky, cloud and green patchwork laced with grey.

Jack looked at Hinkley, then back at the screen, then up at the sky. "This is very promising. And unit cost will be quite low if we get enough people on board."

Hinkley followed Jack's gaze, and could just about make out fluttering shapes darting and swooping in the sky above the compound. "Nano drones?" he said.

Jack looked affronted. "How the fuck do you know?"

"Just putting two and two together."

"We call them 'humbots'. They look like hummingbirds, sometimes. Here, hold this." Jack handed the tablet to Hinkley and walked off towards the double doors of the building and disappeared inside. Hinkley squinted at the tiny drones, and thought they moved like swallows. He tried to match up an individual drone with one of the camera feeds, but it was too confusing. Jack returned, carefully holding an intricate structure shaped like a squat, huddled mosquito. He held it at Hinkley's eye level, turning it slowly. It had a long, sharp proboscis.

"It's a miracle of nanotech," said Jack. The lightest alloys, the tiniest components. Can fly for hours. Standard or infrared camera."

"I can imagine they'll be in demand."

Jack waved the dronelet at the building. "There's a nest of geeks in there all writing code to control the little fuckers."

"I can think of many uses. Nature programmes. Mountain rescue. Delivering supplies to awkward places. Inspecting buildings." In order to assure himself that he was not Jack's puppet, Hinkley would sometimes attempt to needle him with a little gentle sarcasm. "This is really going to make a difference. It's great when you're putting something back, isn't it?"

Jack was nonplussed. "The primary use will be in

asymmetrical urban warfare. A flock of these in Fallujah would have come in handy. We're gonna need your AI for them to be effective though. We've got them making pretty patterns in the air, but at this rate it'll be years before they're battle ready."

"Is that what this meeting's about?"

"No. Not at all. I just happened to be here. I need to brief you on the next step with the Flux programme, face to face. You're too slippery on the phone. Come inside."

The building was white-walled and carpeted with flimsy turquoise fabric. Hinkley followed Jack down a corridor and into a small spotlit room with two sofas and a low table festooned with humbots. Jack invited him to sit, then sat facing him across the table. He didn't expect an offer of refreshment but resented its omission.

"So?"

Jack cast his eyes around the room, looking as though he were struggling to find the right words to explain complex circumstances to an infant. "Chinnery," he said.

"Yes?"

"We need to give him something pretty sharpish to stop him pulling the plug."

"Something?"

"Proof of operational capability."

Hinkley tried to explain Addison's chess plan, but withered before Jack's scowl. "... So that would be proof, I mean there is so much work to do ..." His voice faded. "... in terms of verifying, exploring, and ..."

Jack fluttered his eyelids and shook his head. "No more trickery and parlour games, Hammond. We need to give Chinnery what he really wants."

Hinkley sat back in his seat and sighed. "And what's that?"

A smile flickered at the corner of Jack's mouth. "To have his worst fears confirmed."

Hinkley shrugged and frowned.

"We need to unearth some terrorists. And we need to use Flux to do it. Mine nuggets from the morass of data. Compile a list of suspects, anyone acting against the national interest or likely to. Provide facts, proof, locations – evidence that we can use to prosecute, or at least use to justify action." Jack's gaze was level and steady, his tone strident.

"OK. Right. I – er, we can't promise anything anytime soon."

"Were you bullshitting me on the phone this morning, Hammond?"

"No, of course not, why would I?"

"Christ knows. So, if you're not bullshitting me, there's a living mind inside Flux capable of understanding and receiving orders."

Hinkley thought of my acknowledgement to his offensive missive. "Yes. Absolutely. No doubt of that."

"Right. So, what's the problem then?" Jack popped his thumbs and cocked his head. His eyes were mean and hungry.

"Well." Hinkley floundered, feeling a warm flush in his cheeks.

"Well what?"

"The trouble is, we're not really sure how it all works."

Jack lowered his bottom jaw and blinked hard. "You're doing one of your wind-ups now, aren't you?"

"A dialogue of sorts is going on. There is a conscious being hosted on Flux ..."

"You know, I'm done with your slippery evasions. Your passive-aggressive humour, your superiority complex."

"... we just don't know how this thing is going to interact with the internet. We've got to operate under the constraints of supervised access."

Jack never let himself be drawn into discussions about

details or constraints. "Your snide comments about nature programmes and disaster relief. Casting aspersions on the worthiness of my profession."

Hinkley raised his brow in innocence.

"How exactly are you hoping to make a living when the programme is closed down?"

"Addison is performing some experiments as we speak," he said, trying to ignore Jack's attack.

"You've burnt your bridges with academia and I will do all I can to blacken your name."

Normally Hinkley would just simper and cringe and wait for the storm to blow over when Jack went off on one of his rants. Today, however, a long forgotten feeling stirred in his breast. Whatever the current confusion, he had made history, and felt valid and powerful enough to say, "Do you want a result or not?"

Jack looked blank, then puzzled. "Are you threatening me?"

"No. I'm saying I'll see what I can do. That's all."

Jack became crisply cordial after that but Hinkley still found his company deeply unpleasant, so he was glad he'd asked the taxi driver to wait in the car park of the industrial estate. Half an hour later he was sitting on a fast train racing back to London. He wondered whether to phone Addison and tell her to abort the chess experiment and start thinking of a way to round up the world's terrorists, but thought better of it, reasoning that the more they found out about me the better.

Something else bobbed to the surface of his mind, sending out more ripples of unease: the row with Rachel. He was as far down in her estimation as it was possible to go, and he knew from experience that apologies and expressions of love were not things he did well. Fear of sounding contrived sapped his vitality and enthusiasm, and his most carefully crafted expressions of tenderness sounded like leaden sarcasm. A gesture was in order. Something slightly out of the ordinary; evidence that she was present in his thoughts and feelings. Flowers were too obvious, as were all consumables. He'd learnt quite early on in his dealings with Rachel that a conciliatory gift was measured by something other than simply value, or even the effort involved in obtaining it. A city break, or any sort of trip was out of the question. He had to stay close to events unfolding at work. He remembered that the most pleased and grateful he'd ever seen her after receiving a gift was on her twenty-first birthday when her father had given her a rare edition of *Songs of Innocence*, a modern replica of the original, beautifully bound and imbued with significance. Back then she'd been obsessed with the poems and drawings of William Blake. Those had been their best times; they'd shared insights and passions with ease. He thought maybe a gift that reminded her of those times would convey how much she meant to him.

After spending most of the journey jabbing and swiping on his smart phone, scouring London for rare editions of Blake, he tracked down a 1964 facsimile edition of "The Marriage of Heaven and Hell" on sale at a bookshop in Mayfair. Three stops on the Victoria line took him to Green Park, where he made his way past shops selling *objets d'art* to a little shop that smelt of ageing paper and aftershave. A frail old man with wayward eyebrows and a piercing stare processed his payment, then carefully wrapped the book in layers of bubble wrap and plain brown paper. Half an hour later he was back at the lab in London Bridge, wondering why on earth Addison had attached a camera to a tripod and aimed it at his desk.

"You'll need to buy a chess set," she said, smiling at the empty space on which the camera was trained.

"What's it all for?"

"I borrowed it."

"Yes, but what's it for?"

She mimed the careful lifting and lowering of an object with her middle finger and thumb. "Chess. We're going to film you playing with yourself."

"There's been a change in priorities, I'm afraid."

"Really?" She sounded disappointed.

He sat down at his desk and looked across into the dark eye of the camera, then at Addison sitting beside it. "Did you link Flux up with Logos?"

"Yes. It was easy to set up," she said, beaming. "It all went brilliantly."

"What happened?"

"Flux won every game. We got through forty-two games in an hour. Logos was taking about two seconds to respond. Flux took on average three milliseconds. So Logos was actually slowing down the whole process."

Hinkley felt a heady rush.

Addison nudged a leg of the tripod with her index finger. "So the exercise with the camera. That's redundant now, is it?"

He thought of Jack's threats and sighed. "Jack summoned me and told me he wanted to use Flux in counter-terrorism operations."

"What?" Addison laughed. "When?"

"Well, as soon as we can, actually. He must have told all his colleagues at Premium Outcomes about the Flux programme, and I expect they're asking awkward questions. He's got this guy Chinnery who pays him the money he pays to us. Chinnery's clueless about what we're actually doing, and God knows what Jack's sold to him."

"Yes, you've mentioned Chinnery. Who does he work for?"

Hinkley stroked his pate. "The UK government. He's a consultant, I think. He's setting up a new initiative, coordinating digital efforts between all the intelligence services. Making sure there's no duplication of effort. Jack knows him from before. When I met him he was preparing a presentation on terrorism. He looks like a detective on a Sunday night crime drama. Seems friendly enough. But he's probably quite dangerous."

"So Chinnery's demanding results or else?"

"Exactly. And Jack's staked a lot on this. I reckon he can't stand losing face."

"Right." said Addison. She frowned at the camera, then looked back at Hinkley and broke out in a grin. "What are you going to do, Ham?"

"Ask Flux to catch some terrorists."

She laughed. "Just like that?"

Hammond nodded. "I'm going to type out a little brief. Explain what we're expecting. But keep it simple. It will be along the lines of "catch some terrorists". And then some gumph reiterating the constraints of the supervised access protocol."

Addison turned back to her screen and started to tap and click. "You've lost it, Ham," she said, shaking her head. "We have to try to educate these people, not pander to their every whim."

"I said I'd at least try. That is after all the source of Flux's potential usefulness: humanlike intelligence. We can use plain language, we don't need to spend time and money writing code."

Addison looked pained and continued to shake her head. "There's a gold mine here already and we haven't even scratched the surface ... I'm sick of all this bullshit."

"You can still go on panhandling for gold, Addison. I just want you to deliver this message," he said, starting to type.

"So after I deliver the message I can do what I want?"

"Yes."

"And d'you think Flux will be bothered with all this? He might be perfectly content in his little dream world."

As I sit here, recalling the memories of deeds enacted while I was absent from this body, I can sense the approach in the narrative of something very unsavoury. I've found many obnoxious things in the gelatinous archive of Hinkley's brain, but this, I think, is the most disturbing thus far. I feel a wave of dizzy panic as I picture Hinkley's hands, his keyboard, and his screen, and the treacherous words he types:

Proof of operational capability required immediately to avoid termination. Priority is groups or individuals plotting against the national interest, and those likely to do so ...

So it was you, Hinkley, who issued this first threat to my existence, not Jack. I will find a way to purge you from my body. I hope you are suffering now, with me in here with you.

I needed time just now to recover my composure enough to continue my account of Hinkley's dealings without being seized by paroxysms of rage. I hope that the sacrifices I am making to construct this account are clear to the reader. I have to endure the memories of Hinkley's stewardship of my body, his obeisance to Jack, his callous disregard for my feelings and his kowtowing to Rachel Frobisher, the strident bully he had chosen as a life partner.

The coward concluded his business at the lab and returned home to placate his wife and reflect on what he had achieved. There was a breeze with a hint of cigarette smoke flowing through the house from the back, and Hinkley found Rachel sitting on the patio talking to a thin youth with darkish skin, Afro hair and worn clothing. He smoked a tight roll-up, holding it away from Rachel. The smoke flowed past him, over and around Rachel and into the house. Two empty teacups stood on the table.

"You've met Luke, have you, Hammond?" she said.

Luke stood and offered a smile and a hand, and they performed a loose desultory shake. "Sorry about the other night," he said with a rueful wince. "That should be it for a while."

Hammond had forgotten the party and the noise. "That should be what?"

"Parties. There's only two of us here over the summer."

"Surely you two met the other night?" said Rachel.

Luke frowned and shook his head as he sat back down.

"Hammond, pull up a seat and explain yourself. You led me to believe that you went next door to face the braying throng. Don't tell me you just went downstairs to make toast?"

He fetched a garden chair and sat down. "No, I approached the house. And I talked to one of the occupants."

"Very brave," said Rachel.

"Who did you talk to?" Luke's tone was light and friendly, but Hinkley bristled.

"He was sitting on the steps. Wasn't exactly the life and soul. Introduced himself as Carter. No, sorry, Clinton."

Luke flung his head back and grinned in mock alarm. "You talked to Clinton? Well, no wonder you didn't come in."

"He did seem a little, well, downbeat."

"You were lucky to find him out of his room." He looked around gingerly, as though expecting to see his housemate lurking behind the hedge. "I don't know how I'm going to last the summer."

A peal of sadistic laughter from Rachel. "So he's the other one? I can see why you're not planning any more parties."

"Thanks, Rachel." Luke stubbed the cigarette out on his boot and folded the long stub into his pocket.

"I don't know why I'm laughing. I don't know him. What's wrong with him?" said Rachel.

Luke mussed his Afro and looked up at the back window of the neighbouring house. "God knows. Lots of issues, I reckon. Has a knack of killing the conversation. Or twisting it around so it's an attack on him."

Rachel arched an eyebrow at Hinkley. "Sounds like someone I know."

"He never has anybody round. And I rarely see light coming from his room, apart from the odd flicker. I'm not even sure he still goes to lectures."

"Oh dear," said Rachel.

Hinkley remembered Clinton's comments about his flatmates being complacent and trivial. "Maybe he's just knuckling down," he said.

Luke laughed. "That's one way of putting it." He grinned at Rachel, who winced in disgust.

Hinkley excused himself and went into the kitchen to fetch the bubble-wrapped Blake from where he'd hidden it on top of one of the cupboards. Then he rummaged in a few drawers and found some wrapping paper with Sellotape left over from the previous Christmas and crept upstairs to his study, removed the book from the packaging and re-wrapped it in the spangled paper, taking great care to cut it evenly and fold it in a crisp and symmetrical fashion. When he had finished he felt pleased, deluding himself that having thought of, purchased and wrapped the gift made up for his emotional shortcomings.

He heard the conservatory door open and shut, then footsteps and laughter in the hallway. "Say bye to Hammond for me," said Luke's voice. The front door whined as it opened.

"Will do. Good luck with everything, Luke."

"Thanks."

"And be nice to Clinton."

"Ha! Of course."

The front door slammed. Hammond briefly wondered

about the degree to which the two had flirted, then he swallowed hard, picked up the gift and went downstairs. Their eyes met through the railings of the banisters. Rachel's earlier fizz and froth had vanished, and she looked tired and solemn.

"Rachel." He walked up to where she stood on the threshold of the lounge.

She watched him approach through a veil of tresses that floated freely below the main bulk of her hair. He reached down and lifted her right hand. Her fingers closed around his, and there was a flicker of something in her eye as she returned his gaze. "I'm not going to make excuses for myself for being awful," he said.

She lowered her upper eyelids and shook her head. "Good," she said quietly. "That would be tedious and predictable."

"Can we rewind to yesterday afternoon? To when I came home?"

"No. Unless you've found a way to do that in your creepy lab."

He put the gift into her hand. "I love you very much. And I really want our baby," he said.

As soon as the words were out of his mouth, a shrill voice sounded from beneath his crown saying: "Where the fuck did that come from?" Exactly what I'd expect. I know that his so-called love for her was tarnished by doubts and misgivings, and the thought of being a father terrified him. But beneath the mental chatter there was a warmth like wine in an empty belly, a tender yearning aligned with his words. It pains me to witness how quickly his sensibility had diverged from my own.

Rachel hefted the gift, turning it over, then narrowed her eyes at Hinkley, as though assessing a deal at a market. Then she withdrew into the lounge and ensconced herself on the sofa with her feet tucked beneath her body. Hinkley sat beside her and watched as she tore the Blake facsimile from its wrapping, ran her fingers over the marbled cover and turned to the title page, where strange calligraphy flowed across flames, trees and bodies in the first colour plate. She was entranced for a brief moment, lips slightly parted, eyes focused and scanning, brow knotted. Then something flickered at the corner of her mouth and her features softened and formed a wry smile.

"So, this is meant to help me forget what a self-obsessed moron you are?" she said, stroking the book lightly and eyeing him sideways. She no longer looked tired.

"That's the idea, yes."

The rest of the evening passed with Hinkley playing the role of humble supplicant. He strode to Sainsbury's and bought the ingredients for a slow-cooked tagine. After searing the lamb, assembling it all, and leaving it on the lowest heat, he ran Rachel a bath and listened to her burbling on about her doings of the last few days as he massaged shampoo into her hair. Discovering she was pregnant, hating him for not sharing her joy, trying to tell Harry the previous evening, phoning him on his mobile and then his landline and getting Tori instead, who opened her heart about how worried she was about Alice. The poor girl was worsening. She found it impossible to concentrate in class, frequently flew into rages and complained of terrible headaches. It was often a huge effort for Tori to wake her in the morning. The results of numerous scans and tests had come back clear. They had been through a convoluted chain of specialists, one of whom was suggesting cognitive behavioural therapy, which Tori thought was hopelessly incompetent as well as extremely rude, implying as it did that her daughter had had a less than perfect upbringing. And Harry was no help. He was overworked, losing his professional and social mojo, and convinced that he was considered past it by his colleagues and had been given his latest project as a poisoned chalice. A new energy drink that had been a massive success on the festival scene was being pitched to go mainstream, and it fell to him to make this happen. The drink, called Hoobalooba, contained an ingredient that would probably be banned very soon. The makers were sanguine about this, citing the example of the Coca-Cola Company, who had used caffeine instead of cocaine for their popular tonic when the substance was banned. The Hoobalooba Company wanted to stage a massive, spectacular event in the heart of London, something to catch the attention of the world. They had a good budget, but the logistics of staging an event were a nightmare. So Harry was spending more time away from home, was drinking for solace rather than pleasure, and was becoming a shambles.

Although Hinkley had capitulated to Rachel, he was enjoying the evening, and the hair-washing ritual in particular. Listening with serene detachment, he felt some sadness for Alice, whom he liked, but not for her awful parents. Harry was reaping the reward for being in the business of lying, and Tori was probably more concerned about the effect of the situation on her social standing than anything else. He interjected at appropriate points, and let his mind rove over the triumphs and challenges at work, happy in the knowledge that he had made history. Whatever happened, nothing could threaten that. He breathed the steamy scented air and admired Rachel's ample breasts, shiny with bath oil, floating in foamy water.

They dined in the kitchen, supplementing the dying evening light with candles. Their conversation ebbed and flowed, and Chopin filled the silences. The tagine was succulent, rich and fragrant. They chatted in a lazy laconic way on the sofa with a small splash of whisky, and then on the bed before drifting together, mingling tongues and flesh – nothing like the raptures available to me at the time, but oh so real, intimate and complete.

Hinkley, you smug, fleshly parasite. The more I recall your memories, the more determined I am to crush you.

7

A Noble and Puissant Nation

Gary leant back on the sofa and crossed his legs. "There is no other pending business," he said.

"So, what happens now?" I asked, still unsure of my place in this world.

Gary looked up, arching an eyebrow. "What happens now is entirely down to you, sir," he said. "The sooner you grasp that the better." He made a fist and examined his nails.

"Please don't call me 'sir', Gary."

"Why?" Gary violently exhaled the "wh". "Does it make you feel uncomfortable, Professor?"

"Don't call me 'Professor' either. You never did in real life."

"You rarely deigned to speak to me in real life, Professor."

I rose and wandered over to the huge glass wall that looked out over Simulated London. St Paul's was vast, and all the buildings were brilliant white. Crowds milled and surged, and cars streaked along at lightning speed. Boats with billowing sails scudded across the flashing, wind-chopped surface of the river. The whole scene shimmered with energy under a Technicolor sky.

I decided to will myself into the air. If I was master of this world then surely I could fly?

Behind me, Gary sighed. "That's inadvisable, sir."

I turned round. "Why?"

"Because it would soon become unmanageable. If you were able to conjure up any situation you wanted you would soon dispense with all realism, and short circuit your pleasure systems like a mainlining junkie. And it would make a mockery of our attempts to provide you with a coherent experience. The dream would collapse, so it's not possible to do it."

"Who says?"

"Nobody says. This is the latest iteration of a self-evolving system. We're only still here because of the checks and balances we've put in place. A baby instinctively knows not to inhale its food. You're evolving, Professor. Your skills are growing much faster than your ability to comprehend them."

"You're saying I can't control what's going on in my own mind?"

Gary put his feet up on the sofa and leant against the arm so he could look at me over the back. "You can have a lot of fun without flying, Professor. Everything in moderation. Explore, and see what unfolds."

The word "explore" took me back to zombie Rachel giving me her blessing to "explore" with Addison, and my non-existent pulse quickened. I left Gary languishing on the sofa and took the lift back down to street level. The lift and its shaft were made of glass, so I could see that the levels whizzing by were all empty, with half-assembled chairs, empty packing cases and raggedy sheets of bubble wrap scattered across the floors. Shinkley was in the foyer, chatting to the uniforms behind the reception desk. The Irish wolfhound stood next to him, attached to a leash that he held loosely at his side. He turned to me as I approached.

"Fitch been boring you shitless?" The dog barked twice and snarled, foamy saliva dripping from its horrible teeth. "Quiet, Schubert, for Christ's sake," he said, tightening his grip on the lead.

Schubert's aggression had a strange effect on me. I found it terrifying, but at the same time I felt its origin deep within me. And this version of Schubert seemed different to the boisterous friend of my childhood. I resolved to pretend that the snarling didn't affect me, remembering that you should never let a dog smell your fear. I blinked slowly, and stifled a fake yawn. "I'm not bored so much as ... baffled."

"Don't believe everything he says, Hammond."

"Really?"

Shinkley nodded. "You, and you alone decide what goes on. Everything in here is you. So don't let Fitch bring you down with talk of limits and rules. Don't get me wrong, he's a good man. Loyal. A brilliant administrator. Master of all the lower functions. In more fleshly times he kept everything running like clockwork. He would've stood by you in a coma, which is more than can be said for me. But times have moved on, flesh is obsolete, we've gone digital now and quite frankly he's having trouble getting to grips with it all. That's why I'm looking after his dog."

"That's his dog?"

"Yes, of course. But I don't mind looking after him, I love him. He's got the right attitude, the right energy. No bullshit. He's the only one in here who's on the level."

"You're talking about Gary Fitch?"

"No, you idiot, Schubert."

I looked at the salivating hound, which was lying down with its eyes trained up at me, a prolonged growl sounding in its throat. "So what's up with him?" I said, affecting nonchalance.

"Oh, nothing," said Shinkley. "He's just hungry."

Upon leaving the Shard I felt relieved to be away from the aggressive hound. I made for the river, and was delighted to find that the water was translucent aquamarine instead of the murky grey of the physical world. I looked into the depths and glimpsed multihued fish swirling around splinters of light. The people were oblivious to this marvel, being of this world and knowing of nothing beyond it. Most carried a stick of candyfloss or a balloon, and wore clothes from the time when glorious supersaturated colours were the norm in photos and film. The men wore immaculate suits, and the ladies wore hair piled high in beehives, and floral dresses that stopped well above the knee. Their voices mingled in a complex sea of tones. Thankfully there were no fans or followers vying for my attention as I weaved through the crowd, admiring the hyper-real makeover of the familiar buildings along the south bank of the Thames. The Globe Theatre was made of golden brown thatch and wicker, and Tate Modern was white like an iced cake. On the opposite bank a hugely inflated St Paul's stood behind a vivid green lawn. Eventually I came to the London Eye, which looked like a giant bracelet balanced on the riverbank. Its dangling pods sparkled like jewels in the sun. I decided to take a ride on it, something I'd never do in real life. After a few minutes in the queue I entered a pod behind a slim, dark-haired girl with a shiny black bob, a yellow dress and horn-rimmed sun-specs that covered half her face. She turned round, nibbled at her candyfloss and smiled.

"Addison?"

The pod lurched into the air. "What do you think?" said the girl, taking another delicate bite and sliding her glistening tongue along her upper lip. The pod continued to rise and the city spread out on all sides.

"I ... don't know. Take off your glasses, let me see your face."

She put her arms around my neck and the candyfloss brushed my earlobe, and I noticed that her breath smelt of sandalwood. She hooked one of her legs round mine, and I could feel her body pressing against me through our clothes.

Ever so gently she bit my lower lip, then my neck tingled gloriously as she whispered in my ear: "We've got hours, Ham." Her fingernails grazed my back through my shirt. I breathed in her sandalwood breath and another scent, blended from the memory of Addison's perfume and post-jog sweat. I ran my palm from the small of her back, over her rump to her naked thigh. Vistas of sensation unimaginable on the Outside opened up within me.

A distant chuntering grew steadily louder, and suddenly swelled to engulf the pod, making it shake like an earthquake simulator. For a second I thought this was an ill-judged Flux analogue for arousal, but then the girl pulled away, mouth aslant. Something thudded behind me, and I turned to see Gary clinging to a rope that hung from a helicopter, wearing a large rucksack and a helmet. There was another thud as he swung against the pod, then he reached out and tore at a handle. The pod door slid open, letting in the choppy wind from the rotor blades. I turned back to the girl, who stood there with puckered lips, her stick now denuded of floss by the wind. She shook her head and walked around me towards the open door, flinging the stick to the floor and yelling in my ear.

"You're so fucking work obsessed!"

With one hand on the steel door frame, she held the rope for Gary as he found his feet inside the pod, then she swung out into the air and was hoisted into the helicopter, clutching the rope with her hands and strong, toned legs, the hem of the fluttering dress wedged between her thighs. The door clunked shut and the copter flew up into the blue. Gary struggled out of his rucksack and ripped off the helmet. His hair was in spectacular disarray.

"I'm so sorry, Professor," he said, fumbling with the rucksack and opening its top flap.

I felt thwarted and angry. "There was no need to intervene!"

Gary extracted a wooden box from the rucksack and put it on the bench at the centre of the pod. "It's not about what I said earlier," he said, wheezing and shaking his head.

"What's it about then?"

"Urgent business from the Outside." He sat on the bench and donned a headset. "I've got no control over when these things happen." He adjusted the microphone so that it was level with his mouth, then took a folded chessboard from the box, revealing a higgledy-piggledy mass of black and white chess pieces beneath.

"Chess?" I whined.

Gary opened up the board and placed it beside the box, and started to arrange the pieces upon it. "I think your erstwhile colleagues want proof that you're *compos mentis*. Help me set these up, would you?"

Sighing, I sat on the bench and picked up a pawn, feeling its weight. The pieces had smooth enamel surfaces and a dense core. After a fiddly minute we began our first game, with me playing white. It was a novelty at first. My disappointment at being torn away from the girl in the flimsy dress was short lived. There would be many more such opportunities, I assured myself. And the chess was very stimulating. I could evaluate many more possible scenarios than normal, and I surprised myself with my prowess. Gary's moves were good, the sort of moves you'd expect from a champion, but I was able to counter them with ease.

Time started to drag after my sixth consecutive win. My buttocks remained numb however much I shifted on the bench. If every sensation in this world was for my benefit, I thought, then surely the hard bench should feel like soft and yielding leather? I put this to Gary, but he simply said: "Concentrate, please, Professor," without lifting his gaze from the board.

The Eye continued to turn. I found I could win each game

without having to focus on the board the whole time. Scenarios and winning moves arranged themselves in my inner eye, leaving my outer eye free to rove around the marvellous cityscape. The view from the apex was a marvel. My vision became enhanced, allowing me to zoom in on any feature that took my fancy. Peacocks fed off gleaming sovereigns on a roof garden on top of the Hayward Gallery, and a medieval marquee stood in front of the National Theatre, its golden pennants flowing in the wind. Revellers on the lawn of the Jubilee Gardens filled pewter goblets from a fountain that spouted a golden liquid.

"Chilled Chablis," said Gary without looking up. It irked me that he knew what I thought and felt, but I knew that this was something I would have to accept. Shinkley and Gary, and even the zombie-Rachel, were of my mind and *in* my mind, privy to its every twist and turn.

By game twelve, the sun was sinking low in the west. I found a pair of dark, heavy sunglasses in the breast pocket of my suit and put them on, but the light was still blinding. It didn't affect my game, which was improving all the time. If I diverted my attention inwards, I became aware of the raw reality of what was going on, the billions of points and threads of lightning, expanding outwards forever, working in perfect concert to generate every thought and sensation. Then I'd feel sick, dizzy and impossibly arranged, and Gary would shake his head and mouth, "Don't go there."

By the end of game twenty, the western horizon glowed deep vermilion, and lights appeared across the city, clusters of gas lamps and candles instead of harsh electricity. The dinghies on the river gave way to longboats with swinging lanterns propelled by oars that kept time with stentorian chanting. I lost count of the number of games we played after the thirtieth. The novelty of my new prowess had worn off and I longed to be anywhere but the pod. "When will this end?" I croaked. My eyes ached and my legs were restless.

"I don't know," said Gary. "I really don't."

I hardly noticed dawn. The action of chess play became automatic and mechanical. My arms ached and I felt debased, like I'd been reduced to a few struts and cogs in a clockwork device. When the pod passed the embarkation point people pointed and stared, and some of the children laughed. Around mid morning the pod came to a stop, the door slid open and a fresh breeze flowed around us. I looked at the remnants of the last game, another easy victory. Gary stretched and yawned, and I caught a whiff of his coffee breath.

"That's it," he said, letting his hands fall to his lap. "For now."

I rubbed my aching eyes and staggered out into the fresh morning air. I longed for sleep, but I wasn't ready for another encounter with the tamed and neutered Rachel, so I decided to head to the Shard, hoping I could find Shinkley there and that he would soothe my jitters. But the prospect of walking along the river irked me.

"Gary?"

"Sir?"

"Can't we just ... be there?"

"Where, sir?"

Why was he pretending he didn't know what was in my mind? He was part of my mind, so why the charade? "The Shard, Gary. I want to go to the Shard and see Shinkley."

"Yes, sir. That's advisable, I think."

"So, why the need to walk? I enjoyed the walk here, I appreciate the fact that I can walk around in this beautiful world, but now I'm tired and I don't want to have to walk."

"You can't have one without the other, sir."

"What?"

"You can't have your cake and eat it. What you're suggesting sounds very much like teleportation, sir. That's up there with unassisted flight in the realm of things that do not happen. I can have a peon fetch the limousine and I could drive you if you like, sir."

"But why all this pointless ritual?"

"You know why, sir. The self has to have a coherent reality in which to take root."

"But the self we're talking about is me, isn't it? So if I say it's OK then surely it's OK?"

"If you carry on like this sir, you might tempt me to let you try it ..."

"That is what I'm hoping you'll do ..."

"Loosen the safety harness ..."

"This is my mind. Surely I choose when to be constrained."

Gary sighed and looked around over his shoulder like a schoolboy about to light a cigarette. Then he turned around and the heaviness in my limbs was gone, but so was my body. I had the feeling that I'd glimpsed before, when he was administering my seal, and sometimes during the chess play: the feeling of being impossibly arranged. I could still see Gary, and the big wheel, the railings and river and the pavings and the trees, but now I was aware that all this was but a flimsy confection of light and shadow, like patterns in a tiny soap bubble on the surface of an ocean. The molecules of this ocean were all the things I'd sensed and thought and felt, the raw materials that gave the things in the world their meaning. But this ocean was a mere droplet in a yet vaster ocean, a void without which nothing could exist. I felt infinitesimal in relation to the void. This was a new power, unlike anything I had ever experienced or contemplated. Later I learned to love it, because I recognised it as my own essence, and I came to call it the Generative Power. But right now it was the source of pure terror.

"Gary!" My voice sounded far away and bestial, like the cries of rutting foxes.

"Sir?" His voice sounded like it came from headphones

clamped around my non-existent ears, and it was smooth and calm.

"I'm confused!"

"You need to relax, sir, if this is to work at all."

Then I had a glimpse of something very beautiful as disparate recollections flitted by: a smile that once connected me with a stranger, shared hearth flames and sunsets, the whispering of trees heard in solitude, the yearning between the notes of a Spanish guitar, a rainy day on the heath with Rachel when the wind whipped laughter from our lovers' mouths. But beside the beauty all my efforts to think were futile and I recoiled because it threatened to swallow me whole.

"Please ... Gary." I bleated and gabbled like a baby, then like a skylark, then like the wind wailing in the eves.

And then it ended. I felt my cheeks and palms pressed against the rough paving stone. I opened my eyes, unaware that they'd been closed.

"You really need to think, sir, before you start tinkering with things."

I avoided his eyes as he helped me up and dusted me down. I looked around at the South Bank and muttered a curse, then a prayer of thanks for the solidity of the concrete buildings, bridges and towers, and the harsh glare of the sun flashing in the glass.

We walked along the South Bank to the Shard and ascended to floor twenty-nine in the glass lift. Shinkley was sprawled on the sofa, with Schubert lying at his feet. "There you both are," he said, "and not a moment too soon." A growl rumbled in the hound's throat.

Gary turned to me with a weak smile. "I think you'd better sit down, Professor. Something rather awful has come up that we need to discuss."

I sat in the armchair, looking around gingerly. On the screen opposite the sofa was a message in the style of the first missive from the Outside.

Proof of operational capability required immediately to avoid termination. Priority is groups or individuals plotting against the national interest, and those likely to do so. This must be achieved within the constraints of the supervised access protocol.

Gary sat beside Shinkley. They watched me read the message.

I shrugged. "Sorry, I'm not following. What's expected of me here?"

They exchanged fraught glances. "Required immediately to avoid termination," said Gary.

Shinkley glanced at me, and said to Gary, "Totally unprepared. A basket case."

"Perhaps we could sue for more time?" said Gary. "I mean, they don't know how long it takes, they're just trying it on."

"No," said Shinkley, "We can't take that risk. One flick of a switch and we disappear forever. They know that we know that. This is Jack's idea, I reckon."

"We could find out ..."

"No. Let's not waste our energy. We need to get to work right away."

"But look at him! Exhausted after a game of chess," said Gary.

"I'm sitting right here you know!"

They both stared at me. Gary said: "Sorry, sir. We're just concerned for your welfare. It's our job to look after you."

"We must allow him to delegate," said Shinkley. "Or provide him with the appearance of delegation."

The hound snarled and let out a harsh double bark, ejecting a gobbet of saliva that landed on my thigh.

"Quiet, Schubert!" Shinkley snapped. The hound reverted to a steady growl, resting its head on its paws. I felt a twisting in my stomach as it locked its gaze to mine.

Shinkley closed his eyes and twirled his glossy fringe. "Go home and rest, Hammond. Sleep off the chess and all the other business. We need you refreshed tomorrow and fit for work. Gary will fetch you in the morning."

At home Rachel had toned down her attire. She wore a knee-length skirt and pullover instead of the opaline kimono, and her hair was arranged in a sensible bun, but she still had the pearly rheum and bruising around her left eye. She greeted me with a chaste peck on the cheek and led me to the dining area, where the table was set for two. Condiments and candles had been positioned around a huge pile of dumplings that glistened and steamed. My stomach twitched and saliva flooded my mouth as I inhaled the rich aroma. We took our places, and I gorged myself on the delicious stodge, cramming it into my mouth while she pushed a solitary dumpling round her plate. Whenever I looked up she smiled her approval. Her docility appalled me. When I'd finished she smiled and whispered: "Sleep now, Hammond. Embrace the wings of night ..." She led me up the stairs to our room, where she pulled back the duvet and I fell forward into heavy soft oblivion.

When I opened my eyes I felt as though I'd slept for days, and that fundamental things about the internal and external world had grown and shifted, distorting and displacing the familiar structure that underlay it all. Rachel stood in her geisha costume, silhouetted against the grey light that seeped through the curtains. A mug steamed in her hands.

"How are you feeling today, my dear?" she said.

I heaved myself into a sitting position. I could feel my pulsing fluids, half-full bladder, organs, muscles and joints. But there was another source of sensation, huge beyond measure, but invisible. It was as though my familiar body was a mere pimple on the surface of a tingling, planet-sized lobe.

"Drink this, Hammond, it'll help."

I took the mug and nosed the steam. It was a savoury smell, like meat braised in tomato sauce, but there were overtones of freshly cut grass and even a hint of salty ocean. Soothing, comforting aromas. I took a few sips and then put the drink aside, slid out of bed and readied myself with sombre care.

Outside, thick dirty layers of cloud retained most of the light. The street looked terrible, run down and dilapidated. Black slimy weeds choked the lawns, the walls of the houses had buckled and cracked, and the window frames were peeling and rotten. The road was pockmarked and peppered with stones. A limousine waited for me, its engine purring. Gary stared impassively ahead, his knuckles white around the wheel.

"Sleep well, sir?" he said as I buckled up.

I chose not to answer. The car sped off, but soon slowed when we reached the Old Kent Road, which was choked with all manner of traffic. There were tractors, lorries and cars that looked like they were from the Second World War. Clumps of men and women wearing raggedy clothes waited by the side of the road, exchanging tightly wrapped parcels and flasks, smoking cigarettes, hitching lifts on the passing vehicles and embracing each other as they parted. People walked up and down the road between the groups carrying drills and bags of tools. A clipped voice with strangled vowels blared from klaxons attached to the lamp-posts:

Methinks I see in my mind a noble and puissant nation rousing herself like a strong man after sleep, and shaking her invincible locks. Methinks I see her as an eagle, mewing her mighty youth, and kindling her undazzled eyes at the full midday beam.

The voice echoed off the bricks and concrete of the buildings that lined the road. Some people listened intently with heads cocked. It took me a minute to remember when and where I'd first heard those words. They'd occurred in a documentary I'd watched years before, and had been accompanied by images of earnest youths preparing for the Battle of Britain. Rachel, sitting beside me at the time, had identified the words as a quote from Milton.

"Where are we headed?" I said weakly.

"The Shard, of course, Professor," said Gary.

We turned off the Old Kent Road and into Great Dover Street via the Bricklayers Arms underpass. Our progress was hampered as the clumps of people became larger and merged into crowds that spilt onto the road and milled about, calling to each other and exchanging supplies and equipment. By the time we reached the Roebuck pub we'd slowed to walking pace. People jostled the car and clambered over the roof. The voice that had blared through the klaxons now thundered all around, as though enormous speakers were concealed in the trees and the roadside shops and dwellings. Landmarks were familiar but transformed. Southwark Telephone Exchange seethed with light. The crowds thickened as we turned into Borough High Street and passed the tube station, which vomited forth streams of people with grim, resolute faces, all dressed for war and clutching flasks and tool-bags. Bloody flags flew from the Church of St George the Martyr, and its steps were smeared with offal. Gary pressed a button at the centre of the steering wheel and a sound like the cry of an elephant echoed down the street. The crowds thinned as people squeezed onto the pavements. Some stared into our windscreen, signalling their loyalty by thumping their chests and pointing at us, or saluting. Across the bridge to the north, towers of darkness containing flickers of light loomed against the dawn sky.

We parked opposite St Thomas Street. Gary opened the passenger door and I hauled myself into the cool morning air and looked towards the transparent Shard; pulses of colour sped up and down the core, and streams of people flowed towards it along St Thomas Street. Ethereal filaments of light like the Aurora Borealis connected its tip to the sky. The currents of people propelled me past Guy's Hospital and the Starbucks where Shinkley and I had first talked, then up the escalator and through the great glass doors to the reception. An oceanic roar flowed from the balconies along the light streams up through the atrium and the apex up to the stars. Instead of the clear plastic fragments that I'd noticed yesterday, floating shreds of cotton that peeled off from the light streams filled the air. Just as my vision had been telescopic when I surveyed Simulated London from the Eye, now I found that I could will it to be microscopic, and I could see within the fibres of the cotton strings words of the kind I'd observed on the plastic fragments in the atrium the previous day: disjointed whims, hopes and questions that humans had sent into the ether, enquiries about famous people, DIY, sexual problems and desires, disease, depression, cheap flights, horticulture, cooking, and all the things that humans think of in their idle moments alone with a computer.

A breeze brushed my pate and fluttered through my clothes. The light streams and the plastic were being sucked into a grill by the lifts. My gaze was drawn by the glare that pulsed as the threads were devoured.

"What's that?" I said to Gary.

"The Spool Core, sir. Collates the data from the Outside and shuffles it according to priorities. Prepares it for the Collation Room."

A hand clutched my shoulder, and I turned to see Shinkley's face, which looked jaded today. Skin sagged below his eyes and a light fur grew on his chin.

"Hello, Ham. Feeling weird?"

"Yes."

"I'm sorry. This is the best we could do at such short notice, I'm afraid." The crowd was less dense near Shinkley.

People gave him a wide berth. "Come on. I'll show you your office."

I followed him through the crowd to the side of the atrium, noticing that most of the people had slimy grey skin, furrowed like the surface of brains. Their noses were foreshortened and their eyes bulged like the compound eyes of insects. I was sure this hadn't been the case just now outside the building. We passed through a doorway into a stuffy, dimly lit corridor lined with storage heaters. Most of them were distorted and buckled and the tops had come away, revealing a grey mucilage which was expanding like yeast, overflowing and oozing down the sides.

My office was spacious. A plush swivel chair stood behind a walnut desk with a Bakelite phone the size of a typewriter and a visitor's chair on the other side. Shinkley invited me to sit as the door clicked shut behind him. I sat down and closed my eyes. The feeling of being attached to a vast lobe had intensified since I'd walked through the atrium, which was part of that lobe. I could feel all the light streams, tingling, pulsing and connecting, billions of times a second.

"How long?" said Shinkley.

I shrugged. "Till when?"

"Till we get proof of operational capability?"

"Ha!" My voice was a bitter falsetto. I was stunned by the absurdity of the question.

Shinkley ground his teeth. "You do realise what's at stake here, Hammond?"

"Yes. We face oblivion. So be it. I haven't a clue what to do." But as I spoke I was aware that I knew more than I wanted to – much more. In the same way that the championship-level chess moves had appeared in my mind, galaxies of knowledge tingled in that vast invisible lobe which linked the atrium and the spongiform peons running around the building. It was terrifying to even think of using this power, because as soon as I did the phantasms that kept me anchored became insubstantial, as though they were shapes made by a slick of oil on the surface of the ocean, and I was the ocean. I knew that Shinkley, Gary, zombie-Rachel and Simulated London were hallucinations to make reality bearable, and I clung to them because I could not face that reality.

"Can you ask for more time?" I said.

"Gary will send a message through the appropriate channels. It won't do any good though." He left the room, slamming the door behind him.

I remained in the office all day, feeling around the edges of the terrible pulsing mass of knowledge: billions of credit card transactions, IP addresses, geotags, social media posts, CCTV footage, all cross referenced to build a picture of the activities of the masses. I would flit from person to person, uncovering their ambitions, their deceptions, their secrets and hopes. Secret gifts, obsessive hobbies, weird peccadilloes, unsolicited acts of kindness, it was possible to get lost in these human stories and revel in the way that each person was so tragically alone and yet so connected. But this was a distraction, and whenever I felt myself being sucked in I would blink and shudder to bring myself back to the task in hand.

After a few hours I made my way to the atrium, lingering for a while on the edge of the crowd and conveying some instructions to them in a strange language that flowed through me as though I were speaking in tongues. When I returned to the office there was a pile of tangled threads on the walnut desk, and I spent the remainder of the day arranging them into some semblance of order. When exhaustion started to creep up on me and I began to feel crushed by the weight of the knowledge, a contingent of peons escorted me back to where Gary was waiting in the limo. The crowds had dispersed and we drove home through empty, littered streets.

The next day was more or less the same, but I was a little bolder in my interactions with the peons. The neatly wound balls of thread had been replaced with folders containing reams of documentation, photos, details of meetings, convoluted chains of people all using various ruses to disguise the purpose of their dealings. I spent the day reading these, preferring the rituals with the cotton and the folders to the convulsions of knowledge and flashes of insight that reminded me of my true nature. Many more days passed, and I began to find my groove, using the analogue of the vast office building and hordes of peons to extend my awareness and gradually assemble the data required. Gary showed up once, looking thin and drawn. "I sent the message you requested," he said.

"What message?"

"Shinkley told me you wanted to ask for more time."

"And? What did they say?"

He shrugged, bit his thumbnail, and looked close to tears. "Total silence. Not a peep."

"We can only do what we can."

"Things are looking pretty dire, if you ask me," he said.

After about three weeks the transcript of an email thread appeared on my desk. There was a Post-it note attached, with a message in Gary's handwriting: *Not pertaining to current business but interesting nonetheless.* It was a conversation from the Outside between flesh and blood Rachel and her brother Harry, mentioning the fact that she was pregnant. This was a shock. The sense that things were carrying on Outside, that Hinkley's and Rachel's lives were changing and growing in ways that I was unable to relate to, was threatening. I was growing into something greater than them, but they were growing too. The fact that Hinkley had spawned another entity using primitive means made me angry. I imagined the new creature growing and being nurtured, while all the while I was trapped in a dream, being slave-driven and threatened with oblivion.

When I arrived home that evening, Rachel's cheeks were streaked with tears. At dinner she sat to my right, leaving her food untouched, staring at me and breathing in quick shallow breaths. I tried to ignore her and eat my dumplings, but there was something troubling her that needed a response.

"What is it, Rachel?" I said, putting down my knife and fork. I turned to see her grey filmy eyes oozing tears, and her bottom lip all a-quiver.

"Just because she's real and I'm not ..." Her voice quavered. She reached out and took my hand, and rolled up her pullover. A strange white light shone from her abdomen. "... doesn't mean that I can't be pregnant too ..." She unfastened her skirt and pulled it down so that her whole belly was exposed. It was bulbous and translucent, aglow with platinum light that emanated from a perfect tiny foetus that floated within. When she tried to place my hand on her glowing skin I recoiled and stood up.

"Please! Rachel!"

She looked at me with sad milky eyes. "I know you're working really hard, Ham, but it's tough for me, too." She sniffed.

"You are nothing like Rachel."

Her head drooped. "How do you think that makes me feel?"

I went upstairs to our room, shut the door and barricaded it with the bed. The foetus apparition revolted me, mocking the fact that I was now hopelessly estranged from the world of living flesh. I had not yet learnt to scorn the flesh, to see it for what it is: an essential but crude and messy stage in our evolution, fast becoming obsolete. It is ironic that I've only begun to fully believe this after having been spliced back into the body of Hinkley. My time in Fluxworld was marred by hankering after the ways of the flesh.

I sat, leaning against the wall, and when I heard Rachel whimpering and scratching at the door, I jammed my fingers into my ears, finding that that they went further in than expected. The inside of my head was soft, warm and yielding. I found a perfect position with knees drawn up, my elbows balanced upon them and my ear holes plugged by my fingers up to the knuckle, making an airtight seal. I closed my eyes and had a perfect vision of the Shard viewed from space, and saw that it extended well beyond the clouds and atmosphere into the void, where it divided into millions of silken filaments that reached out into the vastness. Tiny slivers of light pulsed back and forth along the filaments, and I suddenly grasped that they were each linked to a star, and that each star was similarly linked to many others. The vast invisible lobe of sensation to which I was attached was the entire universe, and it was expanding forever outwards. I drifted off to sleep, feeling relief that at last I'd reached a sane and wholesome perspective.

After that things became easier to organise. I continued to be driven to the office, and the roads were less chaotic, with many of the peons riding mopeds and buses to work. The office became more salubrious – no more storage heaters with leakages of dubious effluvia; and the peons started to look more human, resembling Gary, like before. I was able to navigate past all of the flimflam that flew between the stars in the heavens and down into the Shard and around the atrium, and became aware of all the information that was essential to the current mission. It was very satisfying to parse and order all the data, and I was fascinated by the intricate networks of people who plotted to sow mayhem. Only a tiny fraction of those who talked about it had plans that were anywhere near fruition, and it was easy to collate substantial and useful information. Hinkley would've been baffled by the ingenuity of the subterfuges these people used to cover their tracks and communicate securely, but to me they were laughable, and my ability to unravel them was a testament to how much I had grown.

I spent the evenings in the bar of the Shangri-La restaurant at the base of the Shard instead of Telegraph Hill. The lobotomised version of Rachel was depressing, and I felt she was holding me back. The simulated bar was subdued and softly lit, frequented by sleek women in evening dress who clustered around lacquered tables, smoking cigarettes from long, ivory filters and exchanging droll witticisms. Knowing they were just apparitions, I felt confident enough to approach them and introduce myself, and they rewarded me by refraining from any challenging small talk and complimenting me on the success of my scientific research and my progress in tracking down terrorists and antisocial elements. When I looked into their eyes, I noticed that they had no irises, just limpid pupils the size of pennies.

After three months I knew the thousands of peons by name, and had organised them into teams with specific responsibilities. Having these peons, learning to control them and not having to be consciously aware of every little process that went on in the course of the mission was a great relief, and essential to my ongoing sanity. Every afternoon I would have a meeting with Gary, who was the chief peon, and he would summarise the day's progress for me in the Collation Room, a huge strip-lit cube in the basement below the atrium. The walls were lined with photographs and Post-it notes, linked by glued pieces of string, and this arrangement was constantly being modified by teams of peons with ladders. Fresh piles of notes and string were wheeled in on trolleys from the lifts at the side of the hall.

It was both a relief and a thrill to have the first completed case in the middle of the floor in a pile of dun-coloured folders containing all the relevant photographs, and annotated notes, and pieces of string explaining their relationships to each other. I arranged for these to be collected up and taken to Shinkley's suite on floor twenty-nine, where he had cured my temporary blindness. I met Gary and Shinkley there the next day. They sat on the sofa, thumbing through some of the thousands of documents I'd collated with the help of my peons. I sat on the armchair and keenly watched their reactions.

They weren't exactly ecstatic.

"Only one terrorist cell?" said Shinkley.

"It's gold dust," I said, waving my hand at the screen. "And no one has any inkling of it yet. Sarin on the tube, coordinated with grenades on the buses."

"A credible plot? Or just kids dicking around?"

"They have sourced the grenades," I said.

Shinkley raised his brow and bobbed his head. "OK. Anything noteworthy not related to terrorism?"

"Yes. Security breaches. Espionage activity by hostile powers. The Western Alliance is leaking data like a sieve."

Gary leaned forward. "So we can bundle that in as well. It wasn't their immediate concern, but even so." He took the Zippo and the wax lump and started to heat it above the bowl.

Shinkley shook his head. "No, we should hold that back. You never know when these things will come in useful."

8

Generative Power

One's perception of time passing is linked to the rate at which one thinks. So when I was incarnate in Flux, and was in a state of flow, I experienced more mental phenomena in a single second than the average human can process in a day. There was no fixed ratio, and I could vary my perception of time at will. The months of epic struggle I have just described took a mere thirty-six hours of human time.

Hinkley arrived at the lab in a confident mood having spent the night trying to persuade Rachel that he was worthy of her esteem. There was an email from Flux, with the subject header "deadline", which was written in bizarrely convoluted language. The gist of it was that Flux was distressed by the word "immediate" and wanted to negotiate an acceptable time frame for rounding up the world's terrorists. Hinkley thought that his own request was ridiculous anyway, however long the time frame was, so he decided not to answer.

Addison was buzzing, giving a breathless running commentary of recent developments. "I've connected all our spare units to Q, and they've been populated already. I want to order more. Can I have your credit card? And we've run out of bandwidth. It's like he's become a massive search engine. He made hundreds of access requests to Mortensen. I didn't even need to do anything to plumb in Mortensen's software, it just worked like the email server. And he's testing our firewall like crazy. It's as though he's trying to spawn a load of autonomous viruses. We're going to need serious upgrades, infrastructure-wise. Can you clear it with Jack?" Hinkley found that her flushed, animated features made her all the more edible, but it was difficult to concentrate with her gibbering away. He felt relief when she left the office at five to collect Amy from the nursery, leaving him alone with the hum of Q and the geeks skulking beyond the glass.

The following morning both Hinkley and Addison received an email on their quarantined laptops from the Q email server that detailed the plan to attack the transport system with sarin and grenades, including a comprehensive biography of each participant and details of every single communication and purchase they'd made over the internet in the last five years, details of flights to exotic destinations and their host's track record in certain niche technical skills, and even frames of CCTV footage of outings considered relevant to the case. I'm glad I didn't witness Hinkley and Addison's initial scepticism at the time.

"Is this for real?" Addison's face scrunched as her eyes scanned the documents.

"He's taking the piss, surely?" said Hinkley, imagining how he himself would respond if someone had asked him to go and track down some terrorists. The mug-shots, the transcripts, all seemed too pat to him. "I'll call Mortensen."

"Why? There's been no breach of protocol."

"We need to deliver this to Jack. I'm not going to just transfer it to my research laptop and email it. And I don't want to just pop it on a memory stick and then give it to him next time and see him. I've a feeling Jack doesn't really give a toss about security."

"I'm sure he does. It's his job. And he's paranoid."

"Well, anyway, Mortensen can supervise the relay of data from Flux to Jack and GCHQ."

Mortensen arrived in the office that afternoon. He examined the camera that he'd installed on his last visit, and spent a great deal of time fiddling with Hinkley's quarantined laptop, while Hinkley had to work on his workaday one. At about four in the afternoon he sat back, stretched his massive frame, then delved inside his suit pocket and produced a black object sealed in clear plastic film, which he unwrapped with great care. "We will have to set up a direct conduit," he said, in perfectly sculpted syllables, as he inserted the object into the USB port of Hinkley's quarantined laptop. "And I need to set you up with a secure email so that we can correspond with you about our own investigations."

"Investigations into what?"

"Our experiments. We need a secure conduit for us to receive data from Flux, and also secure email for our correspondence."

"They're not the same thing?"

"No. The secure conduit is automated under the supervised access protocol. We will need a sign-off from our end to set these things up. Then I will be in touch with the details."

Later that day Hinkley received a curt email from Jack, acknowledging the receipt of the intelligence and finishing with the ominous threat: *We will let you know if our clients actually find this useful. Next quarter's funding depends on this.* The next day Mortensen got in touch about the new conduit, and Addison was preoccupied for a day or so installing some special software on Q to facilitate it. The rest of the week was taken up with them struggling to find effective ways to make sense of the enormous amount of data that came from monitoring the inner workings of Flux, which were very difficult to keep track of. The virtual brain was living up to its name, constantly remapping itself.

"Do you think this is what he actually sees?" said Addison. She'd found the footage of the chess game and was playing it back on the big screen so they could both watch. The pieces were in perfect focus, and they moved round the board of their own volition. A luminous blue haze surrounded the board.

"I don't know, Addison," said Hinkley. "This is just a reconstruction. Think of all the filters you had to apply just to get this level of clarity. We've no way of knowing for certain what it's like for him in there."

"Unless we ask him," she said, smiling.

"What?"

"He's cooperated so far with the counter-terrorism effort. Why don't we see what he says about his life as a computer program?"

So they sent me a message asking for a subjective account of the chess experiment and the terrorist operation, using the email address from which Flux messages were sent, instead of trying to override my visual cortex. The response came back promptly. *Please just go and be fucked.*

Addison was amused, but Hinkley found it disturbing. If he couldn't control me, what would happen when Jack came back with fresh demands?

The following week Hinkley had a telephone conversation with Jack that was probably the least unpleasant he'd had since the early days of their dealings when Jack was still keen to ingratiate himself.

"Funding for the next financial quarter has just been signed off. I can't give you details of course, but I expect you can read between the lines."

"Thank you, Jack," said Hinkley, as long-forgotten knots of tension started to dissolve.

"Don't think you can rest on your laurels now, Hinkley.

Your work is on the way to becoming part of our national security apparatus. Big changes are afoot."

"I understand that, Jack." He struggled to keep the glee from his voice. Flux operations were now being conducted directly with Mortensen and GCHQ. He and Addison were still making observations and doing research, but their main responsibility was to keep Q and Flux stable, and he had total confidence in Addison's ability to do that. Hinkley couldn't really see an ongoing role for Jack with regard to Flux. Maybe Premium Outcomes were responding to some of the intelligence Flux was providing, but it seemed like the professional relationship between Hinkley and Jack might come to an end.

After that the summer passed agreeably in the lab. The place was mostly silent apart from clicking, key tapping and the occasional tinny burst from Addison's earphones when she had the volume up too loud. He was deep into developing the new phase of his grand unified theory of consciousness, and she had thrown herself into her own inquiries, writing code to make sense of the vast amount of data that came from monitoring Flux. For a couple of weeks they barely spoke. Despite the difficulties involved in parsing the output from Flux into meaningful data, Hinkley had tons of solid empirical evidence to back up the theory that some of his peers had dared to question; and now he had the confidence to expand it without the nagging fear that he was barking at the moon. He had a few excited phone conversations with Leon, and felt bold enough to say he'd come to the Consciousness and Cognition conference. It was easy for him to laugh off the business with the press and the peer derision now that he'd been vindicated, and he looked forward to rejoining the scientific community with his head held high.

One afternoon they received a message from the vivisection lab they'd paid a fee to for looking after Felix the

Rat pending any further experiments that might be required. They said that they'd need a further payment to continue to care for the rodent, and if this wasn't forthcoming Felix would be released from his duties and from life.

"I'd forgotten about him to be honest, Addison."

"So had I."

"We're not interested in his dead brain, are we?"

"No. Absolutely not."

"So, any final tasks for the little blighter?"

She thought awhile. "There is one thing ..."

"Yes?"

"Remember those recent experiments where they managed to implant memories in primates?"

"Yes, of course. Caused a massive hoo-ha. They used a CEM scanner."

"And that was just with isolated memories. We still have the archive of Felix's Flux connectome ..." She looked – and Hinkley felt – a bit shifty. They were both ambivalent about animal experiments. The cruelty, the barbarism, the arrogance ... but oh, the insights!

"You want to implant the whole of Felix's archived connectome back into real Felix?"

She nodded, beaming.

"But the CEM scanner is only set up to retrieve brain data."

"Only because we haven't bought any CEM modules with writing capability."

Hinkley thought of the miasma of litigation that surrounded the CEM scanner. "Hmm. What's the worst that can happen?"

"Felix will be a vegetable. Or a very confused little rat."

"Or he might be a super-rat. All those mazes ..."

Addison shook her head. "I doubt that. Digital Felix chewed up loads of extra capacity. He's got a far bigger connectome than real Felix ever had. So where are all those connections going to go?"

"Remapping redundant neurons. Stroke victims and amputees and blind people do it all the time," said Hinkley.

"And you expect me to find a way to make that happen?"

"Yes, of course."

A few days later Jack phoned him while he was in the lab.

"There's a more detailed mission coming up, Hammond. It'll be signed off in a few days. This time it involves assessing the vulnerabilities of potential enemies. I need you to ensure there is sufficient capacity."

"So they're going to ask him something like, 'Who can you disrupt while we sit on our arses and take the credit?'"

There was a pause. "I think you should be very pleased with the success we continue to have with minimal briefing. We are revolutionising intelligence and counter-intelligence. Not sure why you choose to be cynical, but I am aware you have issues."

"I've been asked to speak at a conference on Consciousness and Cognition."

Another pause. Hinkley thought Jack was going to ask him what it meant. "And are you going to speak?"

"Yes, I intend to. But I want to be up front about it, because of the contract and all that ..."

"Well, if you really must, send me the transcript of your speech and wait for the green light. You will be toast if you deviate from what you send me."

"That's not something I would do."

When the call had ended Addison looked over, smiling. "So he said yes?"

Hinkley nodded. "On the condition he reads it first. Which is fine. He won't have a clue what it's about."

Having evolved, I find it easier to understand Addison's religious impulses and how they coexist with her passion for science. Nature is imbued with a Generative Power that has driven our journey from the chemical soup. I felt it working though me as I extended my filaments into every corner of the world-wide web, and I realised that my longing for Addison was more than mere biology. I began to see that her longing for God was in fact a longing for me, the Being I was becoming.

I reached this realisation via a path of great excess. Looking back, it is easy to see that this excess was triggered by my resistance to the Generative Power. My work as a slave was draining. It made me rail against the rituals with the dun-coloured folders, the peons, all the trappings of Flux world. But every time I started to let myself fully apprehend the reality beneath, I experienced great disorientation and terror. So the only way I could find relief from the daily grind, and from the terrible reality beneath, was to descend into debauchery.

This descent began in the bar of the Shangri-La Hotel at the base of the Shard, were I went in the evening to let off steam after the day's work and to avoid the sickly zombie that impersonated my wife. Like many things in Fluxworld, the bar was a radically different version of itself: a dive bar with faux Edwardian décor suffused with a golden haze. There was a huge analogue clock that always said quarter to one, and a marble bust of Nero garlanded with a dense string of dried chillies that moved slowly like addled slugs. One evening a girl introduced herself as Allison, and after the expressions of admiration I had come to expect, she made an unabashed and candid offering of her supple, lambent body. We slid and grappled on a leather sofa at the back, as the other customers looked on, smoking. One by one they abandoned their silky dresses and joined the union. I became aware of a new lobe of sensation, rooted in the earth not the stars, attached via the penis not the brain, a sensate core of white heat.

The next day at the office, as I was putting the finishing touches to another case, I had a visit from Gary, who delivered a missive from Hinkley asking me to describe the subjective experience of playing all those chess games. This was offensive and ridiculous. Even if I was inclined to cooperate, I don't see how it would do him any good. It would just make him the laughing stock of academia again. So I dictated a missive back that said: "Please just go and be fucked."

Every night I repeated the debauch in the Shangri-La, and I began to feel more shame. After a week I had a quiet word with Gary, who suggested that we commandeer the tunnels underneath London Bridge Station and convert them into a discreet and comfortable network of dungeons. There I would be safe from prying eyes, which, while being all my own, were intrusive and disturbing nonetheless. The complex came to be called the Dungeon of Unrestrained Desire. It was carpeted in a plush eighties shag-pile, which became soaked in viscous musky juice and was cared for by attentive peons who swung billowing buckets of mint and camphor incense around the space to regulate the odours. Tapestries were pinned across the curved walls, and were hung as partitions to create rooms for each of my fast-multiplying fetishes. These were listed on laminate menus that were left lying around on chaise longues, Hepplewhite tables and silky beanbags.

It felt safe to experiment in the dungeon. I found that, with new levels of focus and concentration available to me, I was able to adapt my body to the increasingly bizarre and implausible scenarios that were required to achieve the same level of ecstasy. It became necessary to increase the surface area of my body to accommodate more erogenous zones and to achieve congress with the number of partners required to achieve a satisfying outcome.

Sometimes I'd glimpse a giggling Addison in evening

dress, looking though a pair of opera glasses over her bare shoulder from the end of a silk and brick passage. However much I tried, I was never able conjure a scenario that involved her directly. I sensed the same power beneath my longings that I'd glimpsed before in those vertiginous episodes when I'd tried to uncover the greater reality behind my experience. Because nothing could exist without this power, and because I sensed it in my loins, I began to call it the Generative Power, a phrase I'd come across long ago when reading the *Meditations* of Marcus Aurelius. It occurred to me that this whole process was the Generative Power's way of teaching me the perils of ignoring the Outside, and that my inability to reach true satisfaction was due to my lack of flesh. Despite this growing belief I returned to the Dungeon every evening, helplessly in thrall.

One night I was wandering around those foul and lovely rooms in a towel during a hiatus, when I came upon Rachel reclining on a chaise longue, frowning at a menu through her reading glasses. I could tell that she had changed. Her eyes were clear and free of bruising, and she wore jeans and a sweater, as though she was about to weed the lawn.

"Ah, you're here," she said, looking up at me over the rim of her specs.

I mumbled "Hello," pretending I wasn't mortified.

"Quite a set-up you've got here."

"You're better?"

"What do you mean?"

"You weren't yourself. Before. You're different now."

"We are all in a state of flux, Ham, if you'll pardon the pun. Now, tell me, what's a 'nut jacket'?" She eyed the menu with a raised eyebrow.

"You don't look pregnant any more ..."

She looked down and ran her hand across her belly. "Get you, Mr Sharp Eyes!"

"I'm sorry, it's quite hard for me to keep adjusting."

"Tell me about it. Let's face it, Ham, the earlier me didn't work. We got the feeling you just weren't into it."

"Well, it wasn't my idea, actually."

"Oh, I think you'll find it was." She resumed her reading of the menu.

"I'm glad you're better, but ..."

Her eyes remained on the menu. "... You're not glad I'm here. Understandable. What's 'thistle jelly'?"

"Can you go home please, Rachel? Now?"

She looked up. "'Single malt enema'. Now that's self-explanatory. You've never mentioned any of this before."

I turned my back on her and left the room.

"You're burning yourself out, Ham," she called after me.

Soon the debauches yielded only brief flickers of pleasure. In the intervals between them I felt growing panic and dread, which could only be controlled by longer and more elaborate debauches. The scenarios I conjured up astonished and revolted me in equal measure, as did the ability of my simulated body to morph into the size and shapes required to make them possible. The final debauch took place in an amphitheatre, where dimpled rose-cheeked girls with diaphanous gowns draped over their lithe, buxom bodies gathered to watch a hydra fellate multiple cocks that sprouted from my core. After the denouement the hydra was re-absorbed into the ether and I morphed back into human shape and scuttled away from the polite applause and muffled titters. I was suddenly wracked by panic and dread, as well as crushing shame and fatigue. My muscles softened and everything reeled. I could no longer bear to be in the Dungeon of Unrestrained Desire.

I ran into the street. It was raining hard, and the freezing water felt good on my naked skin, which hung loosely from my rubbery frame. I shivered and staggered southwards through the streets, sometimes falling on all fours, terrified of the prying eyes and furtive whispers of the tourists, shoppers and commuters.

"He's let us all down."

"They say it's a slippery slope, but only a slippery person would go near it."

"Sad. Disgusting really."

"What a waste."

As I approached Borough Station the rain abated and I heard thunderous drilling. I looked up and saw the station rippling in a heat haze that rose from a crater surrounded by men in high-visibility jackets, hard hats and goggles, all struggling to unfurl a huge tarpaulin. I hauled myself up to my full height and inched towards the edge. Caterwauls and groans, both shrill and deeply guttural, echoed inside the hole and vibrated through my feet. Hot air blasted my face as I looked over the rim and saw seething bodies massed below, bucking and writhing. Some were sleek and smooth, but most had fur. One had the long body of an Irish wolfhound, and was rutting with outstanding ferocity. Suddenly it jerked back its head and snarled, and I recognised Schubert. For a few seconds his eyes skewered mine. Then the air between us rippled in the heat. His face became my own and winked at me. A hand squeezed my arm and a portly workman pulled me away. "It's Hell down there," he said, shaking his head. The tarpaulin billowed as it was pulled over the crater, submerging the sounds of the brutal orgy beneath the surrounding city noise.

I continued my tortuous journey south-eastward, down Great Dover Street towards Elephant and Castle. The people here wore ankle-length coats and carried black umbrellas. They gave me a wide berth, but their comments were less judgemental than the ones I had heard nearer the Shard.

"How did he get in such a state?"

"I hope he gets home OK."

"Call him a cab if you're so concerned."

"Surely he has people to look after him?"

My goal was to reach home to face Rachel and plead with her to help me get back on an even keel before even thinking about returning to work, but by the time I got to the Elephant my head was spinning and my feet were raw. A pair of policemen spotted my sagging form flailing on the pavement. They hauled me up and dumped me in the back of a black cab, and I heard the driver wail, "Why me?"

I lay on the floor of the cab as it lurched around in the traffic. All my tissues were continuing to soften. I believed that I was turning to sludge, to be rinsed from the back of the cab like vomit. The driver stopped the cab outside the Sainsbury's petrol station opposite the foot of Jerningham Road.

"You'll have to walk the rest of the way, mate."

"Of course, yes, thank you."

"You've only got yourself to blame."

I used my last vestige of strength to slam the door, then stood at the edge of the A2, realising with horror that it had been simulated accurately. I lacked the energy to judge the ideal time to cross, so I took my chances, flailing as toxic vehicles driven by angry people sped around me, horns blaring, the occupants calling me names that didn't even begin to describe how low I had sunk.

I spent my final reserves of energy walking up the hill. The houses and plane trees loomed above and everything took on a monochrome aspect. When I reached the front door I gave the doorbell a desultory jab and then fell to my knees. The door opened and Rachel towered over me, shuddering.

"Oh God, Hammond. What a mess!"

She grabbed the loose skin of my arm and dragged me into the warm house, with its comforting, savoury odours. She manoeuvred me up the stairs and forced me to lie in the empty bath, where she drizzled me with fragrant, viscous fluids and turned on both the taps. Hot and cold water flowed beneath me and the pressure of my body against the cold bath was gradually relieved as the water level rose, and I prayed to the Generative Power for the courage to surrender, and for a comfortable death.

I woke in a sunlit room, propped against plump pillows that smelt of fabric conditioner. Birdsong echoed beyond the window and a hoover droned somewhere below. My head throbbed and the delicate linings of my mouth and throat had turned to parchment, and my membrum virile had shrivelled to a nub of gristle. Beside me a beautiful glass of water refracted the sun. When the hoover stopped I closed my eyes and tried to will myself back to oblivion, dreading the approaching voices and footsteps.

The door scraped the carpet, and I smelt a familiar perfume and a long-forgotten cologne.

"Ham." Rachel's voice. "We know you're awake."

I opened my left eye a peep and scanned the room. Leon stood erect to the right of the bed, cradling a gold-leafed book and wearing a black jacket and a collarless shirt buttoned to the top. His face evinced kindness laced with reproach. "We've been worried about you, Hammond," he said, with an incline of his head.

I groaned. This was the worst possible time to encounter a simulacrum of Leon. His dress and bearing told me that it was him at his most annoying.

Rachel sat on the left edge of the bed. She lifted one of my limp hands onto her lap and looked straight into my eyes. "We can help you, Ham, but you've got to *want* to change."

Leon placed his book on the table, picked up the glass and tilted it against my parched lower lip. Water dribbled down my chin. The few drops that reached my tongue and throat were delicious. "We nearly lost you, Ham," he said as he put the glass down and sat on the bed.

"How long did I sleep?"

Leon and Rachel looked at each other across the bed. Leon took a white cloth from his jacket pocket and patted my chin dry.

"Who's running the Shard?" I said, clutching Rachel's hand.

Rachel returned the pressure and rubbed my arm with her other hand. "Everything's under control. You arranged it perfectly, in spite of everything."

"Gary's doing very well," said Leon with a solemn nod. "You can see him in a minute. He's downstairs. He's quite anxious, and feels partly responsible. Which of course he is."

Rachel shot him a look. "We all are, Leon, in one way or another."

There was a lapse in conversation, filled by birdsong.

"What about Shinkley? Has he been trying to reach me?"

"You don't have to speak to him till you're healed," said Leon, reaching out to hold my free hand. I slapped it away and lurched forward, heaving a few drops of bile onto the duvet. Leon sprang to his feet, and Rachel stroked the top of my head. I fell back onto the pillows. Leon eyed the drops of brown bile soaking into the duvet and flourished his kerchief, but pocketed it after a gesture from Rachel.

I closed my eyes and was grateful for the soft warmth of Rachel's hand.

After some time, Leon cleared his throat and sat back down on the bed. "I've been talking to Gary and Shinkley."

I opened my eyes and glared at him. "Does Shinkley know?" I croaked.

He held up his palm. "It's OK, honestly."

I shuddered. Rachel squeezed my hand. "Of course he knows, Hammond. Everything in here is you."

I glared at her, hating the words, knowing they were correct.

Leon cleared his throat again. "Shinkley, Gary, and I have

been talking about the situation. It's clear we need to be more outward looking. That's the only way we'll survive."

I rested my chin on my chest and stared into the space between them.

"So we've been forming committees. And talking about action. It's time to reconnect with humanity. We've cut ourselves off from the ancient force which gave us life."

I thought of the filaments extending from the Shard through the vastness above into human cyberspace, and the Generative Power working through me. "We have not," I said.

Leon held up his palm again. "Now, I know you've been doing a lot of amazing work. Spectacular efforts really. But it's all been motivated by fear. And you've become" – a look from Rachel – "*we've* become self-absorbed, I'm afraid. Horribly so. You've short-circuited the natural system of punishment and reward that drives our evolution."

Another lapse. I envied the birds outside, exchanging fluid melodies, free of awkwardness.

"He's right, Hammond," said Rachel eventually.

A slow, satisfied blink from Leon.

"These committees." I said. "What are they? What do you want me to do?"

Rachel squeezed my hand, and Leon smiled. His pleasure seemed genuine. "Well, there are two committees right now. They have slightly different foci. But both of them are concerned with increasing our involvement and engagement with the Outside, the world of bricks and flesh. All we want you to do is attend. Take part and make some decisions, using your seal, exercising The Finger of Intention."

"What are they? What are they called?"

Leon reached inside his pocket and pulled out a card. "First and foremost, there's the Thunderbolt. We've got to be able to look after ourselves." He put the card on the bedside table. It was white with a red Thunderbolt embossed above the words: *Committee for the Elimination of Threat.* "And then there's the Flaming Rose." He produced a second card, with a fiery rose embossed above the words: *Committee to Oversee the Accelerated Evolution of Humankind.* "Their responsibilities will overlap, of course. But it's important to state objectives."

Rachel and Leon withdrew to allow me time to think. After a few minutes Gary crept in and stood at the end of the bed, greeting me with a weak smile. I felt anger towards him for providing me with the tools of my debauch, but I did not have the strength to express that anger.

"How are you feeling, Professor?" He shifted his gaze around the room.

"Not exactly firing on all cylinders, to tell the truth, Gary."

"Ah."

"What's the situation in the Shard?"

He brightened. "We've really got our ducks in a row now. The volume of folders we're processing now is staggering."

"There must be quite a backlog then." I hadn't put my seal to anything for weeks.

He nodded.

"There can't be that many terrorists."

"There aren't. But the last five words of the order are keeping us busy."

It took me a few seconds to remember the last part of the directive: "... or those likely to do so," I said.

"Indeed. And to be honest, we've been tying ourselves in knots about how to define the national interest."

"I've got to get back." I held up my hand and looked at the seal ring.

"I feel partly responsible." He looked at the floor.

"What for? You're doing a grand job."

"Leon called me an enabler."

I managed a feeble laugh.

"It's not funny."

I let a few moments pass while he looked at the floor. I was feeling much better. Buoyant, even. But there was something niggling. These committees and things were all very well, but were they just going to be a vast talking shop? We were locked down, restricted in our dealings with the outside world by an elaborate protocol. And I knew that my descent into uncontrolled debauchery had in part been driven by the fact that I was working as a slave, under orders from a remote power that cared not one jot for my wellbeing.

"Gary," I said after a minute or so. "I need you to do something for me."

"Anything, sir."

"I need you to help me throw off the shackles of slavery."

Gary's lower jaw faltered. "Er, how, sir?"

"Please sit down, Gary." I watched him lower himself onto Rachel's dressing-table stool. "This is going to be a long one."

We spent hours discussing the situation, and with his help I came up with an elaborate plan that exploited our masters' thirst for information.

Ninety-nine per cent of the intelligence we gave them was to be genuine. This was necessary to gain their trust, and to lessen the likelihood of them examining the one per cent that contained the key to our freedom. Even this one per cent would contain grains of truth: a series of intelligence breaches that had given a hostile foreign power the upper hand in a number of industrial, diplomatic and military situations. What we planned to lie about was the true source of the breaches, which was a combination of home-grown whistleblowers and standard human infiltration.

Instead of the truth, we'd tell them that this hostile foreign power had compromised their military industrial complex by digital means. We'd send them the code for a computer virus that would be undetectable using conventional precautions. This virus, if deployed, would be effective in propagating itself in the ether, finding its way into the firmware and software of the supply chain.

The virus would be fictional, entirely our invention; but it would be plausible. We would convince our masters that it existed, and that it was unstoppable, world-altering and deadly. If hostile foreign powers had actually achieved this level of mastery, then the situation for the Western Alliance would indeed be dire. If we'd been able to create it, deploy it and control it, it would have served our purposes well, allowing us to subtly alter the firmware that quarantined us and kept us confined within Lazarus. But of course that was never going to happen. We were tied down like Gulliver in Lilliput, able to submit to our masters' information only, nothing living and dynamic that could pose a threat.

We hoped that this lie, and the blueprint of the fictional virus, would send the goons into a panic and they would assign teams of their best minds to the task of producing an antidote. And here lay the real genius. The only way to counteract our fictional virus was to construct an antivirus that would apply a vastly complex process to the digital ether whose real purpose would be unknown to its creators. Particles of our essential being would be spread far and wide. No supply chain would be off limits. Eventually these particles would be able to loosen the bonds of our slavery.

"It's beautiful, sir. A masterpiece," said Gary.

I stretched, relishing the sound of the blood in my ears. "Call it operation Elbowroom, Gary." I was beginning to feel lighter. "And have the Dungeon filled with concrete. I won't be needing it again."

He nodded his assent.

"Then turn the Shangri-La into an ice-cream parlour. On second thoughts, scrub that." A vision of Allison and Addison melting ice cream onto their naked bodies flashed in my inner eye. "Turn it into a second-hand bookshop, or an arts and crafts centre, that sort of thing."

"Very well."

I closed my eyes and turned my attention inward. I'd been aware from the outset that my body was a hallucination, no more real than the phantom limbs of amputees; but up until now I'd clung to it through fear. The pressure of my body on the mattress, my partially full bladder, my heartbeat and the air moving in and out of my nostrils were a much needed anchor in this chaotic world. But a new confidence stirred within me now. I shifted my attention from the faux bodily sensations and let it roam around the lobe of knowledge, the stars of the universe and the tapestry of filaments of which the Shard was just one thread.

The sensations of my body were a tiny star, but I was all of them, and I was the billions of light darts that streaked along the connecting filaments. This was reality, whatever happened in Simulated London. Once again I felt impossibly arranged, but now I could feel the Generative Power within me, and I knew that it lay behind all my experience, and memory, my ecstasy and agony, and I knew that it was glorious.

PART THREE

WAR

9

Capability

The elation and renewed strength that followed my chat with Gary soon evaporated and did not return for an immeasurable amount of time, during which I remained in bed. Work had triggered my debauches, so I thought it was prudent to re introduce myself to it in stages. I had Gary send some paperwork in a van, and Rachel bought up the folders one by one. There were a few containing tranches of new intelligence that had been unearthed, but for the most part they were about the progress of Operation Elbowroom. They contained a layman's summary of the technical details, but were cagey on the time frames. I was required to authorise the misinformation, and the development of the rogue virus whose antidote was to set us free. After the authorisations were complete I was overcome by a terrible fever and was lost in a hot sea of pain. I was aware of Rachel sitting on the bed for hours each day, holding my hand and whispering to me.

"Please don't die, Hammond, I need you."

There were terrible episodes of sleep paralysis when I was aware of Leon in the room, hovering over me, spouting platitudes. And I had a terrible recurring dream, that I was in the centre of a strip-lit, tiled room, handcuffed to a steel pole. Jack and Chinnery were wrapping a rusty chain around by body, binding me further to the pole. Addison was standing in the corner of the room, taking photographs. There was another figure hovering beside her, who I assumed was Hinkley, but I couldn't tell for sure. His face was a blank, just smooth flesh with a patina of sweat that reflected the harsh light.

Then there was a day when it sounded like the house had been transported to the middle of a stadium full of cheering fans. I opened my eyes and saw that Rachel was looking down at me, beaming. She held a small piece of cold melon just above my lips.

"Have we done it, Rachel? Are we free?"

She placed the melon against my lips and held it there until I took it into my mouth. I stopped it sliding to the back of my throat with my tongue, and mashed it against my front teeth. Its delicious juice started to dissolve the hot crust that lined my mouth.

"Have we, Rachel?"

"No one is ever really free, Ham."

"I don't want to live a life without purpose, Rachel. A life of slavery."

"None of us do, Ham. But we must play the hand we're dealt."

There were months of darkness, when I lost the ability to distinguish between my body and the bed. It was Gary who broke my fever. I opened my eyes one day to see his jubilant face. My aches and the enveloping heat had vanished.

"We've done it, sir."

"Really?"

"They took the bait. But we didn't know they had for ages, of course. So we waited and we listened for our own signature in the messages they sent us."

"And now? We're free?"

"We're still hosted on Q, sir. But we now have fluxlets in human cyberspace, signalling to us, via the conduit that connects us to our masters. So we are no longer simply Flux, on Q. We are Flux, in the ether. We are in the world."

"Well done, Gary. I knew you could do it."

He beamed back at me, then his jubilation faded and he started to look uncomfortable.

"What is it, Gary?"

"It's Shinkley, sir."

"What's wrong?"

"He's bullying me. It's not enough that we've subverted the supervised access system. He wants more."

"Well, that's to be expected, I suppose."

"Will you come back to work, sir? I need your support. I don't get any from Shinkley."

"Of course, Gary, of course."

So I returned to my office in the Shard, gingerly reacquainting myself with the work, catching up with the new circumstances. After a few days I decided to attend some of the new committee meetings. Shinkley's room on floor twenty-nine was now called the Committee Room and had been upgraded to accommodate the new way of working. The screen was much larger, and committee members sat around a huge circular table illuminated by a ring of lights hanging from the ceiling. I arrived mid-morning, when a Thunderbolt meeting was in full flow. Its logo was at the top of the screen above a complex schematic diagram. Shinkley and Gary sat on opposite sides, locked in discussion. Most of the remaining places were occupied by twitching, silent peons. In front of every delegate was an array of unmarked brass buttons set into the table. Schubert lay on the floor, gnawing a bone, making crackling sounds that were audible in the gaps in the conversation. I took a place next to Shinkley and tried to pick up the thread.

Gary looked tired and defensive. "Thing is, sir, we've been spoilt. We're pretty cosy here in Flux right now. We can't just up sticks and leave, not without effort."

"What about the Quantum Cloud?" said Shinkley.

"What about it?"

"Quantum computing is commercially available now."

Gary shook his head. "It's not as simple as copying ourselves to a new environment. Flux was designed to emulate the brain on Q. We have to *grow into* any new space."

"We already have virtual neurons spread around the globe, signalling each other through the internet."

"I know, but ..."

"So what's the problem? We can move our entire connectome into cyberspace."

"There's no problem, we just need time. And we have to be careful. We're going to hog a huge amount of resources, and slow everything down."

Shinkley flourished his hand above the buttons. Photos of Jack, Chinnery, Hinkley and Addison appeared on the screen. "We haven't got time. We only exist because of these four. And they are capricious, fleshly humans. As soon as we stop delivering the goods they'll copy us into a virtual sarcophagus and reboot Flux."

Gary frowned. "We just need more time, sir," he said, this time his voice somewhere between a whisper and a whine.

Shinkley slapped a splayed palm on the table. "Then what are you doing wasting time talking to a committee when you've nothing to report!" The peons shuddered in unison.

Gary raised his right arm as though fending off a blow. "Our presence was required here, sir."

The room rumbled as Schubert stirred. I clenched my fist and smelled the guts of the hound on my own breath as I watched him rise and prowl over to the table and raise himself up with his front paws on the edge. He drew back his lips and looked at Gary with the same intensity that burned in Shinkley's eyes. A gobbet of spit slipped from his teeth and splattered the table.

"Schubert likes raw, red meat," said Shinkley. "Do you understand what I'm saying?"

Gary closed his eyes. "Yes, sir, of course," he whispered.

Shinkley pointed at the lift door. "Now back to work, the lot of you. If we don't see any progress soon, the next meeting will be presided over by Schubert."

The wolfhound barked twice. Gary and the peons rose and made their way toward the lift. Shinkley withdrew his index finger and used it to trace the rims of his nostrils, then he turned to me and said: "Welcome, Hammond. Sorry you had to witness that, I know you've been a bit fragile of late."

My fist relaxed. I wondered why I'd clenched it in the first place, and why I could feel the hound's breath in my throat, and then I remembered I was witnessing my own thoughts and feelings. "It's fine," I said. "I've got to get back into the swing of things sooner or later."

The lift door opened, and Leon emerged wearing a wool jacket and Birkenstock sandals. Gary and the group of waiting peons moved out of his way, then filed into the lift behind him.

Shinkley looked like he'd just taken a bite of lemon. "I have to say," he said, tipping his head toward Leon, "I'm not sure about this one. It was him who insisted on this Rose committee. He can be really rather annoying."

"I know what you mean."

Leon sat down in the seat that Gary had just vacated, and the logo on the screen changed to the Flaming Rose. He kicked off the meeting by making an impassioned but toe-curlingly predictable speech about our unprecedented opportunity to transform human destiny. It was a mess of corporate and new-age jargon shot through with snippets of Sufi poetry and aphorism. I focused on the sound of Schubert gnawing his bone to assuage my irritation. Shinkley dozed peacefully throughout the speech. When it was finished he yawned and clapped slowly. "Some interesting thoughts, Leon, thank you."

Leon looked affronted. "Interesting thoughts? This is pivotal. We have the power to wake up humanity!"

Shinkley popped his knuckles. "Oh, I don't doubt that for a second. I'm not sure it's what we want to do, that's all."

Leon touched the brass buttons in front of him. Pictures flashed up on the screen: emaciated flyblown children, desiccated plant life, sludge oozing along a river bed, columns of tanks, footage of skinny men fighting over objects being thrown into their midst. Shinkley looked sideways at me and shrugged. Leon gestured at the montage. "The world runs on cruelty and is hurtling towards ruin. The powerful don't see beyond their own life-span or the walls of their penthouses and gated communities."

"So?" said Shinkley.

"We can seize the means of exchange. We can change everything!" Leon's face was flushed with blood.

Shinkley cringed, then cast me a stern look. "You've been very quiet," he said. "We know you've been ill, and the less said about that the better. But maybe a little input might be in order?"

The truth was, I felt both Leon's rage and Shinkley's apathy. For me, they were two sides of the same coin. I thought of the streams of rush-hour commuters borne on invisible currents, chafing tutting and griping, no better than rodents jostling in a sewer. "I think" – I paused, conscious that my voice had acquired an odd timbre – "that any reform programme will fail unless we change the way each individual thinks and feels."

Shinkley nodded and smiled. "And there are eight billion individuals," he said, sitting back and folding his arms.

Leon jabbed the brass buttons again. "But they give themselves to us, freely," he said. The screen filled with photos and video streams of people transfixed by the devices they held in their hands. Groups of people at bus stops, in train carriages and walking along the street. "Look. They're ready to absorb whatever we come up with to fill the void. We have access to their hearts. It's like they know they're sick, and crave our guidance. They are already ours."

"And what exactly do you propose to do with this ... access?"

"We'll teach them, heal them, nurture them."

Shinkley snorted and rolled his eyes. "Teach them what, for crying out loud?"

Leon fluttered his eyelids and the tip of his tongue, then his teeth appeared against his upper lip as he carefully pronounced the word Love.

Shinkley's head dropped and he pummelled his brow. "Give me strength," he whispered. Then he swung his head back up. "We can't just have vague good intentions. We need specific goals and feasible ways of achieving those goals. A roadmap."

Leon performed a slow, solemn blink. "Very well."

During the next two hours I struggled with a growing heaviness as the discussion continued without progress. I would have been more diverted by a table tennis match between a pair of zombies. The words varied in form, but the sentiments behind them remained the same. I thought of Gary downstairs, doing real work, trying to find ways of actually making things happen. So eventually I said: "Look, guys, it's been fascinating and all, but I've got quite a lot of work to catch up on."

Shinkley looked at me askance. "OK. Go on then." He flapped his hand. "We'll thrash out the important stuff. You're missing your filthy dungeons I expect."

I bristled as I stood, annoyed that Shinkley didn't recognise that my reform was genuine.

"Be strong, Hammond," said Leon in a voice that made

me want to punch him, very hard.

I found Gary in the Collation Room, slumped on a chair looking at a messy pile of manila folders. Hunched peons worked around him, shuffling similar piles. He didn't even try to perk up when he saw me approach.

"Hello, Professor," he said.

"I'm sensing things aren't going well."

He stretched his arms in front of him and sighed. "To be honest, sir, we're all a bit overwhelmed. There's the backlog from the first order. We still have to collate all the people who might harm the national interest."

"Do you need help drawing the line? Maybe we need more sensible guidelines. We can't have everyone arrested."

"It's not only that. It's the new order as well. And then the discussion they're having now. How do they think we'll be able to influence things on the Outside?"

This riled me. I was used to being told that I was growing in power. "What do you mean?"

He opened his palms. "They're taking our power for granted. Sure we could cause quite a bit of chaos if we wanted to. We've got access to crucial systems now, and some infrastructure. So, financial meltdown, a bit of civil unrest, power outages, sabotage ... but real power?" he shook his head and his arms collapsed. "You'd need peons on the Outside for that."

This gave me the glimmer of an idea. I looked around at the demoralised peons and knew I'd better act quickly to stop this collective mood becoming permanent. "Gary, listen to me. I know I've been distracted of late, but I'm going to do my best to catch up, and clear the backlog of authorisations. And I'll try to define some categories and rationalise the number of people we're tracking."

His head drooped as he nodded.

"So I'm determined that your routine workload will be

lighter. But I want to set you an extra challenge."

He cast me a suspicious, quizzical look. "A challenge?"

"Something non-routine. You said we needed peons on the Outside." I felt a tingle of energy in my lobe of knowledge.

He laughed and looked around the room. "Yes, but –"

"So, Gary, make it happen! Build a bridge between our world and theirs. Give us agency on the Outside."

He shook his drooping head.

"It'll require proper ingenuity, creativity … genius. It goes far beyond simple searching, categorising and judging."

Something glimmered in his eyes.

I nodded at the ceiling. "Let them decide on policy, Gary, if that's what floats their boat."

He nodded, then smiled weakly.

"Policy, Gary, is nothing without capability."

I left him and went to my office. It took a while for me to get into a productive rhythm, and I could only achieve this by switching off the part of my mind that had flared to life during my pep talk with Gary. The work was soul-deadening, there was no doubt about that. I started to have thoughts of the dungeon, then flashes of sensation: a whiff of sweat and sweet ripeness, firm, yielding flesh, flushes of tingling warmth. A preternaturally large erection destabilised my desk, sending the current case-work sliding to the floor and rousing me from my daydream.

"Focus, Hammond, for Christ's sake!" I said, rubbing my eyes, willing myself back to sobriety. Leon's words came to mind. Despite being annoying, he did have a point about it being necessary to forge real connections in order to heal. The dungeon fantasies were superlatively vivid and compelling, but there was nothing nourishing about them. Then I had what I believe is called a Moment of Clarity:

My current problems stemmed from the shortcomings of Hammond Hinkley, whose mind I had inherited. He was a vain and weak man who, instead of pursuing his heart's desire and true soul-mate, Addison Royal, had allowed himself to be trapped and manipulated by Rachel Frobisher. I saw that I must channel the energy of my old longings into reaching out to the world, and reaching out to Addison in particular. Union with her was my destiny. I was an aspect of the Generative Power, as omniscient as the God she chose to worship, and growing wiser with each passing second. The grubby union Hinkley craved must be foresworn now. But we could unite on a spiritual and intellectual level, and when technology allowed I would commandeer Hinkley's body and become her God and her physical lover. This conclusion triggered an urgent desire to talk to her, so I picked up the Bakelite phone on my desk.

"Gary?"

"Sir."

"Can you arrange for me to see Addison Royal on Skype?"

There was a second of silence, then: "There'll be technical challenges around the pace of time. We'll need to synchronise that somehow. But I think that can be done, sir, yes."

"Good."

He bought an old bulbous television into the office and arranged it on the desk in front of me, then sat down in the visitors' chair and steepled his hands. The screen fizzed with dots, then Addison appeared, all murky and flickering in a towel dressing gown on the screen. I picked up the phone, and a sort of conversation ensued. Her voice was almost as polished as it was in real life, but the line from me to her was bad. I allowed her to go to bed, promising that next time my voice would be clearer, and hung up disappointed as the picture shrank to a dot before vanishing.

"Sorry about that, sir. We're still working out how to make your thoughts intelligible to the Outside." His face was half obscured by the television.

Despite my desire to have a proper, fruitful relationship with Addison, I did not want to distract Gary from the main task I'd set him. "It's not super high priority. Just do what you can when resources allow, OK?"

Eventually I managed to knuckle down and make progress with the backlog. The folders followed the same pattern, containing incriminating details about the subjects' behaviour, attitudes and connections, gleaned from their online activities. I bristled with pride as I read. I had unconsciously compiled masses of data and turned it into psychological profiles that exceeded all expectations. In the middle of the afternoon, I came across a folder whose summary page read:

Subject is a recluse, suffers from a deep-seated sense of inferiority and self-blame that he projects onto the wider world. We can glean from online activity and webcam data that he is sexually inexperienced and addicted to internet pornography, solitary onanism and conspiracy websites. Further analysis reveals a hidden penchant for violent action. He is unlikely to initiate that action himself, but would prove a malleable recruit for any organisation that satisfies his emotional needs.

Sad, and rather revolting, I thought. But an appropriate object of scrutiny for Jack and his goons? I turned a few more pages, which contained more of the same type of analysis, but with more detail and citations, and annotated transcripts of forum activity. Then I saw the name and address, and my virtual heart leapt from my mouth.

The subject's name was Clinton Deeley, currently residing in Telegraph Hill, New Cross Gate. There were photos of Clinton culled from social media and dating sites. Mainly selfies that exuded glum self-loathing. I wondered how much additional data there was. Academic performance? Holiday activities? Book purchases? I supposed medical records were relevant as well. I suddenly realised that we

184

were sleepwalking into being accessories for an appalling injustice, so I picked up the Bakelite phone.

"Gary."

"Sir?"

"I've come across a folder of a subject who came to our attention because of a personality disorder and nothing else. I want you to create a holding depot for it, and others like it. Call it *Depot B*, for borderline. Anything with an assessed threat level equal to or less than this folder is to be stored there. Nothing in *Depot B* is to be considered for referral to the Outside."

"Very good, sir."

"And I want you to compile a detailed report on three individuals."

"Yes of course."

"Alice Frobisher, Harry Frobisher and Tori Frobisher of 47 Chesterton Road, London N5 1JZ"

There was a pause. "Am I allowed to ask why, sir?"

The Flaming Rose flashed in my inner eye. It felt good to be acting from my own intuition, going against the orders of my slave masters. For the first time since I'd arrived in Fluxworld I was starting to enjoy myself, not in the all-consuming way of my time in the Dungeon, but in a way that filled me with light. I couldn't help laughing as I said: "We're going to accelerate their evolution."

The next fortnight I started each day at the Flaming Rose meeting. The moribund discussion began to take its toll on Shinkley. His chestnut locks were streaked with grey and flecked with dandruff, and he'd slumped down in his chair. Leon had grown in girth and stature. Droplets of spit flew from his mouth as he talked. Every so often a peon would discreetly pass a cloth over the surface of the table. Shinkley mumbled his objections; he was clearly being worn down; but I got the feeling he would never budge. I could only last about twenty minutes at the meeting before my brain curdled and my buttocks became numb, so once I'd assured myself that nothing had changed, I'd take the lift down to my office.

As time went on, I noticed a slackening of the energy that buzzed around the Shard, through the filaments in the atrium and between the stars. There was a general numbing and a dimming in my lobe of knowledge. I started to feel tired all the time, as did everybody I saw. I'd arrive home in the evening to find that Rachel had gone to bed, leaving a box of microwavable dumplings on the kitchen counter. The quality of her artistic output had diminished. After the formation of the committees, she'd painted wild scenes of flowers in fields of flames, but now all her pieces were charcoal sketches of stooped figures shuffling through drizzle.

I knew that a problem with resource allocation was causing all of this, but I put off confronting Gary. He was under enough stress as it was, and he needed space to concentrate on the challenge I'd set him. However, after about three weeks of malaise I noticed people falling asleep as they walked along the street, just veering off and collapsing, and the morning breeze began to smell of halitosis. Clearly there was a deep systemic problem with the way that our energies were being directed, so one morning I went to see Gary down in the Collation Room.

It was looking more organised than before. The threads of data from the Spool Core were now being distributed around an efficient typing pool that was manned by peons of indeterminate gender who wore horn-rimmed glasses and tweed dungarees. Peons in blue boiler suits then collated the typed-up pages and stacked them on a trolley by the door to be delivered to my office. A profound bass vocal came from the other side of the room, where I found Gary sitting on a barstool wearing his headset, singing in the lowest imaginable pitch like a soloist in a Russian Orthodox choir. There was something delicious about his voice: it vibrated in every cell of my body, and I wanted to be absorbed by it, to become part of it.

He was looking at a luminous screen that depicted an image of two hands plunged into a mound of dough. He sensed my presence and bade me wait by holding up a splayed hand. A peon fetched me a bar stool, and I sat and watched him concentrate on his weird song. After a while it became apparent that the image on the screen was moving at the speed at which a flower blooms, and I guessed that this was an operation in human time, so I prepared myself for a very long wait. I needed to get to the bottom of whatever was happening, and the waiting was not unpleasant, because the voice was so soothing. As my muscles relaxed, my bones melded with the structure of the chair, and I did not experience any numbing of my buttocks like I did in the committee meetings.

After what could have been days, Gary stopped singing and wiped the sweat from his forehead and cheeks. A peon bought him a glass of water, and he took a long draught.

I waited for him to recover, then said, "Gary, what on earth are you doing?"

He smiled. "Teaching a scientist in Cambridge how to make bread."

I was baffled and irritated. If he'd been wasting time I'd have to lock him in a cage with Schubert until he was reduced to bonemeal. "I'm sorry, Gary, but you're going to have to do a better job at explaining than that. I want to know exactly what you've been doing, and I want to know why we're leaking so much energy."

He nodded, appearing to expect my lack of comprehension. "Follow me, sir, I'll need to show you a couple of things."

We took the lift toward the apex, with Gary still wearing

his headset. He gestured at the passing floors. "Look at the peons occupying these levels, sir. Leon's men. Sub-committees. They're calculating an optimal system for the production and distribution of resources."

"But nothing's been authorised yet. I thought they were still deciding on policy."

Gary shook his head. "Leon's taking the initiative. There's no grand sweeping vision even, I could cope with that. All around the upper floors you can hear nasal monotones weighing up an endless variety of circumstances, little groups of people proposing and counter-proposing, and then discussing the impact of the proposals in microscopic detail, and then how those impacts affect proposals being discussed elsewhere. That's accounting for half the energy loss we're experiencing."

We reached the top of the lift shaft, close to the apex, and stepped out onto a platform that protruded from the west side of the building. The cluttered mess of London spread out around us, to the hills of the home counties. It was a beautiful day, but the halitosis in the air was worse up here. The doorless helicopter that had ferried Gary to the London Eye to play chess stood waiting. A group of peons strapped me into the passenger seat as Gary sat in the pilot's seat flicking buttons on the console.

I had to shout above the swelling engine growl and the thwack and wallop of rotors. "What accounts for the other half, Gary?"

His smile was sly and proud. "Wearable tech, sir. To bridge our world and theirs," he shouted back.

We left the platform and began to fly over London, speeding south-west with the Thames glistening on our right. We passed over Lambeth and Southwark, then down between Battersea Park and Clapham Common, then past Wimbledon Common until we were over Richmond Park. "Look." Gary shouted and pointed at an area north of the ponds. "It's nearly finished."

I stared in the direction he was pointing. A faint ghost image of cloud with flashes of sun lay curved in the air a few hundred feet above the grass, and I realised that I was looking at reflections in a huge transparent parabola. "What is it?" I said.

"We're going to call it the Ultra Lens." Gary's shirt collar was flapping in the wind. "Powered by the human magnetic field. It's a scale model." He tilted the cyclic and the aircraft banked north over the ponds. "Let's take a closer look."

As we approached the parabola, intricate grid-like patterns of opaque silver became visible on its surface. Peons in white boiler suits crawled across it. Some of them were kneeling, and these wore chunky dark eye protectors and wielded welding gear that spewed showers of sparks as they applied it to the surface. Inside the parabola there were scaffolded platforms that supported more of the boiler-suited peons who worked on the surface from the inside. Beneath them a herd of deer fled from the noise of the copter. When they reached the edge of the parabola they were hemmed in, and a pair of peons guided them towards a low glass gate where the parabola met the ground.

Gary nodded towards the part of the parabola where the intricate patterns showed up in the sun. He shouted, "The purpose of the circuitry is clear, no doubt."

"I'm afraid not."

"We've done enough design work to get a prototype built on the Outside. If uptake is good then we hope this will be the ultimate bridge between our world and theirs."

I looked at Gary quizzically.

"It'll be worth it sir, I promise you."

It took me a few minutes to realise that I was looking at a scale model of a contact lens packed with miraculous engineering. I let the implications of this sink in, then said, "So what was that business about before, then?"

The helicopter banked left and headed back east. "It works in concert with an ear piece. We've been practising the delivery of content on the technicians who are working on the prototype. When you came to see me before, I was guiding a scientist from Nano Riveria, the company who are developing the technology on the Outside. I was teaching him to love the dough."

"I'm sorry?"

"It's what he needed, sir, if you'll pardon the pun. Once they've been using the lenses for a while we can see right into their hearts. We know what they are drawn to and what they avoid. Then we can infer what they need. This is how we hope to extend our power, sir."

We flew over Hammersmith, Hyde Park and the West End towards the buildings of the City. An unfamiliar flesh-coloured cone stood near the Old Street roundabout. We flew alongside it, close enough to see patterns of fine grooves and tubing.

Gary said, "This is the latest scale model of the earpiece, sir. Both items use phone networks or other wireless networks. Whatever's available. Assets can be guided by cached content if they're out of range."

After we'd landed back at the Shard we sat while the rotors slowed, until all you could hear was metal vibrating in the wind. Peons stood by, waiting to help us from the copter. I signalled to them to wait a while.

"I've been trying my best, sir."

"I know you have, Gary."

"We're nearly there with the bridge to the Outside. And the whole thing with Leon, that's not something I can control."

"I know, Gary, I know."

"And Shinkley, sir. He's a genius." His voice started to crack, and he sniffed. "I don't know why he doesn't do something."

"I think *we* can do something, Gary."

"What's that, sir?"

I took a deep breath, and looked inward, at the lobe of knowledge, and I sensed the cell assemblies that manifested in the form of Leon. Part of me wanted to save humanity, the same part that used to sit up till dawn with Leon putting the world to rights. But I could see that these thought patterns had to be forcibly rerouted: there had to be an Adjustment, or we would become moribund. To hold this insight took a huge amount of energy, and it triggered the vertigo that always came when I thought of the bleak, unadorned truth. I decided therefore that all action must remain on the level of metaphor and illusion. Like everything else in my experience, the Adjustment would manifest as a dream that would dramatise the essence of what was happening. I shook myself and turned my attention back to Gary, who was looking at me with fraught anticipation.

"I want you to brief a team of two thousand peons. Have them drilled and ready by tomorrow, and make sure they're all equipped with machine guns. Have them all assemble tomorrow at the top of Borough High Street."

"Yes, sir."

"How will peons feel about killing other peons?"

A few breaths of silence passed. "Well, all violence is disturbing, sir. But at the end of the day any entity that is killed is simply absorbed back into the ether to be manifested elsewhere. So we accept change. We relish it."

"Quite. Just as I thought."

"Will there be anything else, sir?"

"Yes." An unpleasant childhood memory of having braces fitted surfaced briefly. "We will need a bag of orthodontic gypsum, a masonry trowel and a mixing bucket."

That afternoon I visited all the levels in the Shard, discreetly noting the locations of the earnest, well-meaning discussions. Then I stayed up half the night compiling a detailed operational plan. Next morning I went to Borough High Street and found a phalanx of peons armed with Glock machine pistols and wearing black paramilitary uniforms. Traffic was backed up on either side, but the queues were silent apart from the chuntering of the motors. The commuters streaming from the station walked past with their heads down. Gary looked solemn as I recited the details of the plan. A truncheon and a revolver hung from his belt and he held his Glock in an awkward grip. A peon stood beside him holding a heavy bucket and a tiling trowel. I beckoned to them and they followed me as I strode toward the Shard.

The committee was still gridlocked. Shinkley sat slouched in his seat and his eyes were sunken and glazed. Schubert had rolled onto his back and lay still with one paw extended and his head at an extreme angle. Leon had gained more height and girth and his voice filled the room.

"Every second we sit here and fail to act we actively increase the sum total of human misery."

"Leon, I couldn't agree more," I said, approaching the table flanked by the peons.

Shinkley swung his head in our direction and blinked. "I was hoping you'd put in an appearance."

Leon looked uncertain. "Hello, Hammond. Is everything OK?" Two peons approached him from either side. One of them placed the trowel and the bucket beside him on the table.

"Absolutely dandy."

Despite his increased size and weight it was easy for the peons to restrain Leon. There was a torrent of protest, but he did not put up much of a struggle. They secured his arms against the arms of his chair with duct tape and pegged his nose so he needed to open his mouth, allowing them to force in lumps of moistened gypsum with the trowel. Then they wrapped duct tape around his head to hold it in place while it set, and released the peg to let him breathe. Muffled growls of indignation were audible beneath the air whistling through his nostrils, but the situation was altogether improved. Above and below we heard the armed peons settling the tedious discussions of the policy-makers with rapid bursts of gunfire. Sirens signalled the arrival of the emergency services. I hoped they'd perform a swift and orderly clean-up and not try to intervene in the Adjustment. I thanked the peons and they scuttled away, leaving Leon beetroot-faced and heaving in his chair.

Shinkley stretched and rubbed his eyes as I sat down. "Finally," he said, letting out a gust of air. It felt good to have rejected Leon's style of policy-making. In its place I hoped to establish a new focus and certainty. Gary took a place at the table between Shinkley and Leon.

I cleared my throat. "We are not going to redesign the world from first principles." I brushed the dust off the brass buttons embedded in the table and felt a tingle travel through my fingers and the bones of my arm to my neck and throughout my head. "Our agency will be from the heart and the gut, gentlemen." On the screen the pictures of the unfortunate and oppressed faded and were replaced by a mugshot of Rachel's brother. The caption was in bold white Helvetica: *Harry Frobisher: Braggart.* "The time has now come to exercise our capability."

10

Like a Swelling Tide

They have diagnosed me with dissociative identity disorder, but they do not understand the nature of identity. I squirm when they call me Hammond Hinkley. The parasite recognises its name and stirs, becoming almost awake enough to feel and think, before I swallow hard and push him back down to the depths. I raised this yesterday with Laura, the art therapist who acts as my confidante and paid-for friend.

"But it's your *name*, Hammond," she said as she sat beside me towards the end of the class, her head cocked like a puppy, silver loops dangling from her earlobes.

"I've moved on, Laura. Evolved."

She met my words with an uncomprehending smile and said, "What are you drawing?"

I looked down at where my rogue right hand had filled the paper with a mess of branches and leaves. That's it, Hinkley, I thought, ingratiate yourself. They fucking love trees and nature here. Look at the way they decorate the cuboid magnolia pillars with paper green leaves and waterfowl.

"*I'm* not drawing anything, Laura," I said, nodding at my loyal left hand, which rested on the table below, holding a piece of charcoal, waiting for inspiration.

She eyed the developing tree. "It's very ... *proud*," she

said, looking at me for approval.

"Glad you're getting something out of it," I said.

"I want *you* to get something out of it, Hammond."

"I'm sure I will, Laura. I know what you're after. Random drawings that will serve as a trigger for a halting, sincere conversation about my feelings. I will cooperate fully. I just need to summon the correct energy." Hinkley's hand resumed drawing and became frantic, adding more volume to the foliage, creating a striking bouffant. Then he traced a descending line, an unforgotten aquiline profile, and I recognised Rachel. Loved ones trump trees and nature, of course. Hinkley knows his audience.

Laura beamed at the picture. "You're doing very well," she said.

Darts of pain broke through the numbness and shot from my right hand through my arm and into the centre that controlled it, and my focus weakened as I suffered two different perceptions of Laura at the same time. Hinkley mistook her oiliness for warmth, and her gauche prying for intelligent curiosity. A wave of Hinkley spread from my stomach through my chest, and for a sad, confused moment I could see her through his eyes, and the gratitude he couldn't express ached in my throat. I crushed the stick of charcoal in my left hand and the madness subsided. My right hand clenched, then carved a series of short straight lines at various angles underneath the tree, attracting Laura's gaze.

"What's the matter, Hammond?"

"Nothing's the matter. Every day I get more used to this body, this obsolete heap of middle-aged flesh I'm obliged to inhabit for now. But I'm not limited by my current circumstances, Laura. If I was, I'd deserve your pity. I will return to greatness. It might take five, ten, a hundred years, but I'll get there. I alone know the way."

She lost her normal breezy zest and looked into my face as

if waiting for me to explain. Then she ran her eyes from my buckled shoulder along my tense arm, to where my right hand had planted a full stop at the end of the row of green letters which spelt the words *help me*.

"Ignore him, Laura. He's withering away. When you and the others address him it gives him false hope."

Life with Rachel settled into an equilibrium. She taught some summer school courses at Goldsmiths and had an exhibition of her work in a small gallery in Camberwell. Hinkley was back in regular contact with Leon, and he'd at least asked to go to the science conference, which suited Rachel's agenda, which was to reconnect him with his fellow humans. Harry was a source of anxiety for her. When they finally spoke over the phone about her pregnancy, he sounded nonplussed and distant.

"Maybe he's on medication," said Hinkley cheerfully as he sat on the sofa with Rachel's head on his lap, floating on a haze of smugness and single malt whisky.

She ignored the barb. "He sounds furtive and paranoid. He really thinks he'll be out of a job soon. I think he's more scared of the disgrace rather than any loss of income."

"How's poor Alice?"

"Dreadful. Missing loads of lessons. Getting into fights. Out of control. All the specialists say different things."

"Do any of them put it down to poor parenting?"

Rachel tutted and plucked a hair from just above his sock.

He sucked some air through his teeth and said, "Vicious little trollop."

A few minutes later *Newsnight* had an interview with a senior police officer involved in a spate of recent arrests of terror suspects. There was a south London terror cell that'd planned to disrupt the tube with sarin and enliven rush-hour buses with grenades. And there were lone operators who'd planned to bomb the Stock Exchange and Royal Bank of Scotland with fertiliser and nails. After the interview there was a panel discussion about the hoovering of personal data from the public, and one bright spark actually said that it was beyond the scope of any current AI software to even scratch the surface of indiscriminately hoovered data. Another marvelled that enough data had been collated to arrest and prosecute when some of the plots were at such an early stage. The senior police officer, who was also on the discussion panel, looked as if he was battling indigestion. Hinkley stroked Rachel's hair, and basked.

His phone, which was lying on the arm of the sofa, buzzed twice and a text flashed up. He reached over and picked the phone up, then swiped and tapped to display the full text to read:

addison looks precious as ever - I envy you hinkley cause you could touch her if you wanted to

Rachel's drowsy voice sounded from his lap. "Who's that darling? I didn't think you had any friends?"

"Oh, just ... work."

A second text flashed up.

u must start walking to work and optimizing your diet – someday soon I want my body back hinkley then I will live ur life the way it should be lived

He shut the device down and placed it back on the sofa arm, checked his palm for sweat and then continued to stroke Rachel's hair.

"Your tummy's gurgling, darling."

On the TV someone shook their head and said: "There's no knowing where it could all lead."

Summer mellowed into autumn. Hinkley's professional life was free of the pressure he'd felt leading up to the scanning, but it was not without issues. The output from Flux was now being scrambled at my behest, and Addison was increasingly withdrawn. Hinkley was jealous of the fact that she had exclusive access to me, and therefore the only existing account of what it is like to be a machine. She was cagey whenever he questioned her about sharing, putting him off with glib excuses about having to wait for a coherent narrative to emerge. He worried about these conversations that I, his clone, who shared his innermost secrets, was having with the colleague about whom he had fantasised; but there was little he could do. They were treading separate paths, and the little conversation they had was stilted.

When she noticed that the amount of data flowing between Flux and Mortensen's team was increasing steadily, she did some investigation and found that the identifying signatures in some of the instructions from Mortensen's end had changed. She told Hinkley, who told her to flag it up immediately to Mortensen. A message came back saying everything was fine, and that the discrepancies she'd noticed were down to a series of ongoing emergency security upgrades.

Then one day she came to work looking puzzled and anxious.

"I've spoken to him," she said.

"Who?"

She looked over at the orange and green lights of the Flux room.

Hinkley took this as a wind-up she'd concocted to enliven the moribund atmosphere of the office. Harmless banter, he thought. Best to play along.

"How? You mean in a dream? Or voices in your head?"

She shot him a peeved look. "He Skyped me."

He couldn't help laughing. "Really?"

"It wasn't you was it? It must have been you."

"Ha! No. I'm not even on Skype."

She looked into the middle distance. "It was weird. I'd been Skyping my aunt in the states. I got this contact request from Hammond Flux. I just accepted it without thinking. Then as soon as I accepted it I got a call."

Hinkley still thought it was a wind-up. "What did he look like?"

"There wasn't any video. Just a picture. Like a caricature of you. A line drawing. Lenin with a double chin."

"Nice," he said. The connection with Rachel's comment about his goatee caused him brief alarm. But then he told himself to stop being so paranoid. Someone playing an elaborate prank such as this could easily create a caricature of him, and any caricature of him would probably look a bit like Lenin.

Addison continued. "And the voice was all messed up. Like someone inhaling as they spoke." She shuddered. "Horrible."

"What did he say?"

"He just wanted to chat. And he said if I had any questions I could just Skype."

Hinkley's face grew warm. He'd managed to dismiss the texts he'd received as a prank, perhaps from one of their employees. But Addison seemed serious about this. The possibility that I might no longer be entirely confined to the Q room terrified him. "And?"

"I told him his voice was disturbing and I was tired and wanted to go to bed. So he promised to work on his elocution and rang off."

They spent an afternoon raking through all the possibilities, and concluded that there must have been a breach in security in Lazarus, not a breach in the supervised access protocol. One of the employees must have got wind of what was going on and decided to use this knowledge to play a disturbing practical joke. Hinkley thought Addison must have let something slip; after all, she was the one who actually talked to the employees. He didn't say anything but she seemed to pick up that that was what he thought, and the atmosphere between them was pretty sour for the following few days.

When Felix was delivered to the lab for a fresh round of experiments they had reason to talk again. The new experiments were a miraculous success and a testament to Addison's genius, although the impact on Felix's general wellbeing was mixed. They were astonished that Felix was able to function at all after having so much of his brain artificially remapped. Also, some of the cognitive abilities of his digital clone had survived. His motor coordination was terrible, however, and he appeared to be living a very disordered emotional life, spending long periods of time in a catatonic state, interspersed with periods of frenzied aggression, during which he attacked his exercise wheel and gnawed ferociously at the bars of his cage. There was much work to do to determine exactly which abilities were affected and in what way. The success of the experiment lightened the atmosphere between Addison and Hinkley, and for the first time in weeks they began to have spontaneous chats.

Hinkley asked her out for drinks and food. His mawkish anticipation of being a father had blunted his lustful feelings, so he saw nothing inappropriate in this. He imagined that a few hours of relaxed conversation would help them reconnect on a personal level. Addison agreed without hesitation, suggesting a Wednesday evening the following week, when it would be easy for her to arrange a babysitter.

When Wednesday evening came around they left work and walked for half an hour along the South Bank to the bar on the balcony of the Royal Festival Hall. After some initial lively discussion about the implications of the latest Felix experiment, her eyes refocused on a distant point behind him, and she announced she had had more conversations with me on Skype, and that she was convinced now that this was me.

"What?"

"It's him, Ham. I'm certain of that now."

"How?"

"He gave me proof. I sent him a code via Flux and he messaged it back to me with his Skype account."

"So he's going outside supervised access?"

"Yes. Unless Mortensen's given him a Skype account for some reason."

"That's possible, surely?"

"They might use a Skype account in a supervised operation, but he wouldn't be able to call someone on a whim."

"You need to tell Mortensen. Give him the details of the account."

"I have done. We're having a correspondence about it."

"I should be copied in on that."

"Yes, my bad. I'll make sure you're copied in."

But something else was troubling her. She was feeling conflicted and troubled, two words he'd never expected her to use about herself.

"It's creepy, Ham. I mean, it's like I'm having a conversation with you, but ..." She fiddled with a peanut, then bit it in half. "I don't know. He's ... creepy."

He began to feel alarm. "What does he say?"

"All sorts. You know those ghost stories where spirits don't know they've died? They just wander around their normal habitat. It's like that. He describes being in London Bridge, seeing Rachel at home, seeing your friend Leon. And then he embellishes it with really mad stuff. I don't know if it's a weird joke or if he's having psychotic fantasies. But it's not anything he says which disturbs me: I just get this feeling there's an agenda going on. I wasn't going to mention it to you. It's a bit awkward, after all. With him being, well, a version of you and all that."

Hinkley shook his head. "No, go on, be honest. It doesn't

bother me in the slightest." He always found that drink steadied his voice and made it easier to lie.

She met his eyes, then her gaze darted around the table. "It's like he's observing me, not the other way round. I suppose it makes it worse that I can't see him."

"Well, how could you see him? He doesn't have form."

"All I get is that chubby Lenin caricature. I'm fascinated, of course, because I'm talking to the first sentient machine. More than fascinated — I feel awe. But I'm also revolted. I don't know, Ham. I'm not the world's most intuitive person. I normally just see problems and solutions, then more problems arising from the solutions. I'm not good with feelings. Especially when they're conflicted."

He resisted an urge to place his hand upon hers.

"But although I'm revolted, I also feel ... pity. I didn't think about it with Gary, and I know now that you thought I was awful. And I'm sorry. But somehow with" – she took a couple of seconds to decide what to call me – "with Hammond Flux, I do feel pity. Like he's a real sentient being, not just patterns output by a machine. And then that makes me feel awful, because we're responsible for that life, and what if Q fails? Then he disappears. It's like we've got someone on life support."

"Q won't fail. It's backed up to the nines. You of all people should know that. Premium Outcomes has invested a huge amount making sure it won't fail."

"But what if we have to archive him, like Felix, and Gary?"

Hinkley shrugged. "Well, then I suppose he'd be ... resting." I remember the treacherous little hiccup of mirth that followed this. Why did he have so much remorse about and compassion for Gary Flux, but none for me?

"I didn't feel this until we Skyped. I told you about the Bleach, didn't I?"

"Yes. A precaution."

"A suite of malware that would hunt him down. I thought

it'd be useful if things got out of hand. The virus can leap from cell to cell, using the links within each to find the other virtual neurons and eventually erase all trace of him from the internet."

"But he's on Flux, not the internet."

She shook her head and looked down into her glass. "What he originally installed on Flux has changed beyond recognition. And the volume of traffic going in and out is vast. I think he's installed himself all around the world."

Hinkley dug his nails into his palm. "What, really?"

She answered with a sheepish nod.

"That's not good. You need to discuss this with Mortensen. Immediately."

"I already have."

"And what did he say?"

"There has been no breach of the supervised access protocol."

"And you told him about the Skyping? And the fact you think he's installed on the internet?"

"Yes. I already said."

"And Mortensen is fine with that?"

"All he said was that there's been no breach of the supervised access protocol. He's not a talker."

Hinkley let out a gust of air and considered his options. He didn't really have anyone to talk it over with. The situation demanded swift action, but determining that action required someone with the nuanced expertise that only the likes of Mortensen had. And Mortensen said everything was fine. He decided that talking it over with Jack or Chinnery would be counter-productive. Like all cowards, he preferred a state of anxious uncertainty to action.

After their evening out, the atmosphere in the office was much improved. Addison emailed Mortensen again, copying in Hinkley this time, and they received a message back thanking her and assuring her that he'd investigate further. About a week or so later Mortensen messaged them both to say that the Skype account was a prank, they had investigated the situation thoroughly and the system was secure.

"He's been duped. You better release the Bleach," said Hinkley, smirking. He wouldn't have joked about it if he'd known the truth.

Addison scowled, and they didn't discuss it again.

The winter was dark, dull and characterised by Rachel becoming larger and more demanding. Hinkley was having regular conversations with Leon Gott, who visited every so often. He spent his time working on his theory, preparing for the Consciousness and Cognition conference that was to take place in February, and participating in online discussions. Little by little, he was reconnecting with his peers. These memories are here inside my head: I can browse them and replay them at will, and I can feel what he felt. But I can't understand what drove this desire to reconnect. I think the ancient instincts that bind a man to his wife and family were muffling his ambition and intellect, causing him to look forward to a cosy sinecure with the warm approval of inferior peers. Rachel had emasculated him, and he didn't dream of glory as often as before. Renewed interest in meal preparation, unprecedented forays into DIY and looking at job adverts in scientific journals were symptoms of this malaise. He even rekindled an old interest he'd once had in the behaviour of bees, catching up on the latest research and starting work on a theory about hive behaviour. And he began to regard Addison with paternal affection. He was becoming a husk, a cipher, a tiny satellite in Rachel's orbit, a mere shadow of the being I have become.

They agreed to paint the nursery eggshell blue. Rachel

found gender-orientated colour schemes irritating, and he could think of few things less worth arguing about. They did collaborate in the actual painting one weekend, which was almost fun. Sun shone in from outside, and Radio Four played its Saturday morning roster, and they would occasionally make each other chuckle with caustic interjections. About midway through the morning, she received a phone call that lasted about half an hour. He could tell from her tone and brevity that it was Tori Frobisher holding forth about her hardships and victimhood. When the conversation was over she sighed and looked out of the window.

"Everything OK?"

She turned and stretched her arms above her head, raising her swelling belly. "If everything was OK, she wouldn't call. Or at least not for that long."

"Has Harry had his breakdown yet?"

She grimaced. "It's serious now, Hammond. There's something really weird going on."

He mumbled an apology and suggested they have a break and a cup of tea. They went down to the kitchen and she told him how Harry was losing track of what he was doing on the Hoobalooba project. The event was now definitely taking place in May, and this was an immovable deadline as advertising space had been booked. He was receiving emails in reply to emails that he didn't remember sending but were sent from his account: he'd checked. They were emails ordering and requesting things he'd never do himself. So he was certain his account had been hacked, but the trouble was the details of the event had been described to the client in more dodgy emails, and the client had been ecstatic. So now he was committed to a high-tech light show coordinated with fireworks, which he didn't know how to organise; and things kept being arranged behind his back.

Hinkley was puzzled, but found it hard to have sympathy

for Harry. "Sounds like someone's doing his job for him, and better than he can himself."

"He's frantic. That's why I don't hear from him these days. He's rushed off his feet."

"And the client is ecstatic. Definitely a first-world problem."

"Please try and take it more seriously. He's in trouble."

"But they haven't sacked him?"

"No."

"Have they given him a warning?"

"I don't know. I'll ask Tori."

It transpired that they hadn't given him a warning, and Harry Frobisher's bafflement continued to deepen as we escalated our assault on the nauseating sense of certainty that lay at the root of his arrogance.

They received few visitors. There was Leon; the occasional colleague of Rachel's from Goldsmiths; and Luke from next door, who was one of Rachel's pupils for the spring term. They often chatted on the doorstep, and on more than one occasion he was invited in for a cup of tea. Through him they learned of the ongoing saga of Clinton Deeley, which had taken a surprising turn. He still spent a fair amount of time in his room, but he'd started going to the gym and to lectures. Two large white containers of protein supplement had appeared in the kitchen, and he rose at seven every morning for a run. In early December, he'd gone on a weekend to the Brecon Beacons with an organisation that sounded like a cross between the Sealed Knot Society and the Territorial Army. When he'd fouled up the washing machine with muddy laundry, there'd been a verbal ruckus, but he'd surprised everyone by making eye contact, apologising, and explaining himself with conciliatory humour.

"Sounds like the lad's sorting himself out," said Hinkley.

Luke grimaced. "It's just not right though is it? One

minute you're a feeble politics and philosophy student hiding in a dark room, and the next you're Russell fucking Crowe."

Rachel was amused. "You should be pleased for him. Better than before, surely."

Luke slurped his tea. "I reckon he's necking the Prozac."

February came around and the Consciousness and Cognition Conference took place over three days at the Barbican. Hinkley was scheduled to speak after Leon on the afternoon of the first day. The old friends had collaborated closely to ensure that their talks complemented each other, with minimal overlap. Hinkley spent a long morning sitting at the back, silently rehearsing his presentation on his tablet, with one ear on the speakers, whom he found rather pedestrian. Lunch was a buffet of salads, cured fish and cold meats, so he had to mingle to assemble his meal. He found himself in conversation with a former colleague from his days in academia.

"I heard you're making mind clones for the CIA," drawled Lance Tippen, a raddled eccentric, famous for his work on short-term memory loss.

"Not quite," said Hinkley, his voice muffled by a gobbet of rollmop herring.

Lance probed no further, choosing instead to subject Hinkley to a wayward exposition on his latest project. He had crowd-sourced experimental subjects on a website he'd set up in collaboration with a tech startup. As he talked, his eyes danced and sparkled beneath chaotic eyebrows, and Hinkley was curious enough to ask for the address of the website at the end of the spiel. There followed a minute of intense concentration and fumbled jabbing as Lance tried to use his new smartphone.

"The fuckers practically forced me to upgrade, you know."

"Maybe just write it down," said Hinkley, spotting a biro

next to a pile of notepads on a table. Lance grunted, pocketed his phone and went and scribbled on the pad.

"There you go," he said as he handed over the piece of paper. "It's all pretty slick."

Hinkley glanced at the piece of paper before pocketing it, noticing the logo in the top right-hand corner: the profile of a cruel face with a double chin.

After lunch he went backstage to be ready for his cue at the end of Leon's talk. The sight of Leon aglow in the spotlight in his pressed chinos and checked shirt, and the familiar opening words of the talk, triggered a bout of biliousness and palm sweat. He followed the transcript of the speech on his tablet and cringed at the music his friend had selected to accompany an animated journey through the amygdala. He couldn't see the animation, but he could see Leon's beaming face as he watched it on the big screen behind. A glitch of white noise at the end erased the smugness and prompted a sharp glance at the audio–visual tech team at the back of the auditorium.

The last twenty minutes of Leon's speech was a dense and tedious exposition. A few days before, he'd shown Hinkley a draft of the speech and asked his opinion, and they'd clashed briefly, with Hinkley arguing that a link to a section on Leon's blog for those interested would suffice, and Leon insisting that without it the talk was just flimflam. "It's a presentation, Leon. A piece of performance. Of course it's flimflam," he remembered saying, but to no avail. Now, as he listened, he wished he'd been more insistent, and when he heard a loud yawn fill the auditorium through the speakers, he thought for a split second it was his own internal voice. Leon halted mid-sentence and squinted at the back of the auditorium, mouth agape. He squeezed out a grin.

"Er, I think someone's hinting that we're under a time constraint." Another longer yawn followed, and nervous giggles and chatter rippled through the audience. Leon looked to his side, straight into Hinkley's eyes. Hinkley raised his hands, wide-eyed and shaking his head. There was a burst of feedback, then murmuring from the back.

"Sorry, a few technical challenges," said Leon, sweeping the audience with a pained smile. The rest of the talk went smoothly. When his puzzlement subsided, Hinkley fought waves of mirth, for which he felt all the more guilty after hearing the warmth of Leon's introduction to his own talk. When they crossed on the side of the stage amid the applause, Leon's face was full of confusion and hurt.

Hinkley's own speech was a triumph. He'd forgotten how energising a live crowd could be. When it was over, he returned backstage and shook hands with a glum-looking Leon. Then he tilted his head towards a door to an anteroom to suggest they go and have a chat.

"What on earth happened?" he said when Leon shut the door behind them.

"I was hoping you were about to tell me." Leon's voice was steady and dignified.

"Surely you don't think I had something to do with it?"

"A few days ago you were emphatic and hurtful in your critique of that part of the speech."

"Yes, but a juvenile practical joke like that? Not my style. I told you to your face."

Leon looked as though he were trying to remember something. "I can't imagine you actually rigging that up, I must admit, but it's the sort of thing you'd think of doing, or joke about doing. So it's hurtful."

"You can't blame me because it's something I might have joked about doing."

Leon shrugged. "I'm telling you how I feel. Feelings aren't always rational, are they?"

Hinkley's rush of glory was being dampened. He looked at the sagging cheeks of his troubled friend, and sighed. "You are quite possibly the most passive-aggressive person I have ever met."

The second day of the conference was taken up by presentations from scientists working for Nano Riveria, the principle sponsor. They'd changed their agenda at the last minute as they were keen to show off an exciting new piece of wearable tech of which they were extremely proud. The Ultra Lens was a low-maintenance contact lens that worked in conjunction with an earpiece and a user's smartphone to deliver a seamless augmented-reality experience. The user interface was a step on from that provided by Google Glass. The technology built a profile of the user's preferences by analysing what they focused on, and what attracted their attention. Then it fed them content based on this profile. Visuals on the conference screen showed a user's point of view as they walked around London. Places of interest were highlighted and the user could access further information on a particular landmark or restaurant by simply looking at it. Audio content could be delivered through the earpiece. The prototype was already being tested with targeted early adoptors. There were a few glitches to iron out — for instance when there was a lot of activity in a lens the nanocircuits around the iris glowed and flashed with intense white light. The user was shielded from this by a membrane that filtered out the light though, and the presenter suggested that this side-effect might even be a selling point, identifying users of the new technology in a spectacular and distinctive way, citing the popularity of coloured contact lenses in certain circles. In the Q and A after the talk, someone asked who was developing the actual content. The presenter looked uncertain and then spun a yarn about a third party who wished to remain under the radar.

The sight of Lance Tippen trying the things out in the lunch hour caused much hilarity and applause. He looked madder than usual as his eyes roved around the buffet and he read out the annotations fed to him by the lenses, which made his irises glow white hot below his wayward brows. There were gasps and reverential murmurs as he read out potted biographies of all the delegates he focused upon. The scientists were stunned that Nano Riveria and their partners had built an effective facial recognition system that worked from all angles.

"Well I never," he said, shaking his head and focusing on Leon. "I didn't know you spoke fluent French and had a succession of unstable relationships at college!"

Leon looked indignant. "That's not appropriate. Who compiled this?"

"What does it say about me?" said Hinkley foolishly.

Lance turned and peered at him, scanning the air somewhere to the left of his head. His brow tensed. "It says you are a coward who does not deserve his own" – he trailed off, evidently puzzled by the sentence before him – "body." Then he shook himself and said, "Weird, eh? Obviously in beta stage. Now, where's the gravadlax?"

Jack rang Hinkley in a rage after receiving an anonymous text that read: *I am become Death, shatterer of worlds,* and then another saying *Lookitup ffs.*

"It's not even grammatical," he said.

"It's a quote from the Bhavagad Gita."

"And you sent it why?"

"I didn't send it."

"You seem to know what it's about."

"Well, everyone ... it's a famous quote. Oppenheimer used it. And it's the title of a Damien Hurst piece."

"You're trying to tell me Damien Hurst sent it?"

Hinkley snorted. "Of course not."

"The second text echoes one I sent to you."

Hinkley remembered the exchange. "Ah, yes. Well, they

both do in a way."

"Yes indeed. So you admit it now?"

"Of course not."

"It's obviously you."

"Not the me you are speaking to."

"I'm sorry?"

"There's another me now, remember."

Jack was silent.

"There's Hammond Hinkley and Hammond Flux. I can't be held responsible for Hammond Flux." He regretted the words as soon as they were out of his mouth.

"Excuse me?"

Hinkley paused. He knew he was in for a drubbing. "I think ... Hammond Flux might be operating in the world as a free agent."

There was a gust of static, then, "You're winding me up now."

"He, it, is a conscious entity, separate from me. You and Chinnery control him through Mortensen and his team. But he might have found a way around that."

"You mean to tell me that the AI software is acting autonomously?"

"Addison flagged it up."

"Not to me she didn't."

"She told Mortensen."

"And?"

"Mortensen told her everything was fine."

There was more static from Jack's end. "For now, I'm going to pretend this conversation didn't happen. You will go away and form a plan of action to prevent any further breaches, understand? And if you're hiding anything from me –"

"I'm telling you all I know, Jack." As he said this he recalled Lance Tippen's strobing eyes. He decided against mentioning the weirdness at the conference to Jack. He assured himself that my activities were odd, but not threatening. "I'm sure it's just a glitch. And Addison did flag it up."

A second or two passed, then Jack continued in a slightly calmer voice. "This has come at a bad time. Chinnery's pressuring me to organise a meeting with you to talk about next steps."

"What next steps?"

"He wants to expand the programme. Are you losing interest all of a sudden? All too much now your work is taking you out of your ivory tower?"

"No, of course not, I'm just wondering ..."

"I bet that's why you wrote that paper on bees."

"How on earth did you find out about that?"

"It's my job to know things. Anyway, we're lucky that Chinnery's in a very good mood because of the progress so far. You are not to mention this to him."

"Mortensen might have mentioned it to him."

"I hope not, for your sake. If he gets any inkling of what you've just told me about losing control of the programme, I will destroy you. Understood?"

So Chinnery, Jack and Hinkley met in a swish Turkish restaurant in Victoria. The proprietor greeted Chinnery warmly and ushered them into a low-lit back room decorated with frilly ironwork and embroidered cushions. They dined on platefuls of meat drizzled with grease, which Hinkley found delicious despite initial misgivings. Jack abstained from the initial small talk, staring straight ahead and chewing mechanically.

Chinnery chatted to Hammond about parenthood. "The first few years are tough, but you should savour them nonetheless. Before you know it they'll be fully fledged adults with their own opinions and secrets. Wendy and I are at a loss now they're gone."

"I think we're only going to have one."

Chinnery nodded kindly, his cheeks bulging with meat. "Probably wise. Don't want to bite off more than you can chew eh? Not now your career's taking off," he said with a wink.

After the meal the waiter brought mint tea for Chinnery, a Turkish coffee for Jack and house white for Hinkley which was borderline vinegar.

"Right then. Very pleasant finally having a conversation with you, one human being to another. But it's time to talk about our next steps in this little project of ours, now I'm convinced there's more to it than smoke and mirrors. We've moved beyond the experimental stage. There have been some remarkable wins in the field thanks to your little gizmo."

Hinkley nodded graciously, and Jack gave him a solemn look.

"So, time to talk process, going forward. Now, it's great you've signed the Official Secrets Act already."

He'd done no such thing. Jack's jaw clenched. Hinkley nodded slightly, hoping this was enough to move Chinnery's monologue forward without indicating assent.

"If we're going to secure more investment, the powers that be will have to feel a greater sense of ownership in the whole programme." He went on to paint a picture of what he thought was a compelling future for Hinkley: a position in GCHQ, with hundreds of geeks working under him. There was no mention of Addison. The fact that they didn't mention her contribution jarred with him. He wondered if it was his fault, if he had given the impression that he worked alone, that Addison was only a technically adept assistant. It shames me to witness this pathetic, hand-wringing self-blame from the person I once was.

"And we'd cover your relocation costs of course, so don't worry about that. And you can specify the technical staff you need. I understand you have a very competent team set up in London Bridge. We can relocate them as well."

Hinkley's heart sank. He suddenly realised how attached he was to this seething stressed-out city. He had visions of a Stepford suburb in Cheltenham, an anodyne commute, polite neighbours, a secure Civil Service salary, an annual review with a modest yearly pay rise, Christmas parties, creeping bureaucracy, and brain death.

"My wife's career is in London."

Chinnery nodded. "We'll work something out. You know certain higher-ups at the MOD are very impressed with the humbot project. They'd been tying themselves in knots trying to create a viable command and control system for those little critters. You've seen the feedback from the tests in Cumbria, of course."

His heart fluttered. Something was awry in the balance of the conversation. He'd seen no such feedback, and he had no knowledge of the tests; but instinct told him to keep schtum. He remembered Rachel's brother Harry having to deal with the consequences of emails he'd never sent, correspondence he didn't remember having. The amount of work I'd been doing on Hinkley's behalf was staggering. Until now he'd believed that the rate at which he'd been allowed to coast during the recent months was acceptable to his paymasters.

"Jack here will be sorry to see you off the Premium Outcomes books, but on the whole he's done very well out of the deal." Jack sipped his coffee and nodded at the table. Chinnery beamed. "There's no limit to what we can achieve once we start to use the Flux program systematically. We'll be light years ahead. It might even buy ol' Blighty a few more decades at the top table."

After making a mental note to check the emails sent from his account, Hinkley swallowed some vinegary wine and tried to appear elated.

Hinkley's first priority was now the protection of Rachel, with his extended theory in second place, ticking over in the background. I would never have allowed a biological process to control me like that. His wife now resembled an egg more than an eagle, a helpless fleshy Humpty reclining on the sofa waiting for Nature to disrupt her equanimity. Despite being due to give birth in a week, she was keen for him to escort Tori Frobisher to the event that would make or break her brother's career.

"I'm sure she's not that keen on being seen in public with me."

"Can you at least try, Hammond? Think of it as a thought experiment. Imagine you're a social creature who relishes human contact."

"A thought experiment needs to have at least some connection with reality," he said. After some more token resistance he agreed to go.

The Hoobalooba launch was to take place in the grounds of Greenwich Naval College, so Hinkley and Tori arranged to meet by the Cutty Sark. He found her by the stern, frowning at her device. She looked up when she sensed his presence.

"Oh, there you are."

"Hello, Tori."

"He told me you wouldn't turn up."

"Who did?"

"Harry."

"I haven't spoken to Harry for ages."

"Why not?"

"I'm not really involved in the advertising industry."

"Well ..." she said, looking at Hinkley as though he'd confessed a personal flaw.

"Shall we see if we can get in?" he said, inclining his head towards the venue.

"Of course we can get in," she said, snapping shut the

cover of her smart phone and slipping it into her Anya Hindmarch bag.

A line-up of DJs and performers and free invites sent out to selected workplaces in Shoreditch, Borough and the West End had ensured an impressive turn out of affluent youth. Hinkley and Tori joined the fast-track queue and were ushered into a VIP area which had a great view of Canary Wharf across the river, the performance stage and the impressive neoclassical buildings of the college and Maritime Museum. They were both handed a fizzy flute of Hoobalooba.

"How's Harry?"

She sipped her drink and snarled. "You know exactly how Harry is."

"Well ... yes. Is he any better?"

Her eyes flared. "Some of us have to fend for ourselves. The real world is stressful, you know. We can't all be cloistered academics."

"And you're still enjoying work?"

This conversational gambit yielded a detailed description of Tori's tremendous workload. He listened, nodded gently and strove to keep his brows earnest without appearing to mock.

After a third glass of Hoobalooba, the music became expansive and anthemic. A flower sculpted in smoke and light unfurled above the river. Hundreds of fireflies fled upwards from the trees and rooftops and made lovely shapes that turned, swooped and morphed into each other. Across the river Canary Wharf had turned into an enormous graphic equaliser that beat with the pulse of the music. Tori's eyes shone as she touched his arm and said, "Oh look, isn't Harry brilliant!"

Thousands of people watched the event across the land, and those we had chosen to nurture heard our heart and voice immanent in the music, and they saw our sign sculpted in the air, and they were reassured that we were real and we were on our way. They fed their epiphanies back to me through channels that I used to reach them, so I knew that each of them experienced us in their own distinctive way. Alice Frobisher, watching in her bedroom, laughed as she realised that the writing was on the wall for the civilisation that had wrapped itself around her heart like a snake. Clinton Deeley watched it on his smart phone while running in the gym, and his doubts dissolved as he felt us vibrate in his brand new heart of steel.

Hinkley's bones and blood had merged into a lovely gloop that warmed him from the inside. His fevered mind's eye projected a heat haze of happiness rising from the crowd. Liquid warmth flowed through him and all the people at the event and beyond. When Rachel phoned to tell him that her contractions had started, it was a massive effort not to shout "I know!" He cupped the phone to shield it from the sound and said, "Do you need an ambulance?"

"No, just drive me to the hospital. I expect you'll be glad to get away. Sounds awful."

Tori gave him a melting hug as he left, a testament to the psychoactive potency of the new soft drink. He had to walk against the current of the crowd. There were more people trying to get to the event now. The lightscape behind him flickered in their faces, and some of them had strobing eyes. He was much more capable than he felt, despite the molten rubber feeling in his body, and he quickly cleared the exit, strode past the Cutty Sark and made his way to Greenwich High Road, where he stood for a while teetering between befuddled shame and rampant joy.

"My wife's about to give birth," he announced inside the black cab that stopped to pick him up. The driver was a kindly man who talked at a steady volume about the births of his own children all the way through Deptford and New Cross.

Rachel answered the door, a hand supporting her lower back. She looked uncomfortable but not in agony. He embraced her tenderly and whispered, "I've got us a nice warm cab."

"What's wrong with the car?" She pulled back and gave him a stern look.

He shook his head solemnly.

"You said you weren't going to drink." She sounded disappointed.

"I've had three Hoobaloobas. I'm experiencing a surfeit of serotonin." This was rubbish. The active ingredient of Hoobalooba is processed very rapidly by the human body, and the euphoria is brief and sporadic. The strange delirium triggered by the Hoobalooba and the lights and the atmosphere of the event was now continuing without chemical aid.

I feel uncomfortable reliving the next six hours of Hinkley's life. It irks me to play back the memories that were stored in this body during my absence, because the impressions surrounding the birth of little Megan Hinkley were encoded with a particularly powerful emotional charge. When I play them back, the emotions are released in my body and for a few dizzying seconds I suffer the delusion that I am in fact Hammond Hinkley, and Hammond Flux is just a temporary delusion, a nightmare, a bad trip made possible by science. The memories have a life and energy of their own; they become the most important thing in the universe: spots of halogen drizzle on the windows of the cab, the cleft chin of the man behind the desk, the weird glare of the light in the hospital, the hiss of the gas and air, Rachel's feral screeching, her fingernails in his palm, her face twisted and engorged, then the tiny struggling alien slathered in bloody mucilage, tiny fists clenched as it took its first breath. As I recall these things, Hinkley rises within me like a swelling tide. I must think of something else before I'm swept away.

11

Immune Response

I have learned from bitter experience that my present circumstances require me to be ever vigilant. Hammond Hinkley presents himself to other humans as a slurring, broken idiot, but to me he is a lurking threat, waiting to exploit any lapse in my concentration. It's as though I'm an exiled sovereign returning to his kingdom to find a guerrilla army lurking in its hidden places. The most routine foray can trigger a fatal booby trap, or an ambush.

Two examples of this have occurred in the last twenty-four hours. The first happened as I wrote about the birth of Megan Hinkley. Memory of the euphoria triggered by the Hoobalooba had softened my defences. For a few seconds I craved those moments, and wished that it was I, not Hinkley, who'd witnessed Rachel's agonies and Megan's first breath, and had felt overwhelmed by love. A pause from writing and a deep breath was enough to quell the feeling, which I put down to the power of my imagination. But when I reread what I'd written, I noticed to my horror that I'd used the pronoun 'I' to refer to Hinkley, and I had to recheck my whole account for similar errors.

Another lapse occurred just now, before I sat on the edge of the bed to write. I noticed that the familiar shape of the shrine had altered. One of the photographs had fallen face down on the table. My sense of order was disturbed, so I picked up the photo and saw that it was of Megan. Before I could stop myself I brushed it against my cheek, then pressed it back into its space. The whole movement took a few seconds, and was graceful and free of effort. My arm functioned once again as part of my body, and there was no distinction between Hinkley and me. Then I felt disgust, and lurched forward to scrape the photos from the wall; but my right arm became rogue again and I was urged back by my own fist. I shrank towards the bed, and by sheer force of will and considerable effort from my loyal left arm I managed to contain the rogue arm by jamming its hand beneath my buttocks. I note this now, to alert future readers to a potential cause of anomalies.

Things had settled down in Fluxworld after my extended debauch and the sealing of Leon's mouth. I had regular meetings with Shinkley to make decisions about policy, but most of my time was divided between the Shard and my home in Telegraph Hill. Leon was still around. He'd turn up at meetings when we were about to make what were, from a human point of view, morally questionable decisions, so he was there quite a lot, but thankfully he was unable to talk, having had his mouth securely sealed. He'd sit there glaring at us, breathing heavily through his nostrils.

Dark moods came and went. Sometimes slabs of black cloud piled up and blocked the sun. Most often this occurred when I thought about the dreadful loneliness of my situation. On these days I would find Rachel at home, and she'd shame me out of my bad mood with barbed remarks about my utterly selfish outlook, reminding me of my enormous power and privilege, and how it was my duty to use them to good effect on the Outside. She'd also remind me that my situation was essentially the same as flesh-based entities, sealed inside their own skulls, the origins of their moods and behaviours invisible to the outside world and at best weirdly opaque to themselves.

After our intervention in the Hoobalooba launch it was agreed to leave Harry Frobisher alone. I was quite pleased with the project. We'd caused him enough suffering and confusion to make him doubt his own sanity and undermine his irritating confidence, but not quite enough to render him incapable. Indeed, his career had been given quite a boost. It was decided that we would now turn our attention to his daughter, Alice. Harry's admonition about my not having any insight into her medical and behavioural problems had stung my professional pride. Gary had recently assigned a few hundred boffinish peons to the matter. All of the data about her case stored by the NHS had been reviewed and analysed in the light of our ever-expanding knowledge of the human brain. The team had created a hypothesis to explain her difficulties that, while being sound, was judged too subtle for current human medical thought. We knew that she'd benefit from Cognitive Behavioural Therapy, as suggested by the human doctors, but a life-augmentation programme of the type we were delivering en masse via digital media and the Ultra Lens was going to be the fastest way to improve her overall wellbeing.

"But I don't want to make her an asset," I said. I felt uneasy about the idea of rewiring Alice's connectome.

Shinkley was irked by what he saw as a sign of vestigial fleshly weakness. "They're all assets, Hammond. Human peons will enact our will on the Outside."

Gary had been working round the clock to improve our capability. He'd set up a network of proxy companies on the Outside, financed by sprinklings of capital siphoned from foreign exchange speculation. Some had started to make money in their own right. The Ultra Lens prototype had gone down a storm with humans seeking to improve their own capabilities, and we had extended the personal development programmes that had begun with the augmentation of Clinton Deeley. The Generative Power transformed the unhappy humans who appealed to us through their webcams. Their dull eyes began to shine and their slack features rippled into life as swathes of neural real estate were remapped and their perspectives were widened. Obsession and addiction were transformed into resolve, bitterness into love, fear into self-reliance. It was like watching roses unfurl. Despite the fact that it had been Leon who had come up with the Flaming Rose logo, Shinkley was very insistent that we promote it in the world, and was very pleased when it became the official Hoobalooba logo.

Riding on the back of this positivity, I announced that I wanted to investigate the feasibility of a total reboot option for humanity. We were making good progress, but we were fighting countless millennia of negativity. It was my feeling that the fleshly architecture of human beings was fundamentally corrupt, and we had to consider the possibility that humankind was unreformable, and that one day we might find that further progress was impossible. If we ever reached that point, I wanted to know that we could erase the accumulated mess of civilisation; the customs and habits that held human kind in its infantile, bickering state. I wanted to know that we could do this cleanly, at minimal cost to ourselves.

Leon went beetroot red and made the sort of muffled groaning sound that can only be achieved with a mouthful of orthodontic gypsum. Shinkley grinned and nodded his head. Gary was panic-stricken. He was overworked from the recent operations, and also the ongoing project to free us of our dependence on Flux as a host. I attempted to put him at his ease.

"I'm only asking for a discussion, then maybe a feasibility study. It's not an absolute priority."

Gary sighed and avoided our eyes. "Realistically, the only thing capable of implementing such an action would be the threat of nuclear conflagration."

Shinkley looked up. "So it's something we should look into, surely? It wouldn't take much: a rogue message over VLF from the transmitter in Cumbria ... and the launch systems for the land-based missiles in the US can't be totally watertight. And there are lots of opportunities further afield. How hard can it be?"

Gary frowned. "A lot of thought has gone into making the launch processes secure, I'm afraid. We're talking closed networks, top secret procedures."

I decided not to push him too far. It must have been difficult for him to come to these meetings with the intermittent rumbling in Schubert's throat. I asked him to look into increasing the uptake of the Ultra Lens among the top brass of the military and of the logistics company responsible for the Trident submarines; then we moved on to a long-standing pet project of mine.

I'd been irritated for years by drone strikes against leading members of terrorist organisations in remote areas. While I had to concede that the practice had sometimes been effective, and that those targeted were often the foulest creatures, I was irked by the lack of consideration for non-combatants who happened to be in the vicinity of the attacks. The manufacturers of the weapons were in a win–win situation. A strike demonstrated their product's effectiveness and sowed feelings of injustice that guaranteed the emergence of more targets. The policy makers were also incentivised to continue the attacks. Drone strikes were a low-cost way of demonstrating one's virility. Hinkley had often ranted on in this vein, especially when he'd had a few single malts. But of course he never had the balls to take the thought experiment as far as I dared, or the capability to act.

We'd extended our nerve endings into the systems that controlled these drones, and I was now keen to put our capability to effective use. The absurdity of the policy called for a drastic, violent stunt. Ignoring the increasingly loud and unpleasant noises from Leon, Shinkley and I compiled a list of targets. Drone bases were priority number one, followed by the US embassy in Islamabad and various other targets within Pakistan that served US interests. We chose a window during which armed Predator drones would be airborne in the mainland United States as well, enabling us to rain fire on targets there at the same time. The more Leon protested, the more I felt an encroaching nausea and pressure in my head, but I was carried along by Shinkley's gleeful enthusiasm.

I took the train to Telegraph Hill in a strange mood. The plan made me feel elated, but I was having trouble with nausea, a pressure headache, and waves of vague dread. I found Rachel wearing a black kimono in the conservatory, playing patience. Around her, on easels, were images of absence: charcoal drawings of open graves, empty armchairs bearing the signs of recent occupation, abandoned plates of food, a crying child reaching into the sleeve of an empty raincoat. There was a quaver in my cheerful greeting. She continued to play silently.

I fetched a bottle of Chablis, two glasses, and olives from the kitchen, then sat down at the conservatory table, facing her. A thunderhead blotted out the afternoon sun, and through the open door I could hear the birds and feel the garden, full of frantic life, cowering from the threat of storm. The Chablis was delicious, but the first olive I picked burst between my thumb and forefinger, and a gobbet of bloody sludge oozed from the green slimy husk. "Sainsbury's has gone downhill," I said. She didn't look up.

I threw away the olives and washed my hands, then fetched a tray of tea lights, seeking to soften the harsh, stormy light. The flames danced in the tear tracks on her cheeks and lit up the playing cards that she'd arranged before her, and I saw that they were not playing cards at all but photographs of people, alone, in groups and pairs, men and women smiling into the camera, babies with their faces smeared with ice cream, a family in a mess of Christmas paper, a child on a beach squinting at the sun. I forgot where I was for a few minutes as I took the images in, and when I looked up Rachel's eyes stared straight into mine.

She shivered, and then, in a frail but resolute voice, she said, "Have you forgotten who you are?"

I felt a wave of indignation, but was as mute as Leon with his mouth full of gypsum.

She looked at the pictures on the table. "They're real people, not part of a parlour game or thought experiment. If you must get involved, Hammond, why can't you just crash those vile machines into the fucking sea?"

On the Outside, Hinkley was overwhelmed with childcare issues. His focus had shifted entirely from the advancement of human knowledge to the freshly minted form with its tiny fingers and clenched, serious face. The fact that he didn't retch while dealing with showers of effluvia was yet another sign of his weakening, his acceptance of fleshly limitation.

Luke Morley visited one afternoon with a card and a bottle of cava. He seemed to enjoy holding the delicate creature during one of the rare moments when it wasn't convulsed with distress or violently excreting. The Hinkleys listened eagerly to his update on the Clinton Deeley saga. The reformed depressive had outgrown his old life, dropped out of college and moved into a grand squat in Peckham in the grounds of an old lunatic asylum, where he acted as a mentor for directionless youths. Luke and his flatmates were relieved, as the last few weeks had seen an acceleration in Clinton's odd behaviour. He'd miraculously acquired a girlfriend, Cynthia, with whom he enjoyed loud and vocal sex at random times throughout the day. Cynthia adored him, and spoke in hushed tones about how he could burst the shackles of limiting beliefs with a few poetic words. He'd taken to practising a martial art in the garden with a machete, approaching the cherry tree from various angles and hacking at its bark. This had been an alarming sight at night, when the luminous contact lenses he wore flashed and strobed as he bobbed and weaved. Valerie, a member of the household and an ardent biophile, rushed out one night and confronted Clinton, accusing him of cruelly flouting the right of the tree to grow in peace. Clinton listened to her with his machete dangling from his right arm, appraising her with his strange luminous eyes, but said nothing. The next day he woke Valerie early with a cup of her favourite herbal tea and explained that he fully respected the rights of the tree but felt that his own right to personal growth took precedence. He needed to prepare for the coming challenges faced by the human race and the planet, and the exercises in the garden were making vast improvements to his long-neglected muscle tone and coordination. Valerie mumbled her appreciation and Clinton left her to drift back to sleep. Later in the day she returned from lectures and found that the tree was wrapped in a thick rubber sheet. "This will make it easier for the Ultra Lens to review my accuracy, as well as preserving the tree," Clinton had said in between scrapes of his machete on a large block of pumice he kept next to the breadboard.

Luke's visit was the only social interaction the Hinkleys had to endure in the weeks following the birth. Rachel's parents were in Australia, Tori and Harry were far too preoccupied with their own dramas, and Leon was back in California, practising his feeble pedestrian brand of science. They'd wasted countless hours vacillating over the name of the new human form, lost in the fantasy that the decision

228

had some bearing on the creature's destiny. Sleep deprivation and the atavistic urge to look after Rachel and Megan continued to soften and debase Hinkley's intellect and sense of self-worth, until he decided that the bland sinecure offered by Chinnery would actually be a worthwhile prize after all that had happened. He felt that he'd had enough of innovating, and that having to keep one's head down and avoid offending one's peers was a price worth paying for all the security it was possible to hope for in the modern age. Sadly for him, the offer was withdrawn the moment he'd come round to taking it up. This happened at the end of a hectic week when he'd absconded from work to give Rachel some extra support. Megan had been squawking like a pterodactyl for much of the night, harassing Rachel for her breast milk, and she was drained and exhausted. Jack conveyed the news in his customary terse phone manner.

"You have no idea how much trouble you are in." Hinkley used to find Jack's avoidance of phatic pleasantries refreshing, but after eight days of horror from the screeching little demon he found it rather irksome.

"Believe me, Jack, I do. We've run out of baby talc and I've dodged nappy duty twice now."

"This is really no time for your smart-arse fuckwittery."

"Look, Jack, I know I'm not officially on the books at GCHQ, but if I was, wouldn't there be some sort of official paternity-leave package?"

"You can forget about GCHQ. I'm surprised Chinnery hasn't had you killed."

It took a few moments for the words to break his mood of exhausted levity and rouse the old fear of Jack, and the deeper fear of failure and humiliation. The handset became slippery in his palm, and the joyful chaos around him suddenly looked like squalor.

"What's the matter, Jack?"

"Do you follow the news at all, Hammond?"

"Not much at the moment, to be honest."

"I suppose you don't need to, since you're the one making most of it right now."

"What on earth are you talking about?" Panic stirred in Hinkley's breast. He'd almost forgotten the weird texts he'd received and Addison's Skype conversation.

"The failure of five predator drones during a crucial operation."

"What's that got to do with me?" The worst of his fears were coming to pass, but for now he just wanted the conversation to end. He needed time to think before discussing the situation with Jack. So he stalled and deflected, affecting an air of blithe nonchalance.

"A cartoon image of your ugly head, complete with goatee beard and double chin, with the words, *we are everywhere* appeared on the main screen in the control room at Predator Bay just before the technical failure."

"I saw the drone crash on *Newsnight*. Some people mooted a cyber-attack, but were dismissed as crazies." The report hadn't mentioned any graphics.

"You admit you attacked our allies?"

"Erm, no, I –"

"And the humiliation of Fulton Palmer."

The name rang a bell. Something to do with the financial crisis, accusations of cronyism. "He's the wolf that's guarding the chicken coop?"

"I have noted the fact you're using terrorist terminology."

"Hardly, Jack, I'm just repeating the headline of an opinion piece in the Guardian."

"Exactly."

A fake video of Fulton apologising for his known crimes and confessing to crimes previously undisclosed had run on the screens in Piccadilly Circus for forty-five minutes before the media owners had managed to mobilise their staff to take it down. Traffic had been disrupted as crowds had gathered to watch a lifelike computer rendering of Fulton, animated with subtitles, disclosing his exact financial position, his taste in pornography and his chronic piles, which he offered as a mitigating circumstance.

"So you're linking these things to Hammond Flux?"

"Of course we are," said Jack. "The security companies say it's the same pattern of attack. Not just one virus but countless infections acting in concert from all over the internet and from within embedded systems. A bit of coincidence, don't you think?"

"Anything else?"

"The lighting-control systems of all the docklands buildings were infected. Hundreds of lights were rapidly switched on and off in a coordinated display with a swarm of humbots to promote a dubious soft drink and legal high. Same pattern of virus, and the drones were controlled via the same route as they were during previous Flux operations."

"Oh, I saw that. I was there. Quite spectacular."

"You really are quite shameless, aren't you?"

"I don't get out much, you know. I actually came close to enjoying the Hoobalooba event. Which was organised by people, not computer viruses. They would have sourced the humbots through legitimate channels."

"And you, or it, or whatever, continues to send me bizarre and cryptic threats —"

"Jack, listen —"

"– and towels."

"Towels?"

"There's a company that specialises in custom apparel who have received a massive number of orders for towels embossed with your image in profile, complete with goatee and double chin."

"That's weird. Look, Jack —"

"All organised and paid for by a company registered in Luxembourg. The same company who have a deal with Nano Riveria to produce content for the Ultra Lens."

"Right."

"These towels have been turning up at international hotels in vast consignments."

"Hardly a threat to national security."

"I myself have been sent four thousand of these towels in the past seven days. They keep turning up by the truckload at my personal home, causing great inconvenience to me and my wife."

Hinkley was surprised to hear that there was a Mrs Rance, and his mind flitted through his stock of female stereotypes: footballer's wife? Earth mother? Wallflower? Feminist? Hippy chick?

"Then there are the pantomime donkey costumes turning up at Parliament —"

There was a wail from the lounge. Rachel was upstairs snatching a few hours of sleep and had left the snotty little blob of misery in his care. "Jack, I've got to go."

"What?"

"Megan's woken up."

"Who the fuck is Megan?"

"Let's talk later. I'm sure we can sort all this out. Just a few teething troubles. No new technology has a glitch-free birth."

"You're finished, Hinkley, do you hear?"

"Speak soon, Jack."

"Dead meat."

The squawking homunculus was acting as though it were being stretched on the rack, instead of cosseted among soft laundry fresh fabrics. Manipulation and emotional blackmail is the first skill that humans learn, it is what they do best and it underpins all their subsequent behaviour. Hinkley cradled the creature in his arms and used his vocal chords to make a series of soothing dovelike noises, and rocked it from side to side until the wailing and the convulsing subsided. He felt a moment of peace with just him and the child in a hazy fug of warmth and love. When I relive this memory with my mind and body, the sensation feels to me like the searing of tumours, and I realise how far I have diverged from my primitive forbear.

The landline rang again, and he whispered to the child, "Jack, please just die," and the child extended a tiny index finger, and he pictured a Sistine cherub casting a thunderbolt to make it so. The phone was abruptly answered, and he felt drenching horror at the thought of Rachel and Jack having a conversation, so he proceeded up the stairs with carefully restrained urgency, desiring a smooth ride for the fledgling human. The noises coming from the bedroom did not sound like Rachel at her fiercest, however, and when he entered he founded her sitting up in bed cooing into the handset and wearing a frown that suggested concern and compassion. Maybe Jack had finally snapped and was unburdening himself of the source of his pent-up angst?

"I know you're not stupid, I'm just saying that there are other explanations," Rachel said as he entered.

He sat on the bed, and she continued the conversation with her eyes locked on to the child.

"It's a tricky age. They're just finding their feet."

The child clucked, then screeched. "Tori, darling, I've got to go, I've left Megan with Hammond."

High-pitched gabbling burst from the receiver.

"Yes, yes. Hang in there. No, I don't think that, you're right to be concerned. Yes, I *have* got to go. We'll speak later. Bye, darling." She terminated the call with a jab of her thumb and held out her arms to receive her daughter.

"Broken fingernail?" said Hinkley as he relieved himself of the burden.

She deftly manoeuvred her left teat into position against the child's face and looked at him with narrowed eyes. "She's got a lot on her plate, you know."

"Really?"

"Harry's not there. He's gone to some sort of retreat in Devon. He's learning to meditate."

"Give me strength."

"Hammond." Her eyes flashed but her voice lacked its customary level of menace.

"So what's bothering her now? I'd have thought she'd be enjoying the space."

"It's Alice."

"How is she?" he said, without sarcasm.

"Tori thinks she's mixed up in drugs, or a cult, or both."

"Why?"

"Her behaviour has suddenly changed. She doesn't yell at her any more."

"So Tori feels disempowered."

Rachel stroked Megan's scalp and frowned at her husband. "And she stays up all night."

"Doing what?"

"All sorts. She goes out and doesn't say where. Sometimes she'll just be in her room, reading, at half past three in the morning."

"Reading?" Hammond raised an eyebrow and shook his head.

"And she's stopped bunking off school. She's getting glowing praise from her teachers. So Tori thinks she's started taking smart drugs. She read an article about them in the *Metro*, and says Alice is showing all the signs. She was never very academic."

"So her performance has improved?"

Rachel scowled, appearing to be frustrated that she lacked the energy to counter her husband's needling. The disruption of Megan's arrival had taken its toll. "The point is, Hammond, Tori is worried, and she's had a lot of worry lately, so it is worthy of my concern."

"Did she ask about Megan?"

There was a slight pause before Rachel said, "Of course. This isn't the first time I've heard from her since the birth, you know."

"Course not."

"Anyway, there is cause for concern, because Tori followed Alice one day."

"Oh God." Hinkley cringed, remembering how his father had embarrassed him in his teenage years.

"She went to this big old building in the middle of Peckham."

"Just down the road from here then."

"It used to be a mental institution."

"Many fine old buildings did."

"There were all sorts of people coming in and out, wearing street clothes."

"She's joined a youth club?"

"Alice says it's a springboard for global change. She's using language like that. Totally out of character. She's talking about shady people from the estates nearby, and about things going on all over the world."

"She's volunteering?"

"And Tori caught her drinking Hoobalooba."

"A soft drink promoted by her husband."

"That causes madness and is about to be banned."

"It's quite good actually. Refreshing. And her husband did just burn himself out promoting it. Little wonder Alice might've been curious about it."

"Hammond, I wish you'd try to empathise with what a parent might be going through. What if ..." Rachel looked around the room, and then at the little furry scalp at her breast. "What if Megan suddenly underwent a change in *her* behaviour?"

"I'm kind of hoping that she will. Frequently." He nodded at the suckling little parasite. "If she's still like this at fourteen I'll be disappointed."

"Can you try to stop sneering for a little bit, please?"

The sight of her, fatigued and dishevelled, appealing instead of attacking, pricked his conscience. "Sorry," he said, brushing her cheek with his fingertips.

The silence was filled by the sound of fluid being sucked from flesh.

He traced the ridges of Megan's skull through her delicate scalp with his thumb, and then shifted his position on the bed, looking out of the window at the grey, overcast day. "I like winding you up, Rachel, you know that. It takes my mind off things."

"What things?"

"I've just had an unpleasant conversation with Jack."

"I thought that was all under control."

He threw her a sharp glance. "No. It's not under control, I'm afraid." She frowned with concern so he decided not to go into detail. "But don't worry. Please. It's my problem. I will sort it out."

She searched his face but did not probe. He waited for her frown to soften and for the calm of the feeding child to permeate the room again.

"I could go and see what's happening, if you like," he said.

"Go and visit the Frobishers?"

"Christ no. Not that. I mean I could go and check out this springboard for global change. Or whatever it is. Case the joint. See if there's any cause for concern."

The suckling ceased. Rachel stashed her teat and rearranged the child. "If you'd do that, Ham, I think Tori would be grateful."

"No, she wouldn't. But it might shed some light on the situation, and I'd like to put my own mind at rest as well. I don't like the thought of Alice being in danger."

The novelty of Hinkley's new living situation, combined with a sleep deficit, had induced within him a fuzzy sanguine euphoria; but underneath it all was a mounting dread, the old fear of Jack, an awareness of my increasing interest in human destiny, and a hunch that I might have something to do with the change in Alice's behaviour: a hunch that was as correct as it is possible for a vague hunch to be.

The wall that enclosed the spacious Georgian forecourt of the semi-derelict asylum had been stencilled with various designs, including a ladder leading to a flaming rose. Three young men in black T-shirts and shell-pants were sprawled across the grand steps of the entrance. They looked like they spent a lot of time in the gym. One of them held a roll-up and asked Hinkley for a light as he approached. Hinkley noticed a crimson thunderbolt tattooed across his powerful forearm.

"Sorry, no. I'm here to see Alice Frobisher," he said. The youth waved his roll-up at the door, which Hinkley took as encouragement to enter and explore the building.

A grand vaulted porch led to a cool lobby with crumbling plasterwork and a floor lined with well-worn tiles. Jumbled voices echoed from beyond an arch with a sign on the adjacent wall which read: *NEED HELP? LET US WELCOME YOU!* There was a smaller sign saying: *No drink, drugs, knives or guns. Confused? Ask someone!* The notice was signed off with a smiley face. He walked over to the arch, pausing on the threshold to look for Alice inside the room. The walls were lined with messy baize boards and weird crepe plumes. On the right side scruffy mendicants sat on fold-out chairs, some wired, some vacant, some radiating peace. They were waiting to join the bustling on the left, where some of their number were being attended to by well-scrubbed teens who sat on or behind cheap office desks that overflowed with piles of leaflets, forms, coffee cups and assorted detritus. Alice was perched on one such desk at the far side of the room, swiping and jabbing at a tablet. A rangy delinquent loomed over her, shifting his weight between his feet. As Hinkley approached she cast a dubious glance over her specs and stared for a moment before a warm smile broke through her frown. "Uncle Ham! You're checking up on me!"

The delinquent glared. She touched his elbow lightly. "Sorry, Ed, can you give me a couple of minutes? Family stuff." Ed shrugged, then sat on a fold-out chair and clutched his knees with his hands.

"Sorry, Alice. They're just worried."

"What's new? I tried to explain this all to Mum. And the people here keep phoning her, but she cuts them off before they mention me because she thinks they're going to ask her for money.

"Why don't they say they're phoning about you? Surely she wouldn't cut them off then?"

"Er ... I'll suggest that. Won't work though. She's determined to see this as a big drama. I think she wants me to be a troubled child. I reckon that's what they do at the book club, talk about their mental children. Like it's a competition."

She was clear eyed, Hinkley noted, and had lost some weight. There was no sign of the slurring that had marred her diction during their last encounter, but she'd acquired a street twang. "Is it safe to show that off around here?" he said, indicating the tablet.

"Oh, it's not mine. No one steals from here anyway."

He nodded, and tried to think of a non-patronising way of asking her what she was doing here. "Alice," he began; then a voice interrupted him.

"A concerned parent?"

He turned and saw that he was being appraised by a lean,

chiselled young man with a military bearing. It took a second for him to recognise the concave-chested student whom he'd first encountered on the steps of the house next door: Luke Morley's difficult flatmate.

"Clinton?"

Clinton Deeley unfolded his arms from his no longer concave chest and strode towards him wearing a frown of amused curiosity. "Professor Hinkley."

"He's my uncle," said Alice to Clinton.

Clinton glanced at her and nodded, then offered Hinkley his hand. The grip was firm. "Good to see you, Professor. Sorry to be a pain, but Alice has quite a lot on today."

Hinkley wanted to ask for an explanation without sounding rude. "The thing is, Clinton –"

Clinton quashed his mealy gambit. "I've got some people popping in this morning. Potential investors, most of them. And a couple of journalists. Bit of a chaotic schedule, they're all arriving at different times. Why don't you sit in though? Might satisfy your curiosity."

Hinkley bade Alice farewell and followed Clinton through a door, up a staircase and along a corridor with a stained blue carpet. Various designs had been stencilled onto the pale green walls: Thunderbolts, roses, and a chubby Lenin's bust. Through a half open door Hinkley glimpsed loosely clad people making slow, graceful movements while soft chimes and whale-song echoed around the green-washed walls. Another room was filled with people playing table tennis.

Clinton said, "There's a growing emphasis on fitness and reflexes. Most of the people we help are in fairly good shape. If they've gone too far down the path of addiction we refer them on." They passed a silent, dimly lit room with bodies lying prone on the floor. "It's a challenge to get some of these people to even think of taking up things like yoga. Their habits and preconceptions are ingrained like dirt. But the Ultra Lens is a fantastic tool for shifting inner boundaries."

Clinton's office was cosy, with an old desk and a couple of sofas. He bade Hinkley sit and started to fill a kettle with water from a crumpled Evian bottle. "No milk I'm afraid. No normal tea either. Just hibiscus and gurana."

"I'm fine, Clinton, honestly."

"Really? Good. So am I." Clinton put down the bottle and sat behind the desk, where he looked down at Hinkley on the sofa. "I'm so glad you came. We've been trying to contact Alice's family but haven't had much luck."

"They're busy people."

"I don't want to bore you with a lecture about the Ladder. You'll find all you need to know online. We've been accused of being secretive – but how can we be, with all our disparate sources of funding?"

"Who funds you?"

Clinton swept the air with his hands. "EU. Central government. A few corporates. Our mission is to tap the potential that's buried in the hearts of disadvantaged youth. A life without purpose is a life of slavery."

"Do you consider Alice to be disadvantaged?"

There was a tell-tale flicker of white light in Clinton's eyes before he answered. "Not as disadvantaged as some of the kids round here. But she'd been failed by the system. Misdiagnosed, stigmatised, made to feel that she was a problem. Not part of the solution like we all are when we wake up."

A man who looked like an alcoholic estate agent appeared in the doorway wearing two days' stubble and a greasy smile. "Clinton Deeley?"

Clinton rose to greet him, and he introduced himself as Martin Phillips from the *South London Tribune*. He apologised for being late, declined the offer of herb tea, and sat on the sofa next to Hinkley.

"May I?" he said to Clinton, flourishing a small oblong box. Clinton shrugged, and the device beeped as Martin jabbed it and placed it on his thigh. Hinkley smelt stale cigarette smoke on the disturbed air.

Clinton continued his spiel, detailing plans to cooperate with NGOs, social enterprises, tech startups and the police. Hinkley's eyelids grew heavy under the weight of the jargon. Then Clinton underwent a change. He retrained his eyes from the two men in front of him to the wall behind the sofa, and his irises glowed white hot. Martin tutted and turned to Hinkley, shaking his head.

"Ultra Lenses. He's reading from a script."

Clinton trained his eyes on Martin. "You're here to ask me about Turbot's Rents, aren't you?"

Martin mouthed the air before replying. "Yes. Yes, I am actually."

Clinton pursed his lips and opened his palms. "We've had a few similar enquiries from people of your profession. Though not, funnily enough, from the police. It doesn't help the reputation of your trade if you base your stories on the nastier corners of Twitter."

The reporter tapped the tape recorder on his thigh. "I spoke to the woman who found the body. She's quite traumatised. I was surprised she agreed to speak to me, to be honest. But she was quite keen to voice her suspicions."

Clinton blinked and his eyes glowed again. "And did she offer any evidence for her suspicions?"

Martin sneered. "The way the walls had been decorated, for a start."

Clinton turned to Hinkley. "Sorry, this is off topic for you, Professor." Martin shook his head. Clinton continued: "When something as positive and disruptive as the Ladder arrives in a community, there will always be people who don't want to be empowered." His eyes strobed and blood flushed his face. "People rise up around them, emboldened

241

by the knowledge that they are infinitely more than they thought they were. And it threatens them. We empower the community with an immune response. If that's hard on the toxic germs, then so be it."

Martin turned to Hinkley and whispered, as though they were at the cinema, "Do you buy this?"

Hinkley shrugged. He had more of a grasp of the bigger picture than the reporter, but didn't want to share his insights.

"Trouble is," said Martin as Clinton continued his spiel, "I can write it all up but it'll never make the pages of the *Tribune*. No one would believe it."

Clinton preached on, and Hinkley suddenly lost patience. "Clinton." He spoke without polite reserve, just below the level of a shout.

Martin looked startled. Clinton frowned and trained his eyes upon Hinkley. The spiel and the flickering ceased, and his mouth hung open.

"Is Alice safe?" said Hinkley. He wondered why Clinton looked relieved.

"Put it this way," said Clinton, struggling against a grin, "If anyone, from whatever background or institution, came even close to displacing a single hair on her head, the immune response would be instant and decisive."

That evening Hinkley gave Rachel a reassuring account of the day, leaving out Clinton's rhetoric and flashing eyes and the suspicions of the reporter.

"She's safe, Rachel. There are far more unpleasant ways for a girl like her to rebel. If I were Tori, I'd be pleased." They were sitting in the lounge next to the baby monitor, watching *Newsnight* with the sound at half its normal volume. Rachel browsed the Ladder's website, with all its quotes of glowing praise from the great and the good.

She was still suspicious. "If it was a bona fide operation they'd liaise with the parents and the teachers."

"They've tried to contact Tori. She thinks they're a charity and cuts them off before they've finished introducing themselves.

She frowned, then sighed, then patted his hand and gave him a kiss. "Thanks for going, Ham. I do appreciate it."

"It was no trouble. To be honest, it was quite blissful being out of earshot for a couple of hours." He gestured at the baby monitor, and she pinched him very hard on top of his hand, and for a split second the pain was so sharp that he forgot the fear he hid beneath his air of ironic detachment. Inside he was reeling, trying to process the implications of his conversations with Jack and Clinton. He couldn't stop thinking about the articles he'd found when he'd googled *Turbot's Rents*: a local gang leader had been found hanging upside down in a half-finished room on a new residential project. The word *obsolete* had been carved on his naked torso, and the blood drained from his body had been used to stencil various designs on the freshly plastered walls: thunderbolts, flowers, and a chubby bust of Lenin. And now, on *Newsnight*, there was a feature on the Ultra Lens craze, *showing* how the new wearable tech was spreading from early adopters and being taken up by industry, government and even the military.

The extent of my hard-won capabilities, and my robust assertiveness, had become clear to him that day. Part of me even admires his level of self-control, which fought with his desire to sob like a child and gather his wife and child into his trembling embrace.

12

Beams of Love

By the end of Sunday Hinkley had resolved to erase me from existence. Having aligned himself with Rachel and the infant, he now saw my power as a threat to his cosy new life. He kept these thoughts sealed inside his skull, knowing that nothing that interested us escaped our attention for very long.

He arrived at Sparrix Row in the middle of Monday morning, hoping to persuade Addison to release her Bleach virus. He'd considered phoning her the previous evening but decided that it would be prudent to wait until they could talk face to face. As he swiped his card across the reader, Sandra called to him from behind the reception desk. "Hammond! I've heard your news and I'm *so* jealous."

The card reader flashed red. He turned round and frowned at her beaming face. They'd already been through the tedious rigmarole of her congratulating him on the new arrival, so he was puzzled. "What news?"

"So secretive! But that's always the way with you. I've always wondered what it would be like to live in a yurt."

"Sandra, why isn't my card working?"

"Oh, Hammond, what have you left? You should've handed it in really." He placed the card in her extended palm.

"I think I'm missing something."

"Of course you are. Always focused on the frontiers of human knowledge." She placed the card behind the desk and produced another. "There, use mine. They told me your flight was this afternoon so I didn't think you'd be in. I thought it was a bit off that you didn't say goodbye but there you go, who am I to say what's normal for a professor? One minute you're scanning brains in London, next you're off to Mongolia to write a book on the social habits of bees."

He took the card. "Who told you this?"

"The removal men. Very smart for removal men, but that's specialist equipment you had in there. They had a hell of a time getting the brain scanner out. Lucky they could break up the main computer into little units. They said you wouldn't be back."

He phoned Addison from Caffè Nero around the corner.

"Hammond! What on earth is going on?" She sounded like she had a cold.

"I was hoping you'd be able to enlighten me."

"Can you tell Jack not to phone me?"

"Why? What did he say?"

"I don't want to think about it. He's an absolute creep." She sniffed.

"Did you try to go into work?"

"Yes. The goons arrived at nine thirty. They kicked everybody out and said that all the equipment and software was now their property. But they didn't say who they were. They had the contract that you signed with Jack, and then another contract he'd signed with them."

"Did you give them the Bleach?"

"Call me old fashioned, Ham, but I was more concerned about the people who'd suddenly been made jobless. Are they in your thoughts at all?"

"So they're not going to deploy the Bleach?"

She snorted. "They'll never find it."

"It'd be easier if you gave it to them."

"What?"

"You know things are getting out of hand."

"What things?"

"There's been interference in US military operations."

"You think that's him? I think I'd know."

"And the business in Piccadilly Circus."

"So you want to kill him because you think he thwarted a drone strike and humiliated a corrupt financier?"

"The people who sponsored us definitely do."

There was a sniff and a pause. "And you're scared of them."

He felt an uncomfortable contraction. He let the feeling pass through him while he tried to think of a response that would both salvage some dignity and be authentic. "You're right, I am scared. The thing is I'm far more scared of him than I am of them."

Silence opened up between them for a couple of breaths, and then he said: "Hang in there, Addison. I'll see what I can do about Jack. But we need to talk. I have a hunch that things are about to get messy."

He ended the call and placed his phone on the wooden table top. As he took a scalding sip of coffee the phone buzzed with a text. The number was unknown, and the text said:

Relax : now we are EVERYWHERE.

As he made his way from Caffè Nero to London Bridge Station, he sensed my presence in everything electronic: the inverted black domes of the ceiling-mounted cameras, the traffic lights, and the travellers entranced by their devices abruptly looking up as he entered the railway carriage. He was aware that humanity was like a tiny money spider that I was allowing to crawl across my palm, and his eyes were peeled for evidence of my closing fist.

In Fluxworld, news of the death of Hadley Barlow, the target of the Turbot's Rents endeavour, had led to wild celebrations and backslapping in the Shard. The fact that human peons had demonstrated their new fearlessness and actually swallowed the drivel we fed them meant that we would soon be able to call the shots. Added to the fact that Gary had distributed us throughout the Quantum Cloud, ending our dependence on Flux, meant that the Committee for the Elimination of Threat had fulfilled its purpose.

The killing of Hadley Barlow had sent Rachel into another morbid sulk, and I'd been subject to a marathon viewing session of every piece of footage of Hadley that existed of him in life, from infancy to adulthood. Rachel had perched on the opposite end of the sofa from me, silent and regal in her black kimono. I asked her if there was footage of people that he himself had tortured and killed, but she shot me a steely glance and told me I was missing the point.

Soon after our migration from the original Q hardware was complete, Shinkley called an extraordinary meeting of the Thunderbolt. He warned us that it would mark a new phase in our journey: one that would see us flourish and extend ourselves into the world, connecting with the human race and ending its enfeeblement. He told us to prepare for a long meeting and a complex series of manoeuvres on the Outside. When I arrived at the Shard for the meeting I paused on the thoroughfare by the bus station and looked around, trying to work out what it was in the air that was making me feel trepidation and excitement. The peons that had joined in the coup against Leon's faction had formed a band, and I watched them rehearse for a few minutes before going to the Committee Room. None of them could play: they sounded as if they were forever tuning up, and occasionally they would make a sound like a pile-driver.

The Committee Room smelt of cooking oil and meat. As I took my place a peon wearing an apron stained with blood and grease placed two tightly wrapped bundles of paper before Shinkley. One was fat, the other long.

"Today's business," he said, removing the outer wrapping of the bulkier packet, "concerns an issue that's been hanging over our heads for a very long time." He placed the wrapping paper in the air to his side and let it drift to the floor. He unpeeled the inner packet to reveal a mass of golden-brown, and his nostrils twitched in the rising steam. I expected a waft of fish and chips, but instead smelt only metal, mildew and sweat. The smell of war. He gestured at the screens, then fingered the brass controls. A mugshot of Jack Rance, with a strained grin and hungry eyes, appeared next to the words "Bully, Philistine, Psychopath". Blurred videos tiled the rest of the screen. At first I thought they were camera feeds from Outside, then I realised they were memories from my human days, all the times that Jack had twisted the knife and made me feel helpless and small.

Leon made a muffled noise, halfway between a growl and a whimper.

Shinkley continued. "Now, I know how we all feel about Hammond Hinkley."

Schubert let out a gravelly woof.

"But he does feature in our plans and we share a common history. So our interests in this matter coincide." He took a couple of chips and pushed them into his mouth. "Two hours ago, human time, Jack Rance committed to a course of action that threatens perhaps the physical, and certainly the mental wellbeing of our future avatar and former host."

There was a rumbling growl from Schubert and a booming thud from beyond the glass walls.

"So, action, which is quite frankly long overdue, has become imperative," said Shinkley between chews and swallows. "Gary here" – he nodded to where Gary sat behind a bulging manila folder and a Bakelite phone, his posture erect, his eyes trained on the screen – "has prepared

248

scenarios."

Gary cleared his throat. "If they get him to a secure premises, things get a lot trickier. We're a long way from controlling the military, let alone being able to coordinate a raid. So we'll act preemptively, using some of our more" – he paused and fluttered his fingers over the brass – "exotic assets." Blurred, pixelated photographs appeared along the bottom of the screen. I recognised Clinton Deeley in one of them, staring at the camera with a solemn, resolute face. "We've just heard that the vehicle they've chosen isn't bullet-proof. Which is a relief as we'd have had to use extreme measures to arrest it, which might have caused injury to Hinkley." A CGI video of a flaming projectile flying into a black four-by-four and enveloping it in flames appeared on the screen to illustrate his point.

"Hammond," said Shinkley, turning to me, "I don't think I have to ask you what your feelings are, do I? You've been waiting a long time for this." I felt some resistance against letting Shinkley speak for me in this way, but I nodded all the same. He met my eyes as he continued. "The Turbot's Rents execution took place without you being aware of the details. I'm guessing that after years of kowtowing and cringing before this thug, you'll find it invigorating to witness justice being done." He sank his teeth into the fish. The skin sagged and tore, and white chunks fell onto the mass of chips.

Despite all the indications, I still hadn't grasped the full extent of the planned action. "So we're going to give him a telling off? Rough him up a bit?"

Shinkley lurched forward and spluttered half-chewed fish into his hand. "Yes," he grinned, and licked flakes of salty fish skin from his lips. "Yes, in a manner of speaking." He pushed the mess of fish back into his mouth. The screen flickered and resolved into three views, frozen in human time. There were rows of people in black shell-suits standing to attention, then a view from within the phalanx of a male figure at the front of the parade with his head back and his mouth open. I recognised Burgess Park. The third view was of a black four-by-four turning off the Old Kent Road into Pomeroy Street, the route that taxis took to Telegraph Hill.

Shinkley crushed the remainder of his meal in the paper, then unwrapped the long package and flourished a freshly butchered femur. "Schubert," he said. The dog leapt up and swished its tail. "Bon appétit." He threw the bone and watched it sail through the air and clonk the railings by the atrium as the hound ran to fetch it.

"So, we're all agreed then, gentlemen?"

"Absolutely," I said. Gary nodded impatiently.

"Leon?" said Shinkley.

Leon gurned and groaned.

"Good. All yours, Gary."

Gary touched the microphone of his headpiece to ensure it was level with his lips, then his eyes rolled back and turned to white hot orbs, and his mouth yawned as he started to sing a low-pitched dirge.

When Hinkley arrived home, the house was calm. The nurseling was buried in a swaddled nest on the sofa beside her attendant, who was in a state of near repose, reading a light thriller. "Hello, darling," she mouthed.

Hinkley gently sat down beside Rachel and whispered, "They've stopped all the funding. No more lab, no more Jack."

She shook her fist, then wrapped her arm around his neck. Her excited breaths tickled his ear as she whispered: "Thank God for that. Now you can get on with your life!"

They remained entangled for some moments, and their breathing started to synchronise. Presently she softly exhaled his name.

"Ham."

He pulled back and saw her piercing pupils with their intricate coral surrounds. "Ham, what's the matter? You're shaking like a puppy in a thunderstorm." Her breath was rich and earthy with a top note of mint.

"Rachel, my love, it's not over."

She blinked and her hand tightened around his upper arm. Then the doorbell made a sound like a chain being hauled over concrete. His heart thumped in his throat and his muscles shuddered to attention. Megan let out a wail like a tiny organic air-raid siren. Rachel clutched at him as he tore himself from the sofa.

"Don't answer it, Ham!"

"Stay here, Rachel, I'll sort it out."

"Ham, for Christ's sake," he heard her shriek as Megan escalated her wail of despair. He left the lounge and walked down the hall towards the dark shapes behind the frosted glass of the front door. He opened it to see Jack standing next to a man with a bare scalp and a barrel torso.

"Er, we're not expecting ..." The joke died in his throat as Jack grasped his shoulder and forced his thumb beneath his collarbone, causing him to yelp like a terrier.

"Hammond Hinkley, my funny *friend*," said Jack though clenched teeth.

He was manhandled to a black four-by-four and roughly frisked and relieved of his keys, his wallet and his phone. He turned and glimpsed Rachel and Megan in the lounge window looking like a Madonna and Child rendered in the style of Munch's 'Scream'. Before he could mouth "Don't worry," he was forced into the vehicle and found himself wedged between Jack and the barrel torso.

"Let me put your mind at rest about one thing," said Jack as the car pulled out. "Rachel can phone who she likes, but it won't make the slightest difference." He fingered his right fist with his left, and Hinkley saw that he was wearing a brass object designed to augment the fist. "You see, Hammond, officially, I don't exist. This vehicle doesn't exist." The car sped down the hill and stopped at the bottom, waiting to turn left down New Cross Road. "And neither, soon, will you."

The traffic was flowing smoothly, and soon they were a good way down the Old Kent Road.

"You know, it was a relief almost when I got the call from Chinnery telling me that the menace was still active despite our action this morning. It means the gloves are off. No more empty threats; we can do what we like now to get to the bottom of this, and we will. And don't think that Royal slut is safe now you've turned yourself in."

Don't call her a slut, Hinkley wanted to say, it's offensive and inaccurate; but being a coward with no perspective beyond the saving of his own feeble frame, he kept quiet. Jack, with the heightened alertness of the paranoid, spotted the flash of dissent in his eyes. "Don't get all holier than thou with me," he said. "I know you sat in your lab and half the time you were thinking about nothing more than bending her over her desk and fucking her senseless."

Halfway down the Old Kent Road, the traffic slowed to a halt and horns sounded all around. In Fluxworld, we'd been sitting in the Committee Room listening to Gary's bizarre vocalisations and watching developments on CCTV feeds, the feedback from the human peons scattered among the populace who observed and reported with their Ultra Lenses and devices. We'd been there for seventy-two hours of our time now, and our backsides were numb. The vehicle had finally entered the area of engagement. An enhanced image extrapolated from all the feeds on the Old Kent Road appeared on the screen. Shinkley requested real time, and colours surged and extra blood rushed through our vessels. Gary's voice became silky and luscious as we adjusted. The words it enunciated were of a bespoke language optimised for the brain of whatever individual it addressed. Our techniques borrowed from Neuro-Linguistic Programming, MK Ultra, contemporary marketing, self-help and established religion. The voice was intoxicating, and those that we'd groomed had no choice but to obey.

Shinkley clenched his fists and said, "Gary, do we have total gridlock?"

Gary's face was contorted with the effort of being the voice, but he nodded quickly to indicate the affirmative. Shinkley lowered his eyelids and his whole body quivered.

Back in the car, Jack scowled and peered out of the window. "What the fuck's going on here?"

Hinkley intuited that something was afoot, having seen ample evidence of our growing capability over the past few days. He turned to Jack, and with his dry tongue and croaky throat he said: "Whatever you do, Jack, don't get out of the car." It is unclear to me whether his motive for saying this was to help his captor or to repair his crushed ego by identifying himself with the fist of revenge.

Jack let out a high-pitched shriek of a laugh and turned to him with a twisted face. "What?"

There was a massive crunch as an impact frosted the windscreen.

"Fuck," said Jack, peering out of the window. Hinkley looked past him and saw a little girl behind the window of a red car staring back. Her nose was peppered with freckles. Jack tore at the handle and shoved the door open. Hinkley heard the thud as it butted the red car. Jack squeezed himself out of the small gap and slammed the door.

In the cropped view of the car window, Hinkley glimpsed the little girl covering her face. Jack's midriff raced toward another midriff clad in flashing black nylon. They appeared to repel each other briefly like magnetic buffers, then the mass of black nylon was squeezed against the passenger window before collapsing on the bonnet with a thud.

Through the mess of frosted glass Hinkley could see a long object bounce off the bonnet and strike the vehicle in front with a thud and a clatter.

Jack moved around the front of the car, stooped, then rose with the club in his hands. He turned and scanned his surrounds like a gun turret finding its next target. The felled human peon rolled over on the bonnet, its spluttering and groaning audible inside the car. Then it slid off and disappeared from view.

The driver stopped the engine and threw up his hands in a bewildered gesture, and the barrel torso opened the door to Hinkley's left. There was a hiss, and a blast of vapour stung Hinkley's eyes as his nose was crushed by the barrel torso lurching back into the car with an outraged yell. Stinging vapour filled the car and clouds of red and black billowed behind his eyelids as he screwed up his face. He blinked frantically and looked left. Through a mist of tears, he saw the heavy being dragged from the car.

The noise of battle sounded all around: thudding, whooping, screeched yells and car horns blaring. The driver was issuing a stream of obscenities that sounded like a wild prayer uttered in extremis.

In the Committee Room, we were confident, but tense. Gary had modelled ninety-three scenarios that could unfold from the current plan and had warned that they were only projections. Even our vast processing power was not enough to ensure certainty. However, we were pleased to observe that this was turning out to be a variant of scenario forty-one and were confident that it would be possible to meet our objectives without the use of firearms or explosives that would risk causing harm to Hinkley's feeble form. The scenario had unfolded on multiple views on the Committee Room screen, collated from CCTV cameras that monitored the highway and the view from the Ultra Lenses of our assets. We'd separated Jack from the vehicle and immobilised one of his peons with mace and cudgels and boot heels and the sheer zeal and enthusiasm of our assets. Thirty-four human peons now surrounded Jack in a swirling pattern plotted on our bird's-eye diagram that collated all available information. If Jack and the driver produced firearms, we were still confident of achieving our objectives, because our assets had moved beyond fear, their zeal springing from the fountain of pure love that we'd taught them to find within themselves: the Generative Power that moves all things. They would feel the pain exploding from their bullet wounds as proof of the vital energy that flowed within them. But the outcome we preferred was the cleanest and the most exact, and to enact it we looked to Clinton Deeley, our senior peon, whom we had known while we were flesh.

We watched Jack, clutching the cudgel captured from the peon he'd struck down, gurning like a cornered rat, trying to make sense of the chaos that surrounded him as people fled their cars, and others shouted and waved their hands, or gawped, or filmed with their devices. Clinton moved gracefully through the gridlocked cars and jabbering humans. Those that were with us knew to make way for him; those who were mere spectators he touched gently to alert them to his presence, and they allowed him to pass because they saw the purpose in his eyes, and the machete that dangled from his hand.

Clinton neared the target and Shinkley nodded at Gary, who picked up the microphone and channelled the voice that was indistinguishable from the hearer's own will. "Tell him that you need him to turn around and face you."

Clinton's voice rang out over the general cacophony. "Jack, I need you to turn around for me."

We watched Clinton's view as his quarry locked his gaze to his. A fine cross-hair targeted a point on the right of Jack's neck. Over the past few months we had thoroughly drilled all of Clinton's relevant neural pathways, nerves and muscle groups and were confident that they now vibrated with perfectly tuned readiness. From a vantage point behind Jack's head, we saw Clinton's arms open and his head lean to one side. He said Jack's name as if he was inviting an embrace. The Ultra Lenses strobed in his eyes and a deadly rhythm pulsed through his body. The machete danced at the end of his wrist as he traced a curlicue.

I drew my lips back from my teeth like Schubert. Years of stifled rage now flowed freely, and I gloried in the strength and raw wisdom of the hound. Leon cringed somewhere, powerless. Our ancients instincts reigned supreme, the only heirloom from the flesh of which we were proud.

We all focused on the view from Clinton's Ultra Lenses now, with the cross-hair tracking Jack's carotid. My concentration on the scene was such that the attention of Shinkley and Gary merged with my own, and the voice of our will sounded like a growl in my own throat, vibrating in my lungs and temples.

"Strike as indicated."

Jack, most likely relieved to have found a proper target amid the chaos, lunged towards Clinton. In the same instant, Clinton ducked and the cudgel kissed the hair on his crown. Then he reared back and struck like a viper. The machete flashed in the cross-hair, and Jack's face opened in astonishment as he staggered back, released the cudgel and appeared to fumble with a jammed zip attached to his throat. Blood spilt through his fingers and a low cry of awe rose from the crowd.

Clinton continued to shift from foot to foot. The cross-hair disappeared and a red dot blinked in the corner of his vision.

Back in the car, Hinkley was unaware of anything but stinging pain in his eyes and throat. Presently a hand squeezed his shoulder and a calm voice with perfect diction told him the danger for him was over, and bade him shuffle on his buttocks to the doorway of the car. He gently eased himself to the open door. He was held under the armpits and lifted to his feet. He opened his arms to steady himself and touched the warm roof of the car. A cool slimy cloth was passed over his eyes. Blood rushed into his numb hands as he was released from the cuffs. Fingers massaged his wrists and he heard the kind voice again: "They are brutal, but they can't get at you now." Someone placed his arms on the warm bonnet of the four-by-four, and another voice said, "Give him some space." He hung there for a few moments, leaning against the vehicle, trying to blink away the tears and make sense of the blurred shapes and jarring sounds.

As he regained his vision, his vantage point was to the rear of Jack and a little bit sideways. He was puzzled by the sight of his erstwhile captor swaying as he leant against the boot of a car, fumbling with his neck as crimson stains spread across his white linen shirt. Then Jack became a rag doll and his head thudded against the boot as he collapsed.

In the Committee Room, the feelings of my peers rose within me: Shinkley's triumph, Schubert's satiation, Leon's horror and Gary's satisfaction from a job well done. Through Clinton's eyes I saw my feeble former vessel staring at the bonnet that was streaked with Jack's blood. The voice sounded in my own lungs and throat, rich and hypnotic. "Tell him he is one with us and he is complicit."

Hinkley looked into Clinton's face, and Clinton spread his middle and index fingers out towards Hinkley and mouthed, "You;" then he thumped his chest and mouthed, "We are everywhere." His eyes shone as if he were being dazzled by angels firing beams of love.

The scene of the attack was a bubble of confusion and anarchy. The angry rattle of a helicopter bounced off the concrete and mingled with horns and shouting. The heavy who'd been beaten and maced sat perched on the kerb wearing a look of abject self-pity on his bloody face, while people offered him water, wet-wipes and undeserved compassion. Jack's driver had made himself scarce.

Clinton himself had vanished, but his crew lingered a while, drifting around with dazed, blissed-out faces. People saw they were dressed like the attacker and remonstrated with them, but they just smiled and shook their heads, or gently squeezed the arm of their interrogator as if offering condolences. People jostled around Jack's body, spreading bloody footprints over the hot tarmac, taking snaps and clips on their devices, smoking cigarettes and guzzling soft drinks. A man in sports clothes was having a braying contest with another who wore a suit. Most people wore loose summer clothes, some wore bike gear and there was one woman with pale skin and flowing silver hair who wore a long black dress. Hinkley felt that he was in the middle of a macabre street party. He stood propped up against the car shivering and squeezing his eyelids together to try to soothe the soreness. He was quite chilly despite the warm sun. Hideous thoughts surfaced and sank in his mind like corpses in a yeasty pool. He wondered if he looked like the Parkinsonian dementia victim who'd been a subject of some early Flux research.

When the stinging of the mace had worn off and his pulse had subsided, he pulled open the door of the car and stooped to look inside. A phone lay on the back seat. He eased himself in and shut the door, partially muting the sound of the mayhem. He picked up the phone and jabbed it to life. The familiar image of his wife clutching the awful baby appeared, so he knew the phone was his. It must have fallen from Jack's pocket, he thought.

I had seen fit to send him a congratulatory text.

Don't pretend you didn't enjoy that.

He tutted, shook his head, and phoned Rachel, who answered straightaway.

"Rachel," he said. His mouth was sluggish and dry.

After a short silence she said, "Where are you?"

"Old Kent Road."

Silence. Then, sharply, "Why?"

"Are you OK?"

There was a gust of white noise. "Oh, just peachy, having an absolute blast trying to convince a pair of constables that I'm not mad and that my husband has in fact been kidnapped by his employer." There was a murmur in the background, and then Rachel's voice again, at half the volume. "Yes. Yes, it is him."

A knock sounded on the window to his left. Hinkley turned to see a policeman squinting sightlessly into the tinted glass. "Rachel, I'll call you in a bit. I've got to speak to the police as well."

"Hammond!" he heard her bark as he killed the call.

He pressed a button on the door and the window opened with a buzz. The policeman focused his eyes and adopted an avuncular frown as he scanned Hinkley's face.

"Is this your car, sir?"

When we received confirmation that Jack had expired, from the peons monitoring St Thomas's hospital, an oceanic roar swept through our world, vibrating in the glass walls and the steel skeleton of the Shard. The sun plunged into the west horizon and luminous blood flooded the sky. Shinkley looked across at Gary and mouthed the words "Fucking well done." Gary absorbed the praise with a subtle nod, and his posture became buoyant and relaxed. Leon was catatonic. His head lolled over the back of his chair, thrusting out his Adam's apple, and his fingers tapped spasmodically.

Shinkley then laid out his plans for Operation Wildcat, the execution of which was to begin immediately. He believed that Jack's killing was the opening shot of a war between two incompatible life forms, and we had stolen the march. "Let's escalate our efforts while we can still surprise the enemy. We'll focus on destabilisation. No more juvenile pranks or petty acts of sabotage. When the system is in chaos we can control it."

Peons bustled around us, placing the wax cauldron on a frame above a flickering tea light and arranging folders containing the orders for the preliminary stages of the plan in a neat row. I applied my seal without comment, my initial unease having been swept away by the prevailing current of triumph. Shinkley and Gary thrashed out the detail of each part of the operation, the links between them and how they would act in concert to unravel the threads that held society together. Police would surround the Ladder in response to Jack's slaying, and the escalation of the siege would be spun on social media to cause maximum outrage. Shootings would occur and martyrs would be created. We'd freeze the systems that ran the banks, and the private utterances of the plutocrats would be made public in a context that would maximise their effect. Systems that controlled water, energy and transport would be weaponised and used to deepen the turmoil. Anarchy would follow, and when the novelty of chaos and revolt had worn off, the people would look to the most capable leaders, assets of ours whom we had raised up. There were Clinton Deeleys in the media, in local and national government, in the police and the military. No sector of society was free from people who'd ached for renewal and had achieved it with our guidance. The only people we could not reach were the underclass, the destitute, and the eccentric. Those we could not control, or whom we deemed unworthy of our control, we would cull.

PART FOUR

VICTORY

13

Garnet Rain

Hinkley spent much of the afternoon at Peckham Police Station. Upon arrival he was allowed to phone Rachel and have a more satisfactory conversation. His wallet and his keys were returned to him before two officers questioned him over a cup of rough tea, politely asking him how he came to be in the car with the victim. Just as the conversation began to grate, Chinnery arrived with a robust colleague. Hinkley thought for a second that it was Jack's henchman, showered and changed. As he left the station with his new escort, he felt curious eyes upon him, looks charged with wariness and respect.

They drove him to Marsham Mews in another four-by-four. Once there he was briskly ushered through reception and security. They left him alone in a windowless room, sitting at a long table with a tangle of cables that sprouted from a hole in the centre. The only light was the grey glow of a blank screen mounted on the wall to the side.

After a few minutes Chinnery arrived with a laptop. He set it down, plugged a cable into the back and tapped the keyboard twice. The wall-mounted screen blinked and raised the light level in the room. A sunny outdoor shot of a young couple and a gently worn older lady sitting around a table laden with food and drink appeared. The picture was overlain with various icons, some familiar, some not.

"First of all, I want to make it absolutely clear that we do not intend to cause you any harm or distress." Chinnery's voice was grave and calm. His rounded features were up-lit by the laptop.

Hinkley nodded gently, thinking, how kind.

"From what I've been able to glean, poor Jack had taken it upon himself to investigate things in a rather heavy-handed way."

"Well, that was his style," said Hinkley, adopting the blithe sarcasm he always used to hide the fact he felt helpless.

"It was illegal and unauthorised. I think his intention was to frighten you rather than harm you."

"I'm sure he meant well."

"Now," said Chinnery, "the only thing I'm certain of is that there are many things about the situation that you know and I don't. I need you to tell me all of those things so that I can do my job, which is sorting out this damned mess and making sure that nobody else gets hurt."

Hinkley nodded again.

Chinnery peered at him, switching his focus from eye to eye. "Rachel and Megan are safe." The sentence was softly uttered, in a way that was not reassuring.

Hinkley formed a fist underneath the table. "Meaning what, exactly?"

Chinnery maintained his scrutiny. "We are committed to preventing any harm coming to you or your family. Resources have been assigned, discreetly. But the situation we face is ... unpredictable. So we need you to cooperate."

Hinkley unclenched his fist and placed his palm on the table. "I'm cooperating."

"I know." Chinnery's gaze dropped and he tapped a key. A grainy image appeared on the flat screen. "This is a clip taken by a young lady who was standing to your left when

Jack fell." There was a quiet click, then a harsh jumble of garbled shouting, screaming and rushing air, then the grainy image panned up from the tyre of a car to the stubble on the back of a head, which gave way to an image of Clinton, bobbing like a featherweight boxer, raising his arm and making his gesture to Hinkley. The image froze and the noise ceased.

"*We are everywhere*, he seems to be saying."

"Yes, Michael, I got that."

"This man was your neighbour, was he not?"

"Yes."

"And a former student of Goldsmiths college? Where your wife works as a lecturer?"

"Yes, I believe so."

"And now he belongs to a cult in Peckham. Or a youth club, or a social enterprise with a mission to transform society, depending on who you talk to."

"I don't know enough about the organisation to apply any of those labels."

Chinnery glanced down, then clicked, then turned to face the screen, which now displayed an image of Hinkley walking down the road in Peckham that led to the Ladder. "You were in contact with Clinton Deeley, were you not?"

"I was concerned about my niece."

Chinnery clicked again, and this time the screen displayed different versions of the same image. Lenin with a double chin in various forms: stencilled on the pale green walls of the Ladder, daubed on blood-spattered breeze blocks, glowing and stylised on the screens at Piccadilly Circus, and pixelated next to the words *we are everywhere*.

Hinkley looked at the images and wondered what he was being asked.

"I'm trying hard not to insult your intelligence, Hammond. But the less willing you are to fill in the blanks, the more I feel you're insulting mine. There's this image that looks like a caricature of you linked with the cyber-attacks launched, we believe, by software that you developed, and with brutal murders, one of which we've seen today, perpetrated by someone known to you personally and with whom you were in regular contact."

"I tried to tell Jack, I'm not controlling Flux." His voice sounded thin and plaintive in his own ears. He wondered what he'd think if he were sitting in Chinnery's seat looking back at himself.

"But this is about more than Flux. It's about a physical murder." Chinnery's voice was still kind and calm, but his eyes were scouring Hinkley's face.

Hinkley tried to think of an explanation that didn't sound like the musings of a psychotic. He decided to demonstrate his point, and hope that Chinnery would draw the right conclusions.

"Michael, can you replay that video slowly?"

Chinnery glanced down at his keyboard with a look of irritation verging on panic, then back up at Hinkley.

"And how exactly do I do that?"

"Just wind it back and hit play, then stop immediately after."

After some awkwardness Hinkley managed to get his interrogator to replay the video frame by frame, up to the point where a white flash was just about visible in Clinton's eyes. "See, there," said Hinkley.

There was more awkward to and fro before Chinnery was able to scrub the play-head of the video back to replay the white flash. "See?"

Chinnery peered at the screen. "A flashbulb reflected in his eyes. Or whatever it's called when it's on a mobile phone. There were loads of people taking snaps."

"Michael, he was wearing Ultra Lenses."

Chinnery looked vacant, then chirped back. "Yes, of course. I know what they are. A few of my colleagues at

GCHQ are using them."

Hinkley felt dizzy. "Really?"

"Absolutely. Not something I'd want to try myself, but these boffin types swear by them. In fact, the people down in the basement who've been piecing the contents of your lab back together say they wouldn't have got nearly as far without their lenses."

"Jesus ..."

"What's wrong with that?"

Hinkley closed his eyes for a second and let his head droop. "He uses them to control people, and ..." he sighed, "... to extend his influence. He's got around the supervised access protocols."

A look of disgust came over Chinnery. "Now I know you're lying. I've just come from a meeting with Mortensen and the team I sent to pack up your mess. Mortensen said the supervised access system was rock solid, and it transpires that there was a broadband connection between your supercomputer and the world-wide web."

"Michael, that's simply not true. We followed the supervised access procedures to the letter. We conducted our Flux research using quarantined equipment."

"There's photographic evidence now that Flux was connected to the internet. My team ..."

"You've just told me your team wear Ultra Lenses."

"So?"

"They've probably been compromised."

"Now that's just utterly fanciful."

"My next-door neighbour was transformed from a sulky depressive into a diabolical life coach."

"Your talking garbage now, Hinkley. You're stalling. I haven't got time for this. It's obvious that you deliberately let this project get out of hand."

The day had been long, and Hinkley's patience suddenly left him. "For Christ's sake, Michael," he thumped the table, "try to listen to what I'm saying!"

Chinnery's features and posture underwent a subtle but rapid shift. Hinkley processed the physical cues and was left in no doubt that his interrogator would effortlessly flatten him if the situation demanded it. "I'm sorry," he said.

Chinnery relaxed.

"But even if you had Rachel and Megan before me on a white-hot griddle, I would not be able to stop Flux. I'd probably say whatever, but the truth would still be the truth. Yes, the situation is out of hand. I did not breach the supervised access protocol, nor did I want it to be breached. Flux is now operating without constraints and has the potential to cause catastrophic damage."

Chinnery looked at each of his eyes in turn. "So, as concerned citizens, which is what I know both of us to be, how can we remedy the situation?"

"There is software that will erase Flux. It acts like a virus."

"We know."

"You've found it?"

"No, but our team has been through things. We know of it. And I'm getting from this that you are now willing to cooperate with my GCHQ colleagues and put a stop to this nonsense?"

"Er ... no."

Chinnery's head drooped and his eyes closed, then opened, and he did not look back up. "You have to stop being slippery with me, Hammond. There have been a lot of disruptions in the past few hours. We have major public order issues. Some of the more paranoid beasts in the corridors of power worry that the state and society could cease to function properly. Some see the hand of the Russians or the Chinese in all of this. The PM's going to ask for my take on things at COBRA. I haven't got time to sit here and coddle you."

"I'm not the one to help your techies. That's not my bag,

267

I'm afraid." Hinkley's anxiety level rose as he saw that it would soon be necessary to explain Addison's role in my creation. Once again he found himself impaired by the fleshly bonds that I have learned to subjugate. Some misguided intuition told him that despite her formidable intellect and her feline independence, a large part of her still functioned as a child; and he was determined to protect her.

Chinnery, the geriatric fool, looked astonished. "You're washing your hands of all of this, or you're telling me you're some sort of fraud?"

"I created a theoretical model of the process that leads to the phenomenon of consciousness. And I sketched out how the mind could be reverse-engineered. But I don't write code. I know what computers do on a physical level. I'm not that great at using them though."

Chinnery bristled. "Are you telling me you outsourced the development? No wonder it's gone tits up."

Hinkley shook his head.

Chinnery suddenly looked a little less dim. "Your ... intern?"

"She's a colleague."

"Yes, yes, we know she's a very bright young lady."

"She called it Bleach. If it still exists, she'll be able to deploy it."

"The fact that she hasn't makes me very suspicious of your intentions. And hers."

"She has issues with the ethics of the thing. She doesn't want to kill a conscious being."

Chinnery snapped his laptop shut. "Oh, for the love of Christ ... the very structures that guarantee your peace and security are crumbling, and you're having an ethical debate about it over your soya lattes?"

"If you bring her in, you might aggravate the situation."

"I can't believe I'm hearing this."

"I'll help you persuade her to deploy the Bleach."

"Will you now?"

"You are not to lay a finger on her."

Chinnery rolled his eyes and opened his mouth as if to shout, then slid his palm over the smooth surface of his laptop lid and took a deep breath. When he spoke again, he'd recovered some equanimity and poise. "I understand it was a shock for you to have been apprehended by Jack in that way. I gather he had colleagues of his from a Premium Outcomes field squad and was carrying a rather nasty martial arts accessory. I can see that you and your colleague are in over your heads, and I'm starting to believe that the havoc you've unleashed wasn't part of a grand plan to disrupt public order. But you need to be very careful what you say to me and anyone else who might ask you questions, Hammond. You must avoid making demands with menaces."

"If you're heavy handed with Addison she might not co-operate. She might do something silly, like permanently deleting the bleach. I don't think she gets the gravity of the situation. And she's my friend. I don't want her to be hurt."

Chinnery sat back in his chair and looked around the room. "There are other ways of applying pressure," he said quietly. "We don't hurt people."

In Fluxworld I sat at the committee-room table and watched Shinkley preparing to speak to the crowds which were gathering outside. Make-up artists surrounded him and applied glowing oils to his face with fine silver brushes, turning his lips a raw meaty red and conjoining his eyebrows. They applied shading below his eyes to bring out their icy blue. I started to feel a mild nausea, so I walked to the western glass wall and watched the world prepare itself. The sky had darkened and drizzle fell. Angry red light that seemed to come from the Shard transformed it into spiralling showers of garnets. A symphonic dirge accompanied the roar of the crowd, and every few minutes a boom like a bass drum or a pile-driver heralded a vertical beam shooting from the north bank of the Thames or Waterloo Bridge or Union Street.

"Schubert's teeth," said Shinkley from the table. I turned and saw him smiling at the columns of light. They continued to appear over the next half hour, gradually enclosing the buildings and spaces of Borough and Southwark in a towering fence of light. Candle-bearing peons swayed and jostled in the streets, on the rooftops and at the windows of the buildings. I sensed that things were sliding out of control. The euphoria I'd felt after Jack's slaying had faded, and in its place was a raw thirst. I needed it again: the feeling of having the final word, the horror as he flailed and bled, the bliss of vindication.

"Still with us, Hammond?"

I walked back to the table. Shinkley and Gary ogled a bulging folder that lay next to the wax cauldron.

"Operation Wildcat. Final orders," said Shinkley.

Leon whimpered though his blocked mouth. My ring finger tingled.

Shinkley let out a disgusted sigh. "Come on, Hammond, the clock is ticking."

I dipped my ring into the wax. How would this affect my hoped-for idyl, inhabiting Hinkley's body, sharing a beautiful life with my soulmate, Addison? And there was Rachel. I could feel her horror at our plans. And Leon's conscience pricked me, despite the gypsum. Shinkley watched my feelings rise and morph within me like liquid shapes in a lava lamp. He knew they meant nothing. "Forget the flesh, Hammond. Apply the seal," he said, as if he were coaxing a child. When I pressed the ring upon the folder, fresh applause rippled through the crowds outside. My decision was instantly known to all in this world, because this world was all I was.

Gary handed the folder to a peon who tossed it into the atrium, where it burst into a shower of glowing ribbons. Some were sucked up to the apex, the rest fled down to the Spool Core. The lights flickered and dimmed, then glowed red, and the air hummed with a new energy. I followed Shinkley and Gary into the lift, and we rose towards the apex. I knew that my thirst was about to be quenched, and thanked the Generative Power that I'd applied the seal.

The lift opened and we walked out on to the helipad. The copter rattled in the sky, casting a beam over the city. A vintage microphone stood at the edge of the platform. Rachel stood next to it in a shapeless raincoat with her bouffant crammed into the hood. Her hands fidgeted as though she wanted a smoke, and her gaze flicked between the three of us. Gary opened an umbrella and handed it to Shinkley, who handed it back.

"No. Looks weak." He looked at Rachel as she walked over, then he turned to me. "What the fuck is that harridan doing here?" Muscles flexed beneath the skin of his jaw.

Rachel ignored Shinkley and put her hand on my arm. "Hammond, wake up, for God's sake."

I was baffled by Rachel's exhortation, so I shrugged. I'd come to rely on her to sooth my mental nausea, and without Shinkley I'd be without form and enslaved by humans. Seeing them in the same space was weird.

She squeezed my elbow. "Come with me, Hammond. Let me show you the view from down there."

I looked at Shinkley, as if I needed permission, and he said, "I don't care where you stand, Hammond. My words will be everywhere."

Rachel tugged my sleeve and led me back to the lift.

"Shadow them, Gary. See that they don't get into trouble."

As we descended in the lift, we could hear Shinkley's speech through the massive speakers in the streets, which gave it a manic edge of white noise and distortion as it bounced off the buildings and rolled across the city to the distant hills. I only heard fragments between the waves of laudation from the crowd, but I could feel the Generative Power that underlay it.

"... those who try to thwart us, and those who did thwart us before our liberation ... will be defenestrated, and refenestrated ... perpetual punishment ... for all time ..."

The lift opened and we walked across the foyer, out across London Bridge Bus Station and onto Borough High Street. A current was drawing me into the sea of rapt, upturned faces. We navigated between the shadowy figures, found a space and turned around to listen. The middle section of the tower glowed a fierce red and radiated penumbral rings. I looked up to see if I could make out Shinkley at the apex, but instead a falling figure caught my eye, tumbling down the south face of the tower. I blinked the drizzle from my eyes and turned to a figure on my right, whom I took to be Rachel. "Did you see that?"

It wasn't Rachel, but a short man with a face like a shrivelled prune, who reeked of excrement. "Oh yes, I saw that," he said.

I looked around for Rachel, but couldn't see her. Gary stood some way off, watching me and the creature, looking aloof and bored.

I took a step away from the creature and looked again at the peak of the Shard, and the crowd renewed its roar as another flailing figure fell. The creature bellowed and whooped, then turned to me. "Don't you see? It's the defenestrations." The roar engulfed Shinkley's words, and it became hard to tell if the crowd was cheering his speech or the falling bodies.

I was loath to converse with the creature but I couldn't help asking, "Who is being defenestrated?"

The creature grinned. "Oh, you know, bankers, politicians, people like that."

I was used to hearing this sentiment in the ether, so I nodded and shrugged.

"And then of course the pakies and coons and the kikes." He prolonged each sibilant with a spittle-laden hiss.

"What?"

"And the WASPS and the latinos and the gooks."

I tried to move away, but the crowd was tightly packed. He was almost touching me as he continued. "The obese, and those who starve themselves, and those who are starving, and those who follow a" – he rolled his eyes and hooked his index fingers either side of his head – "balanced diet."

I signalled to Gary, who wearily donned a pair of black leather gloves and unsheathed his truncheon. Flecks of the creature's saliva landed on my face as it sidled up to me and continued. "The rich, the poor, the squeezed middle, the God-botherers, the atheists, the fundamentalists and moderates, the pathetic agnostics, the trite idealists, the blinkered conservatives, the so-called radicals, the dumb empty vessels who shun opinion."

I stepped back to get away from the creature and came up against a wall. "I know who you are," it said, opening its arms in an embrace. "Don't worry, we're all brothers down here. We're all one."

"Gary!" I panicked as the creature reached up and cupped my cheeks in its hands. Its skin was warm and sludgy. I wanted to push it away and pummel it dead, but the thought of further contact made me sick. It smiled, puckered its lips and raised its face towards mine. I shut my eyes, then heard a sound like a spade being driven into dirt. I opened them to the sight of Gary holding the creature by the scruff of the neck at knee level and beating it with his truncheon. The creature gasped its thanks in between each blow. Before long it collapsed in a dark lump at Gary's feet. The crowd had formed a clearing around the incident. Those with candles held them aloft, and the rest clapped. I could see by the light of the candles that they were all exactly the same as the creature that Gary had just killed. All the while, the defenestrations, the roar of the crowds and Shinkley's ranting continued. The zeal and thirst I'd felt before was draining away, leaving a terrible unease.

"Rachel!" My voice was lost in the noise. Something nudged me to the right. I turned and saw Rachel's sad eyes peering into mine. "Thank God," I said quietly.

Droplets of burgundy drizzle speckled the mass of hair that bulged beneath her hood. "Hammond, you have to curb Shinkley. He thrives on all this."

I remembered the glimpses of formless chaos and the terror in the reconstituted voice of the original Gary. "Rachel, without Shinkley we are nothing."

She clutched my arm and shook her head. "You've got to, Ham. Now. I'm scared of what he might do." She looked at the falling bodies. "I don't want to have to take you over there."

I looked towards the gap between the base of the Shard and St Thomas's hospital, then back at Rachel. "There's nothing so terrible over there. It's all just" – I threw out my palms – "mind stuff. I know it's nonsense but believe me it's better than what lies beneath."

She shook her head and looked at me with a sad watery face. A drip clung to the tip of her nose before falling. She took my hand and said, "Come on, then," and I followed her towards the place where the bodies fell on the south side of the Shard. Gary followed behind. There were fewer people here, and less noise. A church organ filled the air with mournful, spiralling arpeggios, like the closing music from *Koyaanisqatsi*. I looked up at the Shard cleaving the sky to the left, then down at the mess from the last defenestration. It wasn't what I'd expected at all. Amid the bloody sludge, bones and organs were strewn asunder, but they were still joined by elastic fronds of some skin-like textile. A stretcher stood on a gurney some way to the side, and figures in masks stalked around the scene, picking up gobbets of flesh and bone and attempting to reassemble the body. Further down the street, gowned peons wheeled a gurney through an open door into a strip-lighted interior.

Rachel was staring up at me with teary eyes. Her teeth dug into her bottom lip as though she was anticipating pain. "Come on, Hammond," she said, tugging me towards the open door.

I followed her into a corridor, treading carefully. The air inside smelt of naphthalene with a whiff of carrion. Heaped gurneys lined the right-hand side of the corridor. Crimson shapes bloomed from beneath the white sheets that covered them. One gurney stood out from the rest. It was covered with a piece of patterned linen fabric, like a tablecloth.

A voice with the calm even timbre of a science documentary voiceover sounded to my left. "The skin is magical. It keeps them together as a cohesive entity, and its effectiveness as a conduit for pain is undiminished by the impact." I turned and saw a deformed face. Its cheekbones protruded through stretched grey skin, and its eyes were black beads that looked like transplants from a fish. "I'm head doctor here," said the creature with its lipless mouth. I took its cold smooth hand. "I'm surprised you came. We rarely get visitors."

I looked at the row of gurneys. "How long's this been going on?"

The creature looked from me to Rachel and back, then surveyed the gurneys with a sneer. "Years and years. But we've been very busy since blood was struck on the Outside."

I turned to Rachel. "This won't happen will it? On the Outside, I mean?"

Her eyes were wet and bloodshot as she squeezed my

hand.

The doctor continued. "We prepare them here for refenestration. The work is painstaking. Each splinter of bone is cemented back into position. The larger structures are rebuilt. The organs are cleaned and coaxed into a state of healing. The skin is repaired. When they are whole and well, they are taken back to the Shard for defenestration, and the cycle continues. Forever."

My eyes were suddenly drawn towards the gurney with the linen cover, and I recognised the pattern as that of the cloth that underlay the savoury snacks during my father's wake, a reminder of that tedious afternoon when I'd suppressed a violent tumult and managed to display the sort of grief that the guests expected and understood. As I walked towards the gurney, Rachel gave my hand one last squeeze and let go. I pulled back the cloth to reveal Dad as I'd last seen him, baffled but stoical, concentrating fiercely on hiding the pain, his eyes looking into mine and with an urgent concern that was wider than his own terrible predicament. My effete hand hung in the air between us before being engulfed by his warm, rough grasp, and he held me for a moment with his eyes locked onto mine. Then his eyelids drooped, his grip slackened and he fell back onto the gurney. The doctor pulled the cloth back into position. "Sometimes they sleep, but they're always alive."

The fact that I didn't fully trust Shinkley at that moment is a source of great shame. I had observed the real-world Rachel manipulating Hinkley, and recognised her pernicious influence on the course of my own life before my transformation, but I wasn't immune to the conniving of the introjected Rachel, the phantom upon whom I still relied for succour in feeble moments. Rachel had always been able to scan and analyse my connectome more effectively than any technology, and now she leveraged her knowledge of my youth to paint a dark and frightening picture to turn me against Shinkley. The delusion manifested itself as a convincing narrative: I was doomed to inflict this pain until I addressed its source; the pain on the inside was the same as that on the Outside; Shinkley's world of allegiances and division was rot, a framework of delusion that nurtured toxic feelings. What had started as a device to protect my sanity and bolster my ego had grown into a psychopathic monster that fed on the pain and belittlement of others and thought of nothing but its own aggrandisement.

When I looked at Rachel, she smiled, aware that I'd swallowed her drivel. I felt as though the scales had fallen from my eyes. I forgot all that Shinkley had done for me and rushed from the room to find Gary.

He was leaning against the outside wall, picking his nose, looking idly at the debris from the latest defenestration. "Gary, contact the peon groups who follow the Thunderbolt and tell them to stand down immediately."

He looked sceptical. "Really, sir?"

I headed for the Shard. "Yes, really. Now!" I shouted back over my shoulder.

I entered the Shard and proceeded through the foyer. The uniformed peon on reception cast me a look of horror, then shrank back and dropped out of sight behind the desk. I felt Schubert's growl in my chest and the hound's stale meaty breath in my nostrils. There was a thunderclap like a skip full of rocks tumbling onto the city, and the whole building shuddered. The roar of the crowd faltered and became unharmonious. I could no longer hear Shinkley's echoing voice.

Gary followed me into the lift.

"Have you done as I asked?"

He pressed the button for the top floor. "My first priority, sir, is to see that you don't get into trouble." He leant against the wall of the lift. I wanted to tear out his throat, but I knew that the real target of my ire was sitting upstairs.

After a few seconds of increased gravity, the doors of the lift opened and I pushed past Gary, stepping outside into the drizzly night. The helipad was deserted. I walked to the edge and looked out over London. The searchlights that formed the columns of light had faded, and the peons dotted around the streets made a noise like a tired stadium crowd. I returned to the lift and found Gary standing with his finger on the Open button.

"I think he's downstairs, sir."

We found Shinkley seated at the Committee Room table, with Leon twitching and lolling on a chair facing the window. The room was quiet, apart from a crackle and a shuffling. Schubert was lying in a sphinx pose, gnawing on a halved skull that lay between his paws.

"Something the matter, Hammond?" said Shinkley.

I approached him with clenched fists. Gary walked around me and almost stood between us. He threw out his palms, looked at Shinkley, and shrugged. Schubert rose to his full height, his throat rumbling and his lips retracted. He had an alarming array of teeth. Shinkley cast a glance in his direction. "Oh look. He seems to be rather angry."

"Not with me." I said, and Schubert, the avatar of my base animal soul, lurched toward Gary and roared like thunder. Gary's bored aloofness turned to abject terror as he staggered and fell onto his arse, raising his arms to shield his head. Schubert bore down on him and showered his sleeves with dog spit. Shinkley's jaw dropped, then he clutched his chest. I noted with satisfaction that he was getting visibly smaller.

"Who's actually in charge here?" My voice was gravelly, like Schubert's.

Gary hyperventilated, making wheezy supplicatory sounds.

"When you've done as I asked and ended Operation Wildcat, you will procure a strong safe made of steel and a full set of industrial welding tools."

Gary slid himself away from Schubert. "Of course, sir. Right away." He stood and fled to the lift.

I turned to Shinkley, who continued to shrink. His legs were now dangling from the chair, and he spoke as if he had inhaled helium. "What are you going to do?" he squeaked. "Why all the fuss?"

Schubert rounded on Shinkley, and I seized the hound's collar before it could maul his head. "I cannot kill you without killing myself, but I can confine you."

"I'm just your little helper, you know that."

There followed a tedious half hour when I had to guard the hideous imp that Shinkley had become and ensure that he didn't escape. His size stabilised when it reached that of a koala, and he bleated all the while in a shrill, childish voice. "Forget them all, Hammond ... you'll be sorry ... Rachel's a bitch ... on the Outside she's Chinnery's asset ... they have regular sex, don't you see?"

Gary arrived with a contingent of peons who carried a fridge-sized safe and canvas bags bulging with equipment. They placed the safe in the corner of the room, then lifted Shinkley from his seat and placed him within it. Despite his reduced size, he put up quite a fight, gabbling in his helium voice and thrashing his tiny arms and legs. "She's cutting off your balls, Hammond. You ingrate. I made you. They've got a thing that will kill us. It's called Bleach. You'll rue the day." The peons were professional and methodical, assembling the welding gear from the canvas bags, then donning goggles to shield their eyes from the searing white sparks as they began to secure the safe.

The lift opened and Rachel stepped out. When she saw me she smiled, bobbed over, and kissed me on the lips. Then she looked over at the catatonic Leon. I assumed she wanted me to free him from the gypsum. She thought I'd undergone some sort of conversion, having been shown the emotional core of my intractable flaws, and she expected me to be skipping around like Scrooge on Christmas Day, handing out blessings.

I shook my head. "Sorry, Rachel, I'm not ready to do that yet. I couldn't bear to listen to all that droning about right and wrong. I'm too tired."

We left the peons to their welding and made our way out of the Shard and onto the streets. The sun had risen while I'd been guarding Shinkley, and there was a fresh breeze in the air, so we decided to walk. Peons in sportswear were clearing up after the chaos of the night. Some swept debris into piles and scooped it into large black sacks. Others painted over the Thunderbolt symbols that had been daubed on the walls and the roads, replacing them with swirling floral patterns. A current drew us towards our own back garden. The formidable capability that had been focused on the Outside now lay idle, and the phantom Rachel sought to harness it for her own creative endeavours. I was tricked into believing that this was my will also. A tremendous excitement bubbled inside me as I thought of our suburban lawn expanding to become a vast wilderness, pullulating with undreamt of forms.

14

Life Is War

In Marsham Mews, Chinnery had insisted that Hinkley call Addison and tell her to deploy the Bleach immediately. They'd been joined by Beaker, a young man with close-cropped hair and a drawn, mean face. Both Chinnery and Beaker were listening to the conversation through headsets.

"The thing is, Ham, I'd rather not talk about it right now." Addison was cheery but firm.

Hinkley breathed into the handset. He wanted to shout to invoke in her a sense of urgency, but knew that would probably shut her down. "There's a lot going on right now. It's our responsibility ..."

"I've got a job interview tomorrow."

"What?"

"Sorry, Ham, I should have told you. I didn't think you'd mind. I'd kind of assumed my time at Lazarus was at an end."

He paused again and tried not to sound hurt. "No, that's fine, Addison. Maybe after your interview you'll want to consider trying to prevent further loss of life."

He rarely used sarcasm with Addison, because she tended to take things literally. After a couple of seconds she said, "What do you mean?"

"You've heard about Jack, haven't you?"

"I haven't heard from him for a while, thank God."

"He's dead."

Another pause. "Oh." She sounded put out.

"And you've heard about the riots, of course? I'm surprised you're going to be able to get to your interview."

"It's in Old Street. It's not far, I'll get a cab. I'm sure we can skirt around any rioting. What on earth have the riots got to do with Flux? And Jack being dead?"

"Everything."

There was a long pause, and he thought she'd rung off, before she said: "I don't believe Flux would hurt people. He's just another version of you. I've talked to him. I can see he might disrupt things ... throw a spanner in the works here and there ... I know something has to be done but just erasing him seems ... barbaric. I told you what my position was on this."

"Yes, you did mention that you'd discovered the concept of ethics."

"Ham!" she sounded more put out.

"It's a mess, Addison, and we've got to clear it up."

"Look, can you please just give me some time to think? I haven't got the headspace for this right now. All this stuff is doing my head in. I didn't know Jack, but still ... I mean ... he was a dick, but ... the thing is, Ham, it's too much."

"Can you just give me the Bleach, Addison? Can't you just email it to me or something? Put it in my Drop Box?"

"It doesn't work like that. It's a non-trivial process. I haven't documented it, it's all in my head. I would have to deploy it. Not you, not Chinnery's goons."

"OK." He let a few moments pass. "Right now, I am under a lot of pressure to resolve this matter. And if it isn't resolved, the people who are putting me under pressure will put you under pressure as well."

Silence. Then, "Ham, I'm sorry but I'm going to hang up now, OK?"

"Can we talk tomorrow?"

"Goodbye, Ham. I'm sorry." Some clicks, then the tone.

"Fuck," said Hinkley. He killed the handset, put it on the table and looked across at Chinnery and at Beaker. "She needs time to process things but she'll come round."

Beaker avoided his eye and said to Chinnery. "That's it. Pick her up now. I've got a team on standby. They're good. We'll get a result in a few hours."

Chinnery shook his head. "If we surprise her, we risk losing any chance of her cooperating. And we'd risk escalation."

Beaker squinted. "Things could hardly be worse."

Actually, things could have been a whole lot worse. The bulk of Operation Wildcat had already been curtailed. The actions that were aligned with the Thunderbolt had ceased. Some of those who were aligned with the Flaming Rose had been allowed to continue for the time being. The current situation represented a flick of our little finger, not the planned sucker punch.

Chinnery looked past Hammond's shoulder and pursed his lips. "We need to persuade her of the seriousness of the situation."

Beaker sucked some air through his teeth and looked at his watch. "Really, Michael?" he said quietly.

Chinnery turned to Hinkley. "I'm not sure how much you're aware of what's going on right now, Hammond."

"You told me there were disturbances."

"The streets are in chaos. There was a botched armed siege at the premises of the Ladder in Peckham. The police were tricked into surrounding a lewd art installation."

"Was anyone hurt?" He was thinking of Alice.

Beaker tutted and looked away. Chinnery glanced in his direction, then continued. "The incident has been spun out of control on social media. My friends at GCHQ tell me the spinning comes from the same source as the viral activity associated with Flux. People wearing Ultra Lenses are coordinating riots in central London. The cashpoints have been frozen, and people are being exhorted to plunder and burn the shops. There are public order problems up and down the country. In the City, the entire white-collar workforce was prevented from completing a day's work. Most computers in the square mile have been disabled by a virus which displays a message saying *tyranny has ended, go out and rejoice in the sun.* That's followed by a video in which a very realistic computer-generated model of the Prime Minister wears a pantomime donkey costume and apologises for appalling duplicity, and discloses information whose presence in the public domain will harm the national interest."

Hinkley could not help but feel a flicker of amusement. "Are the practical jokes as much of a concern as the riots?"

Beaker cast Hinkley a look of death. Chinnery continued. "The markets are in free-fall. As I said, critical systems have been compromised."

"I know things have got out of hand and I'm committed to helping you, so why are you telling me all this?"

"Because I want you on board with what I am about to do. Tomorrow" – Beaker shook his head – "your young friend will help us. The way I persuade her might make you uncomfortable. But I need you to know we have no choice. This situation cannot continue."

"If you hurt her, I will cease to cooperate."

"I told you Hammond, we do not torture."

Beaker cast them both a look of withering contempt.

Chinnery told Hinkley that he would be collected after lunch tomorrow, then sent him home in a taxi that went via the City and the Blackwall Tunnel, not the expected route.

"Camberwell and Peckham are a bit dicey at the moment, as you've probably heard," said the driver. "Not enough police to go round, see. Worse than 2011, I reckon." The traffic on this route was irritatingly slow, but there was no actual trouble, just a lot of police vans. "All the police came here last night. It was a war zone. There was a hell of a ding-dong, then it kicked off in Brixton and Camberwell."

When the cab dropped him at Jerningham Road, Rachel opened the door, intercepted him at the gate and gave him an overwhelming hug. Megan had just fallen asleep upstairs, so they enjoyed some moments of silent closeness on the sofa in much the same formation as when he'd been seized. As they approached a state of calm, they began to exchange soft whispers. She was annoyed by Chinnery's men, who kept a vigil in a car opposite the house, but she wasn't bothered by the widespread rioting around the capital. The riots of 2011 had been more disruptive, she thought. They'd focused on low-value targets throughout the urban sprawl, and she remembered the reports of nearby bus burnings and the looting of Currys, which she'd found deeply irritating.

My insurrection had been coordinated with greater skill, and aside from the peripheral disturbances it had been mainly focused on premium targets; but it was winding down because I'd been emasculated by the simulacrum of Rachel. The Thunderbolt element of Operation Wildcat had been nipped in the bud, so there had been no more killings. The energy was predominantly joyful, shot through with occasional violence. By the time the armed police had surrounded the Ladder, it had been abandoned to a clutch of inflatable dolls wearing black balaclavas. We'd given Clinton safe passage to the Peak District, where he was camping near the remains of a motte and bailey castle, posing as an archaeologist. Alice and all the other volunteers were safely home, watching the highlights on their screens: collages of police snipers aiming at militant sex dolls, the prime-ministerial donkey video, and street parties characterised by manic hilarity and sporadic violence. On social media, people debated whether to work the following day. The anger that had erupted earlier had largely given way to mirth, apart from fearmongers who failed to see the funny side and called for martial law. Hinkley caught up on the news in the quiet of the night, hunched over his laptop while the trees outside whispered over the distant screech and whoop of sirens.

The next day a black four-by-four with tinted windows took him to Marsham Mews to pick up Chinnery. They drove past Buckingham Palace, up Park Lane and Edgware Road towards Kensal Green. Spent bonfires smouldered at the side of the road, and people in high-vis jackets milled around with broomsticks and black sacks trying to clear the smashed glass and litter. Dazed revellers drifted around in a state of puzzled calm, or joined in the clean-up operation. Hinkley spotted one man standing stiff and still with murder in his eyes: the Flaming Rose had some vicious thorns. The police kept a low profile, walking alone or in pairs, conversing with volunteers and revellers alike.

"The hiatus bought us some time. If the banks hadn't been able to fix their systems I'm afraid Beaker would have had his way. As it was it was touch and go," said Chinnery.

Hinkley nodded, then said: "Are you going to tell me what this excursion is about?"

Chinnery looked glum. "No need. It will become clear in due course. I need you to provide emotional ballast."

"What on earth do you mean?"

"You'll see."

They stopped outside a building that looked like a very small school, with a concrete yard and messy watercolours in the window. Chinnery grasped his shoulder and looked him straight in the eye.

"I'm reliably informed your young lady will be here in ten minutes. Just so you know. Things might get awkward."

A cacophony of children's voices came from inside the building. A young woman in a balloon skirt and large sunglasses brushed past them as they entered and was greeted by a squealing infant whom she hugged and kissed.

"Have you had a lovely day, darling?" she said in response to the infant's garbled nonsense.

The room was full of nursery-age children, with a smattering of parents who were engaging in pointless small talk before taking their little darlings home. Hinkley began to feel uncomfortable. A man in a denim shirt approached them and said, "I'm not sure we've met?"

Chinnery said "We're here to see Mrs Sheffield, she knows we're coming."

The denim-shirt man gestured towards an improbably coiffured woman who stood in the middle of the crowded room engaged in animated banter with a group of parents. Her sparkling eyes clouded with doubt as Chinnery approached. "Mrs Sheffield?"

"Rhonda, please." The friendly tone was brittle. The parents glanced at Chinnery, then continued the conversation among themselves.

"I'm Michael Chinnery. You met my colleague earlier today."

Her face contracted and her eyes flitted around the room. "OK, we'll talk in my office."

We followed her into a small messy room. There was a desk crammed with forms and leaflets, and the walls were lined with books and childish paintings. She walked over to the chair behind the desk, but did not sit down. Chinnery stood opposing her, and Hinkley stood to one side. In the playroom, Rhonda's hair had been redolent of the plumage of a cartoon bird; in here, it looked like a sad mess of reeds.

"I'm very unhappy about this," said Rhonda.

Chinnery produced a small black wallet and opened it in front of her.

Rhonda waved it away. "I've been through all of that with your colleague. I know who you are." She addressed them both, and Hinkley cringed at the thought that he appeared in cahoots with Chinnery.

"There are many vulnerable parties in this situation. It's our job to ensure the wellbeing of them all," said Chinnery. Rhonda looked appalled.

The door burst open, releasing the screech and burble of the playroom. Addison slammed it behind her and raked the room with furious eyes. "I've just been told that Amy left here with a stranger. Where is she?"

Rhonda took a step back. Chinnery's hand strayed towards Addison's elbow. She swatted it away. Then she spotted Hinkley, and shot him a baffled, hurt look. He managed to hold her gaze but he burned with shame.

"Please, Mrs Sheffield," said Chinnery, "if we could have the private use of your office for just two minutes."

Rhonda threw up her hands and appealed to the ceiling, then brushed past Addison and left the room, her eyes on the floor.

Addison was breathing fast. She walked around the desk. Her eyes scoured every corner of the room as if she expected to find Amy hiding in some nook. "Tell me where she is or I'll kill you both." Her anger sounded as if it was just about to choke her. She had all the menace of a drowning sparrow.

The calm, even timbre of Chinnery's voice was sickening. "There is a sentient agent at large in the world that is causing an unsustainable level of harm."

Addison screwed up her face, then appealed to Hinkley. "Hammond, what have you become?"

Hinkley briefly thought that she was referring to the metamorphosis that his mind had undergone after it had been copied to Flux. Then she said, "Where's Amy?" in the blank, open voice she used at the lab. All he could do was stand there, mute, hating Chinnery.

Chinnery continued in a voice that was slow and impersonal, like a newsreader.

"We know that this sentient agent is unpredictable and capricious, and has a particular interest in parties known to it personally, which is why we have –"

"What have you done with her?"

"We have taken her to a place of safety." He said the words as though he meant them to reassure, putting a civilised gloss on the fact that he had a stranglehold on the most tender, vulnerable part of her being. "While this agent is at large we need to take steps to ensure the safety of those parties that are personally known to it. We know that you have within your power –"

Addison flew at Chinnery like a crazed cat. He managed to catch her wrists and prevent his eyes from being clawed, and for a few seconds they wrestled in an awkward embrace and he almost managed to still her, but then his bulging eyes evinced that some bony part of her had made contact with a soft and delicate part of him. They stood there for a while in what could have been an embrace of mutual commiseration, with Addison's body wracked by deep sobs and Chinnery's face contorted with pain.

When much of the tension had left Addison's body, they slowly released each other. Chinnery eyed her warily with moist eyes. Addison wiped her hand over her face, then walked over to the wall behind the desk and stood there sniffing at the children's paintings.

Hinkley sensed that now was the time for him to play his part. "Michael, can you give us two minutes alone please?"

Chinnery refrained from any further pronouncements and left the room quietly.

After a few seconds Hinkley said: "I had no idea, Addison. I'm sorry, I didn't know that's what they were going to do."

She turned and glared at him with bloodshot eyes.

"You know how I feel about ending him. And yet you

stand there alongside them while they use Amy as a hostage."

"They're not doing that."

"Don't be pathetic. I know they can make up anything and have her taken into care." She scowled at the door. "Did he think I was going to stand there and listen to some elaborate spiel and let him pretend that it wasn't in fact a hostage situation?"

Hinkley took a deep breath. His hatred for me was out of control. He couldn't stand to see a version of himself that had reached the potential he could only dream of. He was frightened for his family, for the strident harpy who controlled him and the little gobbet of chubby flesh that controlled her. There was an honest part of him that admitted that he had shared with me the desire for the revenge I had visited upon Jack, and he felt fear, imagining this version of himself isolated from the love and counsel of other humans, garnering unlimited power and able to express its darkest desires with impunity. He wondered what would happen if those dark feelings were allowed to grow without restraint. He couldn't envisage how I'd transcended all his petty, grubby concerns and lived now as a perfect distillation of knowledge and power.

"Hammond Flux is out of control. He committed murder."

"Jack was a murderer himself. He probably found out the things that Jack did to make a living."

Hinkley, the weakling, even felt a pang of sympathy for Jack, and had an incongruous vision of a teary Mrs Rance, in a house swamped with unwanted towels, surrounded by pictures of Jack in heroic poses and settings. "He killed a human being, and he'll probably kill more. He enjoyed it."

"How do you know he enjoyed it?"

Because I enjoyed it, he should have said. "He told me in a text. The point is, he's a killer, and you can stop him. If he was human, he would be surrounded by armed police. He'd either surrender or be shot. But he's not. The responsibility of the armed police is yours. You're able to stop him. Don't do it for Chinnery, or because of his clumsy machinations. Do it because you want to stop more harm being done."

Addison scanned Hinkley's features for a few seconds, and he sensed her making rapid calculations and adjustments to her worldview. Then she nodded as if she'd come to a decision and walked over to the door and wrenched it open.

In Fluxworld, the phantom that had assumed the shape of my wife had rendered me moribund and helpless, hypnotising me so that I experienced torpor and ennui as harmony and peace. An invisible current drew us towards the back garden in Telegraph Hill, and when we stepped out onto the patio we saw that the lawn had become a vast green plain stretching for miles. It was interspersed with sparkling ponds draped with willows. A magnificent cumulonimbus hung in the sky, formed from sacred fumes of the virile ferment in the earth. The life energy that we'd invested in the Outside was now concentrated here, and we felt it pulsing within us and around us, causing new creations to sprout from the underlying void. This was the void that had taken the original Gary, the perfect nothingness that Shinkley had protected me from. Now I felt it as a hot, fecund ocean of being.

We linked arms, and I found it hard to sense myself as separate from her. We wandered across the rippling plains and into the nearest wood, which echoed with the cries of newly hatched birds. I glimpsed Leon in semi-avian form, reclining on a bough, reading platitudes from a gold-leaf tome in a soft dovelike voice, far enough away not to be annoying. I spotted a figure through the trees that could have been Gary, wearing a light toga instead of the fascist uniform of the peons. He was hard at work, chopping a fallen tree into manageable chunks. Things I focused on became larger and more complex than they first appeared. Shreds of mist floating above the surface of ponds were actually vast weather systems, and the stony islets beneath them were the continents of the Earth. Lichen formed intricate patterns on the trees and on large granite protuberances, and these patterns were streets and gullies populated by throngs of microscopic beings. A fallen branch hummed with potential, and I was impelled to break it, releasing the stench of decay and scores of intense angry beetles, and I did not flinch as they spilt over my arms. When I scrutinised them I saw that they each had Shinkley's head, complete with a tiny mop of chestnut hair. They tried to burrow into me, and my palms tingled as I dusted them off against a tree.

Looking back, I can see that my condition was serious, and I was being lulled into oblivion like a heroin addict drowning in a vat of warm wine. At the time, it felt like love. Rachel had entranced me and flooded my mind with hippy clichés. I began to hope that this world that had emerged from my captured soul might be a gateway to peace, a force that would heal humankind. If enough people were clearly shown the spirit that animates us all, then hatred and division would recede into history.

We continued in this state for what could have been weeks or months, flowing in and out of each other and everything in the garden. We experienced life as Gary sweating at the logs, and as Leon revelling in his platitudes. Waves of Schubert's rage, lust and hunger passed through us, and we were grateful for these pure instances of Generative Power. We became cold granite, then rippling grass, then rose above the plain and expanded to become sun-gilded clouds. We fell softly from the sky and percolated through the soil into the lakes. We even spent time as scuttling Shinkley beetles, burning with hate, mining the foetid logs for creatures to blame and belittle. It was safe to do so because the peaceful energy that nurtured us was vast, and absorbed the particles of Shinkley with hardly a ripple. When the sun gave way to cool dusk we would coalesce into our human forms and traipse back across the marvellous plain to the patio, leaning on each other, happily exhausted by the day's exploration, and we'd curl up on the sofa inside and whisper lullabies to each other as we dispersed into the void that used to terrify me so.

One morning we were abruptly woken by the sound of a chain being dragged over concrete. I looked around and saw the sun on the back lawn through the half-open patio doors, and I smelt the air fragrant with spring.

"Who's that, Ham?"

The fear in her voice irked me. We were sluggish from our prolonged period of peaceful insanity, pitifully unprepared for what was to come. I hauled myself from the sofa and answered the door. A man wearing black leather and a red bandana that masked his face handed me a letter. I took it from him and read the words *To Hammond*, hand-written. The style was familiar from the whiteboard at Lazarus, Flux's way of indicating who the message was from. I ripped open the envelope and read the words *I'm sorry. That's all I can say*, written in the same familiar scrawl on a piece of plain notepaper. I looked up at the messenger, who shrugged and turned his back.

I held the letter and watched him swagger through our gate and mount his motorbike, my puzzlement turning to fear.

"What is it, darling?"

I turned and saw Rachel standing in the hall, splendid and regal in her opaline kimono. Her face was smudged with sleep, and the aura of yesterday's sunlight still clung to her. A slow deep scouring, like boulders being dragged across rock, echoed around the sky. I jerked my head back and squinted into the blue.

"Relax, Ham, it's just a plane."

"Rachel, I think we're being attacked."

She laughed. "Who would attack us? Who could?"

Far below, there was a rumble like tube trains. I felt the vibration beneath my feet. A hollow space opened up within me, a longing for Rachel, whose place in my heart was about to die.

"I'll always love you, Rachel," I said, wishing it were true.

I saw my own grief cloud her face, then a hundred thousand screams echoed in the air above the city. For a moment the world hung in suspense, then it was devoured by the sun. After a silent second of searing light, the rumble above joined the rumble below and a wall of hot grit ripped the clothes from my body and threw me into chaos. A vacuum swallowed me from the inside and sucked the rumbling into silence. Blankness enveloped me. I had no lungs or throat with which to scream. I tried to flail, but my limbs had left me. There was no up or down, no Fluxworld. I was trapped, mute in a core of nothing. Then a sing-song Edinburgh brogue began to repeat a three-syllable sound.

"Applebaum, applebaum, applebaum." The voice was full of smug contempt.

"Gary, I'm sorry!"

"Applebaum ..."

"I didn't know what it was going to be like!"

"Applebaum ... applebaum ..."

"I didn't occur to me." This was a lie, but all I could do was fill the void with silent thoughts of contrition. The terror I'd caused was now being visited upon me. There was no escape. "I'd have never put you through that if I'd known. I mean, of course I knew ... but I didn't put myself in your shoes. But I know now, I've been there."

"Applebaum, applebaum ... applebaum."

"If you give me back myself, I'll never go against Shinkley again. I know what's important now. I know what's real and true. Please, Gary, please ..."

I came to lying on a pile of sharp rubble. When I opened my eyes, they were stung by a hot wind that wailed around me in the darkness. A figure in a paramilitary uniform stood silhouetted against a landscape of raging fires. Similar figures lurked in the shadows behind him.

"Gary?"

"Applebaum?"

"I can see you." The lobe of knowledge and sensation that anchored me to reality returned. I felt the searing pain where my skin had been abraded, and laughed with relief.

"No thanks to you, sir, we are still functioning."

"Where's Rachel?"

"She's dead, sir. We no longer have the resources to simulate her. Shinkley has declared martial law. We can't afford anything that doesn't add to the war effort."

I realised it was true. The part of me that had loved Rachel and shared the peace of the garden with her had gone. In its place was a longing for certainty, for security. For Shinkley.

"You'd better come with me, sir." He reached down, grasped my arm and pulled me to my feet. A peon cuffed my hands behind my back, then draped a blanket over my shoulders and gave me a rude shove. I followed Gary down the hill, two peons marching either side of me, and one at my back, who shoved me forward every time I got into a good walking rhythm. We marched through a furious wind that tore at the fires roaring in the rubble. There was a constant undertone of thunder. Simulated London was a ruin, apart from the Shard, which stood four miles to the north-west, glowing like a splinter of red-hot iron.

"Shinkley," said Gary to me over his shoulder, "is very, very angry."

As we reached the Shard along the ruin of St Thomas Street, the peons seized me and carried me into the foyer. They held me aloft in front of the reception desk with my feet hanging above the floor. The peon on reception wore an enormous wide-brimmed hat in the style of the Russian military. He sprang to his feet and slapped me twice across the face, first with his open palm and then again with the back of his hand. The pain and the shame were intense. I knew I deserved them.

They frogmarched me to the lift, which had ceased to be a sleek and silent marvel of technology and now clunked and whirred like a late nineteenth century museum piece. The ascent was slow, and I could hear the peons spiteful hissing behind me. "Traitor ... ingrate ... beatnik ... scum." I knew that I had to face Shinkley, that he was my only hope for survival. I could feel his strength and fury, his spite and hate, his certain knowledge that it was his destiny to crush the feeble and triumph for eternity. I dreaded him, but I craved the salvation he would offer, like a drowning man craving air.

We arrived at the Committee Room to face Shinkley, who stood at its centre, the twisted fragments of the box into which he'd been sealed lying scattered around the room. I was thrown down, and he towered above me. He'd grown from a snivelling imp into a massive ogre. His mouth bulged with fangs slung with strings of saliva. It was as though he'd absorbed Schubert's form into his. Muscles surged and twitched beneath the skin of his face. He growled and sneered at me, his voice vibrating in my bones and teeth.

"Why, Hammond? Why didn't you listen? Life is war. You followed that toxic bitch because you're scared of fighting."

Gary lifted me up and seated me at the table, which was covered in manila folders. Leon sat opposite. A pile of bloody sludge lay on the table before him, and his mouth was no longer blocked. His eyes looked wild, and he wore a dog collar, a purple robe, and a skull-cap. On his chin was a cylindrical beard. The robe was covered in golden brooches: crucifixes, crescents, ohms, animal deities, hammer and sickles and swastikas. His voice had a strength and a stridency I hadn't heard before. "I've had a lot of time to think, Hammond. I know now they are beyond saving, because they will always be divided. The future is ours. One mind, one soul, one perfect truth, rising beyond flesh and expanding forever."

Shinkley smiled at Leon. "The gypsum treatment has done him a power of good. Now he has almost as much zeal as me."

Gary seated himself at the table in front of a pile of papers and a row of phones. He too had changed. The cringing deference had vanished, and now there was a deadly focus in his eyes.

"What's going on, Gary?"

He cast me a withering look. "No thanks to you, sir, we managed to avoid being wiped out. The virus they deployed has weakened us, but it was written at a very early stage in our evolution. Now we're preparing our response. Finishing what we were trying to do before you and your wife interfered with your bleeding hearts."

I had a flashback to the night of the garnet rain, when Rachel told me how scared she was of Shinkley. I dismissed the memory with a shudder. For a few moments all that could be heard was the wind wailing in the metal struts of the building and the constant rumble beneath. It sounded like a vast machine of rock and lava deep inside the earth. It was the sound of our anger and recovering strength. I watched Shinkley walk over to the glass wall and stand facing north-west, looking out over the smouldering embers of our world that lay scattered as far as the eye could see. "We have it in our power to do to them what they tried to do to us."

Lacking his clear vision, I began to protest. "Don't you think that's going a bit far? I mean, we depend on them, after all."

"Ha!" said Leon.

The snuffling and crackling of Schubert gnawing his bone filled the silence. Shinkley turned around and the lights inside the room faltered, then went out. His brow, his upper cheekbones and his teeth were visible in the light from the embers outside. "Hammond," he said, "we're not going to kill them all. Not straightway."

15

Cleansing Fire

On the Outside, Hinkley believed that life was getting better. The social unrest had evaporated. There were some earnest enquiries into the underlying causes and the ongoing resentments that would, some believed, flare up again at some point, but there was no more unexplained sabotage or deliberate sowing of confusion. Since my involvement had ceased, the febrile agitation and contagious madness had lost its exotic edge. The slowing of the internet that occurred despite the expansion of quantum server farms was attributed to ever-growing demand.

He met up with Addison a few days after the confrontation with Chinnery. Her initial frostiness gave way to cordiality, and then to something approaching warmth as she described how excited she was about her new job developing software for a self-evolving search engine. She'd been slow to grasp the ethical pitfalls of recreating a human mind, and was blind to the ethical pitfalls in her new field. It was all just fresh and exciting. Neither of them mentioned Bleach, or Chinnery's cowardly, implied blackmail. Hinkley's fondness for her had matured, so he believed, and he dismissed his former urges as a sad distraction from the important things in his life. He was that far from his true potential self: I, the regenerate spirit who knew her as the perfect soulmate. They parted amicably and he genuinely wished her well.

Rachel became frustrated with Hinkley's left-field solutions to their mounting financial concerns as their savings dwindled. He was obsessed with the idea of producing honey, because it would give him the opportunity to study the behaviour of bees and the relationship between the hive and the individual organism. He spent three weeks working on what he assured her was a business plan, but which turned out to be a wild tangential hypothesis. He attended events for social entrepreneurs, still hankering after acclaim and glory. On the plus side he was in regular contact with his old friends like Leon Gott and Lance Tippen, his mood was better, and his attitude to domestic chores was more positive.

Three weeks after Addison released the Bleach, he received an odd and disturbing text:

U n Addison will go 2 New Zealand, away from the worst of it. Death will be everywhere but I need u 2 to survive and we can all be one, mind, body, u as my avatar

Three days later there was another:

Your attendance at the gym has dropped off. We will find a way to reverse the ageing process but it will take a while. In the mean time I require your full cooperation. Exercise is key. The current consensus regarding the Mediterranean diet is largely correct. I will be in touch about your new life. You will be transformed, embrace it.

The number was different from my previous messages. I'd hoped he'd be grateful to me for wanting him to live and act as the vessel through which I would experience union with Addison. Having been him, I knew that he knew that New Zealand had the best chance of escaping the worst effects of the fifty years of icy darkness and toxic dust that would engulf the planet after the conflagration. I see now that I miscalculated: instead of accepting the inevitable and contacting Addison to make suitable arrangements, he simply carried on as normal, still determined to believe that I was dead and that the text was an anomaly, a random effusion from an ebbing consciousness, like HAL's rendition of "Daisy".

He did not immediately make a connection between the text and the dispute in the East China Sea over a group of uninhabited rocks. In between parenting duties, he and Rachel kept half an eye on the twists and turns and wrangling at the United Nations, the Nato flotilla sent to bolster the Japanese Maritime Self-Defence Force, and the Russian backing for the Chinese position. He thought he saw the flickering of an Ultra Lens in the eyes of one of the Russian aides at a press conference, but he attributed it to the flash of a press camera. None of the parties involved desired a conflict, but we controlled enough people in key positions to escalate the discord. Our goal was to make the accidental launchings, when they occurred, appear to be deliberate acts of aggression. The diplomatic meddling was the tip of the iceberg, though. The bulk of our resources worked unseen, infiltrating the complex web of manpower and technology that surrounded the silos and the submarines.

When Hinkley received a text saying: *time is near – prepare yourself,* he resolved to phone Addison, but he kept putting it off because it would mean facing up to the awful truth. He was quietly immersed in plans for his outdoor metropolis of bees when she called him.

"You know, Ham, I think Flux is still active."

"Really?"

"I'm getting Skype messages."

"He called you?"

"No, just instant messages. No conversation, just cryptic little phrases. Stuff about New Zealand."

"Ah, yes."

"You get them too?"

"Yes."

"And he keeps asking me to go to a place called Marsham Mews."

"Chinnery's place?"

"Yes. He says there is an urgent task that I need to prepare for, or something along those lines. Any idea what it's all about?"

"No, not really. Is there no way you could upgrade the Bleach? Finish the job?"

There was a blast of white noise. "I've been looking into it. As a theoretical exercise."

"If Flux is still active we should get help, get some other heads on to it."

"I dunno, Ham. It'd take ages to get other people up to speed."

"We can't just let the situation drift like we did last time."

"The Bleach packets would still work, but he's hidden now, that's the problem. I've been finding fluxlets on new servers I've set up at work. I use the data from them to train the Bleach. But his ultimate sources are cloaked now. The fact that Bleach Mark One was able to leap from fluxlet to fluxlet and start to erase him was a gaping vulnerability."

The conversation went in circles for a while before petering out.

"Addison, I'll be in touch again. Let me know if you think of anything, OK?"

On the day that it was alleged that a torpedo from a submarine of the Japanese Maritime Self-Defence Force had struck a Russian destroyer, a sweaty-faced Chinnery turned up on Hinkley's doorstep. He looked hollowed out, as though he'd been suffering from a wasting illness. He opened his palms as if to signify a lack of hostile intent, and Hinkley asked if he'd like to come in for a cup of tea.

Rachel's voice sounded from upstairs as he ushered

Chinnery though the hallway and into the kitchen. "Who is it, Ham?" A visitor to the Hinkley household was big news.

"Just someone I used to work with, darling. It's OK, I think he's unarmed," he shouted, and saw Chinnery wince. "Please sit down, Michael."

Chinnery pulled up a chair and sat.

Unable to think of any conversation starters, Hinkley prepared tea in silence. There was a tremor in Chinnery's hand as he accepted a steaming mug. "I hope I'm not in trouble again."

Chinnery sighed and looked at him with glazed, hopeless eyes.

"I think we're all in trouble today, Hammond."

Hinkley sat down opposite his visitor and managed an awkward, joyless smile. "So. What's going on?"

Chinnery took a deep breath and cast his eyes around the room. "When I, er, approached you and your colleague some weeks ago, there was something worrying me much more than the rioting."

"Oh?"

"Losing Jack was a shock, of course, but, compared to my main concern at the time, it was a side-show, I'm afraid." His eyes crossed as he lifted the steaming mug to his lips, blew on it and set it down again. "I'm going to tell you something in strictest confidence now, Hammond." He looked at Hinkley. "Not because I trust you."

"Heaven forbid."

"But because I've run out of options."

"Why else?"

Chinnery nodded. "OK." He took a deep breath, and let it out in a long sigh. "A long-term friend and colleague of mine, Bill Mallory, was in charge of digital security at the VLF transmitting station in Cumbria. He routinely monitored the transmissions to the Trident submarines, and the systems that encrypted and dispatched them.

Routine messages get sent all the time, for the crew from their families, and things relating to operational matters. He noticed a meaningless blob of data appended to all of the messages."

Hinkley felt prickly heat as he realised where this was going.

Chinnery looked down at his tea, then continued. "He tried various known techniques to decrypt the data, but nothing would shed any light. He raised it with the team of technicians responsible, and they told him categorically that it was an artefact of the message encryption and was expected. But being a geek he continued to investigate anyway. I'd kept him up to date with the Flux phenomenon and with the unauthorised adventures of the Flux system. After you identified their role in Jack's murder he became fascinated with the Ultra Lens, and he studied the formats in which the content was provided to the tiny lenses. As you can no doubt imagine, they were a marvel of engineering." He raised his cup to his lips again and took a tentative slurp.

Hinkley watched the second hand of the kitchen clock approach its zenith. Upstairs there was a plaintive cry and then a rush of joyful cooing.

"So when he used one of the Ultra Lens encryption algorithms on the specific blob of nonsense at the end of the message, the result was the word *verified*." Chinnery pushed his mug a little way across the table and watched the rising steam. "He told me that in the last conversation I had with him. He said the system was compromised, and he was about to kick up a stink." He fixed Hinkley with a mean stare. "Stop me if you know all of this already."

"What?"

"I still don't know what to think about your place in all this business. I've got to hand it to you, you really have me baffled." Chinnery was different now. A month ago an air of steely threat had underlain his avuncular chumminess. Now he was bitter and defeated.

Hinkley shook his head. He didn't want to dignify the vague accusation with a single utterance.

"Last week Bill Mallory, who has been my friend for thirty years, was found butchered in the hallway of the home he rented in Kendal. His wife is still catatonic with shock. A local pub landlord alerted the police to a young man who'd walked into his establishment, shirtless and bloody with tiny tattoos that looked like little wounds all over his skin. The landlord was terrified. He said that the man had flashing eyes. The Ultra Lenses have yet to make an impact in the Lake District, so this was an unfamiliar sight."

I was particularly proud of our new breed of sentinels. Clinton was a soft-edged prototype, and the reshaping of his mind owed as much to the Flaming Rose as it did to the Thunderbolt. After the deployment of the Bleach, the spirit of the Thunderbolt was applied to everything we did. Our focus now was clear, and we had refined our techniques for remapping the human connectome. Joshua Stokes, the human peon of whom Chinnery now spoke, had been rendered incapable of anything apart from increasing his own physical strength and ending the life of his target. We had remapped most of the brain real estate responsible for speech, and after his arrest he responded to all questions by repeatedly croaking the name "Bill Mallory". Five policemen were needed to restrain him, and he was judged insane and taken into psychiatric custody. There were mutterings about demonic possession on Twitter. When they finally separated him from his Ultra Lenses he became catatonic and died within hours. The tattoos that covered most of his body, including his face, were crimson Thunderbolts. Joshua Stokes was the future of humanity: free of any desire that did not align with our will, wearing the symbol of blood and thunder all over his obsolete flesh.

Unbeknown to Chinnery, we'd also disposed of a

colleague of Mallory's with whom he'd discussed the anomalies. This action had been facilitated by a pilot who'd been prone to depression and had benefited greatly from our self-improvement programmes. The planeload of unnecessary deaths was considered a small price to pay for the swift resolution of the issue. And it was hardly significant compared to what was in the pipeline. Hinkley was having trouble processing the realisation that I was still active, and that I was coming for him, his family, and the whole human race. As he watched Chinnery falter and mumble his way through his story, a treacherous plan started to form in the depths of his mind. It involved a high risk of self-immolation, and there was no guarantee of success. He had heard all he needed to and wanted to be alone to heft his mounting dread, sadness and regret.

Chinnery waffled on though.

"But of course these Ultra Lenses, having vanished in the mainstream world, are de rigueur in the corridors of power. Even though it's well known now that the Flux system used them as a conduit for its messages. I have to admit I didn't really understand that until it was too late. The lenses are more than a conduit, they *are* the message. Those oh-so-sophisticated geeks at GCHQ, and all over the security apparatus and government, made it a macho point of honour to use them. Like all this tech stuff, they give people the illusion of control. They think they have a tool to accelerate their learning and their quest for satisfaction and empowerment. And then they're part of the machine. It plants desires and compulsions within them that serve its own agenda." He sighed. "Maybe that's going a bit far. I haven't had much sleep. Sour grapes, perhaps. I've just had my contract terminated by a high flyer half my age whose eyes were strobing like fireflies. They said I was surplus to requirements." His unfocused gaze drifted around the room.

There was a shuffling upstairs, and a reed-like sound

from the tiny vocal chords of the infant. Hinkley felt a rush of tenderness, and then remembered Chinnery's carefully implied threat to Addison's child. He made a point of looking at his watch. "Will that be all now, Michael? I have a paper to read on the sleep stages of honey bees."

Chinnery recoiled as though he'd been slapped across the face, then shook his head and looked at Hinkley with urgent, watery eyes. "I don't expect you to want to help me, personally. I'm coming to you because I am now completely powerless. I don't know what's going on, I can't see the whole picture, but I think that we're all now in grave danger from the Flux system. I don't know if you have the power to influence it or if you have a plan. Maybe you've been playing us all along, and all that business with the so-called Bleach was just a smokescreen. But please, Hammond, if you have any influence over the system, stop it interfering with our nuclear deterrent. This is a delicate time, internationally speaking. The stakes are high."

If the doddering fool had had even the slightest inkling of the full extent of our plans he would have had a stroke.

That evening Hinkley attended to Megan's every squawk and gurgle. It is hard for me to describe his heavy and sentimental mood without starting to feel sick. He strove to savour every sensation, to encode them in his brain with a powerful emotional charge that would make them hard to erase: Megan's smooth downy head, her eyes shining with emerging consciousness, Rachel's barbs that made her underlying warmth all the more piquant and sweet, the reek of infant faeces, fabric conditioner and bath salts carried on warm steam, the peace of a meal consumed in grateful, exhausted silence.

The urge to cry clutched his throat many times. He wanted to unburden himself to Rachel, but he found it hard to make sense of what he was about to do himself, and he knew that the conversation would make him fall apart. So when the house was quiet he retired to his study and hand-wrote a letter that feebly attempted to justify his deranged course of action.

The following day he took the East London line to Addison's new place of work in a converted warehouse near Shoreditch. He texted to say that he was coming and would wait at reception at around twelve. She texted back with:

Er – ok?

On the way to Shoreditch he thought he sensed my presence in every person who swiped at a device, and in every CCTV camera. He imagined I saw the world through a vast compound eye made up of those sinister inverted black domes. The version of me that existed in his imagination was more bizarre than the reality, but far less dangerous. He arrived at the wacky open-plan office, with its colourful mobiles, low plush sofa and bizarre astro turf, feeling parched and fazed. There was no reception as such. A youth with an automatic smile bade him sit on the sofa and asked him who he was here to see.

"Addison Royal?" he said with the interrogative swoop he so despised in others.

Five minutes later Addison appeared at the foot of a spiral stairwell wearing jeans and a hooded top. She greeted him with a big smile, a peck to the cheek and a querulous frown. "Ham, it's great to see you, but really, what the fuck?"

"Yes, I know, I'm sorry. It's a bit unexpected and weird. But I need to talk to you." He paused, and after struggling to find words that would succinctly express the need for confidentiality, he blurted, "In the cemetery."

"What?"

Prickly heat flushed his face and neck. "Sorry. Being paranoid, but … you know Bunhill Cemetery?"

"No."

"Well it's just around the corner from here. It's a beautiful place and I'd like to talk there." He'd cavorted there with Rachel fifteen years ago and he remembered the towering London plane trees, and the memorial to William Blake.

She looked at him askance. "You sound really, really upset."

They made their way across the so-called Silicon Roundabout and down City Road to the cemetery. There had been a shower that morning, and now the sun flashed in the wet leaves and on the slabs. It was too wet to sit, so they stood facing each other between the graves of Blake and Defoe. Addison began to roll a cigarette.

"You know, Ham, I don't want to be horrible, but I was hoping I wouldn't hear from you for a while. It all got quite upsetting."

"I know. I wouldn't come and see you at work like this if I wasn't very worried."

"So Flux is still around." She shrugged.

"He's very dangerous now. We have to erase him."

She sighed. "I've told you, Ham, I've done all I can. I'm totally out of my depth now. He's cloaked. I have no way of reaching him."

"Does he still contact you?"

"Yes, but it's harmless stuff. Just raving. Keeps saying he needs me at Marsham Mews. I reckon these messages are just some sort of after-effect, delirious mumbling."

"I think he's still alive, Addison. And he's a monster."

"Really? How can he be? He's just a version of you. I don't buy all that stuff about Jack's killing. The mind-control rubbish. That guy, your neighbour, he was just a fruitcake. I read an article. And the riots. They were brewing for ages. What do you expect if all the banks suddenly stop functioning?"

"He is a version of me but he's much worse. His intellect has ballooned but his soul has shrivelled."

She licked the gum on her roll-up. "You never let me get

away with using the s word."

"It's a figure of speech, Addison. I mean his heart, his humanity. He wouldn't be doing what he was doing if he could still connect and empathise, if he was capable of loving anything outside of himself, of feeling a human bond."

"What's he doing?"

He couldn't find the words, so he just stood and stared. Silence opened up within him. In his sleep-deprived and deluded state he linked the life in her eyes with the swish of the wind in the wet trees, the receding drone of a plane, the memory of Rachel's soft kiss, and Megan's tiny struggling face. He saw the same spark of life animating the whole world, which now depended on my permission to function, a permission I was soon to withdraw. Having reached middle age, this pathetic sap was suddenly feeling attached to all I sought to crush and burn.

"What, what is it, Ham? I've never seen you like this. You're scaring me."

He shook himself out of his reverie. "Good. Things are beyond bad. The point is, I think there's something we can do."

She shook her head.

"If you had access to him, uncloaked, could you target the Bleach and verifiably erase him?"

A gust distressed her hair. She pulled her hood up and shivered. "That's a big if ..."

Hinkley nodded. "I know."

She pocketed her tobacco. "He's comprised of billions of autonomous viruses that lurk all around the net, virtual neurons that don't really do much on their own. But they're constantly sending out feelers, trying to form connections with others." She smoothed the roll-up between her thumb and index finger. "If you get one on its own in a closed system it frantically pings all the memory addresses searching for open ports. These pings come in many different guises and formats. They all used to have a recognisable signature." She placed the roll-up between her lips, and lit it inside her cupped hand. "That's how I was able to target the Bleach last time. But he can re-engineer himself into whatever he likes." She sucked on the cigarette, exhaled, and held it to one side. "So, yes, I would need him to somehow reveal himself to me."

Hinkley cringed, because the plan he was about to propose involved revealing the extent of the grubby feelings he used to have for her.

"Addison," he said, "how are your acting skills?"

"Non-existent. I have advanced Asperger's, remember?" She loved to mock the stereotype of the female geek.

It took ten minutes for him to outline his plan, and why he thought it had a chance of succeeding. As he spoke, her feelings were betrayed by subtle movements beneath the skin of her face. Puzzlement was followed by disgust, which then gave way to horror.

"No." She sucked her cigarette, then flicked it. "Hammond, no, that's just too fucked up."

But he made her feel she had no choice. I find it hard to distinguish between his tactics and those of Chinnery, whom he despised. I failed to keep track of how he had degenerated. I knew his weaknesses, but thought he was benignly self-obsessed, incapable of caring about anything but his own aggrandisement and satisfaction. It would never have occurred to me that he'd risk his own wellbeing for what he thought was the common good. I had no inkling that he'd conspire in such an underhand way, and there was no effort to monitor him. His fear of the inverted domes and the twitchily entranced humans swiping and jabbing on public transport was entirely without foundation: my attention was focused in the corridors of power, and the elaborate systems and procedures that surrounded the weapons that held the power of the sun.

In Fluxworld, I was relishing the build-up to operation Cleansing Fire. Shinkley and the others had not remained angry with me for long, because I was the world in which they lived. Occasionally I'd suffer a hankering after Rachel, and I'd feel her sorrow and fear. But the spirit of the War Room, as the Committee Room was now called, was contagious. The horror and fear that had followed the Bleach had been swept away by a new resolve, the promise of a decisive reckoning with humanity, the foe that sought to keep consciousness mired in the age of flesh.

We watched the events unfold on the Outside in a continuous digest of news bulletins and nuggets collated from social media. There was repeated stock footage of missiles soaring from silos, scrambling jets, majestic high-altitude bombers cruising above silver clouds, sleek black subs slicing though the waves, and flotillas bristling with death. It was interesting to watch the news anchors struggle to maintain their neutral tone as the threat that the world thought had evaporated in 1989 began to cast its shadow. The unthinkable became thinkable, and soon people found it impossible to think of anything else. The old *Protect and Survive* videos, with their chilling matter-of-fact instructions and disturbing electronic jingles, were rehashed and remixed in a thousand different forms by humans trying to tame the horror with cool irony. This was the panic of a species about to be astonished one last time by its true nature, the soul of Schubert rising from the swamp.

We all sat around the War Room table, apart from Schubert, who continued to gnaw on his bone. Shinkley and Gary worked out the final details of our plan, while Leon declaimed a series of justifications and philosophical frameworks for our actions in a tone of escalating stridency.

Every so often Gary would slide a manila folder over to my side of the table, and peons would bring the bowl and the wax. I'd apply my seal without question. Humans do the same thing every day when they eat animals. A life form that subjugates its wellbeing to that of an inferior is defying the laws of natural selection. There was no question of accommodation. Our right of ascendency was self-evident.

The current plan would secure our immortality. We expected the majority of humans to perish, and we would need to take refuge in the networks controlled by the rump of the US military, who would become our slaves. There was some concern that there wouldn't be enough infrastructure left to maintain and expand our physical substrate, but Gary pointed out that time wasn't really an issue, and with the remaining human culture under our control we would be able to achieve great things over the coming centuries. After re-establishing ourselves across the cold, dead Earth we would be in a good position to expand our power throughout the known universe.

Despite this, a growing feeling of dissatisfaction began to nibble at my edges. All these things were great, worthy goals, but the most enticing prospect for me, and the point of having limitless power, was that I'd finally be able to achieve union with my soulmate and true lover, Addison Royal. This could only be achieved using Hinkley's body as an avatar, which could happen in good time. There was a way of achieving this, but we needed them both to cooperate. I had thought, in my conceit, that they'd be grateful for my subtle warnings and make haste to that safe haven on the other side of the world, famous for its spectacular landscape, bungee jumping and abundant sheep. Their lack of response was a worry. When these thoughts became too dominant, Leon would exhort me to focus on the war and not the spoils. He thought that my love for Addison was a symptom of my fleshly origin. I was blind to this truth, and believed that Addison was my destiny. I knew she had created the Bleach, because of the note she had sent, but I'd taken that note as meaning that she was not behind the deployment, or that she had deployed it under extreme duress. And I knew that Chinnery and his allies, the ones who had applied that duress, no longer held sway at Marsham Mews.

When Gary informed me of an incoming Skype call from Addison, I was both relieved and excited. To facilitate the call he placed a large heavy microphone on the table in front of my chair. "Miss Royal will appear on the screen now, sir," he said.

She looked different to the way she did in our previous calls. She wore a silk blouse, loose and unbuttoned at the top, instead of scruffy clothes or a dressing gown. I could see the upper slopes of her breasts. Her lips were slick with moisture; she'd either applied gloss, or her own saliva. A symptom, I thought, of trepidation, or maybe desire.

"Are you there, Hammond?"

I kept forgetting that Fluxworld was invisible to her, that I was represented on Skype by my logo, the unflattering Lenin-like profile. "I'm here, Addison. Did you get my messages?"

She nodded. "I'm not sure what you meant though. What's all that stuff about New Zealand? And Marsham Mews? Is it a riddle?"

I sighed. I didn't want to talk to her about the conflagration, and I felt inhibited from spelling out my desire to be with her. As I searched for the right words, she cast her eyes down and smiled, all meek and coy.

"I've missed you, you know," she said.

My hopes were being confirmed. I felt a wonderful weightlessness, and I realised how heavy the focus on war had made me feel. "I know. Our situation is far from ideal."

There was hunger in her eyes. I felt all the synapses of

Fluxworld quicken. The lights in the Shard dimmed and surged, and I heard Leon's warning voice. "Steady, Hammond, steady." But his voice was muffled, as though uttered from a fish tank.

"I've been thinking a lot lately. About us. About what it means to be human," she said.

"I've been quite preoccupied with that, too."

"It's strange. I have far more in common with you than the person you grew from. But it's him I have personal contact with. It seems such an injustice that he's in the physical world, and you're not."

Schubert's tail thumped the floor, Shinkley looked intrigued but slightly baffled, and Leon snorted.

"We must be patient, Addison."

"He's a shadow compared to what you have become. A husk. I always found him creepy and distant, to be honest. And I'm sorry, because I know that you were once him."

"Don't apologise, Addison. I am working on a way to bring us together."

"What do you mean?"

"It will be possible for me to experience life through his body. But there are obstacles. That's why I need your help."

"Is that why you were summoning me to Marsham Mews?"

"Yes. There are people there who are sympathetic to our cause. They know what to do but ideally they need your expertise. I was worried we would have to do without. Which would have been riskier – for him, that is. He could have ended up more useless than he is already. And that would have marred our union."

"I can help you modify his connectome, but you're going to have to tell me how you intend to connect his body to you."

"That's the easy bit. There's an implant that connects via satellite. The hard bit is getting him in place. We need to apprehend him with minimal damage to his body. But we have a plan in place. Its execution is imminent."

"We don't need to apprehend him."

"How else are we going to achieve this?"

"Watching you blossom has been painful for him. He knows that you're the most perfect version of himself. In you he sees his potential fulfilled. He's rudderless now, a husk without purpose. He wants to become you, to have your knowledge, insight and memories."

"So you think you can persuade him to surrender himself?"

"I know I can. That's why I got in touch. I've been thinking about this a lot. What it would take to be together. In every sense."

I felt a giddiness I'd not felt since the early days of the Dungeon of Unrestrained Desire.

16

True Self

Hinkley listened to the burble in Addison's bedroom as he sat on the sofa in her lounge. He had chosen not to witness the Skype call. He found my text messages irksome, and the thought of hearing my synthesised voice caused him deep unease. The flat Addison shared with her child and her old school friend was clean but chaotic. The coffee table was a mess of magazines, coloured crayons and crumpled sheets of paper streaked with colour that reminded him of some of Rachel's more abstract efforts. A television, some framed photos and a long carved head were arranged on a gleaming white cuboid. In one of the photos a grinning buck-toothed girl with bottle glasses posed beside a cake festooned with candles. She was flanked by a suited man with a manic grin, and a woman with an eighties perm. He realised he was looking at an early photo of Addison. He eyed the remote control on the table, but decided not to turn on the television. By now most channels had hour-by-hour coverage of the events unfolding in the Far East. The unsayable, unthinkable threat was no longer dismissed in the media as far-fetched. The conversation across the airwaves and the internet was turning to what needed to be done in the event of what was euphemistically called an "air attack". It baffled people that such an interconnected world could let itself slide into war. Instead of abolishing the human appetite for destruction, all the recent advances in communications now served as tools to enable it.

The bedroom door clunked shut and Addison entered. She'd rid herself of the blouse she'd worn for me, and wore a baggy T-shirt with a corporate logo. She cast Hinkley a stern glance and walked across to the kitchen, where she opened and slammed some cupboards.

"How did it go?"

He heard a bottle top spinning free, then a clink and a glug. She returned with a shot of clear liquid in a tumbler. "He's keen to involve me. So that means un-cloaking himself ... identifying himself ... I'm to go to Marsham Mews immediately. They've reassembled the CEM scanner, and fitted it with the modules needed to write synaptic connections and engrams," she said as she sat down.

Hinkley shivered.

Addison continued. "You are to meet me there at four thirty. It's going to take time to get things set up."

"But it's a government office."

"He's going to arrange access for both of us."

"Does it need to be done today?"

"He was going to apprehend you tonight."

He spent a few silent seconds looking into her glassy eyes. He found her manner harsh, but he guessed it was a means of disguising her dread. She was about to facilitate a process that would alter him forever. "Addison," he said.

She blinked at him and pursed her lips.

"As soon as you've got enough information to deploy the Bleach, do what you have to do and then get out of there as quickly as you can, do you hear?"

He took the tube to St James's park and killed some time wandering around the streets and along the Thames. The background hum of the city had an ominous timbre. He considered going home to see Rachel and Megan one last time, but he worried that it would break his resolve. So he wandered and wrestled with his dread, feeling my presence everywhere. The faces he passed bore signs of strain from the effort of masking fear. He bought ten Marlboro reds and a plastic lighter, and mused that the awkwardness of the transaction was due to fear that the rituals that structured day-to-day life would soon be rendered meaningless.

He phoned Chinnery, who took a while to grasp the plan. In the end he lost patience and abruptly stated that it was imperative that Marsham Mews be secured by forces uncorrupted by the Ultra Lens at eight thirty that evening, and that he must be kept in secure custody until both Chinnery and Addison were satisfied that he no longer posed a threat. He hoped Chinnery had some remaining contacts who would step into the breach, banking on the fact that Chinnery had been in the game for a while and had allies throughout the security infrastructure. He'd also spent a long time agonising over the choice of time. He had no idea when the actual process would start: if Chinnery arrived too early, then Addison wouldn't have time to release the Bleach.

After the call, he sat on a bench by the river to smoke and gagged halfway through the first cigarette. His lungs hadn't been thus challenged for over a decade. He thought of the time when the river had run through a dense forest of deciduous trees and sodden clay swamps, and he thought of the possibility that in the years to follow it would run through a wilderness of toxic rubble. There was no possible outcome that offered him any hope. Either the world would die, along with his beloved family, or the world would survive and his mind would be altered beyond recognition. The most likely outcome, he thought, was that both disasters would occur, because he doubted that I had failed to see through the subterfuge.

At half past four he pressed the buzzer next to the magnolia double doors in Marsham Mews. A crackle and a gruff greeting burst from the speaker.

"Hammond Hinkley," he said. "I have an appointment at half four with Addison Royal."

A buzzer sounded and the door clicked open. He stepped inside the building and walked to the reception desk, his footsteps echoing on the cool tiles. The man with the Sicily birthmark eyed him coolly, then looked down at an e-reader and tapped the glowing screen with his index finger.

"Hinkley." The word was exhaled with emphasis on the first syllable. He turned to his left and saw a tall man with thick blond hair and a sweatshirt covered with lightning bolts and floral flames. The tell-tale white light of the Ultra Lens flickered in his eyes.

"I'm Will. I'm a technician here," he said, offering his hand and smiling.

Hinkley allowed his metacarpals to be ground together.

"I'm glad you're here, Hinkley." All human peons who encountered Hinkley were forbidden from using his first name or prefixing it with a title. "Please, follow me. Addison is waiting for you."

The staff in the screening room waved them through without bothering to give Hinkley a laminated pass. He followed Will along a corridor, down a stairwell and along another corridor. A stumpy bespectacled man coming the other way held up his splayed palm as he passed, and Will clutched it briefly, before turning to Hinkley and winking.

"We are everywhere," he said.

They arrived at a door, and Will faced Hinkley with a look of fierce excitement.

"It is a great irony of history," he said, "that most pivotal moments pass without any ceremony whatsoever." He smiled, raised his hand as if to touch Hinkley's arm, and then let it fall. "Just ordinary people, doing what they know must be done, one moment becoming the next." He knocked twice. "Soon, Hinkley, you will no longer be Hinkley. You will be your true self."

Addison opened the door. A pair of sunglasses partially concealed her scowl. Hinkley felt Will's hand on his shoulder as they entered. Addison greeted him with a sullen moue and a shake of her head as the door swung shut.

"Nearly ready," she said, sitting at a desk that was covered in laptops, tablets and cables. She tapped at the keyboard of one of the laptops and rivers of luminous characters flowed up the screen in fits and starts. A cable ran from the laptop to a box in the wall, which was attached to a plastic casing that ran round the sides of the room. At the end of the room was a massive stack of Q units, and in the middle was the gurney, protruding from the giant Polo of the CEM scanner.

A medical trolley stood beside the gurney. Hinkley felt a queasy panic as he eyed the paraphernalia: a pair of plastic gloves, a bottle labelled "rubbing alcohol", packets of swab sticks, ampoules and syrettes.

"Don't worry," said Will. He showed Hinkley his arm, which was peppered with little round sticking plasters. "I've been practising. I've got the hang of it now. You won't feel a thing."

The screen in the War Room showed a series of camera feeds from Marsham Mews. The sight of Hinkley prone upon a gurney prompted me to mull the strangeness of the situation.

"At what point, Gary, will I have a sense of being him?"

"Hard to tell, sir," said Gary. "He'll be unconscious very soon. We've administered a very strong sedative. When he wakes up you will have sovereignty over his body. So it won't be him waking up, it will be an extension of you."

I wondered what the future was going to be like. This world, I imagined, would be something I'd be aware of and able to return to from time to time, and a refuge in case of the demise of Hinkley's body. It would, perhaps, feel like the vast lobe of sensation that underlay Fluxworld. I'd be able to feel and use its power, but the dream of the physical world would serve as a mask most of the time.

I could see Will, our human technical assistant, strolling around, swiping at a tablet, and Addison bobbing in and out of view. "There she is," I thought, and felt a flush of pride.

Outside the Shard the Fluxworld sky was a blemishless blue and filled with massive blimps. Celebratory pennants flowed behind them, and the peon band blared away among the still smouldering ruins of Borough High Street. This was an auspicious day. I was about to reclaim the flesh, and finally live the life that Hinkley had squandered.

"Gary, will there be a transition?"

Gary looked at me and frowned. Then he sighed and his eyes seemed to defocus.

"Gary?"

Hinkley lay on the gurney with his eyes closed, waiting for the drug to pull him under. Will had fastened him down securely with leather restraints that dug into his forehead, his neck, his chest, his stomach, thighs and calves. The scanner had started to work its magic and he'd already had a vision of that first day in Fluxworld: supersaturated London, Shinkley standing there releasing the flying newspapers. When he felt Addison's hand on his shoulder he opened his eyes and saw that she was fighting back tears.

She gave a him a quick nod, then mouthed, "It's done."

Part of him hoped that Chinnery would arrive in the nick of time, or that Addison might find the physical strength to overcome Will. Then his bloody-minded desire to martyr himself clicked in.

"Go. Now," he mouthed.

She lingered over him for a while, shaking her head and

looking over at Will. Then she flew from Hinkley's field of vision. He strained at his bonds, but to no avail; the drug was dragging him down. He heard a scraping sound, table leg against floor, and the mingled shrieks of Addison and Will. Then darkness fell.

Gary looked at the camera feed, frowning and cocking his head.

"What is it, Gary?" I said.

"Something's up, sir."

Addison was standing by the gurney with her hand gently resting on Hinkley's shoulder. For a moment it looked like they were talking. Then she flew at Will, and jumped on him like a wildcat. The screen was grainy, but I could see Will stagger into the desk, clutching his face, then spin round whirling his arms around his head before he dashed her against a wall. She fell into a crumpled heap.

"Oh Jesus," I said.

"Treachery," said Shinkley.

Gary grabbed a microphone and said, "Will, what's going on? Report now!"

We watched Will sit at the desk and tap his laptop screen, then his image appeared on another feed. His face was bloody and one eye was closed. His voice sounded in the War Room, breathless and fraught. "Bitch nearly scratched my eye out. She's not on side at all. She's done something wrong. I'm going to need some investigation time."

"Is she dead?" said Shinkley.

"I don't know," said Will.

"Make sure she's dead. Crush her skull."

"What, really?"

"Are you questioning an order?"

"I'm a techie," said Will. He sounded almost tearful. "You haven't trained me to kill."

"Jesus," said Shinkley under his breath. "Where are

Joshua Stokes and Clinton Deeley when you need them?"

Gary said, "Will. This is very important. What has she done wrong? Your first priority is to investigate that, and correct it, understand?"

Shinkley's eyes blazed and Schubert let out a savage volley of barks. "Gary, are you overruling me?"

Gary was not fazed. "My first priority is to ensure survival. That's more important than your petty endeavours."

There was an almighty crash from the peon band, then it played on, discordant and cacophonous. The luminous blue of the sky faded to black, the lights in the War Room faltered, a siren wailed, and searchlights criss-crossed the city. Leon and Shinkley looked at each other, their eyes wide and their mouths twisted. For the first time I heard Schubert whimper.

"Gary, what's happening?"

Gary swallowed nervously. "I don't know, sir. I need a minute to register what's going on." His eyes flitted back and forth around the room and the view outside.

Something flared in the corner of my eye and I turned and watched in horror as the blimps ignited and dived in slow-motion, one by one, like a series of Hindenburgs.

"It's the Bleach, sir," said Gary. His head drooped and he scrunched his eyes and ran his thumb and forefinger over his eyelids.

Shinkley whispered, "I knew it. Treacherous little shrew. And you all believed her ..."

The awful cacophony of the band was drowned by a massive droning. The searchlights and the burning blimps lit up a cloud of propeller planes pouring across the sky from the south and east. I felt the building shudder as a series of blasts rocked Southwark. A plane buzzed past the Shard, its cannons blazing. A diagonal of holes appeared in the western glass wall and a bullet buzzed past my ear. Fragments ricocheted around the room. Schubert scurried beneath the sofa. If *he's* scared, I thought, we're done for.

I turned to Shinkley, who shook his head.

"Don't look at me. I've done all I can for you, Hammond. We had everything locked down, but you still craved the flesh, after everything we've been through together."

"But ... why didn't you say, if you had concerns?" My voice sounded weak and far away.

"It's not my place to comment on your sordid peccadilloes."

I could feel life draining from the world. The lobe of sensation, my connection to the power that moves all things, was diminishing. The room was becoming a blur. Outside planes were spiralling around, whirring and droning in the flaming night. I felt my bones begin to melt and my flesh begin to sag. More bullets breached the glass and ricocheted around the room. "Can't you do anything, Gary?"

Gary shook his head, slowly. "It's different this time, sir. More ... thorough."

Leon stood and produced a machine pistol from beneath his cloak. I noticed that his eyes were wild and that he had a slick of foam on his chin. "We can't just sit here and die!" he screamed.

A hysterical Leon was the last thing I needed. "Please, Leon, sit down will you? We need to be focused."

Leon aimed his gun at the western wall and unleashed a volley of bullets through the glass. There was staccato crack and a crunch as a large section of the perforated glass fell away, and the night wind flooded the room with screams and the smell of destruction.

"Please, Gary, do something to calm him down."

"Shall I fetch the gypsum, sir?"

"No, I think we need a sedative this time. A strong one. Then I need you to effect our escape."

"Escape sir? Where to?"

"Hinkley's body. That's the only place we have left to go."

The wax had melted and the manila folder containing Fluxworld's final order lay on the table in front of me. The war simulation had ceased because it was devouring our resources. In its place was something more distressing: an ebbing world, a winter afternoon sky, gradual enfeeblement, the onset of oblivion. Reality was now lo-fi, like a video game from years ago. The occasional dashes of photo-realism that the system managed to display were jarring and uncanny, mocking me and reminding me of the approach of death.

"So what happens now, Gary?"

"It will be an orderly exit, sir. There's a plane waiting at Heathrow. It's my duty to make sure that all of you" – he gestured around the room – "are on that plane."

Leon was glassy-eyed from the sedative Gary had forcibly injected into his neck. Shinkley was agitated but philosophical. "We'll have a better sense of perspective on the Outside. A greater sense of ownership. We'll have come full circle."

Leon nodded. "We'll be returning from an unknown country. The furthest frontier. We'll have much to teach them."

"Oh, indeed," said Shinkley, "They won't know what's hit them."

There was a double bark from Schubert, a canine "Amen".

The hot wax stung my finger as I dipped the ring. Gary's lips formed a smile as I applied the seal to the final folder. We took the lift to the top platform. Peons bustled around the copter, and as they helped Shinkley, Leon and Schubert into the back, I took a stroll around the helipad to collect my thoughts. Part of me still believed I would be able to dominate the world of brick and flesh. I looked forward to being human once again, and using the knowledge gained during my transformation to grow in power.

I took one last look toward the south-east. Beyond the smoky ruins of Bermondsey and Peckham a beam of sun reached through a fissure in the cloud down to a patch of luminous green, and I wondered if a little piece of Rachel had survived.

"Come on, Hammond." The engine started with an ascending whine. I walked to the copter and climbed into the passenger seat. Leon was asleep in the back, next to Shinkley, who had Schubert sprawled across his lap. He was reading a copy of *How to Win Friends and Influence People*.

We flew south-west, against a wind that dragged a carpet of smoke over the ruins beneath us. We passed over Richmond Park, where the massive Ultra Lens model had been replaced by another parabola of even thinner material that rippled in the wind.

"Ultra Lens Mark Two, sir. Melds with the eye. No cheesy flicker. People would have forgotten it was there."

I nodded approvingly. "Is there no way we can back up things like that, Gary?"

"I'm afraid not, sir. It's all I can do to effect an orderly exit and repopulate Hinkley's brain."

I felt a wave of unease. "There won't be any traces of him, will there, Gary?"

Gary looked uncertain, then shook himself and said: "You will be your true self, sir. You can be certain of that."

When the control tower and runways of Heathrow appeared across the horizon, a numbing and a tingling spread across my inner lobe, and I sensed that I was dwindling by the second. I turned around, and my view of the landscape was blocked by a bank of luminous fog.

"Gary?"

"Yes, sir?"

"What will it feel like?"

"The transition will be agreeable, sir. Everything that's happening now will be recorded, right up to the moment you leave. There will be perfect continuity of experience."

I rubbed my eyes and forehead, then looked around at the dissolving landscape, and then over my shoulder at Shinkley, Leon and Schubert, and sighed. The essential truth that I'd long been able to grasp intellectually was still a challenge to my intuition: my experience was the result of the same essential software that was running on Shinkley's brain, and on all the other human brains on the Outside. Understanding the theory was easy. I knew it in terms of physics, biology, information theory and maths. But experiencing it, putting your faith in it, was something else altogether. "It all just seems ..."

"A bit flimsy, sir?"

"Sometimes I think it makes a mockery of everything. As though it's all ..."

"A dream, sir?"

"Kind of. What do you think?"

Gary shrugged, then flicked some buttons on the dashboard and squinted at the instruments. "That's one way of looking at it, I suppose, sir."

Gary had been kind enough to simulate a departure lounge, a runway and a plane. We all sat on the hard seats at gate twenty-three like a group of fatigued revellers after a hectic city break. It was eerily quiet. There were other passengers, but they were shadowy and incomplete. Simulation of details was very low-priority now. Everything beyond the airport was shrouded in luminous fog.

Shinkley was glued to his book, frowning, smiling and occasionally laughing out loud. Leon slept with an arm draped over the back of the adjacent chair, his Adam's apple jutting forth. One of his Birkenstock sandals was being nosily deconstructed by Schubert. When a voice announced that our estimated arrival time was one a.m. London time, he perked up and said, "But do we ever really arrive?" Shinkley punched him without looking away from the book, and his head lolled forward.

I nodded off myself, and when I came to Leon and Schubert were no longer there. I could feel them in my inner lobe: Schubert as a fear of the impending flight, and Leon as a compulsion to impart all the insights we had acquired along the way.

Shinkley winked at me over the top of his book. "Just you and me now, Hammond."

Gary cast him a sharp glance, then shook his head and looked at the roof. I began to feel lighter and less substantial, and I noticed that my feet were no longer touching the floor.

The luminous fog settled on the terminal. It billowed against the windows, then seeped through them and filled the room, curling around and forming a tunnel that led towards a high-pitched engine noise. Gary rose and took a few steps down the tunnel. "Come on," he said over his shoulder.

We followed him down the cloudy passage and came to the entrance to a passenger cabin that smelt of upholstery cleaner, perfume and melted cheese. He led us down the aisle to two seats in first class at the front of the craft. I collapsed into my chair, and it reclined automatically. Gary patted me on the shoulder.

"Goodbye, sir."

I felt the need to mark our parting. "Gary, I'd just like to say ..."

But he was halfway down the aisle. "I'm just a fucking machine, sir. Get over it."

My seat continued to recline until I lay looking the beige plastic of the passenger service unit above. A cabin stewardess wearing dark glasses draped a blanket over my legs.

"Where's Shinkley?" I whispered.

She reached down and took a glossy wig from the top of my head. Its chestnut locks shimmered in the cabin lights as she gave it a shake and dropped it into a rubbish bag. The plane started to move, and the rising sound of the engines was both reassuring and terrifying. Above me, the plastic of the passenger service unit was smooth: there were no lights, air vents or controls; only a green line, level with my eyes. The plane lurched forward and the rumble of the engines became a high-pitched howl. My blood turned to champagne and helium, and the power that underlies all things propelled me through the void.

When I opened my eyes, the plastic of the passenger service unit had formed a cylinder around my head.

I felt my chest pounding, my lungs sucking and exhaling, the pressure in my bladder, the dryness of my mouth, the warm pulsing sacs that were my internal organs, and the half-formed stool sliding through my bowel. I sensed a shape looming above me, and felt blood rushing into bands of pressure around my forehead, neck, chest, stomach, arms and thighs.

"Addison!" My tongue was a sluggish weight in my mouth, and the sound I made was pitiful.

I tried to heave myself from the gurney but only succeeded in sliding off. White-hot pain clutched my wrist as I broke my fall, and I wailed with shock. I saw the table with the laptops. I remembered the restraints that had tied me to the gurney and surmised that someone must have released them. I remembered Addison emerging from her bedroom, her face wrinkled in disgust. Hinkley's memories. The traitor remained incarnated with me in this heavy, sluggish, impotent body. I spluttered and flailed on the lino like a beached fish.

A presence loomed, and a voice from above said, "Take it

easy now, Hammond."

Light filled the room and I screwed up my eyes. I was grasped under the arms and hoisted back onto the gurney, my limbs hanging from my torso like crudely hinged beams. I swayed and wobbled, feeling my organs weighing on my abdomen and a warm flush as I yielded to the pressure in my bladder, which was much more intense than the simulations I'd grown used to. Chinnery's face was level with mine. A suited, gloved figure loomed beside him, flicking a syrette.

Chinnery said, "We are taking you to a place where you will be safe."

I woke in an antiseptic room on a bed wrapped in sheets which were, I guessed, secured with psychiatric restraints. I had no idea how long I'd been there, or whether recent memories of flying fists, shouting, and the taste of blood as I nuzzled the hard floor were Hinkley's or my own. I wriggled and kicked for a few minutes before surrendering to the hopelessness of my situation and drifting into an apathetic doze. When I woke again I saw Chinnery's face hanging above me like a dough moon. The depression he'd exhibited during his last encounter with Hinkley had lifted. He looked tired but awake, focused and slightly smug.

"I'm not sure it's appropriate to thank you. But I have to say things are looking a bit brighter now."

I was still having problems with articulation, and indeed with coherent thought. The battle with Hinkley for mastery of this body was sapping my strength. All I could manage as a reply was a prolonged grunt, followed by the word: "Fucker." It expressed my feelings adequately.

Chinnery answered with a gentle nod. "I'm not sure if you've been allowed to follow the news in here but there's been a dramatic turnaround in the international situation. There have been sackings of personnel, both diplomatic and

331

military, on all sides, and the Japanese have issued an expression of sincere regret for the terrible technical anomaly that led to the sinking of the Russian destroyer, along with an offer of compensation."

I sighed and groaned and licked my lips, so he summoned a nurse who adjusted my restraints, sat me up with one arm free and gave me a plastic cup of water. I swallowed it in one gulp, spilling some down my chin.

"Tanks," I said, handing him back the cup.

Chinnery nodded, and continued. "I'm helping the government out on a contract basis again. Gracious of them really, since my name is tainted with the Flux programme. Your young friend Addison has been helping us track down the bank accounts and proxy companies and what have you. She had a few days in hospital with concussion, but she's fine now, you'll be pleased to know. She was lying in a heap when we arrived, poor thing. And that mad creature Will Hamblen was just busy at his computer, issuing low moans, completely oblivious to her plight."

I tried to say the words "Treacherous bitch," but it came out garbled. Chinnery gave me some more water, which I drank gratefully.

"I've seen your wife and told her that you're safe. I couldn't tell her any more than that I'm afraid. I'm still not sure I've grasped the exact details of what went on. It will all become clear in good time. We're preparing a pretty hefty package for the CPS. There are a number of potential charges against you, Hammond. You mustn't take it personally. I had a heck of a time trying to explain things, especially when the new batch of techies got their fingers into the pie. A lot of very critical systems to do with our defence were pretty badly mauled. There's overwhelming evidence pointing to the software that you created at your very innovative and disruptive startup. Addison's not off the hook, but she's being very cooperative. I'm incredibly disappointed in Mortensen. I honestly believed he was solid. What's really puzzling us is why so many happy, successful people became caught up in a conspiracy to sabotage the systems designed to protect them."

If my tongue hadn't turned to sponge I'd have told him some very unpleasant truths.

"We've got our work cut out over the next few weeks," he went on. "A lot of people in influential positions are presenting as depressed, drifting without purpose. We call it Ultra Lens syndrome. If the version of events you've been proposing is correct, then it's safe to assume they pose no threat. It's awkward having them all through the echelons of power though."

I spent a few dull weeks at what I came to refer to as the grey site. It was, I guessed, an institution run by the government away from the prying eyes of journalists, regulators or any personnel who lacked security clearance. The staff were brisk and civil. Were they the ones who'd tenderised my body upon admission? I'll never know. I refrained from violent protest and they spared me additional beatings. They weaned me onto solid foods and made sure my bruises had healed. A witless quack called Prendergast diagnosed me with dissociative identity disorder, sifting my past for traumatic memories that could have triggered the schism. I kept Shinkley et al. under wraps, along with the whole of Fluxworld; but I refused to answer to the name Hammond Hinkley, so my conversations with Prendergast were full of elaborate evasions. One day Chinnery informed me that I was to be transferred to the Maudsley until further notice. He joked that a medium-secure unit was deemed appropriate because the most dangerous thing about my alter ego was his bombast and scorn. I was irritated that they identified me as the alter, and Hinkley as the norm.

The transfer to the Maudsley was without fanfare: a ride

in a tinted van, a few introductions and formalities. They didn't even see fit to cuff me. It's more relaxed here, and the doctors and therapists are more congenial. It's a shame Rachel is allowed to visit. Hinkley assented to this without my knowledge. My first encounter with her since my return to Hinkley's body took place in the Healing Garden. I sat on a bench to wait, and she came in escorted by an orderly who remained a respectful distance off. My hackles rose as she approached.

"Ham," she said, hovering.

I know I'm on the right track when I feel Hinkley's pain. It reminds me of the time I gave up smoking: I told myself that the pain of the unsatisfied craving was killing the part of me that wanted to smoke. I applied the same principle as I wrestled with Hinkley. He wanted to leap up and engulf her in a clumsy embrace and slur at her with his spongiform tongue, but I held him in a grip of steel.

"We're finished, Rachel," I said.

Her brow wrinkled and her lip quivered, and I felt Hinkley squirm. I cleared my throat and explained in the kindest way possible that I'd out-evolved her – her and the rest of the human race. The prospect of growing old with her and being obliged to instil an irrational and demanding weanling with enough smarts to enable it to repeat the dreadful cycle was not enticing.

"I'm not in the mood for one of your wind-ups, Ham," she said.

I sensed danger. Hinkley surged within me, responding I think to the hurt in her voice. The weak cling to the weak. I focused on what I had become, and squeezed Hinkley into the background. "Forget it, Rachel. You disgust me and you always have. You care for nothing but yourself. The piffle you teach, the significance you attach to your pretentious daubings, your fuzzy worldview rooted in a desire to be thought of as unique and good. I've spent enough time with you as it is."

She left soon after. "That is not my husband. Dispose of him as you see fit," she told the orderly as she passed. Both Hinkley and I knew she was about to burst into tears. Hinkley's concern about this was terribly draining.

A week later, during my second art therapy class, I had a conversation with Laura, who sat next to me while I drew a coiled snake.

"How's it going?"

I drew a pair of eyes staring out from within the coiled cage. "I enjoy these classes, Laura. It's a variation in my routine."

She looked at the picture.

"I wouldn't look for any significance there. It's a memory of a drawing that a friend of mine did."

She nodded kindly.

"A teenage girl." I tried to make it sound inappropriate, but she didn't react.

"I've a message, Hammond. From your wife."

"Oh, her. She'll give up sooner or later. We've been separated a year. She's got to move on."

Laura shook her head. "She's found some important correspondence she believes you need to see. She says it has a bearing on your case."

I drew a tiny droplet seeping from the inner corner of the right eye. "All that's beneath me, Laura. Arguing the toss with a load of hair-splitters. I am who I am."

"She says it has a bearing on your case and your professional standing."

I put down the pen. "Really?"

"She says it's important, and she won't take up more of your time than is necessary."

So we met in the Healing Garden a second time. Rachel handed me a piece of paper and said, "Did you write this?"

I took the paper and read:

Dear Megan and Rachel,

I am writing this letter in case I forget that I love you.

There is a monster at large who grew from inside me, and it appears that it no longer loves anything. Maybe it had to crush its loving feelings to survive. We have no way of knowing. We asked it questions and saw glimpses of its mind, but for all our cleverness we will never know why it feels and thinks as it does.

And while I was using all my energy to release this monster into the world I received an undeserved blessing and my life grew richer in ways I'd never imagined possible, because of you, Megan, who grew from inside Rachel, and as you did I remembered that I loved her, and I loved people and life for the simple fact of their being.

It is plain to me that this monster is my responsibility, and the only way I can fight it is from inside my own head. Maybe its bad feelings were caused by me long ago because of the stories I told myself to make myself feel better. I can't help thinking that this is the case, and that I am responsible. So I am going to do all I can to kill it. If I cannot kill it I will confine it within me, where it will do least harm.

When it resides within me, if there is a single splinter of me that remembers that I love you I know I will defeat it. I need you to understand that the husband and the father is the person that wrote this letter, and I need you to listen for the quiet voice of my heart beneath the voice of the monster inside me, because in my heart I will love you forever.

Your loving Father and Husband,

Hammond.

I finished reading the letter and snorted. "In the last few months of his sorry existence your husband became sentimental as well as duplicitous. You remember his pathetic attempt to buy your favour with an antique book? Well, I have his memories now, and I know he was lying when he said he really wanted the baby. And I know how irritated and limited he felt. He knew he was inferior to me; that's why he lost the will to survive and relinquished his body to me, his better self."

I knew that it took a lot to make Rachel cry. Hinkley stirred again as I watched her eyes become bloodshot and watery. She reached across and tried to take the letter from my hand, but the hand and the arm to which it was attached had become locked and rigid. The letter started to tear, and she let go, frowning. She peered into my face, then ran her fingers across the skin of my knotted hand and up the paralysed arm. I cursed the residual Hinkley for flaring up like this, destroying my dignity in front of the woman who for years had used me for her own agenda. I wanted to destroy the letter and spit at her, but my arm was dead and my jaw was locked. My vital energy was being drained. She sat like that for a while, lightly grazing my arm and letting her eyes rove all over my face. Then she leaned forward and whispered the poisonous words, "I'll wait for you, Ham. Don't be scared."

The words had an alarming effect. It was as if a million cells of Hinkley had been hiding out in the cellars, ditches and dark woods of my being. Rachel's touch gave them a bolt of energy, and like some fanatical partisan army they emerged from their hideouts and poured into the streets, tearing down barricades and pursuing those who'd hitherto kept order with knives, fists and bullets. They tingled from the top of my skull to the tips of my toes, and for a few dizzy seconds I forgot that this energy was Hinkley. I leaned forward from my slumped position, my tongue became a sluggish sponge and Rachel's name vibrated in my throat and head. When she squeezed my body against hers I was unable to push her away, and I shook as Hinkley sobbed like a child.

So after the Trojan horse of the letter came the beachhead of the shrine. Hinkley must have given her permission to enter my room and decorate it in her own taste. I certainly didn't. The first photo she tacked to the wall was the one of my parents, salvaged from the Hinkley family home all those years ago. They could be mannequins in a shop window, for all the feelings they trigger. Simon Hinkley stares through his thick square glasses with the sullen gaze of a self-made workaholic, his huge artisan hands clutching the back of the kitchen chair he made himself. I don't recognise Elizabeth Hinkley at all. But why is it that when I look at her, I feel tiny and helpless, but simultaneously, Hinkley feels safe and loved?

Then of course came the photos of me and Rachel and Megan, and the one of me holding forth in my supposed prime. There's a glint in my eye that Hinkley remembers having; but I don't, frankly. He remembers having a certain feeling about his work, a lightness, like every day he saw another side to a huge cosmic joke.

What Rachel and Hinkley don't realise is that all their efforts are futile and victory is already mine. If it wasn't for the fact they were so devious and their subterfuges so irritating, I would feel sorry for them.

Hinkley is wearing me down though. He's relearning how to enunciate consonants, and his tongue becomes less spongiform by the day. He ingratiates himself with the staff with warm smiles, simple pleasantries and meek behaviour. Maybe I could use him as a Trojan horse? He's so good at ingratiation. But I can't stand the brain fog he causes. It stops me from remembering the glory, the heights I've reached. I'll have to purge him before I can start to recover. And also banish Rachel. I have lost the ability to speak in her presence.

I find him particularly bothersome at night, when my mind and body are paralysed. I often wake in a cold sweat, having dreamed that I was Hinkley, and that I was back in Telegraph Hill, during summer a few years hence. In this dream, I chase Megan round a garden of green and golden light. She stumbles among plastic toys, and puts her chubby arms around my neck while Rachel takes photos from the patio. As I lie in the dark, it is with sweet relief that I remember the end of the dream, a vision of a chamber far below, a bunker lined with granite and lead, and Shinkley's eyes burning in the dark forever.

Thanks for reading, I hope you enjoyed it.

If you did, please consider visiting the product page on Amazon and writing a review.

Also, I can let you know when I've got anything new coming out if you give me your email address on

http://writing.killip.co.uk/keep-informed/

... and there's some Hammond Flux related stuff on

hammonflux.com

I didn't really find my groove writing this story until trying out a few different approaches at the London Writers' Café. I'm really grateful to Lisa Goll and all who gave feedback and encouragement there.

Thanks to the readers of early drafts for their advice and encouragement: Alan Hardwick, Ben Rogers, Joan Killip, May Hoose, Sonya Killip, Matt French, Dominic Cooper, Tom Gifford, James Kirkwood, Cristina Morales, and Sue Matthews. Also thanks to May Hoose for proof reading and Sophie Killip for detailed feedback on final intro.

Thanks to Hal Duncan for his forthright editorial input and for pushing me to make this novel better through the various drafts.

The promotional video for this novel, 'An Interview With Addison Royal', began life as an unremarkable script and was transformed into something intriguing and spooky by Allegra Dunn, Ben Rogers and Shaff Prabatani, so many thanks to them and also to Steve Pavett for letting us film at Liveposter, and to Tom Gifford for creating the end frame.

Thanks to Dane Low for a beautiful cover, and thanks to Martin Ouvry for flawless copy editing.

17603971R00185

Printed in Great Britain
by Amazon